The Kindling Heart

Carmen Caine

Edited by Louisa Stephens

Bento Box Books - MyBentoBoxBooks.com

Cover Design by Mehrdad Azadi

ISBN: 0983524025

ISBN-13: 978-0983524021

For Pawkie

BOOK ONE

THE HIGHLAND HEATHER AND HEARTS

SCOTTISH ROMANCE SERIES

THE

KINDLING HEART

Carmen Caine

Prologue

Thurston Hall, Yorkshire, England
Latter part of the 15th century

"Harlot! Whore!" Wat whistled through his teeth as he unbuckled his belt.

Sinking to her knees, Bree mentally retraced her steps as she cowered before Wat on the dirt floor of the cottage.

In the cold before dawn, she'd drawn the water and made the porridge before joining the other peasants in the fields to pull onions. These were hardly the pastimes of a whore. She was cold, exhausted, and hungry.

"I'll not have a whore live under my roof!" Wat shouted.

She'd never understand why her mother stayed with such a despicable man. Strings of greasy grey hair plastered his balding scalp. Years of grime and other things lived under his blackened nails. He hadn't bathed since spring. He reeked.

Wat studied her for the slightest hint of rebellion. His fingers twitched in anticipation.

Bowing her head, Bree forced herself to grovel even as she imagined herself screaming defiantly in his face. The man thrived on ale and anger, one feeding the other in an endless cycle of rage and cruelty. She doubted she'd escape unscathed, but it was worth a try. She forced her eyes meekly to the floor, outwardly subservient, and waited for an explanation of what was amiss.

"Jenet!" Wat shouted, his beady eyes glinting in pleasure. "Come see what your whore of a daughter is wearing!"

It was the first hint.

A cursory inspection of her shoes, dress, and hair revealed nothing. She frowned, slightly perplexed. Last week, her rotting skirt had torn on the brambles, but Wat saw in this a wicked desire to expose flesh. A month ago, one of Bree's brown curls escaped its binding as Lord Huntley wandered the fields nearby. It mattered naught to Wat that the man was ancient, half-blind, and as simple-minded as a child. He accused her of the worst sin: a brazen seduction of the castle lord. She'd paid dearly for both incidents.

Wat gleefully popped his knuckles and smiled. It was a cruel, malicious smile.

"Yes, Wat?" Jenet's tired voice filtered through the cottage doorway. She paused on the threshold. Though her face still held traces of beauty, years of oppression had taken their toll. Her hazel eyes were as lifeless as the limp hair on her shoulders.

"Look at your daughter!" Wat ordered, spittle flecking his beard. "This time she has gone too far!"

Lest they betray her emotion, Bree lowered her eyes and held her breath as her mother subjected her to a nervous inspection.

The silence lengthened.

Finally, Jenet hesitantly cleared her throat.

Wat exploded, "Can you not see? Only a harlot would adorn her hair to catch a man's eye! She is a whore!"

Belatedly, Bree recalled the small bit of dried lavender tucked behind her ear. She loved the scent; it always reminded her of spring. She clenched her jaw, furious at herself. Why, oh why, had she not remembered to remove it? Why had she succumbed to the silly impulse in the first place? She could not afford such errors.

"Be rid of it, Bree," Jenet said flatly, devoid of sympathy.

Obediently, she raised a hand to remove the offending sprig only to have it slapped away.

"That is not enough!" Wat roared. He clenched his belt, a sneer settling on his lips. "Why would you flaunt yourself so boldly? Why?"

Struggling to remain silent, Bree bit her tongue. Hard. She winced as the salty taste of blood spread in her mouth. Soon, she knew her back would be bleeding as well. A cold anger gripped her heart and her jaw clenched.

It was a minute gesture, but it was enough for Wat.

He gloated in satisfaction as Jenet shuffled heavily from the room. She never intervened. She always left the room.

Wat began to hum as his belt arced in the air.

THE TRAP

"A man has the right to discipline his own wife," Tormod MacLeod, Laird of Dunvegan bellowed to the gathered clansmen. "'Tis his God-given right!"

The subdued murmurs of assent following this statement transformed quickly into coughs as Ruan MacLeod strode into the castle's main hall with a handful of men at his heel.

Tormod stood at the high table, chin raised, and from under partially closed eyelids observed his younger half-brother moving purposefully in his direction.

The brothers shared nothing, save the unusual height of their sire. Ruan favored his mother, the daughter of a lesser Spanish noble. His dark hair was thick, shoulder length, and bound by a strip of leather. And his eyes were darker still, were alive with passion. He was lean, muscular, and his movements were swift and virile.

Tormod was quite the opposite, boasting the large belly of a man more interested in being in his cups than anything else. His blue eyes watered continuously in his flaccid face, which was framed by thinning brown locks that clung to his scalp in wispy strings.

It was not in physical traits alone that the brothers differed. Their temperaments conflicted as well. Ruan was hot-blooded, obsessive, and stubbornly loyal while his brother seemingly existed in a perpetual state of lethargy. Tormod excelled in revenge and in the ability to delay a decision for as long as possible, particularly dangerous habits for a Laird of Dunvegan to possess.

The clansmen craned forward for a better view of the impending clash.

"Wife?" Ruan's deep, rich voice resounded as he stalked toward his brother's high table, "My sister is a bairn and has nae even ten years!"

Tormod swallowed a little, but sneered and said, "She was wed proper! Whether ye like it or no."

"Proper? A bairn? 'Tis against church law and well ye know it!" Ruan's lip curled in a scathing smile as he surveyed the men clustered in the hall. "I should have had more than this handful riding with me to rescue a wee lass from the hell that was heaped upon her innocent head! Those gathered here this night are nae worthy to bear the braw name of MacLeod!"

Uneasiness descended upon the great chamber as a mixed chorus of "Ayes" greeted this statement, most of them coming from the men clustered behind Ruan, but the loudest from a lithe young man at his side.

"Well said!" The fearless youth stepped forward. "Aye, we should nae have been so few!" He faced Tormod with a fierce anger terrifying to see in one so young. A few years would truly make him a forbidding man.

Ewan, heir to the Earldom of Mull, was a tall, strapping lad, fair of face and heart. He was the eldest son of the MacClean of Duart Castle, an ancient and powerful clan. His startling blond hair fell loose over his shoulders and he wore the yellow, fine-spun, plaid of his clan with an easy grace.

"May those that harmed a wee bairn rot in hell!" Ewan clenched his fist and spat.

Tormod cut him short with a scornful laugh and said, "Beware! Ye aren't yet Earl of Mull, young cur!"

A murmur of displeasure rippled through the hall at that, and Tormod tensed, checking his anger with difficulty. While the Earl of Mull was a man well-loved, it appeared his son was even more so.

Dropping his voice so only Ruan and Ewan could hear, Tormod hissed, "I doubt our illustrious Earl will be overly pleased when he discovers how Ruan has ensnared ye this night."

"It was my own choice—" Ewan began hotly.

"Aye? It was yer own choice to ferret the MacDonald's bride from his very bedchamber on her wedding night?" enquired the Laird of Dunvegan in a cold, cruel humor. "Your father will nae be happy ye've made Fearghus his enemy once again."

For a brief instant doubt clouded the young man's face. Anger quickly replaced it. "How little ye ken my father!" he retorted.

"Be at peace, Ewan," Ruan said, giving the lad's shoulder a comforting squeeze. Raising his voice, he added, "Be at peace. Ye've shown more loyalty than many a MacLeod here this night!"

The clansmen averted their eyes uncomfortably. They were in an unenviable position. By their own lips, they had sworn loyalty to Tormod. However, their hearts belonged to Ruan.

Unnerved at Ruan's troublesome influence over the clan, Tormod snapped, "I should behead the lot of ye!" His chin jiggled a little as he pointed to the men behind Ruan. "Inciting God-fearing men to break their oaths, stealing a man's wife on his wedding night, and bringing the wrath of the MacDonald on the clan...these are all acts of disloyalty! Aye! Ye be my own blood, Ruan, but ye've scarce shown it this night!"

"I rescued my sister, a wee bairn, and brought her home!" Ruan exploded, temper blazing dangerously as he drew himself to his full height. "If ye dinna protect the innocents of this clan...I *will*!"

He cut a daunting figure. Every line of his lean, hard body, spoke of power.

Tormod faltered, taking a step back but it was a grave mistake. Every clansman witnessed it and every clansman knew it for what it was.

He was afraid of this compelling brother of his and his growing power.

"She is a MacDonald now! Wed proper in a kirk," Tormod said. He wet his lips before addressing the men standing resolutely behind Ruan. "Dare ye risk the wrath of yer laird for this? Ruan is a penniless beggar who can give ye nothing! He has only the braw name of MacLeod and is unworthy of even that!"

Ruan opened his mouth to retort but it was cut short.

"Silence, lad, let it be," a new voice inserted mildly.

Robert MacLeod, uncle to both men, stepped from the shadows to study his nephews. He peered at them, his iron-grey hair framing a stern brow.

"Ye didn't…" Tormod whispered, shocked, unable to finish the question.

"Aye," the man replied softly. Every inch of him exuded a commanding presence. "I too rode with Ruan."

Tormod paled and took a step back in the stunned silence that followed. That his uncle, the most respected man of the clan, would ride with Ruan, was a devastating blow. Unconsciously, he took another step back.

"We are the mighty clan of the MacLeods and we protect our own," Robert Macleod stated with authority. His grey eyes slid over the gathered men before returning to settle on Tormod once more. "Ye ken well enough this unholy union should never have been agreed upon! Cuilen has long been our friend, not Fearghus. Ye've only pulled us into their clan wars with this marriage and we've no cause to be drawn into their affairs! Ye should have been riding with us— nay, leading us—to that accursed pit of evil!" He radiated disdain.

Visibly intimidated, Tormod merely stared. He was at a loss for words. The silence in the hall grew oppressive and then metal rasped as swords were drawn.

"A MacDonald!" someone called in warning.

Ruan whirled. His hand dropped instinctively to his sword.

A short, grizzled man dressed in MacDonald plaids leaned against the entrance of the great hall, observing the proceedings with overt interest.

"I'm Cuilen's man of Dunscaithe," the man said. He raised his hands and stepped slowly into the circle of naked dirks surrounding him. "I bring a message."

Ruan expelled a pent breath.

Aye, Tormod had made a muckle mess.

The MacDonalds of Dunscaithe had long been an ally of the MacLeods until Domnall's Irish sister named Bree and his uncle Robert had fallen in love. Their affair had caused a rift bordering on a feud when the lass had died in Dunvegan. Though that had taken place some years ago, relations were still tenuous. They just might break now, with Tormod's decision to wed his sister Merry to Fearghus, the MacDonald of Duntelm.

Ruan clenched his jaw.

It was a marriage that only the English would make, wedding wee bairns for political gain. His blood boiled in anger, but he took comfort in the fact he'd succeed in procuring an annulment on her behalf. She was a bairn and the marriage was against church law.

The men in the hall were murmuring, eying the messenger with apprehension.

Aye, the Isles had seen more than its fair share of turmoil this past year. With John MacDonald forced to forfeit the Earldom of Ross to the King, the massive loss of land had splintered the MacDonald clan into factions. On Skye, the clan had split in two. Fearghus, MacDonald of the north, was now at war with his cousin Cuilen, MacDonald of the south.

Ruan shook his head.

Of late, Fearghus was behaving as a man deranged. There were rumors he was readying a revolt against the Mackenzies to reclaim the land the King had recently bestowed upon them. He was a fool. Such an action could end only in blood for the Crown solidly supported the Mackenzies. The loss of the Earldom of Ross had proven that.

The MacLeods had no place in these affairs.

Merry's marriage would do nothing but anger Cuilen and cause harm to the clan. Could Tormod not even see his error?

There was a prolonged silence before Tormod lifted his voice, "Take him to my private chambers." With that, he spun on his heel and quit the hall.

"Tormod will ruin us all," someone muttered.

As the chorus of agreement grew louder, Ruan raised his arm.

The clansmen hushed.

"Tormod is The MacLeod," Ruan said, in a tone that brooked no argument. "I'll nae have it said otherwise. This matter of Merry lies between brothers and no one else." He fixed the men in the hall with a firm eye, repeating, "No one else."

They watched him, muttering amongst themselves as he slipped out of the great hall.

Ruan drew his brows in a brooding scowl. His dealings with Tormod had always been poor. Recent events were rendering them impossible. His brothers were obviously convinced it was his desire to wrest Dunvegan from their grasp. But it was preposterous.

Aye, Tormod was childless, but he had four heirs who would see Dunvegan theirs before Ruan ever did. Two half-brothers, Andrew and Michael, along with their sons, stood between them. Ruan would have to see all five men die before Dunvegan would be his. He sighed. How could his brothers think he'd want so much blood to be spilled?

They truly didn't know him.

He sighed again.

If he were wise, he'd leave soon. He pressed his cheek against the cold stones of the passageway.

Dunvegan ran through his blood. It always had, even though he spent precious little time within its walls.

As the fifth son, of a fourth marriage, his father, The Black MacLeod, wanted little to do with him and had given him nothing, save the name of MacLeod. His father had been cruel and given to fits of violence. Ruan had been fortunate to escape.

At a tender age, they sent him to foster with Cameron, the young Earl of Lennox. He'd received the finest education and traveled widely in Cameron's company, spending much time in court, but even more upon the battlefield fighting other men's wars.

His blood family had all but abandoned him, but Dunvegan only grew stronger in his heart with each passing year. The moors, the forests, the stormy seas, were all rooted deep in his soul. Last winter, he'd finally followed his heart and had returned, much to Tormod's distaste and alarm.

Having refused him quarters in the castle, Tormod was horrified to learn he'd been welcomed in the crofts. Ruan preferred them anyway. It was no hardship to harvest the fields and sheer the sheep. It was far better than having a man die by his hand. Living with his clan, sharing in happiness and tragedy alike, was healing to his soul.

Since his return, he'd experienced one calamity after another. Just five months past, he'd given all he owned to pay his mother's ransom in Spain. It was no secret that Tormod and his older brothers had worked in concert with Fearghus to accomplish the kidnapping of his mother by Spanish mercenaries, and for no other reason than to ruin him. They had successfully assured that what little he'd acquired was reduced to even less. In his mind, their steadfast refusal to donate even one shilling to her ransom had all but proven their complicity.

He expelled a breath.

And now, they were using Merry.

Squaring his shoulders, he used the rope spanning the length of the tower stairs to climb the steps three at a time. An image of his tiny sister fled through his mind. The welts and bruises, the eye he feared would never see again. Overcome by emotion, he paused to compose his thoughts, banging his head lightly against the wall.

Aye, he knew the real reason Tormod had arranged Merry's marriage to Fearghus was to show the clan that the half-brother he'd hated since childhood had no control over his own sister's destiny, and that her destiny was a tool to be used against him. He'd always known of his brother's hatred toward him, but he hadn't known the depth of it. Not until now.

A bairn. Why had Tormod used an innocent bairn this way, his own blood no less?

Tears welled as he again felt the cold rage and the utter horror of what his brother had done.

The night before, he'd left Dunvegan with Ewan and a handful of others to spirit his sister away. His plan to kill Fearghus ultimately failed, but he'd succeeded in wounding the man's leg just as MacDonalds crashed into the chamber. Ruan had barely escaped.

In the confusion, Ewan had carried Merry to her uncle Robert who had left the horses to wait in a hidden boat outside Duntulm's walls. When Ruan joined them, they slipped away in the misty night. He would never forget that first sight of his wee sister's face. He'd held Merry close, brushing her matted hair and cradling her to his chest. The tears flowed.

His plan was to take Merry to Inchmurrin, to his foster brother, the Earl of Lennox but he'd fallen asleep in the boat, only to awaken and find they had returned to Dunvegan. Ruan had risen, ready to slay his uncle for this betrayal. Why would Robert, the man he revered as a father, betray him so? As much as he loved Dunvegan, he'd never intended to return knowing the monster serving there as Laird would use her as a pawn whenever he pleased. Merry was no longer safe. He'd yet to fathom Robert's purpose in defying his plan.

But it was too late now. Merry could not move until she healed and regained her strength.

"She's a strong lass, Ruan. She's always been a wee hellion," a voice said, breaking into his thoughts. "And, there's no need to despair over her eye, lad, nae yet. Give it time."

Ruan spun sharply to see Isobel standing on the steps above him. Isobel was his mother's maid, but more a mother to him than his own had been. She was a short, round woman, long past her prime. However, to him, she was the most beautiful and dearest of women on earth. She'd been there from the minute of his birth, holding his heart in a way no one else could.

"She's awake, now, lad, waiting for ye."

Taking a deep breath, he joined her on the landing to kiss the top of her graying head. The gesture caused a tear to trickle down Isobel's cheek. Ruan sighed. She was worried about Merry as well, even though she tried to hide it for his sake. He drew a long breath, preparing himself to see the worst. Ducking under the low archway, he slipped inside Merry's chamber.

There was little light in the small, vaulted room. The glow of the fire didn't reach the bed or its slight occupant. As he approached, a small hand stretched out in his direction.

"Ruan," the thin, wavering voice croaked.

Choking back tears, he knelt beside her and forced his lips to smile. "Ye look much better, my Merry wee lass," he said. It was a lie. He bent down and tenderly kissed the tip of her nose.

She appeared much worse. The shadows accentuated bruises that gave her the most grotesque of appearances. He wanted to scream from pure rage.

"Ruan?" Fear rippled in her voice. He clenched his hands, wanting to rip Fearghus and Tormod to shreds. With a great effort, he forced what he thought to be a reassuring smile. And he promised himself there would be time for Tormod and Fearghus later.

"Ye'll never go back, my Merry wee lass," he vowed fervently, tweaking her chin lightly as he always had. He didn't allow himself to dwell on the mass of black bruises and added, "I swear ye'll be safe now."

Merry let out a sigh of relief. Her small frame shook with sobs.

With his own tears flowing freely, Ruan gently gathered her into a comforting embrace. He suppressed a sigh, desperately wishing he could erase the memory of her cries. He'd hear those sounds until the end of his days. He stayed that way, holding her in his arms long after she'd fallen asleep. He left only when Ewan came to take his place. Ewan was someone he could trust.

He'd scarcely taken a step from the chamber before Robert, Isobel and several elders accosted him.

"I tried, lad," Robert said, greeting him with a sigh and rubbing his head, "I…tried."

An elder brushed his uncle aside, holding out his hand, "Come. The MacLeod is waiting for ye in the hall."

Ruan's lip curled irreverently and he took a calculated step back. He was hardly in the mood to speak with Tormod again.

"Ye'd best go," Isobel chimed in, oddly subdued.

At her strange behavior, Ruan tensed, suddenly alert. His fingers itched for his dirk, but he finally agreed with reluctance and allowed them to guide him back to the hall.

The hall was quiet. The dying fire cast eerie shadows, barely illuminating Tormod and Cuilen's messenger, who was seated by his side. Several men lounged in front of the fireplace; a few perched on the tables.

All of them shifted uneasily as Ruan passed.

"Aye, The MacLeod calls and ye obey, like a whipped cur!" Tormod gave a pompous nod of satisfaction, but his jaw was tense, nervous.

Ruan scowled speculatively.

Slowly, Tormod walked around the table, trailing his hand along the wooden surface. Finally, he stopped in front of him. "Ye've started a war with Fearghus this night and ye'll do as I say now or hang on a tree as a warning to all."

Ruan gave an audible snort, but said nothing. It was true enough.

Arrogantly hooking his thumb under his belt, Tormod addressed everyone, "Aye, Ruan will do as The MacLeod bids. By thieving the McDonald's bride on his very wedding night, he owes us all."

Ruan raised a brow, but remained quiet.

Tormod sneered a little, causing his pasty chin to jiggle, "Ye'll return Merry to her loving husband or…"

All color drained from Ruan's face. With Merry's moans ringing in his ears, sounds no child should ever make, he leapt toward Tormod. "Curse your cowardly heart!" he shouted. "She'll nae be going back! She is a bairn, ye murderous, black-hearted bastard! I've had enough of ye!"

Tormod fell against the table as Ruan lunged at him, his fingers closing about his throat.

"Ruan!" Robert's voice rose above the sudden hubbub.

Ruan fought the hands pulling him back. "Ye'll have to kill me!" he swore harshly, lunging again, but several men moved to block his way.

"Traitor!" Tormod snarled, beads of sweat glistening on his brow.

"I'll have your head on a—" Ruan began as Robert's hand clamped firmly over his mouth, muffling his words.

"Merry is safe, lad!" Robert shouted in his ear. "'Tis you! Ye'll be taking her place!"

It took some time for the words to sink in. They didn't make sense. Slowly, Ruan twisted around, still uncomprehending.

Robert sighed wearily and said, "Aye, ye'll be taking her place, lad." His hands fell to his sides.

Puzzled, Ruan straightened, adjusting his shirt and snapped, "I'd hardly pass for a lass. The McDonald is old, but nae yet blind." A hard edge entered his voice.

A few guffaws greeted these words.

"Aye," Tormod said, lifting his shoulders and speaking far louder than necessary. "Ye'll do as I say. You're not but a dog to follow its master's bidding." Planting his feet apart, he held out his hand with a pleased, expectant smile, as if waiting for a round of applause. When greeted with silence and stony stares, he licked his lips and unconsciously sidled closer to the table.

At this, the messenger stood. Bowing deeply, he addressed Ruan, "I'm Sean McDonald, Cuilen's man."

"Aye." Ruan nodded curtly.

"Cuilen joined Tormod several months ago, against Fearghus, to—"

"Against Fearghus?" Ruan exploded, dark brows rising in shock. He rounded on his brother, shouting. "Pray tell, why Merry was wed to that black-hearted bastard then, nae a week hence?"

Astonished hisses greeted Ruan's words as Tormod's face began to purple.

"I've no need to explain!" he shouted in reply, shaking his fist threateningly. "Ye'll do as I bid ye, or I'll be sending Merry back to her husband this *very* night! I'll have ye wed Aislin, Cuilen's aunt, before month's end—to seal our new alliance—and that's an end to it!"

Ruan blinked, forgetting what he'd intended to say in an instant. He was expected to wed Aislin MacDonald? It was obviously

Tormod's latest attempt to belittle him in front of the clan.

"Cuilen's willing to let the past stay in the past," Tormod said, voice rasping like a snake. "Ruan will marry the woman as I say!"

Marry? Ruan took a deep breath, oddly shaken. The thought of women made him shiver.

For the past several years, he'd shunned all women. He had walked away from his wild past and his life had been blessedly simpler for it. With difficulty, he forced his thoughts to slow down. Aislin was hardly just any woman. Everyone knew of Aislin; she'd long been the source of many a ribald jest. She'd borne four bairns out of wedlock, none of them sharing the same father. Coupled with her love of wine, food, and precious few remaining teeth, she provided ample fodder for humorous storytelling. He'd been particularly eloquent on the subject himself.

Cuilen was a formidable man, though why he'd chosen to marry off his aunt to forge this new alliance puzzled Ruan and he frowned. Perhaps, it was a directed insult.

"Are ye struck dumb?" Tormod asked.

Taken aback, he rounded on Tormod to find him waiting expectantly, almost uncertainly. He opened his mouth, not knowing what to say, but then hesitated, suddenly struck by a new idea. Tormod's purpose in this scheme was difficult to fathom, but he apparently needed his compliance. This could be the leverage he needed to win Merry's freedom. Tying himself to that revolting woman would be a small price to pay for his sister's safety.

"Well?" Tormod prodded again.

Slowly, and with a confidence he didn't entirely feel, Ruan folded his arms. "I've no means to support a wife. You and the rest of my loving kin have seen to that."

Tormod smiled, a cold, gloating smile, even as he shifted his weight uneasily. His eyes darted to the messenger seated at the table and then returned to Ruan. "The lucky bride and ye'll be living here in Dunvegan."

Ruan swallowed. This was by far the worst news. The danger in his life would increase a hundredfold.

"Then, ye'll wed her?" Tormod pressed him.

He wondered, briefly, what might happen if he refused? But then Merry's torn face flashed in his mind, and then all desires fled, save the one to ensure her safety. "Swear, in front of all, ye'll have Merry's marriage annulled," he countered and with only a fleeting moment of hesitation, he added, "...and I shall."

Tormod exhaled, in obvious relief, nodding readily, "'Tis done." He rubbed his hands together, cracking his knuckles and beamed widely at his guest.

Cuilen's man said nothing. He leaned back in his chair and eyed Tormod with obvious distaste.

As expressions of relief circled the table, Ruan frowned.

"Aislin will, no doubt, make a fine wife," his uncle murmured sympathetically, catching him by the arm and offering him a pewter goblet filled to the brim with wine. "No doubt, her time in England accomplished... er... some... um... good."

At this, Tormod threw back his head and laughed, long and mockingly, "I dinna share yer faith, uncle. She is only older and last I heard, as plump as a horse. England sharpened her lust and loosened her morals. She gave the local brewer a son and two daughters to pilgrims!"

The muffled snorts that greeted this comment were quickly hushed. Ruan knew it was out of respect and sympathy. He sighed at the odd twist of events. As a rule, the mere mention of Aislin would signal the mirth to begin, each man claiming knowledge of her latest escapade, each attempting to outdo the other, until all lay drunk on the floor. And as for Aislin's reputation, she'd committed every known crime twice over.

He sighed.

He cared little what Aislin would do once they were wed. He'd marry her, but he wouldn't be spending time in her company. Pushing the wine away, untouched, he prepared to quit the place.

"Aye," Tormod whispered loud enough for all to hear. He leaned close, "She's long past the age for breeding now, though, if she ever had another bairn ye could never be sure of the father!"

Ruan sent him a level look, even as the men behind him surrendered their good sense under the influence of the free-flowing ale. As the comments began, he stalked away.

"At least, she'll be willing in bed!" someone offered.

"Aye...if she can fit in one!" another added.

As rounds of bawdy laughter greeted lewd comments, Ruan escaped the dim, smoky hall to pace the walls of Dunvegan.

It didn't matter.

He had no desire for children. He no longer had the means to feed them. Besides, he certainly wouldn't be spending any time in her bed.

He was done with women and the nets they wove to ensnare men.

THE JOURNEY HOME

"Rest, lass, ye've done plenty this day."

Bree jerked, startled from her reverie and winced a little. "You needn't worry, Afraig. I'm quite well," she promised.

It was a lie.

It had been over a week since Wat last raised his belt, and she was still sore.

"Aye, lass," the old woman muttered dryly, "that bruise is the finest purple this eventide."

Bree wrinkled her nose in Afraig's direction and then leaned over the cauldron, scrutinizing her reflection. Large, green eyes stared back, prominent in a face too thin, and with lips a shade too wide. Unruly brown curls escaped the kerchief that covered the dark purple and yellowing bruises.

"You're a fine sight to behold," she criticized herself and stuck out her tongue.

Afraig approached to give the cauldron's contents a critical sniff before turning an even more disparaging glance her direction. "Aye, ye are a sight scrawnier than a half-fed chicken, love. Ye'll not be finding a proper husband, unless ye plump up a wee bit."

Bree stopped stirring, astounded Afraig would even mention the word 'husband' in her presence.

"Aye," Afraig said, moving away, "that Evil Eye yer offering me, 'tis in sore need of work, now. I'm nae feeling a thing."

In spite of her annoyance, a smile tugged Bree's lips.

Most thought Afraig a rude and intolerable harridan, but Bree knew her gruff mannerisms were only a prickly exterior to guard an unusually soft heart. On the outside, everything about the woman was hard and sharp, from her wit to her bony hands, from the angle of her chin to the cut of her black hair liberally sprinkled with grey.

Life for Afraig had been harsh. Years ago, few had welcomed the highland lover of Lord Huntley. Now that he was old and feeble-minded, his care was widely seen as solely her responsibility.

"Jenet bade ye be home by sundown, didn't she now?" Afraig asked for the third time that hour.

Drawing her lips into a thin line, Bree gave a noncommittal grunt. She added a few more onions to the dye and stirred it far more vigorously than necessary. Her eyes watered. No, she'd much rather peel onions for this obnoxious brew all night. She didn't intend to return while Wat was still awake.

"Lass, 'twould nae be wise to tempt his wrath," Afraig warned quietly.

Bree rolled her eyes and slammed another handful of onion skins into the pot. "He's still in high spirits," she replied.

The last beating had been enough to ensure his good humor a few more days. To her relief, Afraig dropped the matter, and they silently tended their chores.

A short time ago, Thurston Hall had thrived and these very kitchens had been the domain of men. There had been fish, venison, wheat, candles and spices locked in the cupboard. Now, the grey stone manor had fallen into decay and only Afraig, along with the aged Lord Huntley and his niece, Aislin, lived within its walls. Matters darkened each year and with no one capable of protecting them, more tenants left for safer places.

Afraig began to sing.

The soft, soothing lilt of her Gaelic song drew Bree back into the comforting days of her childhood. Whenever time permitted, she'd found her way to Afraig, to eat warm bread slathered with butter and to listen to tales from the Isle of Skye.

Afraig dreamt aloud of the day she could return to Skye, and Bree imagined herself returning with her. They would live in a cottage by the sea and together they would grow herbs and raise sheep.

After living under Wat's tyrannical rule Bree was determined to never wed, and Afraig had assured her that she could live comfortably in Skye as a maid her entire life.

Bree yawned, suddenly aware the song had ended. "What was that about?" she asked.

"Your father will be right ashamed to find ye canna speak his own tongue!" Afraig snorted, slamming a bucket onto the table to wag an accusing finger. "I've tried, Sweet Mary, I've tried, but ye havena, lass!"

Bree looked up in surprise; no one ever spoke of her father.

Once, she had dared to ask her mother who her father was. Her reward had been a sound cuff on the ear. She had only asked Afraig after that, and while Afraig didn't strike her, she always responded with a vague smile and a name. The name changed with such regularity that Bree eventually lost interest. Angus. Brinan. Silas. Edward. Jamie. However, while the names changed, upon one thing Afraig was adamant. Her father was a rugged Highlander, from the bonniest isle on earth: Skye.

Bree hadn't thought of him in years. Why should she? He'd left her with her husky voice, elfin looks, and nothing else, not even his name. The only thing she knew was the vague story she had pieced together: of how he'd arrived one autumn, escorting the Lady Aislin from her latest scandal in Scotland to the respectable Thurston Hall. After two days, he'd returned whence he came, never to be seen again. And then nine months later, Jenet had given birth to a squalling baby girl. She was an unwanted infant, so much so that she'd lived nameless for almost a year before Afraig had taken to calling her Bree.

"Ach, yer Domnall's and no mistake."

Domnall? It was just another name. But, it was strange Afraig would bring up the matter on her own. Shrugging the short-lived curiosity away, Bree's thoughts wandered to Wat and her plans to avoid him, but they were quickly diverted again.

"I've always kent it be Domnall, lass."

It took several moments for the words to register. Startled by the genuine sincerity in her voice, Bree cast a furtive glance her way, holding still lest she broke the spell and Afraig ceased speaking entirely.

"Aye, 'tis why I named ye Bree, after his sister..." Afraig sighed heavily, lost in the memories of the past. "'Twas a sad affair. She loved a MacLeod, and lost her life for it." Her tone hardened at the mention of the name 'MacLeod'.

Intrigued, Bree waited.

"Aye," Afraig said, shaking her head wearily, "Domnall's my cousin, a right fair man. He was nae thinking that night. He could never have wed Jenet as she wished. He was already wed with bairns of his own."

Bree felt a twinge of disappointment. The man was a scoundrel. She sighed.

"'Tis no matter, lass, what's done is done. That was nae what I wanted to speak of." Afraig reached out and patted her wrist, adding, "I've a wee bit of news."

Not knowing why, Bree's heart began to pound.

"My kinfolk are coming for Aislin, after all this time, though, 'twill be a nasty surprise for the lad...but 'tis nae my affair," Afraig checked herself. She affectionately ran a finger over Bree's cheek and said, "Ye should go back with them, to Skye. Find yer father; he's not one to shirk his duty."

Suddenly, the fact that her father was an unscrupulous rascal didn't matter. A thrill crept through her, unbidden. A myriad of questions engulfed her all at once.

"Domnall will treat ye a sight better than Wat!" Afraig heaved a sigh. "The MacDonald has sent for Aislin. He's wed her off to a MacLeod, though. Even a beast of a MacLeod will be sore disappointed in Aislin for a bride. Now, with her expecting another bairn... I'm nae sure he'll take her. I'm fair stumped on what I should do, but 'tis too late. Cuilen sent the message nigh on four months ago and that drunkard just remembered to tell me! Autumn, he said, well, autumn is done!"

Bree stared, trying to calm her rampaging thoughts. With so many things she wanted to ask, she could not decide where to start, but Aislin's bellow from the passageway above startled them both.

"Bree!" Aislin shouted. "More wine!"

An empty wine bottle rattled down the steps, coming to a stop before Bree's feet. She stooped to pick it up, still wanting to ask Afraig questions, but the woman had slipped into a trance, staring into the flames.

As Aislin yelled again, Bree hurriedly grabbed a bottle of wine and ran up the passageway. Aislin was overbearing and dull of wit, but for the most part, kind-hearted. Her temper flared only when the wine was late.

"I'll be having some wine. Be quick, lass!" Aislin grinned, revealing more gaping holes than teeth, "I'm celebrating the wondrous news!"

Aislin lay on her bed. It was a large bed, for she was an enormous woman. Though she was five months gone with child, it was difficult to tell, for her belly always resembled a woman on the brink of giving birth. She appeared far younger than her years, simply because the fat smoothed any wrinkles that attempted to form. With creamy white skin and luminous blue eyes framed by black hair, she must have been lovely in her youth, but now she much resembled a bloated, toothless seal.

Bree handed her a goblet.

Aislin sighed in pleasure and then wiggled her swollen toes and ordered, "Rub them, lass."

Bree stifled a sigh. She hated rubbing Aislin's unwashed feet. Usually, she was able to think of an excuse quickly enough to avoid the entire situation, but she was still reeling from the news of her father.

"I'll be wed soon," Aislin said as she smiled, her chin disappearing into several rolls. "Ruan! He's a sight younger than me, but handsome, I've been told…"

Aislin wiggled her toes again as Bree's fingers closed around them. A waft of air carried the rank odor to her nostrils, and Bree gagged.

The woman didn't notice. Her puffy lids closed as she mumbled about the tall, handsome MacLeod who would provide wondrous pleasures in bed and finally enable her to live as a proper lady in Dunvegan. As Aislin's mutterings lapsed into gurgling snores, Bree scurried out of the chamber before she could wake to summon her back.

Her hands reeked. It took more than one scrubbing to cleanse her fingers of the stench, but she finally succeeded and returned to the kitchens to find Afraig pacing before the fire, highly agitated.

She glanced up as Bree entered. "Ye must leave, love," the woman announced firmly, "and leave now. We canna wait for yer father. Ye'll have to run. I'll think of something!"

Bree blinked in surprise.

"Jenet was just here!" Afraig twisted her hands, obviously rattled. "She and that beastly Wat are… wedding ye off, lass. They want ye home tonight, love, to meet yer… husband. I told her you were in the fields. Ye canna stay. Ye'll have to run…"

Bree stared. It was some time before she could breathe. Wed? Surely, Afraig was mistaken. The woman's lips were still moving, but she could not hear the words.

Her dreams of a peaceful cottage on the sea were crashing around her.

Surely, Afraig was wrong.

Grabbing her cloak, Bree threw it over her shoulders and sped out of Thurston Hall.

Afraig had to be wrong. Her mother wouldn't do such a thing!

Within minutes, she stood outside the squalid hut she called home. It was an eye-sore, the worst in the village. Wat spent his days in a drunken stupor. He relied on his sons to care for it and work the fields; only, they followed their father's fine example instead, drinking and wenching from dawn until dusk.

No, her mother needed her. If nothing else for the simple fact that there would be no one to do the chores if she were gone. She'd never marry her off.

At length, she gathered her courage and crept close to peer through the wide cracks in the door. She could barely make out the thin, hunched form of a scowling man standing before her mother and Wat. It was Raph, Wat's uncle. He was a despicable creature who pinched her at every opportunity. He was filthy, old, and his breath stank.

"…And she's young," Wat belched. "She'll bear children. That should be worth at least two."

Raph tapped his fingers impatiently. "Where is she?"

"Soon. She'll be here soon," her mother twittered nervously. Filling his cup with watered ale, she continued, "A right hard-working girl, she is. She'll make a fine wife."

Bree stifled a gasp. Surely, she'd misheard. Surely, they could not be talking about her. Her mother would never willingly hand her to the man who had trained Wat in every depraved act he knew.

"You've not taught her obedience, Wat."

"Then, I've no doubt you will!" Wat cackled, scratching the exposed flesh of his belly.

"Two sheep is overly much."

"Three!" Her mother disagreed harshly. "We agreed to three sheep. Bree is worth perchance four."

There was no denying the words. Shocked tears burned Bree's lashes. They were selling her to that disgustingly, dirty old man for three sheep.

"Three!" Wat insisted, "You're old. I'll not have Bree returning with brats to feed. Did you bring the sheep?"

Apparently, he hadn't, for her mother spat, "Not until you bring the sheep!"

"I wanted her tonight!" Raph snarled. "I've need of a woman."

"Someone else will have to satisfy that need," came her mother's curt reply.

Bree's heart leapt in hope, but then, she heard the devastating words.

"Not until I get my sheep. You can have her when I have my sheep."

Bree gulped.

She'd believed her entire life that somewhere deep inside, her mother truly cared for her and loved her immensely. However, there was no denying those cold, cruel words. Fleeing to the shadows of the nearby trees, she sank to the ground, feeling ill.

The door opened and Raph emerged, more than half-drunk and slurring his words. "I'll bring the sheep in the morning then!"

He staggered down the darkening lane leaving the village, and it was only when the barking dogs tracking his progress fell silent that Bree allowed herself a deep breath.

For the moment, she'd delayed disaster. Afraig was right. She had to run. She could not return home. They might call him back. Not knowing what else to do, she sped to the castle kitchens, gulping her tears as she ran.

"Afraig!" she sobbed, pushing open the kitchen door. "They are trying to sell me to Raph for three sheep!"

She collided with a firm, barrel chest.

"Hold there!" a deep, booming voice rang.

Startled, Bree pulled back, catching only a glimpse of a bald head before instinctively swinging into action.

Raph had found her.

Emotions flared to life, igniting her very soul as fingers of steel gripped her arm. She screamed a high, piercing shriek. Clawing and kicking, she launched an attack that, judging by the startled grunts of pain, succeeded in striking at least a few of her intended targets.

All at once, the fingers released their grip, and she whirled to escape only to find Afraig blocking her way.

"Let me pass!" she gasped.

Oddly, Afraig grinned, shaking her head, "Stay, lass! Ye will be safe now! Can ye believe the luck of this? 'Tis a miracle he arrived the same day as Cuilen's message!"

"Same day?" the voice was snorting. "That was sent nigh on four months past!"

Too panicked to listen more, Bree forged ahead, attempting to shove Afraig aside, but the woman was stronger than she appeared. After a brief struggle, she was once again caught in a vice grip, this time Afraig's.

It was too much and Bree sank to the floor with a low sob. "Let me go. I beg you! I'll not marry him! I can't! You know I can't! Not Raph!"

"There now, lass." the kindly male voice mumbled from somewhere above. "Surely, there's nae to fear from a husband, now, is there?"

The voice was deep and kind, and the accent strangely familiar. The words shifted into a smooth lilt; odd words ones she almost recognized.

Afraig replied in the same manner and then Bree understood.

Gaelic. The man was speaking Gaelic. Hope instantly replaced despair. Afraig's kin had arrived, not Raph! Wiping her nose on her sleeve, she sprang to her feet, turning eagerly to the stranger.

Like Raph, he was almost bald and what little hair remained was gray, but there the resemblance ended. The man was of medium height and clad in a travel-stained plaid. His face was weathered and lined, but he was not particularly old. He stood stiffly, hunched to one side, observing her with bright green eyes that reflected sympathy mixed with a dash of amusement.

"Are ye done bleating like a sheep?" he asked with a pleasant burr before turning to Afraig. "Yer making no sense, woman."

"Aye, and ye should be listening, Domnall," Afraig chuckled. Brushing him aside to hold both hands out to Bree, she continued, "'Tis a warm welcome ye've given yer father, love, and no mistake! Ye nearly unmanned him!"

Bree froze. Her vision narrowed, blocking everything except the stunned man standing next to her. Time stood still as they stared at each other in mutual shock, and it seemed an eternity before she could breathe and sound once again returned.

Dimly, she heard Afraig chuckling.

Domnall lips parted as his brows climbed into his hairline. "Ye be … daft, woman!" he finally managed in a hoarse whisper.

"She has MacBethad eyes and hair," Afraig snorted. Placing a hand under Bree's chin to tilt it upwards, she added, "Can ye even doubt it?"

"She … she canna be … mine," he murmured, but with words couched in uncertainty.

"Open yer eyes, man!" Afraig chuckled, "How can ye deny her?"

Bree held still, shocked.

After a time, he whispered, "Jenet?"

"Aye," Afraig said with a nod.

Bree winced, not wanting to think of her mother.

"I…" Domnall began, licking his lips several times before falling silent.

"I know 'tis a wee bit surprising," Afraig beamed, drawing them both closer to the hearth, "but while ye adjust to the truth ye've got a fine, wee lassie, I'll finish my words. Aislin's carrying another bairn, so, ye canna take her. That MacLeod will nae want her—bless his soul—even though he be a MacLeod. Why, he—"

"Silence, woman!" Domnall growled. "I'll nae speak of Aislin now!"

Clearly agitated, he clasped his hands behind his mud-caked plaid and began to pace, directing a dark frown in Afraig's direction as she slipped into Gaelic once more.

Bree's heart sank.

Afraig was wrong. This man wanted nothing to do with her. He was obviously less than pleased to discover he had a daughter. Tears slipped down her cheeks unheeded. It was some time before she noticed the silence and the fact they were both watching her curiously.

"There, lass," Afraig consoled, pressing her roughly against her bony bosom. "There's not to fear, I promise ye, love."

Bree clung, weeping, as Afraig stroked her hair with a gentle, soft touch. After a time, she noticed a third hand awkwardly patting her shoulder, and she jerked back in surprise, unprepared to find her father standing close by.

"What's the name, lass?" he asked in a voice unbearably loud, but radiating a soft kindness.

Bree's throat constricted and she found it difficult to respond.

He waited for a time and then dropped his voice to ask again, "What are ye called, lass?"

He wasn't angry, merely inquisitive. She stared, unable to grasp the concept that this stranger, this Highlander, was truly her father!

Frowning, Domnall leaned close and slowly enunciated each word. "Surely, lass, ye have a name?"

Bree opened her dry lips and after several attempts managed to squeak, "Bree!"

Sucking in his breath, he drew back sharply as if he'd been slapped. "Why?" he exclaimed, raising a querulous brow to Afraig. He appeared less than pleased.

"Takes after her, don't ye think?"

There was a short pause before the gruff response: "Aye, though 'tis ill fortune to name her for the dead."

"Nonsense!" Afraig pursed her lips, but there was a cloud of worry on her brow.

Then, the awkward moment was shattered as Aislin swept into the kitchen, the rolls under her chin jiggling with each step. She expanded her arms in a broad, welcoming gesture, bellowing, "Domnall!"

Surveying her wide girth in overt disgust, Domnall snorted, "Ye really are stouter than a highland cow, woman."

Aislin tossed her head, retorting, "Aye, an ye look old."

"A fair disgrace ye are. How can I take ye to Ruan, five months gone with another man's bairn? What have ye done?" Sizing her up and down, he stroked his chin and added, "And woman, how can ye even have bairns at yer great age?"

Aislin's flabby features hardened as the words she began to exchange with Domnall—a mixture of English and Gaelic—quickly transformed into a loud shouting match. It ended abruptly with Aislin turning on her heel, chins quivering angrily as she stormed from the kitchen.

"Sweet Mary, woman!" Domnall barked after her, "Ye could have lived in Dunvegan!"

She returned to hover in the door and hiss, "Oh, but Domnall, I will. I'll be a lady in Dunvegan, and I'll be ready in two days' time!"

Domnall snorted contemptuously.

Aislin smiled, coldly.

"Don't be doing anything foolish." Afraig warned. "Tis too late for actions ye'll regret."

"Two days," Aislin promised sweetly, holding up two fingers and lumbering away.

Heaving a long sigh, Domnall sank on a low stool, burying his head in his hands. "Ye'll be coming with us now, won't ye, Afraig?" he asked wearily.

Afraig moved away, busying herself with the bowls on the table. Her face etched in pain.

Bree knew the expression well.

As long as Lord Huntley lived, Afraig would be at his side.

Domnall studied her from under bushy brows, saying bluntly, "I doubt he remembers those long, hot nights."

It was a cruel thing to say. Bree glared at her father with disapproval, but quickly averted her gaze when she discovered he was looking directly at her now.

"He may not, but I do," Afraig murmured. "Ye'd nae leave Ellin, Domnall, would ye now?"

At that, Domnall sighed, running a hand over his head. Then, he grunted, "Ellin's been dead, nigh on ten years."

Afraig straightened and her face grew pale.

Clearing his throat, Domnall continued in a low voice filled with gloom, "Several months ago... Fearghus sent Dougall's head on a pike."

Afraig's eyes popped in shock.

Bree bowed her head in polite respect. She hadn't heard of either Ellin or a Dougall before, but Domnall's obvious pain revealed they were close kin.

As if reading her mind, Domnall nodded his chin at her and offered the explanation, "Ellin was my wife. Dougall...well, yer brother, my eldest, was struck down in the prime of life. And Catriona..." His voice grew husky with tears. "Aye, my wee Catriona, yer sister. The poor lass died giving birth to a bairn this year past. They both only lived a day."

Afraig's shoulders drooped. "Ye've naught but ill tidings."

"I've no one left."

In the oppressive silence that followed, Bree gazed into the flames. She was astonished a man would mourn the loss of a wife and children. If her mother died, Wat would hardly notice, of that she was certain.

"Aye, 'tis glad I am to have a daughter, and such a fine, wee, bonny lass."

It took Bree several moments to realize Domnall was speaking of her. She caught her breath, meeting his green, twinkling eyes.

"Are ye sure she's nae a wee touched, woman?" Domnall drawled lightly. "Can she speak?"

Afraig chuckled, moving to rest her hand on Domnall's shoulder as they both smiled at her.

"She's a sweet one, Domnall," she said. "Ye'll treat her well?"

"Aye," the man said, nodding. "She's the last of my flesh and blood. 'Twill be right pleasant to have her home, though I'm nae too pleased with the name!" He raised a brow at Afraig. "What were ye thinking, woman, to let her be named that?"

"'Tis a fine name!" Afraig snorted and then added, "And ye ken well enough why I did so. The clan should never have disowned Bree. Her only crime was love, even if she wasted it on a MacLeod." Her tone soured at the name.

"Aye," Domnall murmured, "I suppose. 'Tis time they remember her, especially now with the alliance."

A shiver rippled through Bree's spine.

This stranger, this man, had accepted her as his.

She was truly leaving.

Glancing about the kitchen, she began to feel a strange sense of panic. Raph could not have her now. She should be relieved, dancing for joy, but a cold, clammy feeling gripped her heart.

"Aye, 'tis a bit daunting for ye, I would think," Domnall grunted.

Bree glanced up in amazement that he had read her thoughts.

"Ye wear yer heart in yer eyes, lass. 'Tis plain to see what is on yer mind," he said, chuckling, and touched her shoulder in a light gesture of affection.

As his fingers touched one of her bruises, Bree sucked her breath in pain.

Her father squinted in suspicion, "What's this?"

"Wat!" Afraig spat.

Again, they spoke hurriedly in Gaelic. Gaelic! Already, she regretted that she had not learned it. Yes, she knew a few words, but not enough if it would soon be all she heard. The kitchen walls seemed to be moving, closing about her. She scarcely noticed the strong, stubby fingers grasping her wrist. Someone lifted her hair from the back of her neck, exposing the cuts of Wat's belt. Then, Afraig paraded the bruises, old and new, to the man who called himself her father, still speaking in the strange, foreign tongue. Could she ever learn the cadence of the unintelligible syllables?

Her thoughts were broken as the man began to change. As Afraig spoke, a chilling expression descended upon him like a mask, hard and stony. She hesitated. This man was not one to be crossed. Every line in his body hardened, and as it did, it announced that he was indeed more fearsome than Wat. For when he struck, it would be to kill.

"I'll be seeing this Wat," Domnall said.

The words shook Bree from her stupor.

"Aye!" Afraig's lips split into a wide grin. "When might I introduce ye?"

"Now!"

Bree watched as Domnall stalked from the kitchen with Afraig close on his heels. Neither one looked back in her direction. As their footsteps faded, she hurried to follow and observe the strange Highlander from a safe distance. Domnall was not a particularly tall man nor apparently a wealthy one. His plaid was well worn and his mustard-colored shirt was stained with mud, but he commanded an undeniable presence. There was a frightening, cold violence about him now as he strode through the village, finally pausing in front of Wat's cottage. Dusk was falling fast and it was difficult to see, but he apparently had seen well enough.

As Bree timidly joined them, Domnall turned to her, astonished.

"This is where ye live, lass?" he asked, tilting his head at the dismal structure. "I've seen pigs in less squalor!"

Bree ducked her head in shame.

"Tis no fault of yer own, lass!" Domnall grunted, "If I had known—"

The door creaked open.

Jenet stepped out and squinted at the Highlander. Her mouth fell open.

"Jenet," Domnall said at last, licking his dry lips, "why ... why didn't ye send word? Why didn't ye tell me!?"

With a shrill, contemptuous laugh, she replied, "Why would you want a girl?"

Bree swallowed. Surely, her mother didn't mean it. Then, the soft, rumbling voice of her father astonished her even more.

"She's nae just any girl, woman! She is my daughter. I would always want my daughter!" Domnall was clearly outraged.

Her mother laughed harshly, "Well. You can't have her now. She's to be wed."

Domnall exploded, delivering obviously uncomplimentary words in Gaelic before noticing Jenet's confusion. Switching languages, he shouted, "Ye'll nae be selling my daughter to a lecherous man for a few sheep!"

The joy lifting Bree's heart plummeted at her mother's cold reply.

"Are you certain she is yours?"

"I've only to look at her to see she's mine!" Domnall snorted, brushing the possibility aside. "Dare ye deny it, woman?"

With a pounding heart, Bree searched her mother's face. Surely, it was true! She wanted it to be true. She wanted to believe this man was kind, that he was going to rescue her, and that she truly was his daughter. It seemed an eternity and then her mother's lips parted.

"You may have got her on me, but you've no claim on her now. She belongs to her husband!"

At that moment, Wat chose to appear. He stumbled through the door with a particularly loud belch. His sneering mouth snapped shut as he spied the irate Highlander at his threshold.

Domnall's nostrils flared in disgust, "And ye'll be Wat?"

Wat nodded, suspiciously.

"I'll be having a word with ye," Domnall grunted, striding past her mother and into the cottage.

Wat followed, scratching his belly.

As Jenet moved to join them, the door shut firmly in her face. She stood there, confused, and then whirled on Bree, "What have you done?"

"Jenet," Afraig warned, stepping forward and blocking her path. "Leave the lass be!"

"And you!" Jenet's anger shifted. "You've meddled from the beginning!"

Afraig stood calmly with folded arms, "Let him take her. Bree is his daughter."

"A fact I can never forget!" Jenet snarled, hands clenching into fists. "Domnall and his sweet words that night, before he left…Abandoning *me* for his precious highlands!"

"He was drunk. He—" Afraig began.

A loud crash from within the cottage silenced them both and one muffled cry quickly followed another. Then Domnall's voice could be heard, "Aye, how does it feel, ye lily-livered, fen-sucking, pox-marked witless son of a maggot?!"

Strangely, Bree's heart began to lighten. Never had any dared to speak to Wat so.

"Aye! And if ye as much as look at my daughter, I'll behead ye and yer foul breed, ye worm-ridden bag of filth!"

It was thrilling to hear someone curse Wat. Bree's lips twitched upwards. She wanted to stay forever and simply listen.

The rickety door rattled. One shutter popped open.

Finally, Domnall stepped into the fading sunlight, brushing his sleeves, and adjusting his plaid.

No one else moved.

"Say farewell to yer mother, lass," he gave Bree an encouraging smile. "We'll be heading home to Skye, then."

Jenet reeled, crying pitifully, "Can you leave me?"

Bree stared, stricken, as her mother held out pleading hands. Her mother loved her. She wanted her to stay. She could not abandon her, especially now, with Wat sure to be angry. She took a tottering step forward.

"Think, lass. I'm offering ye freedom," Domnall growled in a harsh reminder. "I'll nae be selling ye to a lusting drunkard for a few sheep!"

Bree flinched.

A loud moan drew their attention to Wat leaning against the door, his face bloodied, and his lips gasping for air. As Jenet rushed to his side, he mumbled incoherently and lifted a shaking hand towards Domnall.

"Aye!" Domnall shrugged unapologetically. "No man touches my daughter and walks away unscathed! No man!"

A strange warmth crept into Bree's heart.

"Come with me, lass. No man will raise a hand to ye. I swear on my life's blood and honor as a Highlander."

"Bree!" Jenet wailed plaintively.

It was only then Bree realized she was walking away. She was leaving. She choked a whispered farewell under her breath.

Picking up her skirt, she ran.

In a near state of panic, she burst into the castle kitchen. What had she done? Did she have a choice? It was too late now. It would be folly to stay. As soon as he recovered, Wat would kill her.

Leaning against the wall, she clutched her queasy stomach, but the sound of approaching voices spurred her into action. She could think later. She didn't want to be present when Domnall and Afraig arrived.

Flying about the room, she grabbed the nearest loaf of bread, a wedge of dried cheese, and a bottle of ale for Aislin's supper. As the outer door swung open, she bolted up the stairs and down the dark passage.

Again, doubt assailed her. What had she done? How could she have chosen a stranger over her own mother? Was he really even her father? Again, she reminded herself she had no choice. Emotions churning, she knocked on Aislin's door. At the muffled response, she stepped inside.

The chamber was dark; she could barely see. Aislin lay on the bed, sideways, as if she'd fallen. A deep crimson stained the counterpane and the glass shards of a wine bottle littered the floor. It was not the first time she'd come upon Aislin drunk. With a sigh, Bree set the tray on the table and lit the candle.

"Afraig…" Aislin whispered, weakly.

Frowning, Bree glanced her way.

It was not wine. It was blood. Blood stained the lower half of Aislin's gown, dripping from the bed to form a pool on the floor.

Bree screamed.

Vaguely, she recalled running to Afraig and Domnall. Their faces had registered complete shock. She followed them back to Aislin's chamber. The second time, however, she remained outside the door.

Afraig cursed. Picking up the broken bottle on the floor, she sniffed its contents. "Ye fool! 'Twas too late for juniper berries!" she hissed, turning to Domnall. "There's naught I can do now."

Aislin moaned.

"Bree, lass, help me fetch the priest," Domnall said grimly. "'Twill nae be long before the end."

It was not, but she did survive the night.

They kept a vigil at the foot of the bed, and the village priest gave her last rites, intoning prayers in a hushed voice. As the sun rose, Aislin breathed her last. Her white lips moved wordlessly as her hand fell lifeless from the bed.

The vision of that grey hand stayed with Bree even as Afraig guided her to the kitchen table. Someone placed a steaming bowl of porridge next to her, but she had no appetite. She merely observed it growing cold.

Domnall and Afraig had been arguing for several hours, speaking mostly Gaelic, but sprinkled with sufficient amounts of English that she understood Domnall wished to leave immediately. The MacDonald must know of Aislin's demise. There was a new bride to be found for the man, Ruan. Apparently, he was so eager to wed he cared not who the woman might be. Finally, when the morning sun filtered through the open kitchen door, they seemed to have reached an agreement.

"Aye." Afraig nodded grudgingly. "I'll trust yer heart, Domnall. But, if he isn't as ye say, I'll skewer yer rotten soul next we meet."

Domnall briskly rubbed his hands together with a triumphant snort as Afraig moved to wrap Bree in a warm embrace.

"Ach, lass," Afraig said with a sigh. She laid her cheek on top of Bree's head, "'Tis time to leave."

Bree yawned, suddenly tired. "Yes," she murmured. "I think I could sleep, just for a bit."

"Leave, lass," the woman repeated. She cleared her throat gruffly. "'Tis time to leave this place and go home to Skye."

Bree raised her head with a growing sense of apprehension.

"Yer father thinks it best nae to tempt Wat's sons into stirring a wee bit of trouble. I know ye'll be weary, love, but ye'll sleep well tonight." A tear trickled down her withered cheek.

Afraig could not be crying; she simply never did.

"Ye'll be safe, soon, far away from this accursed place," the woman was saying.

They were leaving. Domnall was really taking her away. Bree wanted to scream, to shout that she'd changed her mind, but her lips had strangely locked into place.

"Aye," Afraig said, smiling warmly, "but I'll be seeing ye soon, love. I swear it. When Huntley is gone, I'll come home. 'Twill nae be long." She draped a warm plaid over her shoulders and planted a firm kiss on her forehead before glaring at Domnall.

"He's a right honorable man," her father replied, affronted, before leaving for the stables and closing the door with a bang.

Once again, Afraig kissed her, pulling her outside, and speaking all the while. "…and remember, love, Domnall is a fair and just man."

A large, shaggy brown horse stood in the courtyard, flicking its ears and stamping its foot impatiently. It was an ugly beast. Its hooves were massive; she'd never seen the like before.

"He'll see ye properly settled," Afraid was still talking.

She was going away, away from the only place she'd ever known.

She heard Domnall's crisp query, "Where are her thing?"

"She doesn't have any," Afraig replied brusquely.

Bree wanted to cry. She wanted to tell them she'd changed her mind, but Afraig crushed her close in a final farewell and then pushed her toward her father.

It was happening too fast.

With a light toss, Domnall threw her onto the back of the large, brown beast. She clutched the pommel with white fingers as Domnall vaulted into the saddle behind her and with a loud, harsh word drove the horse forward.

Gritting her teeth, the only thing Bree could think of now was how much she hated horses.

DUNVEGAN

"Skye!" Domnall announced, with pride evident in his voice.

Bree stared in dismay at the brown expanse spreading before her.

This cold, wind-swept, endless sea of mud was her father's precious Highlands, her new home. In the far distance, trees dotted the hills, their trunks gnarled and twisted by the perpetually strong winds. Rocks randomly sprouted from the earth, and were covered by gorse, fern, and heather.

This was nothing like the ancient growth covering the green rolling hills in England, with its tidy flocks of sheep. Here, sheep ran wild, perched like mountain goats on the sheer drops of the craggy mountains, with no sign of a shepherd in sight.

"Aye," Domnall murmured. "There is no place like Skye, lass. This land sings to ye."

Forcing a dutiful nod, Bree was thankful he mistook her consternation for awe. Everything in his wondrous isle seemed to be a shade of brown, even the water falling down the cracks in the mountains. It appeared unfriendly and bleak. However, it would be worth living anywhere if she could simply get off the back of the horse.

The journey had been miserable, with one pest-filled Inn after another. Several times, they had slept huddled under plaids in the cold rain. To be finally warm and dry and to eat something hot that was not burned on the edges and raw in the middle seemed outlandishly decadent.

Still, as wretched as the traveling conditions had been, learning more of her father had been unexpectedly pleasant. He was a jovial man, understanding, patient, though far too free with women. Every evening had found him in the company of a widow or a brew mistress. More than once, their morning departure had been overly hasty due to an irate husband riding furiously behind them for a time.

As she traveled for hours on end, with little to do but think, Bree fondly remembered Domnall's beating of Wat. In spite of her best efforts otherwise, she was beginning to trust the man. A little, she firmly amended to herself, only a little. Men were, by nature, untrustworthy, hard-hearted beasts.

"We're home!" Domnall boomed again.

They had reached the crest of the hill. Far below them, nestled close to the sandy shore of an inlet on a bed of rocks rose the mighty, well-weathered fortress of Dunscaithe.

It was a wild place, rough. Here, there were trees, but fierce looking ones. Peat and heather clothed the forest floor. Across the water, she could see hills rising in the distance. More sheep dotted the moors and above them gulls wailed.

A sudden gust of wind clawed her hair, whipping it wildly about her head. As Domnall prodded the mountain horse forward, she wondered, for the first time, exactly where he lived and what a daughter of his would do.

As Dunscaithe loomed larger, she began to hope he didn't actually live in the castle. The cold, brown highland moors were far better than living entombed in a sinister mountain of stone.

At last, they were plodding under the wide-open gates and then lumbering to a halt in a jingle of bits and creaking leather. The courtyard was empty and Domnall made no move to dismount.

Bree held still, waiting uneasily.

Finally, a voice hailed, "Domnall!"

A man approached. He was young but with hair already thinning on top. His hazel eyes were kind, even as his brows furrowed in a disapproving line. He was followed by several others, all bare-kneed and wearing plaids. It was strange to see so many men wearing the same form of dress and all as oblivious to the cold as her father seemed to be.

The man scrutinized her intently, plucking her from the saddle and swinging her down with an easy arm. Apprehensively, she shrank back, but his attention was on Domnall as his deep voice echoed throughout the courtyard. He spoke in Gaelic.

Domnall lifted his hand and made some kind of announcement.

The men gasped, waving their hands in agitation.

Bree strained to decipher the harsh, yet pleasantly lilting slur of words, but with little success. She frowned at herself. If only she'd paid more attention to Afraig and her father on the journey when they had spoken in Gaelic, maybe she'd now understand why they were agitated. She caught the rare word, but was entirely unsure of what a 'sheep's arse', 'cheese', and 'boat' had in relation to each other. It seemed an odd combination to upset so many men.

Domnall's voice rose and the courtyard went silent.

All eyes turned upon her and the balding man gaped in astonishment.

Domnall dismounted, speaking all the while. This time, even Bree recognized the Gaelic word 'daughter'. Nervously, she stepped into the welcoming circle of her father's arm.

The strange man's face lit. He pulled absently on his chin and finally murmured in English, "I...agree...'tis muckle better this way." He exchanged a long level look with his men and then Domnall.

Bree held her breath with a growing sense of unease. She wished she had the courage to ask what they were speaking about, but she didn't.

At last, the man balding man nodded and said in English, "Aye, 'tis a braw plan, Domnall. I give it my blessing. 'Tis a better plan, to be sure. One I'm nae ashamed to support. Aye, I did disagree with Tormod over Aislin, many a long hour, but he insisted. There was naught I could do."

A sigh of relief circled the gathering and Domnall chuckled, squeezing her shoulder, "Bree, lass. This is Cuilen, the McDonald of Dunscaithe. Ye'll be owing him yer loyalty."

Bree blinked and it took several moments to understand that this stranger, dressed plainly in the same homespun plaid as the others, was the lord of a castle. Quickly, she dipped into a curtsey as Cuilen's bright blue eyes bore into hers. She cleared her throat nervously, unable to shake the notion that something was not quite right about this.

"Ach, 'tis right welcome ye be, lass, ye can rest on the ship…as best as yer able," he grunted. He turned to bark impatiently at his men, "Be off! We leave in the hour. There's a storm brewing that I'll nae wait for."

Domnall nodded in agreement.

With an impatient flick of his hand, Cuilen strode away with a sense of purpose. Bree had no time to wonder as her father placed his hand on her neck, guiding her forward.

"Ye've just time to change, lass," he boomed. Pointing to a large woman standing close by, he explained, "Anne here, will help ye. I've duties elsewhere."

Bree opened her mouth, but he left before she could frame a question. She wondered sourly if his duties elsewhere included yet another plump widow. Closing her mouth, she shifted her attention to Anna who smelled faintly of sour milk, but at least her aged face crinkled in a friendly way.

Anna spoke only Gaelic, as apparently did most of Dunscaithe's inhabitants. Therefore Bree spent the next hour nodding at words she did not understand, and repeating the few words she did know over and over again, to show at least that she was trying to understand. Finally, after much prodding and chattering, Anna left her alone with a basin of tepid water.

Peeling off her mud-caked dress, Bree washed herself as quickly as she could. She was anxious to be clothed before anyone returned. Her bruises had faded to a faint yellow, but she was reluctant that anyone should see them.

Grimacing, she shrugged into the rough-spun, yellow dress that was provided to her and snatched the comb to attack her hair. Her thoughts wandered and finally settled on her mother, and the way she had bargained with Raph. Remembering her mother's cutting words brought on an unexpected surge of anger that burned deep within her soul.

"Are ye well, lass?"

With a start, she whirled.

Domnall stood behind her, brows drawn in a curious line. His gaze dropped. "Ach, I'll tend that. How did ye do such a thing?"

Looking down, she saw a jagged scratch across the palm of her hand. The comb had snapped in two. There was only a little blood and it hardly hurt. Flustered, she jerked her hand away.

Domnall studied her briefly. Taking the strip of cloth meant for her hair, he grasped her hand and quickly tied the cloth around the small wound. When he'd finished, he planted a kiss on her forehead. "Trust me, lass. I'll see ye taken care of. I swear it. Now, we'd best go. Cuilen's waiting for ye."

Frowning, Bree followed him to the courtyard. A ripple of alarm coursed through her upon seeing the horse still saddled. To her dismay, Domnall promptly tossed her onto the back of the beast and hoisted himself behind her once again.

"We've nae far to ride, lass," he said, reading her mind. "The boat's nae far."

"Where are we going on a boat?" Bree asked, a little timidly.

He ignored her question and called out a hearty farewell to several gray-haired women as their horse galloped through the gate they had entered a mere hour ago. In moments, they rounded a large jutting rock to join a small party of men seated on horses even shaggier than their own.

Cuilen waited at the head, sitting upon the largest beast. He raised his arm and they wheeled their mounts, cantering down to the beach.

A short distance away, Bree could see a ship bobbling in the restless sea. Dark clouds were gathering on the horizon. She eyed the dipping mast, uneasily.

"Ye've naught to fret over."

Startled, she was surprised to find Cuilen had pulled up alongside them.

"Dunvegan's nae far," he grunted. Shifting to Gaelic, he spoke to her father.

Bree strained to decipher the words, but was interrupted when Domnall lifted her from the horse and tossed her into a small dingy. In moments, they had rowed her out to the ship, helping her board with gentle hands and escorting her to the back. She huddled on the wooden seat under several warm plaids provided by sympathetic and smiling men. Too tired to care anymore, she buried her head in her arms.

Suddenly, an ear-splitting screech strongly resembling a strangled goat shrieked through the air, and she sprang to her feet in alarm.

The men laughed, the most amused being her father. "Aye, lass, 'tis only the piper! He keeps the men rowing."

Several of the men brandished their oars, grinning.

Embarrassed, she eyed the man with the pipes dubiously. She'd never seen such an odd instrument before. Cautiously, she settled back into the plaids.

The journey was torturous.

The piper never stopped playing, striking one melancholy air after another. The sound grated. The ship heaved and rolled, and she soon discovered she much preferred the boney back of a horse. She spent most of her time seized with giddiness and retching over the side. Hours later, her father sat quietly down beside her, an odd expression upon his face.

"Here, lass," he murmured, offering a silver flask.

The pungent smell made her want to retch again.

She hurriedly pushed it away.

"'Twill nae be much longer, and then we'll be home," he reassured, slipping a comforting arm around her shoulders.

Sadness and pain in his eyes caught her attention, pulling at her heart. Pain was something she could understand. An unexpected wave of emotion arose, and for the first time she truly felt this man was her father. Exhausted, she leaned into his embrace and took comfort. Here was a man she could finally trust.

As the day wore on, storm clouds descended and unleashed a torrent of rain that forced them to weigh anchor in a small inlet. They took refuge in a nearby cave. It was cold and damp and Bree slept fitfully. She was relieved when dawn finally arrived, but the wind was still too wild to sail. It was not until late in the afternoon that their journey resumed. By then, she was exhausted, shivering under the plaids and dozing fitfully.

Sometime later, she woke abruptly and sat up in alarm. The banging of the oars mingled with calls from men on the boat. Voices answered them from the darkness around them, and then the twinkling light of torches reflected on the calm surface of the water.

"Aye, lass," her father said as he loomed up before her. "We've arrived."

As the tall, forbidding walls of a castle rose in the gloom, Bree felt a wave of apprehension. "Arrived?" she repeated, throat dry.

"Dunvegan," Cuilen answered, appearing suddenly. He pointed to the dim outline of a castle perched on a small island of rock, separated from the shore by a narrow ravine.

Stiffly, Bree scrambled to her feet, but Cuilen pushed her down.

"The sea-gate is the only way in, lass," he said roughly. "Sit. We'll be there soon enough."

Daunted by Cuilen's cold demeanor, she sat back down as they began the slow approach to the sea-gate. She frowned. Her father had never mentioned he lived in Dunvegan Castle. Several smaller boats appeared out of the mist and joined theirs.

Bree squinted, peering ahead as more torches dotted the castle walls.

It looked like a gloomy place, chilling, with an inhospitable air. The boat hugged the castle wall, and it finally paused by a gate that opened directly into the water. Hands reached out, pulling her up and pushing her through a long, narrow stair cut deep in the rocks leading to the castle.

"Come, lass," Her father's voice boomed comfortingly. He grasped her elbow and pressed her forward.

Cuilen swept past them, joining several burly men as Domnall led her through a smaller door near the kitchens. The smell of roasting mutton made her hungry. Weariness descended upon her all at once, and she staggered after her father up the narrowly winding stairs. Dimly, she wondered if she'd ever get to sleep again.

They entered the great hall.

Tables lined the length of the room with the laird's table at the head. The MacLeod coat of arms hung above the fireplace, reflecting the dying light of the torches on the walls. Close by, stood a heavy iron chest with a lock. Her father pointed to it and told her that within the chest she'd find the famed Fairy Flag of Dunvegan, a treasure of the castle, but being so tired, she found it difficult to concentrate on what he was saying. The tables around her bore the cold, greasy remnants of the evening meal. A few men still lounged about, but most lay already stretched out, snoring amidst the rushes scattered on the floor.

"Drink this, lass."

Someone thrust a cup into her hands. Wearily, she lifted her head to thank her benefactor, but they were already gone.

Domnall pressed her down onto a bench, murmuring, "Wait here." And he was gone.

Gratefully, Bree sipped the warm and spicy contents of the cup. She'd never tasted anything quite like it. With each swallow, a comforting heat grew in her throat and then her stomach. She drained the last drop with regret, but a passing stranger kindly filled it once more. She was nearly finished with what she thought was her third cup when Domnall startled her from the pleasant stupor.

"Come, lass."

She winced. His voice was abominably loud, much louder than usual.

With a hint of impatience, he repeated, "Come!"

Glowering, Bree struggled to her feet. It took several attempts before she succeeded, and she protested when Domnall wrenched the cup from her hands.

Her father chuckled, sniffing the contents. "I see. Mayhap, 'tis best this way."

Clasping her arm, he half-carried her forward. "This way, lass, 'tis nae far. They are waiting."

Wondering foggily who *they* might be, Bree allowed him to support her down a narrow passageway and into a small chamber.

Men filled the room, clustering around a large wooden table. She searched the sea of strange faces, the features blurring eerily in the shadows cast by the dancing fire. They were dressed remarkably alike in mustard colored shirts and brown plaids of various shades.

"Nae what you were expecting, eh, Ruan?" Domnall laughed.

Bree blinked. *Ruan.* The name was familiar, though she could not remember why. Far more pressing was the concern she might retch. Her stomach rolled, and for the first time she suspected just what she'd been drinking. She tripped, but her father caught her elbow, drawing her to the table as the occupants around it began a heated exchange.

"No!" a man's deep voice chafed from close by. "Aye, I agreed to Aislin, nae this one! Find another man!"

"Ruan, lad, dinna be so ungrateful!" someone laughed.

"Gratefulness has naught to do with it, Robert!" the man's baritone continued. "Find another man! I'll nae do this, nae with Domnall's daughter! No!"

At that, Bree tried to focus her blurred vision on the speaker, but was distracted as a large man seated at the table began to pound his fist angrily.

"Silence!" the strange man said, raising his voice.

He was the only one seated in the room.

As his blue, watery eyes swept over her, Bree felt her flesh crawl. This was a cold man, a disturbing one. Instinctively, she drew back, but her father pressed her forward and the voices abruptly fell silent.

The man pinned her with a long, silent look, and then nodding once, growled, "Ye'll do as I order ye, Ruan."

"Tormod, this isnae—"

"Silence, Ruan!" the man retorted. "Ye'll agree to this, or 'twill nae be to yer liking what I'll have done to Merry!"

Bree swallowed nervously.

"Aye," the deep baritone finally muttered.

There was a collective sigh of relief as another man appeared by her side.

The newcomer was dirty. As he began to speak, his beady eyes flitted nervously in every direction but hers. He smelled of fish and wine, and whatever he was saying, it had apparently caught the interest of them all. Bree once again regretted the fact she hadn't put more effort into learning Gaelic from Afraig. She sighed audibly, and then promptly blushed, ashamed of her odd lack of control.

The fish-smelling man shot her an irritable glare as he withdrew a wooden cross from the folds of his sleeve and pressed it to his lips.

He was a priest.

Curiously, she wondered what the priest intoned that kept all enthralled, but as his voice droned on, she once again was unable to resist her impulse to yawn and she did, loudly.

Someone chuckled.

Embarrassed, and no longer able to focus, she closed her eyes and swayed lightly on her feet. Strong, steady fingers closed over her shoulders, and she smiled. Her father was always there when she needed support. He was proving a kind and thoughtful man, a man worthy of trust. He was nothing like Wat.

The rich deep voice which had protested before spoke, its tone rank with irritation. It sounded unusually close. Her father chimed in, speaking her name. One of the hands left her shoulder. Something cool circled one of her fingers. She frowned, bewildered, and lifted her lashes.

A ring circled her finger.

It was far too big.

Turning toward her father for an explanation, she was startled to find him standing across the table instead of behind her. His face filled with what could only be guilt. For several, long minutes, she frowned in confusion, wondering at the firm hands holding her upright before understanding they belonged to someone entirely new. With a gasp, she whirled, to find herself staring at the midriff of the tallest man she'd ever seen.

Dark, smoky eyes caught and held hers for only the briefest of moments, but long enough that she could see resentment roiling within them. She'd only the briefest impression of firm lips, a strong jaw, and dark hair carelessly tied by a strip of leather before the man dropped his hands and moved away amidst scattered, half-hearted applause.

Disconcerted, Bree inspected the ring again, and then faced her father.

Domnall was grinning at Cuilen, holding a cup for someone to fill. "Tis done, then," he said in English with a smile.

Everywhere, cups magically appeared as the wine poured and the chamber buzzed with chatter, this time in English.

"Aye, there's many a jealous maid in Skye this night."

Muffled snorts greeted this comment.

"The wedding night will nae be so trying now, eh, Ruan?" someone chortled. "Bree's a comely lass."

At this, Bree's heart began to race, each frantic beat clearing the wine-induced haze.

"Aye," another laughed. "I wish I'd offered to wed Aislin!"

She held her breath.

"Ach, if ye'd offered to wed that cow, ye would have got one …certainly nae a comely lass. Only Ruan has such braw fortune!"

Bree willed her pounding heart to still. As comments erupted from all sides, she finally knew the truth. Domnall had brought her here to take Aislin's place. He had wed her to this Ruan. It was not even a proper wedding on the steps of a church, but it didn't matter to anyone here. He hadn't cared for her at all. He'd merely needed a replacement. Slowly, she raised her head.

Domnall was studying her closely. "There is naught to fear, lass," he assured softly.

From far away, Bree heard her own voice say, "What have you done?"

A PROPER HUSBAND

"Ruan is an honorable man," Domnall cleared his throat. "I've told ye that. And he'll make a braw husband that will protect ye well!"

She wanted to vomit.

The priest had stood in front of her, binding her to Ruan, and she'd merely noted his dirty nails and beady eyes. She hadn't protested; she hadn't even known. Her consent hadn't been required. Domnall's words on her behalf had been adequate for these Highlanders.

The enormity of her new situation struck her. She was wed to a stranger in a strange country, one in which she didn't even understand the language. She could not move or think. She could do nothing, but stare dumbly as her lips drained of all color.

"Bring the lass some wine," someone ordered. "She's going to faint."

"Or retch," another added helpfully.

Someone plied a bottle of wine between her clammy lips. It seared a path down her throat even as a cold fury took hold deep within her heart. She'd been a fool. Her own father had used her as a tool, but why? To further his place in the clan?

Raising her chin, she stepped forward to clench the table with her hands, not caring what any might think. Lifting her head high, she locked gazes with her father and accused, "I trusted you."

He had the grace to avert his eyes. "Ach, ye still can, lass. I've done ye right, Bree."

Bree's nostrils flared in disgust as Domnall held out his hands in a placating gesture. Just an hour ago, she'd have thrown herself in his arms and taken comfort there. But not anymore.

"Do not touch me!" she hissed, gulping back sudden tears. "I want nothing more of you." It was a vow and one never more fervently felt.

Domnall's shoulders sagged and he seemed to age in front of her, "I'm an auld man, Bree. I chose the best husband to care for ye... and 'twas nae just me. Afraig had her say in the matter. She made me swear nae to tell ye, until 'twas done."

Afraig? The words cut her soul like a knife. Afraig had spent many hours with her, dreaming of their cottage by the sea! Afraig would never have betrayed her this way! Yet, even as her mouth opened in protest to denounce the lie, even as she cursed her father at the top of her trembling voice, in words she'd never used— indeed, words a woman would never dare say to a man— her heart told her it was true.

Afraig's gestures, the half-finished sentences, even then, she'd known the woman was hiding something. Clutching her stomach, she thought she really would retch. Afraig had known. She'd sent her with Domnall to Scotland to marry Ruan. Still cursing, she raised her arm to ward off the blows that were sure to follow such a wicked outburst, but she still cursed.

To her surprise, someone chuckled.

Instinctively, she whirled, astonished to discover it was her newly made husband lounging against the table with folded arms. Amusement flickered in his burning eyes as scattered snorts of laughter circled the chamber.

"Ye've yerself a wee wild one, Ruan," Cuilen commented dryly.

"Aye, 'tis the spitfires that warm a man's soul," someone laughed.

"...And bed," another voice added.

Ruan turned away, and Bree was startled to see Domnall beaming broadly as more wine poured. The men in the chamber viewed her with outright amusement and a deepening interest.

All save one.

The man seated at the head of the table was silent, frosty. His expression made the words shrivel on her lips.

Nervously, she ducked her head and stepped back.

The crowd of men shifted, parting enough so she could see the door. Without thinking, she bolted, pushing through the crowd only to trip over a booted foot and pitch headlong onto the rush-strewn floor.

Hands from all sides pulled her up, hands that threw her into a state of panic. Were they playing with her? Perhaps, lulling her into a false sense of security before the blows fell. Ruan was a tall and strong man; his blows might kill her. Wat almost had, many times, and he was a much smaller man.

Gripped by a growing hysteria, she began to screech. She clawed and kicked with every ounce of her strength, and then the hands let go.

The men melted back.

Leaping awkwardly to her feet, she headed once more for the door. However, this time, she collided with the same muscled stomach, and then an equally muscled pair of arms deftly lifted her upright by the shoulders and held her captive with uncommon ease.

Once again, Ruan's smoldering eyes met hers.

Not stopping to think, she drew up her knee and struck him fully in the groin. He dropped her and doubled over. Dimly, she heard shrieks of hooting laughter. She stumbled back and tripped on the hem of her dress.

Ruan lunged. His eyes widening in alarm as he grabbed her wrist to yank her roughly into his arms.

She screamed again and half choked on a sob.

"I'm trying to save ye, lass!" His deep voice arose sharply above hers. "Surely, ye don't *want* to be roasted?"

As if on cue, the logs in the fireplace behind her collapsed with a loud crash and sent a shower of sparks into the room. However, the fact she'd nearly fallen into the roaring flames seemed of little consequence compared to the dark stranger now scowling down at her.

It was simply too much.

Deep, horrible sobs caught hold of her as she pounded his broad chest with her fists.

Muttering a curse, he let her go. He fell back several paces, and she again headed for the door.

This time, she ran straight into the arms of a grey-haired woman.

"Afraig!" she gasped in hysterical relief.

Lurching forward, she threw her arms about the woman, only to realize belatedly it was not Afraig after all. The woman hugged her all the same. As Ruan exploded into a heated torrent of Gaelic, the woman slipped her arm about her waist.

"I'm Isobel, lass," she said, drawing her through the door. "Ye seem dead on yer feet, love. Let's leave the men to shout on their own."

Isobel led her away as the room broke into a riot of voices. Ruan's and Domnall's rose above the rest.

The woman led Bree up the narrow, steep stairs of a tower and into a small, sparsely furnished chamber. It contained a bed, a large wooden chest, and nothing else. A warm fire crackled on the hearth and the floor was strewn with fresh rushes.

"Ach, lass, they've nae done ye right," Isobel muttered, clucking a little.

Several youths appeared, lugging a large wooden tub. With much effort, they squeezed it between the bed and fireplace and disappeared, only to return a short time later with buckets of hot water.

"Aye," Isobel said as she smiled, bobbing her head. "A nice warm bath will do ye good."

The woman's kindness was her undoing, and Bree burst into a fresh bout of tears.

"Ye'll be safe now, lass," Isobel crooned and enveloped her into a warm, bosomy embrace. "Ye've naught to fret over. There are none better than my Ruan."

The tears dried instantly and suspicion set in. This woman was Ruan's ally, not hers. How could she possibly think she was safe? Bree clenched her teeth. She'd just wed a stranger and the fact she hadn't known, that her father had spoken her vows, apparently didn't matter to these inhabitants of Dunvegan.

Isobel patted her hair and then stepped back, surveying Bree's dress with a critical eye, "Ach, that will nae do. I'll be finding ye something decent. I'll send a bite, but ye'd best bathe whilst the water is hot."

With a sympathetic smile, she shooed the gaping lads out and then followed them to close the door behind her with a firm click.

For several long minutes, Bree remained standing beside the tub, sniveling, before the realization struck her that she was alone. She made her decision in an instant. She'd leave. Anything would be better than remaining where her fate was certain.

Darting to the door, she peered cautiously up and down the narrow twisting stairs and craned her head each direction for any hint of sound. Upon hearing nothing, she gripped the rope that spanned the length of the tower with cold fingers and crept down.

Her mind worked at a feverish pace. Water surrounded the castle, but she remembered that land hadn't been far off. In the flickering torchlight upon their arrival she'd seen the dim shapes of trees and the black shadows of hills. Perhaps she could steal a boat and chance the moors. She could find her way back to England, to Afraig.

She clenched her fists a little at the thought of Afraig's betrayal. Afraig had always known her dream had been to live in a cottage by the sea *without* the danger of a husband. She had led her to believe it was possible.

She took a deep breath. Going back to England was a preposterous scheme, and the voice whispering in the back of her mind coolly informed her it was a ridiculous one at that. She had already traveled across the wilds of Scotland. It had been an excruciating journey. Alone and on foot, with winter approaching, it would be nigh on impossible to return to England. Brushing the voice aside, she convinced herself anything was preferable to remaining in Dunvegan, as the wife of that disturbing stranger called Ruan. He was a huge man. She would never survive a beating.

She was on the bottom step when she heard the actual voices. There was no time to react, and she didn't see the door swing open. She only heard the shattering thud as she collided with the wood.

Pain exploded in her nose, and she fell, ears ringing.

"My lady, what are ye doing here?" an apologetic voice asked, floating in the gloom above her.

Strong arms pulled her to her feet and swept under her knees, lifting her easily as if she were a child.

Fingers gently prodded her nose.

"Tis broken," a deep voice observed, dispassionately.

It was Ruan's.

Then, her father snorted, "By the saints, she's bleeding like a stuck pig!"

A torch appeared and she could dimly see the young man carrying her back up the stairs. His hair was blond, his eyes brilliantly blue. When he noticed her scrutiny, he gave her a wide smile.

"I'm Ewan!" he introduced himself with a cheeky grin. "And I'm right pleased to make your acquaintance, my lady."

Domnall's loud voice sounded from nearby. "Aye, lass. Ewan's a trustworthy lad."

Bree swallowed a gasp of pain as Ewan set her down gently on the bed, in the very same chamber she'd just escaped.

Isobel appeared, gingerly probing her nose and agreeing that it had, indeed, been broken. Faces swam into view. The young Ewan's, her father's, Isobel's once again, and lastly, she saw the forbidding figure observing them all with a brooding scowl, as he leaned against the door.

It was the man, Ruan.

His dark eyes burned through her soul, and she quickly looked away, wishing he'd disappear.

"Ruan's a gentle lad, Bree," Domnall patted her knee. "Ye'll see soon enough."

Bree's grimace of doubt abruptly turned into a howl of pain. Lifting her lashes through the haze of the tears, she saw once more the towering form of her new husband still framing the door. He looked less than pleased. He stood with arms folded angrily and brows furrowed. He was huge. One blow would smite her dead. Her heart fluttered.

"She's a bairn!" Ruan announced, glowering at Domnall. "She's too young, scarce older than Merry! What have ye done?"

Domnall placed an arm about his newly made son's shoulders, "She's of a proper age to wed, lad," he assured. His voice dropped as he slipped softly into Gaelic.

Burying her head in her hands, Bree willed them all to be gone. When silence finally greeted her, she cautiously lifted her head to find her wish granted.

Once again, she was alone.

Immediately, thoughts of escape possessed her once again. She threw back the coverlet, but her feet had scarcely touched the floor when Isobel entered, bringing a steaming bowl and a cup.

"Let me see the nose now, lass," the woman ordered. Her voice held a mixture of concern and amusement, "Ye've got the castle buzzing, ye have. Ruan's got his hands full, doesn't he, no?"

Firm fingers pressed her nose, and Bree choked.

Isobel pursed her lips, "'Tis nae a bad break, but ye'll have a nasty bruise. We've naught to do but hope it'll heal straight, that, and a bowl of milk for the fairies." She stood, smoothing her dress. She stared for several minutes before asking, "Why were ye running down there, lass?"

Bree frowned, searching for a fitting reply.

Isobel chided softly, "Ye'd best nae try it again, 'tis dangerous. The men are drunk now. They would nae think twice of taking their pleasure, be ye Ruan's wife or no. Lassies canna roam safely here after dark. Tormod has seen to that."

Alarmed, Bree recalled the cold man seated in the chamber and the way his eyes had swept over her. So his name was Tormod.

"Ruan will be hard-pressed keeping ye safe as 'tis. Ye'd best help him a wee bit."

At that, Bree drew back, temper rising. As far as she was concerned, Ruan was the same as the rest. In spite of Isobel's faith to the contrary, he probably was a scoundrel like the rest.

"Ach, well..." the woman murmured, sending her a measured look. "My Ruan's nae like the others, lass, ye'll see." She thrust the warm bowl of porridge in her hands and added, "Best eat. Effric's needing me now, so I must be gone."

She left, closing the door with a soft thump.

Speculatively, Bree eyed the door once again.

THE MOORS

Ruan scowled at his scratched hands, Bree's shrieks of terror still ringing in his ears. Wincing, he reached for the bottle of wine, saying, "Ye should have told her."

"She'll make a fine wife," Domnall repeated, for the fourth time, as if by merely saying it, it would be so.

Ruan eyed him. He'd come to know Domnall well, since his son Dougall's premature death. He knew the man was trying to project a confidence he didn't feel, but why he would wed his daughter to him, of all men, mystified him. He thought of her flashing green eyes staring over hands clutching her bleeding nose. She was so small, far too young, and terrified.

The bench sagged beneath the weight of a newcomer, and he glanced up to see Ewan's wide grin.

Ruan groaned and turned to his right only to see the amused face of his uncle beaming over him.

"And why the gloom and despair?" Robert asked, eyes twinkling with mirth. "If yer wife be younger and prettier than ye were expecting and a MacBethad as well, what is the harm? Tormod and Cuilen agree the tie still stands! The affair has worked out nicely, to be certain!"

"She's too young," Ruan growled, sweeping the cup aside to drink directly from the bottle, downing Tormod's precious wine like water. Too young, and from what he could recall, far too enticing.

"She's of age," Domnall disagreed. "And 'tis done. There's naught to change."

"There is still one... minor custom" Ewan said, lowering his eyes suggestively. "The wedding ni—"

Ruan whirled. The young man averted his eyes to stare at the ceiling as if there were something there of great interest. But Ruan knew that Ewan understood him only too well. Ewan knew the exact source of his consternation. He knew that Ruan was done with women, finished with the lot. He hadn't dealt with them in over a few, blissfully peaceful years. An old hag of a wife was fine; she'd fit into his plan. He had no desire to deal with a young and tempting one, one that could wake up feelings that he was better off without.

No, his behavior of the past, the overabundance of wine and women, had overly complicated his life and jaded his soul, turning him into something hard and bitter. He'd no desire to craft himself into another version of his father, known as The Black MacLeod. Everyone had suffered under that man's cruel hand, his mother most of all.

"Aye, the wedding night," Domnall boomed.

That and the great clearing of throats roused Ruan from his thoughts. The teasing annoyed him. This was hardly a matter for jest. How could they expect he would consummate the marriage to the terrified lass, who smelled oddly of lavender? She'd ridden weeks on horseback through the wilds of Scotland and suffered a sea voyage in a storm. She was bedraggled, mud-stained, and bone weary. How could she possibly smell of lavender? Annoyed at the turn of his thoughts, he grimaced.

"Aye!" Domnall beamed with pride. "'Tis uncommon luck ye have. Bree is a rare one — hardy, strong and bonny — as befits a daughter of mine!"

Ruan snorted, slamming his fist on the table. The cups rattled. Glaring, he raised his voice. "Ye canna think well of her, to wed her to a MacLeod."

Slowly, Domnall rose, placing both hands far apart on the table. "I pride myself, second most, in my judgment of men," he said softly, his voice calm, but edged with steel, "and foremost in my ability to exact revenge, in those rare cases where my judgment proves false."

Ruan's gaze didn't falter from his.

"Ye may be larger than me, Ruan lad, but prove me wrong, and ye'll taste another side of Domnall few live to speak of."

The tension in the room was almost visible, before Domnall's mouth eased into a smile. "Though ye be a MacLeod, ye've no taste for violence on women, lad. That I ken well enough, or else I'd nae give ye my last living bairn. I care for the lass, but whether she believes that or no is a different matter."

Ruan clenched his jaw. Aye, Domnall's daughter deserved a far more fitting husband. Why was the man blind? He had nothing to offer a wife. He had no land, no coin, and at present, few prospects in finding either.

Angrily sweeping the wine aside, he reached for the whiskey. Aye, whiskey had been a sin of his past as well, and one he'd long since given it up. He frowned to find himself taking to it once again.

There were several snorts of growing amusement, followed by Domnall's outright laughter.

"A bit nervous, are ye?" Ewan chuckled. "Over bedding your bride?"

Ruan jerked, gripping the bottle tightly.

"Ye'll do fine," Domnall said and gave a mock shudder. "Aislin was an eyesore and dimmer of wit. She truly was bigger than a horse."

"One should nae speak ill of the dead," Robert chided softly.

"Aye," Domnall agreed. He shrugged unapologetically. He gestured to the empty bottle in excuse, "Wine loosens the tongue overly much."

Ruan wiped his brow with his forearm. He didn't intend to bed anyone. He'd suffered far too many ill consequences for the rashness of his youth. He helped himself to more whiskey, knowing in his heart that if a decent woman were to hear of his past and inability to provide for her, she'd run away as fast as she could. He'd be the first to understand. His life was mercifully simple now, peaceful and pleasant, and free of scheming women. He intended to keep it that way.

Robert laid a hand on his arm, cautioning "Careful, lad. Best nae be drunk on the wedding night. Women have a long memory for things of that nature."

"I'll nae be touching her," Ruan snorted, brows burrowing deeper. Despite himself, the thought of those remarkable green eyes framed by sooty lashes started a pleasant hum burning his blood. He grimaced, hoping he was merely drunk. Whatever the cause, he was certain of one thing. He must keep her at a safe distance, where he wouldn't have to see her, to find what else there was besides those startling green eyes.

"Ach now, there's no need to be afraid, lad. The only thing ye must remember 'tis a strong man who shows gentleness to his wife."

His uncle and Domnall's continual sprinkling of fatherly advice suddenly grated on his nerves.

Mercifully, Isobel flung the door open and barreled into the room, but then asked, "Where's yer lady, Ruan?"

"What do ye mean, woman?" Domnall stood abruptly.

"I left her for a wee bit, but now she's gone," Isobel replied, agitated. "I canna find her, and I've searched every nook and cranny."

Domnall swore.

***

Caught in a wave of panic, Bree fled down the stairs once again, unable to believe she was now married to a complete stranger. How could this have happened? Her father had used her as a pawn in some ancient feud. She'd never thought to marry. In fact, she'd always dreamt of returning to Skye with Afraig. The two of them would live in their cottage, growing herbs.

She'd been so naïve.

A little voice in her mind asked why she was running, that surely living here was better than going back to England to suffer under Wat, but she shook her head. No, she'd seen the man. Ruan was huge. Men beat women. It was the way of the world. She'd never survive that man's violence.

Slipping out of the castle had been easy.

Finished with their evening chores, the servants headed for a boat that took them to the village, which was scarce more than a stone's throw away.

Bree had merely to join the line.

Several times, she experienced a wave of doubt, but the fear of marriage kept her moving forward.

The women didn't ask questions; perhaps they were too tired or simply didn't care. One by one, they shuffled into the boat, past an exceedingly drunk youth strumming an oar like a lute and singing loudly. He pinched each woman soundly as she boarded.

Bree grimaced, but submitted to the humiliation in silence.

Finally, with all seated, he dipped the oars in the water and rowed them the short distance to the village and as the bottom scraped loudly on the submerged rocks, the women disembarked.

"Ye'll have us drowned soon, Iain," they grumbled.

"Give a kiss, now, love," Iain slurred with a crooked grin, not caring in the least that all were much older than he was.

"Ach!" they all snorted in disgust, filing past the tipsy lad.

Bree cautiously followed, trying her best to appear as if she'd done it a thousand times before. As she lifted her foot over the edge, Iain gave her bottom a healthy slap.

She yelped, lost her balance and nearly fell back into his arms.

He roared.

A smattering of laughter sounded from the women and for the first time several interested pairs of eyes inspected her with curiosity. With her heart pounding loudly in her ears, she drew her plaid over her head, and strode off with an air of purpose through the village.

Mercifully, no one followed.

In a matter of minutes, she left the last cottage behind and was alone.

She was free. Free!

A twinge of fear assailed her, but she straightened her shoulders and firmly reminded herself that at least she was free.

It was pitch black. Clouds blanketed the moon. The wind blew hard, chilling her to the bone. A blast of wind almost ripped the plaid from her head and it began to rain.

Ignoring the feeling of impending doom, she stumbled forward and tripped, landing face first in the mud. Staggering to her feet, she boldly pressed on, but within minutes sank into a mire with icy water up to her knees. The heather scratched her ankles. She bit back a sob and continued on.

In her wine-affected, panicked state, she hadn't thought to bring food. She'd been gone only an hour, and already her skirt was soaked. Her nose ached and both feet were numb. How could she possibly survive? Doubt surfaced and she felt like a fool.

For a brief moment, she considered returning to Dunvegan, but the thought of the beating she would receive spurred her on. She would likely die in either case, but she would die her own way. With determination, she stumbled on.

As the night aged, matters worsened; each gust of wind seared her wet clothing as if it were a blast of fire. Her throat burned and her reddened fingers stung, responding slower each time she clawed the damp plaid closer.

It was becoming difficult to convince herself that her new course of action was worth it.

There was a break in the trees ahead. The sky was brighter there, announcing the impending arrival of the dawn. Her stomach growled. She'd have to worry about food, soon, but she was distracted by another fall. She felt more water seep into her shoes. This time, it seemed almost warm.

What would happen, if by some miracle she actually made it to Thurston Hall? Would Afraig bundle her up and send her back? Would she, heaven forbid, allow the marriage to Raph? Surely, Ruan was better than Raph?

Tears stung her lashes. Why did she have to wed at all? Not every woman wed, she'd seen plenty that hadn't. Why couldn't she be one of them?

Finally, she staggered into the small clearing and peered into the lifting gloom.

Her heart stopped.

A short distance away, Dunvegan gleamed with its village twinkling on the shore.

She caught her breath in despair.

If she continued, she would die on the moors, crows and other wild things would pick at her bones. For a time, she crouched miserably where she was, her mind reeling with the choices before her.

Dying was much harder than she imagined. Why had she run? Surely, being the wife of Ruan, whatever the man might choose to do, was better than freezing in the cold darkness of the moors. At the thought, she began to sob. She was a fool. Now, she'd willingly be the wife of anyone, maybe even Wat's uncle, if the pain in her ears, neck, hands, and feet would simply go away.

Sobbing at her foolishness, she staggered to her feet.

She would return to Dunvegan and face whatever beating she was given.

At the moment, it didn't really matter if she survived there or not. She was going to die, anyway, if she didn't get out of the wind-torn hell of the moors.

The day passed with her mind in a fog. Her ears were ringing and it was difficult to feel her feet. Gulls wheeled and screamed in the bleak skies above her. She had lost track of how many times she had fallen, sliding down hills only to tumble in a heap at the bottom. Several times she heard hooves, but they were distant, leaving her to wonder if it was merely her imagination.

Finally, she acknowledged what had been a growing fear.

She was lost.

WOMEN

The hounds were baying and Ruan kicked his horse into a gallop as Domnall followed. They, along with many others, had spent the night and most of the day searching for Bree. At first it had been difficult to remain seated on his horse, the wine and whiskey having taken their toll, but the bitterly cold wind had soon sharpened his wits.

Reining at the crest of the hill, he watched the hounds streak to the bottom. It would likely be another false alarm. Domnall paused by his side. The man's face was grey with worry. Night was falling and if Bree was without shelter, they both knew she wouldn't survive.

"We'll find her," Domnall repeated, determined.

Ruan drew his lips in a tight line. The man had said nothing else the entire night and day.

"Aye, well, 'tis no wonder she ran," Domnall abruptly accused. "Ye don't cut a welcoming figure with all those black looks ye favor."

Ruan scowled, temper rising in response. "Oh? And, what cause do ye have, wedding her to a stranger without even telling the poor lass?" He knew Domnall was simply worried and tired. He knew it served no purpose, but it felt good to shout all the same.

"By the Saints, if ye hadn't frightened her to near death, she wouldn't have run!" Domnall shouted.

"'Twas her own father that betrayed her, nae me!" Ruan thundered. In his mind, he saw an image of the drunken, small lass standing in front of him, wild-eyed, lips shaking, as a torrent of curses flowed from her mouth. Most in the room hadn't understood enough English to know what she'd said, but he had. He smiled a little. She was a rare one, standing up to her father and then boldly walking into the wilds of Skye to almost certain death. However, the thought that she'd much rather die than be wed to him was a sobering one.

He furrowed his brows into a scowl.

Domnall was still yelling, "—Yer twisted soul, and as her husband, lad, ye are sworn to protect the lass and ye've done pitifully poor so far!"

Ruan's head snapped back of its own accord. He opened his mouth to retort when Ewan and several others arrived in a thunder of hooves and a spray of mud.

"The hounds have found something," Ewan cut in, pointing.

At the bottom of the hill, the beasts clustered, pawing a mound huddled amidst the dead heather and brittle stalks of fern.

Without a word, they wheeled their horses as one and charged down the hill.

Ruan reached her first.

She was unresponsive, huddled in a small quivering heap. Her skin was cold to the touch. He propped her against his knee, and her lashes fluttered.

"Does she yet live?" Domnall croaked, his voice fraught with worry. He had remained on his horse, clutching the pommel.

Ewan tossed him a flask of whiskey and Ruan pressed it against her swollen lips.

After a moment, she coughed.

Domnall burst into a loud mixture of blessings and curses, accompanied by sharp reprimands directed towards both Ruan and his wayward daughter.

She groaned.

"Best get her back to Dunvegan, and quickly," Ewan murmured, concerned.

"Aye," Ruan agreed, peering down at the puffy nose and cracked lips framed by a white face. He'd been far too drunk the previous night to remember more than a pair of flashing green eyes and brown curls. Now, those eyes remained closed and the curls caked with mud. He felt a wave of guilt. Domnall was right; he'd frightened the poor lass out of her wits. It was no small wonder she'd bolted.

He slipped his arm under her knees, preparing to lift her to his horse. At his touch, Bree's eyes flew open. With surprising strength, she lashed out and he lost his balance, dropping her with a curse. She managed to run a few steps before sinking to the ground once more.

Domnall's voice rang, filled with pride, but with an undercurrent of worry. "Aye, she's a MacBethad, she is, a strong lass. Come! Ewan, leave the man to his wife. I've need of a fire and ale... let's leave the man to his wife."

Wife. Ruan cringed. The word was an uncomfortable one, even to think of. To his horror, Ewan mounted his horse.

"Aye," the blond lad agreed. "And I've words that must be said to the hound-master, never have I seen such poorly trained beasts!"

Ruan opened his mouth to protest, but in a creak of leather and jingling bits, Domnall, Ewan and the others moved up the hill, leaving him alone with Bree. He cleared his throat nervously, unexpectedly at a loss for words.

Minutes passed. She remained where she had fallen, with head buried and half-sunken in the mud.

Beginning to wonder if she still lived, he tentatively prodded her shoulder with a finger. With a gasp, she groveled deeper in the mud, throwing her arms to cover the back of her head.

Ruan blinked, recognizing the gesture for what it was. Countless times, he'd seen his mother cower before his father in the same manner. How could the lass even conceive he'd beat a woman, much less one in her precarious condition? Insulted, he barked, "On your feet! I've need of a fire and ale myself!"

Belatedly, he regretted the harsh tone and words. He should not have been surprised that she'd promptly burst into tears and shrink back from him even more, but he was.

Overwhelmed, he exploded into a string of curses entirely directed at the disappearing backs of Domnall and his kin. Why had they abandoned him with this terrified female? He'd probably slay her from sheer fright. Scowling, he reached down to lift her up, but she shrieked and tried to crawl away, flopping helplessly like a fish in the throes of death.

Unnerved, Ruan took a step back.

She was on the verge of hysteria. If the truth be told, he was himself. He shouted, several times, calling for Domnall, or anyone else, for that matter. He was either deliberately ignored, or they had moved too far away to hear his pleas.

Biting back another growl, he came to a decision. It was obvious that words were useless at this point. The sun was falling fast. She could just as easily weep in Dunvegan. He didn't have to stand in the cold, bitter wind when he could be warm and dry.

Yanking her unceremoniously to her feet, he tossed her lightly over his shoulder. Trying his best to ignore the panic-stricken sobs, he strode to his horse. He had to get her back to Dunvegan and out of the wet clothing before she became ill or died from pure fright.

Gritting his teeth, he heaved her into the saddle.

Women!

Time had undoubtedly proven that he'd never understood them, and this one promised to be the worst of the lot. In less than two days, she'd already caused more than her fair share of trouble.

She began to shake, teeth chattering, as he mounted behind her. Valiantly, she resisted his attempts to wrap her in his plaid. Secretly, he admired her strength of will. After a few moments, she fell weakly against his chest, shaking like a leaf and allowed him to cover her warmly.

Filled with pity, he kicked his horse forward. Domnall and the others had all but disappeared in the gathering darkness. He glared, wishing they had waited, but Dunvegan was not far. At the top of the next hill, he paused to force more whiskey between her chattering teeth.

She tried to fight him off, and he grinned. Her strength of will was remarkable. Vainly, he sought words of comfort, but unable to think of any, plied more whiskey between her lips instead. She sputtered and pushed it away gasping for breath, whimpering. Belatedly, he realized he'd almost drowned her. He shoved the flask in his belt, frustrated. Why had Domnall abandoned him with his precious daughter and why had Ewan, of all people, left as well? He'd done so much for the lad. It was a poor way to repay him.

The wind tore over the moors, chilling his bones and sending Bree into another bout of uncontrollable shivering. With a muffled exclamation, he kicked the horse into a gallop. Keeping his gaze focused, he concentrated only on reaching Dunvegan while trying his best to ignore the hysteria of the woman now named 'wife'. To his immense relief, she quickly fell into a whiskey-induced stupor, and he accomplished the remainder of the short journey in silence.

The evening meal was long over, but most were still drinking by the time he strode into Dunvegan's hall with Bree thrown over his shoulder like a sack of meal.

Slowly, Tormod stood, eyeing the mud-caked form. "If ye don't beat her for running, I will," he grated.

Ruan's upper lip twitched in the prolonged silence that followed. He was exhausted, cold, and unnerved, possessing little tolerance. He hadn't missed Tormod's eyes raking Bree the night before, a leering, openly lustful gaze. No one had. Almost snarling, he replied, "No one... no one touches my wife, and ye least of all!"

The vein on Tormod's temple began to throb.

"Ach, now," Domnall said, clearing his throat. He rose from the table, adding, "The lass dinna ken she was to be wed. She'll nae be causing ye trouble. She'll settle in."

"Aye," Cuilen agreed, though his face expressed doubt.

"Best get her to bed, Ruan lad, afore she catches a chill," Domnall ordered, moving to join him.

"Aye... bed," a loud whisper sounded from behind.

Ruffled, Ruan swiveled to search for the offender, but met only serious expressions, albeit with twinkling eyes. Swearing even louder, he stalked through the hall roaring for Isobel as he carried Bree. He stormed up the stairs to his newly assigned chamber. Under his vicious kick, the door crashed open, banging loudly against the wall. In several great strides, he closed the distance to the bed and dropped Bree unceremoniously upon it.

She was appallingly white, her nose swollen and purple. She squinted in confusion, at first, but upon recognizing him, burst into a flurry of flailing limbs. He easily captured her wrists, but gently this time, washed with guilt for the way he'd just tossed her on the bed. He'd behaved heartlessly. Sheepishly, he gave her shoulder an awkward pat.

Abject terror crossed her face.

Ruan opened his mouth, intending to assure her he meant no harm when a scuffle from behind made him whirl. Domnall hovered in the doorway. A shadow of a smile played on the old man's lips as Ewan peered over his shoulder. What they found so amusing Ruan could not imagine. Masking his discomfiture, he growled, "Well? What are ye staring at?"

"No need to bellow like an ox!" A hint of humor tinged Domnall's voice as he stepped into the chamber.

Further words were left unsaid as Isobel bustled in, wagging her head back and forth. She placed a plump hand on Bree's forehead, clucking, "There, lass, caused yerself a fair bit of trouble, haven't ye now? Ye'll be feverish. 'Tis hardly surprising."

"She's a strong one. She's a MacBethad, and..." Domnall began.

Annoyed at his repetitious rambling, Ruan gave an exasperated snort and fetched his flask of whiskey. When he was ill, it was always of immense help, if not by giving him strength, then by allowing him to pass the time in a pleasant haze until his body recovered. Ignoring Isobel's protests, he forced more of the liquid down Bree's throat.

She sputtered and revived enough to reward him with a pair of flashing green eyes. The intensity of here emotions was captivating. Fascinated, he brought the flask to her lips once more, simply to see if she'd do it again. She sent him a look of pure venom and tore the whiskey from his grasp to fling it with all her strength.

He ducked, but not before it grazed his cheek.

Aye, the lass certainly had spirit.

He chuckled.

"Ye've met a match, Ruan lad." Domnall's voice held a note of laughter.

Ruan stiffened. He was surprised that he'd forgotten their presence. Hastily, he stepped back, adopting a fresh scowl.

Bree struggled to sit, finally settling for propping herself on her elbows. Facing her father, she accused hoarsely, "You swore you would protect me!" her voice was barely audible, but the desperation in it was heartbreaking to hear.

"I have, lass," Domnall replied calmly and gave her ankle an affectionate squeeze. "I found ye a strong man, one who will defend ye and fill yer belly with food and bairns. A father canna protect a daughter more."

Bairns. Ruan jerked as if slapped. Wife. Unnerved, he fished for the whiskey in the rushes, managing to rescue the remainder from spilling. He'd planned to ignore Aislin. He wanted nothing to do with a real woman. Aye, and what real woman would want him? He could give her nothing. Aye, not even love. He was too bitter and jaded for that. Wiping his mouth on his sleeve, he stalked to the door, only to find his path blocked by several young lads bringing in a wooden tub and buckets of hot water.

"I need ye here!" Isobel shoved him back while shooing Ewan out the door. "Make use of yerself, lad, and see to Merry. She'll want to know Ruan has returned."

Ruan prepared to tell them that he'd attend to Merry himself, but an angry outburst from the bed caught his attention.

Bree stood on wobbly legs, less than an arm's length away.

"Father?" she croaked in outraged disgust. "Afraig never knew which man it was!"

She snatched the whiskey from Ruan's hand and swallowed a large mouthful.

Domnall's face split into a wide grin and snorted, "Aye, and there's all the proof I need, lass. With yer eyes, temper and the way ye be downing that whiskey, I could hardly deny ye!"

Bree snorted, in very much the same manner Domnall just had before falling into a fit of coughing. She began to waver unsteadily.

"She's going to fall," Domnall noted mildly, making no move to help.

She would have, if Ruan hadn't caught her. He sent Domnall a pained look. He did not much care for the soft feel of a woman's body pressed against his. He didn't need some green-eyed lass, especially Domnall's daughter, waking feelings better left dormant. He grimaced, annoyed to be reminding himself, yet again, that he was through with women.

All at once, he noticed he was still holding her, apparently at the same moment understanding dawned in her face.

Bree launched into another attack, jabbing his midriff and raking his skin with her nails.

"Be still, ye wee hellion!" Ruan bellowed, pinning her wrists behind her back.

For a moment, he thought she was going to retch; her pasty skin seemed almost yellow. Purple and black streaks adorned her nose and cheekbones. Marriage to him hadn't served her well. In two days, she had transformed from a lass with bright green eyes to a drowned, underfed chicken. As her foot grazed his shin, he winced, quickly amending the thought to a mean-spirited, drowned, underfed chicken.

Another well-placed kicked wrenched a new succession of curses from his lip, but as her tears began to flow—real ones—his exasperation fled. Of all things, tears affected him the most. One slid down her cheek. Succumbing to a wave of pity, he wiped it gently with his thumb.

Bree gulped, frowning in a way he could not fathom.

For several long minutes, they stared wordlessly at each other.

Finally, her cracked lips opened. She wailed, "I'm not wedding anyone!"

Gazing down into the bright eyes brimming with tears, Ruan sighed, "Aye, 'tis a wee bit late, lass."

It was supposed to be comforting, or so he thought, but his response seemed only to renew her resistance. Balling her fists, she struck his chest, but more in blows of frustration than anything else. In spite of his best efforts, he grinned. Battling to the last breath was something he could understand, even for a hopeless cause such as this one. Lips twitching, he easily recaptured her wrists in a single hand. They were unusually small hands, perfectly shaped.

The fingers jerked free from his grasp. Startled, he met her eyes once more.

"You'll die if you touch me!" her slurred threat ended with a hiccup, rendering it anything but intimidating.

He could smell the whiskey on her breath.

His grin widened.

Her hand fumbled near his belt before closing over the hilt of his sword. Assuming a fierce expression, she attempted to frighten him. "I'll sever your manhood whilst you sleep!"

To emphasize the statement she tugged at the blade, several times.

On the third attempt, the sword cleared the scabbard almost an inch.

"Aye," Ruan laughed outright, his lips curving into a suggestive smile. "But 'twould take even a larger blade; ye've nae a prayer if ye canna lift this one." His hand closed over hers. Not as a deterrent, but simply to watch her eyes flash defiantly once more.

As expected, they did, and he felt an unexpected tingle of desire creep down his spine. Shocked, he caught his breath. What ailed him?

Had he forgone the company of a woman so long that anything was tempting? She was hardly appealing in her physical state and, frankly, she smelled like a pig. Why was he staying? He should be walking away. Unnerved, he pried her fingers from his chest and pushed her back as if she were poison, nearly falling into the tub. With a curse, he regained his balance and shook his hands as if ridding himself of her. Yes, the less he saw of this particular female, the better. She was disconcerting.

Straightening his plaid, he prepared to leave.

Domnall stood next to Isobel, both silent, and both smiling.

He flushed, startled. Again, he'd forgotten them. He felt strangely exposed, but Isobel didn't allow him to dwell on it.

"I'll be needing ye now, lad," she declared, scuttling forward. "The lass needs a washing and—"

Ruan jerked in dismay. In faith, did they believe *he* would bathe her?

"By the Saints!" he swore, shouting at the top of his lungs. "I've had enough!"

Nearly tripping over the tub again in his haste to leave, he bolted.

At the foot of the stairs, Domnall caught up with him.

"Ruan, lad, a word with ye!"

Gritting his teeth, Ruan spun on his heel with exaggerated slowness.

"Ye'd best be getting yer arse up the tower and to the wife," Domnall said. He seemed inordinately amused, but his tone was commanding. With an ever-widening smile, he added, "'Tis yer wedding night."

Ruan stared.

"The sanctity of this marriage canna be questioned, lad, there is—
"

"Is there trouble?" Tormod's voice slithered through the darkness. "Did she run, again? If she has, I'll flog her within an inch of her miserable life!"

Ruan whirled to find his brother observing them from under the arched entrance. His paunchy face was cold and hard.

"Touch her and ye'll be gutted like a pig, Tormod!" he promised passionately. "Is that simple enough to remember?" It was not that he felt the need to protect his newly wed wife. Well, perhaps he owed the lass for such a miserable start. No, he told himself, he simply desired to be done with Tormod, once and for all.

Tormod paled in anger.

"All is well," Domnall inserted smoothly, placing a restraining hand on Ruan's shoulder. "The lad's on his way to his bedchamber even now."

Cuilen and Robert appeared behind Tormod.

Ruan swallowed, appalled, and then Domnall was pulling him up the stairs.

"Ye don't have to touch her," the man hissed in his ear at the chamber door. "Just stay the night, that's all that is needed, lad."

Domnall's strong arm caught him off-guard, thrusting him into the room and Ruan stumbled, catching his balance. He straightened to find Bree slumping in the wooden tub, in the most peculiar manner; eyes closed and mouth open, seeming more dead than alive.

Isobel's brows formed a grim line as she said, "Come here, lad."

He held still, not intending to step closer to that alabaster expanse of naked skin.

"Come here!" Isobel ordered uncharacteristically. "And be quick!"

Ruan obeyed out of mere surprise. Rarely did Isobel speak sharply to anyone, and as he drew close, he understood. Scars and healing bruises covered Bree's exposed shoulders and back.

"She's been ill-used, the wee lass," Isobel said with thin lips.

He scarcely heard. He stared at the fading injuries. The journey from England must have been excruciating.

"Ye'd best be careful," Isobel warned, wiping her hands on her skirt. "She's drunk."

Ruan turned to her, baffled.

"Ach, lad, she's slipping."

Bree's nose was perilously close to the water.

"I'm nae staying here," he said quickly. He stepped back, but Isobel was already gone.

He cursed vehemently, but a gurgle from the tub brought his attention back to Bree just in time to observe her sinking blissfully under the water. Swearing again, he grabbed her hair and tipped her upright.

She coughed, sputtering for air, but her eyes remained closed.

Involuntarily, Ruan peeked at her back once more. She was painfully thin. Her ribs and spine sharply outlined. Scars from past whippings laced her back. He wondered who had dared to treat her so cruelly. He could not think of much that would warrant such punishment. Certainly, nothing a slip of a lass could do. He knitted his brows in a brooding frown.

The minutes passed and he waited impatiently for Isobel's return. He faithfully rescued Bree each time she sank below the surface. Finally, he sighed, acknowledging that Isobel had truly abandoned him. As Bree slouched again, he lifted her out of the tub in a smooth motion accompanied by a loud growl of frustration. Averting his gaze, he carried her to the bed, though carefully, and swiftly covered her with a blanket.

For a time, he stood mesmerized by the strangely fierce lass, unable to believe the recent chain of events that had tied his life to hers. He felt a ripple of admiration that she'd fought so valiantly, with such injuries. There was a strength there he'd seen in few, man or woman.

With his heart stirring in the most uncomfortable manner, he moved to take advantage of the still-warm bath water, reminding himself once again that he was finished with women. Aye, what decent woman would want him, anyway?

THE LASS IS DAFT

Bree burrowed deeper into the softness with a smile. She must have fallen asleep on Aislin's bed. The woman would be far from pleased, but she savored the moment with guilty pleasure. A sudden image of Aislin's pale face with the priest praying over her unleashed a host of memories.

No. Aislin was dead.

Groggily, she forced her heavy lids to open.

She recognized only that she was not in Thurston Hall. The grey light of morning revealed a small hearth, a chest, and a wooden tub wedged between it and the bed. Puzzled, she slowly sat up, strangely sore.

It was then that she saw him.

A man sprawled half across the foot of the bed, half on the floor.

She screamed.

He leapt to his feet, dazed, reaching instinctively for his sword but bumping against the wooden tub. Losing his balance, he fell heavily. A cold wave of water rose to deluge the bed, and its iciness jolted her memory.

Ruan.

Yes, the man struggling to his feet, shaking his wet shoulder length hair, the man with the scowling brows and dark, angry eyes focused solely on her was her husband. Her father had simply delivered her to him. Her *husband*.

Her scream abruptly shifted into a squeak.

She ducked her head, frantically searching the clutter of memories returning all at once. The priest had been standing in front of her, blessing her with hands unwashed for months. She'd tried to escape several times. Her nose had been broken.

Gingerly, she felt the swollen tip.

She'd slipped into a boat and then wandered on the moors. The howling wind had been so bitterly cold it had almost burned. She'd lost sensation in her toes and finger.

She shuddered.

The thought of dying had been much easier when not faced with it.

At present, she was willing to do anything rather than be wet and cold again. Almost anything, she amended quickly, anything that didn't have to do with the man glaring down at her. There was no need to fret. He'd be so furious that she wouldn't survive the day.

Heart pounding loudly, she waited, trying in vain not to think. The minutes passed. The silence lengthened. Finally, unable to bear the suspense a moment longer, she opened an eye.

She was alone.

She scanned the room, half expecting him to jump from the shadows, but the chamber was small and there was no place for a man of his size to hide.

Then, she saw the open door.

He had gone.

Bree expelled a long breath, not knowing whether to be relieved or worried. She was exhausted and she ached. She didn't have the strength or desire to attempt another escape. Yet, neither did she want to be there when Ruan returned.

A fine shift and gown lay on the wooden chest next to the bed. Shivering, she glanced down and caught her breath in horror. She was unclothed. Flushing hotly, she reached for the clothing and dressed quickly, making her mind up all at once. She had to find her father. He had created this chaos, and it was his duty, his obligation, to mend it. She'd demand he take her away from Dunvegan.

Wanting to avoid Ruan at all costs, she forced her weary bones to carry her out of the chamber and down the stairs. The passageway at the bottom appeared empty, but she'd scarcely left the safety of the tower before the sound of advancing feet sent her scurrying to the nearest door. A quick peek revealed a dimly lit but empty chamber, and she slipped in.

Her relief was short-lived.

As her vision adjusted to the darkness, she saw that it was not empty after all. In the corner stood a man, the cold one who had remained seated during her wedding. He'd observed her with watery blue eyes that made her flesh crawl. Ruan had called him Tormod, and she vaguely recalled him to be Ruan's brother. He leaned against a chair holding a book, but he was not looking at the pages.

He was watching her.

"Bree," his eyes dipped over her body. "Aye, 'tis time ye knew me. I'm the laird, The MacLeod."

Bree swallowed.

Tossing the book onto a nearby table, he strode forward.

She watched him draw near, knowing she should curtsey, but it was impossible to move. He was standing close, too close. She could smell the whiskey on this breath. Panic flooded her. Much to her horror, his eyes seemed focused upon her breasts.

"Ye aren't much to look at now," he tripped over his words. "Aye…but ye'll be as ye were. Soon, I'll warrant."

The sun had just risen, and the man was already drunk. Mercifully, the door to the chamber opened, and he jumped guiltily. With his attention distracted, she escaped the room to flee down a passageway and run up a narrow flight of steps. Poised at the top, she took a deep breath and trembled. She'd just bolted from the Lord of the castle's presence. He'd be furious at her impertinence. How could she explain herself, how could she tell him that he'd simply stood too close? She wrung her hands.

"Bree!"

She cringed.

Tormod had followed.

He was likely going to beat her. Succumbing to fear, she ran forward, half stumbling in her haste to the bottom of the steps and into the open air. She squinted in the intense sunlight, gradually becoming aware of men, many of them, eyeing her curiously.

Tormod bellowed from behind and she ran across the courtyard and through the nearest doorway.

***

Ruan leaned against the remains of the ancient wall with a brooding scowl, determined to enjoy the warmth of the sun, but failing miserably in the attempt. Images of Bree's white, terrified face filled his mind.

He shifted uneasily.

Aye, the wee lass should be frightened. He was a MacLeod and a son of The Black MacLeod himself. She should be afraid. He frowned, unaccountably disturbed that she was. It was an odd twist of fate that had entwined them. He hadn't expected the tragedy of his sister's forced marriage to affect his own life in such a manner. He'd been meaning to leave the place, now he felt trapped.

Why had he listened to Robert's soft words that he should stay? Aye, his uncle was persuasive. He loved Dunvegan with his very soul, but he could not live under Tormod's thumb. He had to leave. Once he had secured Merry's freedom, he'd take her to Cameron. He owed Bree nothing, but why did he feel like a scoundrel for thinking of abandoning her? Then, there was Domnall. How could he betray the man so? They had shared more than one battle. Domnall's son had been one of his closest friends, and he had few friends.

He shifted guiltily.

A shower of dirt and stones rained upon him, splashing into the loch below. Shading his brow, he peered up and then sprang to his feet in alarm.

A woman ran the outside of the curtain wall, hugging the rocks. As he watched, she tripped and slid down the steep incline directly above him. She managed to check her descent, and stood poised on the edge, as if weighing the decision to continue.

The moss-covered rocks were slippery and jagged on this side of the castle. A false step wouldn't end well. He was confounded why she'd attempt such a thing when there were serviceable steps nearby. He opened his mouth in warning, but abruptly closed it upon spying Bree's long, wavy brown locks.

The lass was daft. There could be no other explanation.

Yet, even as he arrived at that conclusion, he spied Tormod barreling down the steep steps leading from the castle wall to the loch below. Seeing Ruan, he pulled up short, finding it necessary to shout, "I was merely speaking with the lass!"

Aye, his brother would be one to torment her. He was unholy enough. An anger arose deep within Ruan's chest. He clenched his fists. He took a step forward, lip lifting into a snarl of its own accord.

Tormod shrugged. Looping his thumbs in his belt, he retraced his steps and disappeared back into the castle.

Ruan could not pursue him for Bree suddenly emitted a yelp and proceeded to topple his way. He was there, catching her deftly in his arms but losing his balance in the process. He saw the wide green eyes and a nose even more swollen and purple than before. Then, they were rolling, miraculously avoiding the jagged rocks but collecting bits of bracken in their clothes before landing in the shallows, a tangle of arms and legs.

Ruan was cold and he growled, not particularly in the mood to be wet yet again. Rising to his feet, he offered Bree his hand in assistance.

She refused to look at him. Instead, she sat in the shallow water, sucking in her breath in shock.

"'Tis fair cold, best get back to bed before ye catch ill," he said, moving to lift her.

Bree scrambled clumsily to her feet, obviously wanting to avoid his touch, but her wet skirts knotted about her knees like a rope and pitched her directly into his arms. She was soft, shapely. For a brief moment, his blood coursed hotly in his veins, but then she sneezed, startling him into control. Scowling at his temporary lapse, he firmly pushed her away.

She was looking worse each time that he saw her. Her hair clung in damp strings fastened to her pale, bruised face and her ripped gown revealed scrapes and bruises. His scowl deepened, wondering if he surveyed Tormod's handiwork. She sneezed again. They were still standing ankle deep in the cold water and while it wouldn't harm him, she was obviously already ill.

"Best get back to the tower," Ruan ordered, gruffer than he intended.

Her teeth began to chatter as she lifted her foot, but slipped on the slick stones. He tried to steady her but somehow her elbow dug into his stomach. He grunted, taking a step back, but lost his own footing and tumbled back into the loch, once more doused in freezing water. A whimper gurgled from under him, and to his dismay, he discovered this time he'd taken the poor lass with him, half-landing on her.

Sounds of hooting laughter reached his ears, but he ignored it. His pressing concern was for Bree. He hoisted her to her feet, filled with remorse. "I'll nae harm ye," he offered as comfort, half carrying her out of the loch. The poor lass deserved a better life than he'd given her so far. "Best get warm before ye take ill."

She didn't seem to hear.

"'Tis a wee nippy for a swim, Ruan."

Several men had gathered at the top of the stairs, his uncle Robert, Domnall, and Ewan among them, all grinning. He shot them a withering glare, but another sneeze from Bree made up his mind. Ignoring the good-natured jests hurled his way, he unceremoniously tossed her over his shoulder once more and strode up the steps without speaking a word.

"Ach, yer hands are full with that one, lad," Robert's eyes crinkled in amusement as he passed by.

"Aye," Domnall agreed, but there was a worried glint in his eye. "Would ye expect ought else from a lass called 'Bree'?"

"Nothing less, Domnall, nothing less," Robert murmured. A shadow of sorrow fell across his brow.

Ruan frowned. He'd heard tales of Bree, Robert's love, and her short stay in Dunvegan. She'd died of fever, though some claimed it was fairy mischief while others swore it was her weak Irish blood.

Suddenly, Bree sneezed. He clenched his jaw and pushed past them all. He made his way back to the tower to drop her once more upon the bed. Belatedly, he recalled her bruises and prepared to apologize, but it was too late.

She'd fainted.

She was not moving. Someone should remove the wet clothing. A bluish pall had settled over her skin. With a growl of frustration mingled with a large dose of guilt, he pulled a dry plaid from the chest. Tossing it over his shoulder, he returned to the bed and gripped her torn gown.

She exploded into a flurry of scratching nails and biting teeth.

"I'm trying to help ye!" his temper flared, but his words ended in a grunt as a knee connected with his groin. Dropping to the rushes on one knee, he drew a long breath, but when something bounced off his head, he decided he was done.

An ankle, a particularly slender and pleasing ankle, stepped over him on its way to the door. He grabbed it and gave it a sharp twist. She fell, landing across his chest. In moments, she was on her back as he straddled her, her hands effectively pinned to her sides.

"Be done, ye wee hellion!" he shouted. The last day had found him kicked, punched, and drenched, several times. A red welt graced his cheek. His head pounded. Aye, but she was hard on a man!

Large, green eyes stared back at him. Flashing eyes that gave him pause. An image of the shapely, slender ankle fled through his mind accompanied by the memory of soft curves and naked breasts in the early morning light. He shook his head in the attempt to clear his thoughts, focusing on the purple, swollen nose, streaked in different colors. It was a charming nose, a nose belonging to a fierce and fascinating, wee lass, who…

Alarmed by his wandering thoughts, he drew back, shouting, "By the Saints! I'll nae dishonor a daughter of Domnall."

It was more of a reminder to himself than an offer of comfort.

She began to shake. Her lips and skin were almost purple.

"Ye look horrid," he said, throwing the plaid on top of her. "Aye, would be best to wear this."

She simply stared at him.

NOT A WIDOW

Bree was too exhausted to move. Her throat hurt, her ears rang, and her stomach convulsed as a violent spasm overtook her. Dimly, she was aware of Ruan hovering over her, brows drawn in a line. Once more, he picked her up and placed her upon the same accursed bed in the same accursed chamber that seemed destined to forever be her prison.

As a shadow fell over her she cringed, closing her eyes. When the minutes passed uneventfully, she slowly raised her head.

Ruan stood next to the bed, his expression unreadable. His eyes caught and held hers for a time before asking, "What were ye doing outside the castle, lass? Were ye trying to run?"

Run? She shivered uncontrollably, remembering the icy water. She could not explain, even to herself, why she'd bolted. She just had. Tormod had made her uncomfortable. She merely stood there. The words stuck in her throat as her mouth convulsed.

"Answer me, woman! Did he touch ye?"

Bree jerked, surprised at the question. Surely, Ruan was not implying his own brother would be so unholy.

"Well, best stay out of his way. I've no trust left in the man." Ruan stooped to pick up the plaid from the floor and tossed it in her general direction. "Wear that."

She tried to move, but her body refused to obey.

"Faith," he said dryly after a time, a ghost of a smile playing on his lips. "There's naught about ye to entice a man. I've no intention of ravishing you."

Alarm rippled through Bree. In all her frightened panic of the day, she hadn't considered that. Her pressing concern had been a beating. She'd entirely forgotten the inhabitants of Dunvegan considered this man, this stranger, to be her husband. Most likely, he'd do as he pleased. Here, in the opinion of all, she was his possession.

Panicking, she leapt off the bed, lunging for the door, but he moved to block her. She succeeded in doing nothing more than launching herself into his arms. She screamed, blood-curdling screams.

"By the Saints!" he cursed. "I should bind ye hand and foot!"

Then, miraculously, she was free. Again, she'd managed only a single step before strong arms encircled her from behind, trapping her. With two, swift jerks, Ruan yanked her fine new shift off with practiced ease. His hands were hot against her cold, naked flesh. Mustering what strength remained, she struggled, knowing there was little she could do. A rumble of laughter caused her to meet the smoldering, dark eyes, only mere inches from her own. They were odd, those eyes, filled with neither rage nor lust, but amusement only.

She froze.

Ruan grinned.

She didn't know how long they stood there before he deftly tossed her over his shoulder. Once again he dropped her upon the bed in a rough, but oddly gentle manner. He quickly tossed the plaid over her naked flesh with a dexterous swirl and proceeded to roll her in it. With her hands trapped, she could do nothing but move her head. He propped her up against the headboard.

Wiping his hands, Ruan studied his handiwork, a smile quirking in the corner of his lips. "Ach, ye wee spitfire… that should keep ye in hand for a bit."

Bree stared. Several jagged scratches graced his chin, below a smudge of blue on his cheek. She gulped. What man would fail to exact vengeance for such un-wifely behavior? Well, he had her now, bound and helpless. She waited expectantly for the violence to erupt.

He leaned closer and smiled.

She watched him from the corner of her eye, wincing.

"Why was she screaming?" said a voice from behind them.

Ruan straightened and Bree followed his gaze to find the tall young blond man who had gently carried her after she'd broken her nose.

Ewan.

"Why was she screaming?" Ewan repeated. His blue eyes were hard but his voice soft.

Brows knitting into a scowl, Ruan remained silent several moments before replying, his voice deadly, calm. "Are ye asking what I think ye are?"

"Aye," Ewan flushed, but held his ground. Pointing to Ruan's scratched chin, he pressed, "What happened, then?"

Ruan's mouth dropped open in astonishment.

"It sounded like—"

"Be gone!" Ruan exploded. Striding toward the door, he roared, "Go, before I treat ye to the thrashing you deserve!"

Oddly, Ewan's face flooded with relief.

To Bree's utter astonishment, after a perfunctory bow in her direction, the young man left the chamber. He was apparently satisfied. It was astounding. Ruan hadn't answered the question in the slightest. Instead, he'd threatened bodily harm and Ewan had merely smiled in relief. What manner of men were these?

Growling, Ruan kicked the door shut with such force it rattled on its hinges.

Bree swallowed. How could Ewan infuriate the man and then simply leave? She wanted to cry. She was trapped by the plaid and alone with an enraged beast of a man.

Catching her eyes upon him, Ruan stalked to the bed.

Too afraid to breathe, she could only watch, aghast.

"I'll nae have ye trembling in such a manner!" he barked.

It would be much easier to faint. She willed herself desperately to faint with no success, but then to her amazement, the man's demeanor softened.

With a deep sigh, Ruan wiped his forehead with the back of his arm.

"I've no intention of touching ye, out of anger or lust, lass," he smiled. It was a bitter sort of smile, "Aye, I've no desire to be wed, less than even ye have, and 'tis no secret how little ye wish it!"

She blinked.

"Aye!" Ruan began to pace. Muttering as if merely thinking aloud he said, "I only agreed to this unholy union to save my sister Merry. Once I win her freedom, I'll have this mockery annulled. So, ye've naught to fear. I'll nae see it consummated, though ye best let Tormod and the others think otherwise."

Bree caught her breath.

After a time, he sat gingerly on the edge of the bed.

Heart pounding, she could not resist the attempt to inch away.

Catching the movement, a gleam entered his eye and he smiled once more.

"There's no cause killing yourself to run, lass," he assured softly. "I've no desire for a wife, I'll nae be touching ye. I respect Domnall and I'd nae harm his last living bairn. He knows that. It must be why he dreamt up this daft scheme. Once I have Merry's freedom, we can have this thing annulled."

The sincerity in those dark eyes was difficult to doubt. Bewildered but wary, Bree strove to subdue the hope kindling deep within her heart. With a growing difficulty, she reminded herself he was a man. Her father was a man. Men, by design, were simply untrustworthy. Her father had betrayed her. Why would Ruan be any different? She could not allow herself to trust him in the slightest.

"Aye, I'm hardly a fit husband for a daughter of Domnall," Ruan scowled, brows deepening into a line. Then, he shook his head and his lips curved in a rueful smile. "Ye look dreadful."

Leaning close, he slapped her playfully on the knee.

Bree choked in shock.

He seemed rather surprised himself. Jumping hastily to his feet, he hovered uncertainly, when to his obvious relief a knock on the door shattered the awkward moment.

Ruan opened the door and Ewan's grinning head appeared and spoke Gaelic with a soft urgency. With a warm smile her direction, the lad was gone as quickly as he'd come, closing the door with a loud grating squeak. With a violent curse, Ruan pounded his fist against the bedpost.

Bree bit her lip nervously as she watched him stalk to the chest, peeling his wet shirt along the way. When his plaid quickly followed, she came to the disconcerting realization that he'd forgotten her entirely. Never before had she seen a man unclothed and certainly never one standing so grandly naked in so careless a manner. It was disturbing, yet, if she were honest to herself, strangely and oddly fascinating.

She hadn't actually looked at him before. She'd been trying to run the opposite direction or had been too drunk to recall anything more than his immense height and voice rife with annoyance. Closer inspection revealed he was quite young himself. His shoulders were broad. His arms were well-muscled and his stomach hard. He was handsome; exceedingly handsome. In spite of her best intentions and the entire situation, her eyes drifted curiously down.

Blushing, she stared. While she was horrified at her boldness, she was also strangely mesmerized.

All at once, Ruan remembered her presence. Startled, he drew his plaid about his waist. A series of indecipherable expressions crossed his face, and then he hurried out the door without a backward glance, dressing himself along the way.

Perplexed, emotions in turmoil and extraordinarily drained, Bree closed her eyes.

***

She was hot. Burning. Crying for water one moment and freezing the next. Her throat seared with pain. Her head pounded and each breath was an enormous effort. Repeatedly, she felt the murky, frozen water of the loch closing in over her head. The icy water filled her lungs, chilling her very soul.

Voices called her name. More than once, a deep one resonated in her mind, ordering her to drink. Whiskey. It scorched her throat, making her vomit. Sweat drenched her body. Finally, after what seemed an eternity, she could breathe.

Utterly worn, she fell into an exhausted sleep.

"Take this, lass, it slockens the cough."

Someone pressed a cup to her lips. Steeling herself for the revolting taste of whiskey, she was pleasantly surprised with a salty broth.

"Aye, a strong one ..." the voice said. It was overly loud, irritating. "Broth is a sight better than that infernal drink Ruan forced down ye."

It must be her father. Only Domnall had such a bothersome voice. Slowly, she lifted her lids, squinting in the light, and found him at her side, face drawn and haggard, but green eyes twinkling brightly.

"Ach, ye worried us, Bree," he scolded affectionately, touching her forehead with a calloused palm.

Bree smiled feebly in return. For one, blissful moment, she felt safe, as if she belonged and then her smile faded. Her father was the man who had betrayed her; wed her to a complete stranger.

Domnall chuckled, delighted, "Aye. Now, there's a flash of the MacBethad spirit!"

"She's a MacLeod now," Isobel commented dourly.

"She'll always be a MacBethad, woman!"

Bree knit her brows, puzzled and strangely tired. How long had she been ill? Closing her eyes, she drifted off to sleep once more.

At first, the days passed in a patched, hazy sort of way.

Domnall kept a constant vigil by her side assuring her she was safe. He told her that Ruan was gone with Tormod to speak with the Mackenzies and to join Cuilen on raids against Fearghus. Apparently, relations with Fearghus had deteriorated once again. Domnall explained the feuds in detail, along with the role of the Mackenzies now joining the fight, but she could not keep it straight. She listened only because she liked her father's company and the fact that he'd chosen to remain at her side.

It meant little to her that Ruan was away fighting. She didn't know the man. If he were to die, she'd be a widow. She was indifferent to that prospect, but then felt guilty that she was. She settled for relief that he was gone and hoped he'd take his time in returning.

The morning was bitterly cold. The sun was unusually bright and for the first time since she'd fallen ill, and Bree thus felt somewhat alive. The window was open and she could hear the sound of a small waterfall. It was pleasant. With a grateful sigh, she stretched full length only to gasp at a small form hunched nearby.

Perched on top of the chest, a pair of brown eyes materialized. The eyes seemed far too aged for the young body they inhabited. One lid was nearly swollen shut, a mass of yellow bruises dusted both cheeks. A young girl, black hair twisted in a severe braid, observed her with an unblinking stare.

Bree licked her dry lips uncertainly.

For a time, the small girl seemed content to just sit, but then she whispered something in Gaelic.

Bree shook her head, uncomprehending.

The youngster frowned, but obligingly switched to English. "Ye'll be learning the Gaelic, 'tis nae proper to speak English. I'm Merry."

Merry. The name sounded familiar.

"I'm Ruan's sister," Merry offered, straightening the hem of her dress.

At the sound of his name, Bree unconsciously drew the blanket closer.

Shouting filtered through the open window. They were the sounds of angry men. She shuddered. She was still in Dunvegan. Violence hung in the air.

"—And Ruan has four languages in him," Merry was still speaking. "He can read... Can ye read?"

Read? She shook her head, wondering why she'd do such a thing.

"I can," Merry announced. "Ruan has taught me."

A stilted silence fell and they eyed each other for some time before the young girl pointed to the clothing folded at the bottom of the bed.

"Isobel found ye a new gown."

Under Merry's watchful eye, she slid from under the warm covers to inspect the dress. Lifting it up, she saw The MacLeod plaid folded underneath. She studied it, disheartened. It would be a surrender to wear it. She turned her attention to the dress and slipped it on.

It was simple and for someone larger than herself but in a serviceable state with only one worn spot on the skirt. It was cold and she shivered, eying the plaid. She hesitated, but quickly caved. She never wanted to be cold again. Grimacing, she flung it over her shoulders.

Merry had moved to straighten the bed, smoothing the coverlet repetitively in an almost obsessive manner. She clearly found it comforting. Not wishing to disturb the child, Bree peered through the small window into the courtyard below.

A few men milled about, shouting angrily. They were large, violent, and fierce. Several had dark hair, and she could not tell if any were Ruan.

She shuddered involuntarily.

"Ruan will come soon," Merry's voice broke into her thoughts. "He's gone to slay Fearghus for ..."

The child's voice trailed off, and she gestured to her eye. It was enough for Bree to understand that Fearghus had been the cause. She swallowed a gasp. How could anyone harm a child so? Besides Wat, she added grimly to herself.

"'Tis nothing. Ruan will set it right," Merry said. She lifted her chin firmly and gave the bed a final pat. "'Tis time for the midday meal. Come."

The meal had apparently ended, there were few left in Dunvegan's main hall when they arrived. The massive fireplace burned low, unable to penetrate the gathering gloom. They sat timidly at a table in the corner, and a kindly woman brought a loaf of bread along with a platter of meat and pears. Bree ate hungrily, but Merry spent her time tearing up the bread in little pieces and positioning them in lines along the table.

"You should eat," Bree said, and offered her a chunk of meat. When Merry didn't respond, she pushed it closer and repeated, "Eating will make you strong. You'll heal faster." She was beginning to sound like Afraig, she thought.

Merry regarded her suspiciously and Bree thought she'd slap it away.

"I supposed I should trust ye," the small girl agreed, albeit grudgingly. "Now that ye wed Ruan, we are sisters."

Bree frowned, not wanting to hear about Ruan.

Neither spoke the remainder of the meal. Merry only ate what Bree offered, making no move to eat on her own. She concentrated on her lines of bread, fretting if they didn't share the exact length. Bree eyed her curiously; she was an odd child. But Dunvegan was a peculiar place. They had both just wiped their hands clean when Domnall's voice from behind caused her to jump.

"Ah, Bree! 'Tis satisfying to see ye about, lass."

She bobbed her head in greeting, not knowing whether to be pleased or stoic with him.

"'Tis time ye met Effric," her father said. "Tormod's lady, the Lady of Dunvegan."

"Effric is daft," Merry cocked her head sidewise. "She spends her days staring out the window. No one pays her any heed."

"Aye, but she is the Lady of the castle," Domnall boomed. "Mayhap a wee bit of Bree's company will do her good."

"Bree?" Merry gaped at him incredulously. Adopting a visage far too old for her years, she added, "Then, ye ken naught of Effric's madness. She'll hate Bree more than any other."

"Why is that?" Bree asked, disturbed, but Merry frowned and slipped away, obviously wanting nothing to do with this Lady of Dunvegan.

"The lady was a wee bit enamored with Ruan in times past," Domnall shrugged the matter aside. "'Tis no matter now. Come."

Uneasiness rippled down Bree's spine, as he cupped a hand under her elbow and guided her forward.

"Aye, she is Tormod's third wife and one to pity, lass." Domnall leaned close to her ear and pointed to a chair placed facing the fire. "There!"

Bree had noticed it earlier, but had assumed it was empty.

As they drew closer, a face peered around the back of the chair. A woman rose as if to greet them, clutching a small ornamental cage that housed a yellow bird.

A rank, disagreeable odor pervaded the air. As Bree stepped closer, it was apparent something was dreadfully wrong with Tormod's Lady. From a distance, Effric appeared quite lovely, but upon closer inspection her blonde hair lay limp, and unwashed. Her gown was wrinkled and as stained as her bare feet stretched out beneath it. She was a young woman, though she hardly seemed it. And by far the most astounding thing about her was that the source of the unpleasant smell that made it difficult to breathe was the Lady of Dunvegan herself.

"Lady Effric," Domnall addressed her, bowing respectfully. "May I present ye my daughter, Bree."

The woman stared vacantly, apparently having lost interest.

Domnall cleared his throat, adding softly, "Ruan's wife."

The words had an astonishing effect. The dull blue eyes focused instantly.

"Bree?" Effric repeated.

"Yes, my lady," Bree swallowed, dipping into a nervous curtsey.

Effric said nothing for several minutes and then suddenly screamed in pure rage, "Is this true? Is this true?"

Involuntarily, Bree stepped back.

"What is this?" Isobel queried as she hurried into the hall, followed by a heavily pregnant woman with flaming red hair.

"Ruan is wed?" Effric screamed. "Wed?"

"Domnall!" Isobel cursed, sending the man a sour glance. "Hold yer tongue, man! I said a wee bit of company and nae to mention the lad!"

"She was nae responding, woman!" Domnall explained brashly, appearing very unapologetic. "I dinna ken she'd—"

"Ruan wed to this whore?" Effric shrieked, whirling to slap Bree across the face.

Bree reeled back, clutching her cheek, shocked more than hurt, as Domnall roared in anger. He captured Effric's wrist to twist it behind her back. There was a short scuffle.

Effric began to wail, "'Tis a lie! Ruan is mine! 'Tis a lie!"

"Ach, lass," Isobel sighed, shaking her head at the Lady of Dunvegan. "Ye've feigned madness so long ye've finally surrendered to it. 'Tis hard to feel pity, after the things ye've done."

"Ruan is mine! He'll always be mine!" Effric gave a high-pitched screech.

"What is done, is done, lass," Isobel replied, in a matter-of-fact tone. "If ye care to remember the games ye played to be Lady of Dunvegan. Ye got yer wish. Yer Tormod's wife, nae Ruan's."

"Marriage means naught to Ruan! He's slept in more marriage beds than any other!" Effric screamed. Pointing at Bree, she added, "I'll have that whore hanged!"

At that, Domnall bellowed, "No one calls my daughter a whore, even ye, lass, as daft as ye are!" Grabbing the writhing woman about the waist, he half carried, half dragged her out of the hall, Isobel close on his heels.

As Effric's screams faded, the red haired woman waddled forward with an apologetic smile, her hand resting upon her expectant belly.

"Aye, the poor lass truly is mad. She hasn't spoken in months to anyone. We thought she'd just fade away," she remarked. "I'm Jenna."

Jenna was tall, young, and quite beautiful. The freckles dusting her nose matched her hair in the most charming of ways. She was bright, filled with life, and possessed the knack to make one feel at ease.

"I heard ye've been ill, poor lass, best sit before ye faint. I'll rest with ye a wee spell, until Domnall returns," Jenna said. Patting her protruding belly with a proud smile, she lumbered to the nearest bench.

Uncertain, Bree gingerly took a seat opposite her and rubbed her stinging cheek.

"The bairn will be here soon..." Jenna began proudly, but fell abruptly silent.

A newcomer shuffled into the hall. It took Bree several moments to recognize him as the priest who had presided over her wedding vows to Ruan. Not that she'd vowed, she thought bitterly. Her father's word had been enough. Straightening her shoulders, she faced him as he moved their way.

His graying hair still hung in grimy strings, and his nails were even dirtier. Together with his rumpled robes, he was quite the unkempt figure. His watery eyes were cold as he viewed Jenna with open distaste.

"Only a wanton would boast about a child of sin," he accused, by way of greeting. "Ye should be on yer knees, praying for yer lost soul."

Jenna's lips tightened perceptibly. "Ach, Silas, and a braw day to ye."

The priest shrugged before sending Bree a venomous glare. "A godly wife submits!"

Jenna snorted, "'Tis a fine way to greet yer brother's wife," she observed pointedly.

Bree's mouth fell open. This priest was Ruan's brother?

"A pious wife obeys," the priest continued unperturbed. "Your screams were heard to Dunscaithe!"

His brows furrowed into a line, reminiscent of Ruan, and as he towered in open disapproval, Bree's heart quailed. For all his slovenly appearances, he was an intimidating man. She wanted to shout that she'd done nothing wrong, but the words stuck in her throat. What courage she'd managed to foster was rapidly disappearing.

"Confess!" Silas ordered, menacingly.

Bree swallowed, wanting to explain, but it was difficult to focus as the man's gaze dropped, lingering on her breasts in quite an unpriestly manner. Her apprehension turned into shocked indignation.

"I've nothing to confess," she said tightly, though her voice shook. The words had been hard to say. Still. She'd said them.

Jenna chuckled, delighted. "Find other souls to save, Silas."

Glowering, Silas hissed, "Fear the fires of hell, harlot!"

Jenna shrugged, dismissively.

Turning back to Bree, Silas observed her a moment before wiping his forehead and then storming from the hall, disappearing down the same passageway Domnall had carried Effric.

"Aye, let him pray over Effric's twisted soul," Jenna grunted. "'Tis odd Effric spoke today, but then, she's always pined after Ruan. She's a petty one, had a cruel hand before she succumbed to the madness. I'd much rather have her silent than back to her old self, but Isobel thinks there's something yet to save. I'm nae so sure, lass."

Bree nodded in agreement. It was obvious that Effric had been Ruan's lover. The thought evoked no jealousy whatsoever. Ruan was welcome to any woman's bed as long as it kept him from hers.

"'Tis a dark place, Dunvegan," Jenna muttered, shifting on the bench, seeking a comfortable spot. "It dinna use to be."

With growing apprehension, Bree watched her settle.

Finally, Jenna smiled, "Ah, 'tis muckle better."

Dutifully, Bree smiled in response. Twisting her fingers tightly in her skirt, she waited for Jenna to expound upon the strange inhabitants of Dunvegan, but the young woman only yawned before drifting off to sleep.

After a time, when Domnall showed no sign of returning nor Jenna of waking, and Merry was no longer in sight, Bree moved stiffly to her room in the tower. She lay awake long into the darkness of the night, fretting.

Ruan had been clear in that he'd no intention in claiming marital rights.

Could she trust him? Oddly, she wanted to. The thought of wandering the cold moors made her shiver, she could not face that again. The unbalanced behavior of Effric and Merry was worrisome. Silas frightened her and Tormod even more so.

But there was nowhere else for her to go. She was stuck in this dark castle with these disturbing people.

It was a long time before she drifted into an uneasy sleep.

THE MAD LADY OF DUNVEGAN

"Up, ye lazy whore!"

Bree bolted upright.

"If Domnall hears ye call her that, ye'll pay," Isobel's voice calmly inserted itself in the cold dawn. "And ye promised to be pleasant, lass. Bree's a companion for ye."

Bree squinted, barely able to discern the outline of two women.

"Up!" Effric shrilled, apparently heeding Isobel's warning.

Stiffly, Bree slipped out of bed.

"I'm Dunvegan's Lady, and nae you! Ye'll nae be lying abed!" Effric spat, reaching to slap her cheek, but Isobel snatched her hand back in time. Effric glared, but twisting her hands behind her back, she continued. "Ye'll work here and nae get any special treatment! The scullery wench ran off last month, and ye'll take her place!"

"Nay, Effric, Bree's nae to be in the kitchens. She's a companion for ye when she isn't helping me," Isobel sighed, still holding Effric's hands. "Mayhap music would soothe ye. Bree, can ye play a lute?"

Bree shook her head.

"Then, needlework would do ye both good."

Effric bit her lip, she seemed ready to argue, but a piercing look from Isobel swayed her mind. "Then, ye'll attend me, Bree. Now, get up with ye!"

Under Effric's critical eye, Bree hurriedly donned her gown as she wished in vain that Isobel had been quiet. She'd much rather have cleaned the gloomy kitchens of Dunvegan than serve Effric personally. She followed Effric through the shadowy castle, wondering what the woman had planned. Several times, she caught a glimpse of Merry following.

They arrived at Effric's chamber.

It was large, the furnishings finer than she'd ever seen before, with small furs cast on the floor, and an even larger one on the bed. Several chairs with ornate embroidered cushions stood next to a table. Behind it, a small tapestry graced the wall.

Effric walked to the window seat, picking the cloth on her sleeves, and proceeded to stare out silently at the sea loch.

Not knowing what else to do, Bree stood patiently in the middle of the chamber, hands folded contritely behind her back, while Isobel bustled about with several baskets of thread and a loom.

"Ye love yer needlework, lass," Isobel clucked. "Mayhap ye should start a new one. Ye could do one of yer canary, love. Ye love the wee one so!"

"Bree must leave," Effric addressed her in a shrill voice. "She doesn't belong here."

Bree agreed with her whole-heartedly and could not resist a nod.

Isobel sent her a dour look and then corrected Effric calmly, "She canna leave, my lady. There's naught to be done now."

Bree glanced at the floor, feeling a little ashamed.

"She'll nae live in the keep!" Effric slammed her fist on the table, her blue eyes filled with tears. "Nae here!"

"That is atween Cuilen and Tormod," Isobel said. She shook her head firmly before addressing Bree, "Love, fetch a bowl of porridge for Effric, would ye now?"

Grateful for the reprieve, no matter how short, Bree did as Isobel asked. All too soon, she returned. She placed the bowl to the table as Effric rocked back and forth. Before she could react, the woman lunged, sweeping the bowl aside to splatter the contents in all directions. Grabbing handfuls of Bree's hair, she began to wail and yank viciously.

Bree sank to her knees, her head in agonizing pain.

It was several seconds before Isobel managed to extricate Effric's fingers from Bree's hair.

"Ye are the lady of Dunvegan!" Isobel reminded sharply, pulling Effric back to the window. "Behave as such!"

Effric began to weep. Seizing a hairbrush from a nearby table, she threw it at Bree, "Out of my sight! Stay out of my sight!"

Bree fled.

Not knowing where else to go, she returned to her chamber to find Merry tidying the room.

"Ye'd do better to leave this place," the young girl said, running her hands across the blankets repetitively to smooth the wrinkles.

At that, Bree heaved a loud sigh. Tears briefly stung her eyes, and she moved to sit on the edge of the bed, but at Merry's disapproving frown, moved to the chest instead.

Like it or not, she was stuck here. She rapidly blinked the tears away. All she had ever wanted was to live in a cottage with Afraig and grow herbs.

"Ruan is taking me away from this place," Merry said. "So... they canna send me back."

"Back?" Bree sniffed, grateful for the distraction from her own problems.

"Aye, back to Fearghus," she murmured, pointing to her eye in an awkward gesture. "He is my husband."

"Husband?" Bree gasped in shock. She shuddered. Squaring her shoulders and adopting a wide smile for Merry's benefit, she took a deep breath. They wouldn't think of husbands. Instead, she'd recapture happier times and, perhaps, help this child if only for a few, brief moments.

Not knowing what else to do in the awkward silence, she thought of Afraig's stories and began. "Have you heard of the tale..."

***

The next week found Effric despondent, reacting to no person or thing. Isobel, who clearly cared for the Lady of Dunvegan, stayed by her side.

"I'm sorry she hurt ye, lass," Isobel said, while giving her a warm hug. "She's just nae herself, love. Ye'd best stay out of her sight for now. There is no need to cause the lass more harm."

Bree was happy to comply. She spent the time with Merry, huddled under the plaids in her tiny chamber, recounting every story she could recall. To humor the young girl, Bree tried to speak as much Gaelic as she could, and was soon surprised at the ease with which the language began to flow from her lips. She'd apparently learned more from Afraig than she had realized.

Merry listened to Bree's stories in fascination. Each day, the young girl's bruises faded a little more and the swelling in her eye lessened. She still found comfort in her rituals of straightened the covers and lining her bread on the table, but she hurried through the ceremonies a little faster each day.

A week or so had passed in this pleasant manner, and Bree had almost regained her full strength. Only the slightest hint of tiredness remained. Merry had taken to cuddling up with her at night, and she had found the small girl's companionship a great source of comfort.

One morning she awoke to find Merry perched on top of the chest. Her tiny face beaming a wide grin.

"I can see!" she whispered ecstatically, pointing to her newly opened eye. "I can see!"

Bree laughed, her heart lightening at the news. She swept the small girl into a hug. They danced boisterously about the chamber, singing and giggling from the pure joy of it.

Suddenly, the door crashed open.

Hearts pounding, they jumped apart.

"Where have ye been hiding?" Effric demanded, her mouth twisted in suspicion. "And who have ye been with?"

Bree craned around Effric, searching for Isobel, but there was no sign of her.

"Well?" Effric prompted with a malicious snarl. "Ruan will nae be pleased to find his wife's been lying in another man's bed!"

"Bree has been with me!" Merry interrupted hotly, moving to

stand in front of Bree with hands upon her tiny hips. "And I would say Ruan will nae be pleased to hear what ye've to say of his wife, but 'tis no matter! No one will believe ye!"

Effric started guiltily and her nostrils flared. She raised her hand, as if to slap Merry but then thought better of it. Instead, she hissed, "Follow me! The both of ye!"

Bree hesitated. Where was Isobel? Should she even listen to the woman? Isobel had told her to stay away from Effric. She bit her lip, uncertain what to do.

"Isobel will nae be helping ye now," Effric said, seeming to read her mind. "She's in the village, midwifing another of Tormod's brats!"

Bree stared in surprise. The woman certainly didn't seem mad. Unsure, she took a timid step forward. Merry's hand slipped into hers, and they both followed.

Effric led them to her private chambers where she ordered them to stand in the center of the room until she bid them elsewise. She threatened that whenever either of them were tempted to move, she'd throw something their direction, a brush, a comb, or a cup.

There was no sign of Isobel and no one else seemed to care what Effric did. Several times, Bree was tempted to take Merry and run away, but she was not certain of the consequences of such an action. Effric was, even of unsound mind, the Lady of Dunvegan.

As the afternoon sun approached, the disturbed woman began to pace in front of the window, muttering to herself. Finally, in her most contemptuous voice, she ordered Bree, "Wench, bring me food!"

She had obviously meant it to be insulting, but Bree was grateful for the opportunity to escape her presence. With a curtsey, she followed Merry to the narrow passageway that led down to the kitchens.

"She's horrid," Merry whispered, skipping alongside her. "But she doesn't frighten me."

Bree nodded in agreement. She wished she could honestly say the same, but Effric did scare her. She didn't agree with Isobel that she was harmless. There was something unsettling in the woman's eyes.

The cook in the kitchen glowered, but shoved a wooden trencher her way. She'd just picked it up when a sudden scream from Merry pierced her ears. She leapt out the door to see a large, blurry shape outside the kitchen, reaching for Merry as she screamed again.

Bree's heart pounded. Certain that Merry's husband had returned to take her back, a deep rage surged within Bree, and not quite knowing what possessed her, she charged forward, swinging the trencher at Merry's attacker.

Merry screamed louder. Someone else was shouting. As Bree swung at the huge form, she saw the face of Merry's assailant. The eyes were dark, smoldering, and widening in shock.

Ruan?

But, it was too late.

The trencher struck him full on the shoulder and on the side of his head. Bread and mutton stew arced in the air as he caught her wrist, twirled her, and trapped her against the wall.

Bree gasped.

She was pinned beneath his heaving chest. She could feel the cold stones biting into her back.

Ruan winced, rubbing his ear and shaking his head before fixing his attention upon her. Paralyzed with fear, Bree could do nothing but wait. Minutes seemed to pass, the eyes boring into hers were unfathomable, and then his lips opened.

"Aye, but... aren't ye ...a wild beastie," he breathed, speaking with difficulty.

Bree opened her mouth to answer, but managed only to emit a nervous squeak.

Ruan frowned, puzzled, and said "I dinna ken ye, lass!"

She swallowed and tried again, but without success.

His chest began to jerk in silent spasms, but it was not until his eyes crinkled with amusement that she realized he was laughing.

"I left ye nigh dead." his lip twitched. "I thought to be visiting a grave, not defending myself from a wee vixen attacking me with the evening meal!"

Bree held still. How could he be amused? Suddenly, she could no longer bear his intense scrutiny. She dropped her eyes to stare at his lips. They were strong, well-defined, as if carved from stone. They were a bit disturbing. Oddly ashamed and confused to be staring, she again averted her gaze to the deep crease in his cheek, and then noticed the hard jaw and the dark hair, carelessly tied back by a leather thong.

All at once, she was acutely aware of the weight of his body. His hard muscles pressed against her. The heat of his skin was strangely unsettling.

Color rushed to her cheeks.

When she met his eyes again, Ruan's demeanor altered.

She was not certain what she saw in those dark pools, but she instinctively knew it had nothing to do with anger and violence.

Oddly, it frightened her more.

Pressing her against the wall a little harder, he murmured, "I've spent nigh a month in the muck, fighting for my life against the MacDonalds. I've escaped with nary a scratch only to come home and find myself attacked by a wee slip of a lass!"

Her throat constricted but she succeeded in croaking, "Merry screamed…and…"

"Defending her with naught but a trencher and looking like that will only bring trouble to ye both," he warned in a low voice.

Bree knotted her brows in confusion. Something in the man's expression made her heart pound. Intending to push him back, she placed her hands on his chest, but it was a mistake. His chest was broad, hard, and muscular. He was disconcerting, yet at the same time, thrilling.

"Hold still," he commanded, but the tone in his voice belied the harsh order.

Blushing, she tried to wriggle away.

Ruan's jaw clenched.

Cursing under his breath, he moved back, but his eyes dipped, roving quickly over her figure.

"Ye'd best nae be wandering about this place, especially this night," he informed her tersely. "The men are drunk and women are scarce here."

Bree swallowed, taking a nervous step back.

"Aye," Ruan continued, eyeing her thoughtfully. "I'll be sore pressed in keeping from your bed."

The sound of muffled laughter informed her they were not alone.

Domnall, Robert, and several others she failed to recognize were crowded close near the kitchen entrance.

"Them!" Ruan corrected quickly. Clearing his throat awkwardly, he stressed. "I meant... keeping them from your bed!"

It was not until she noted the faint duskiness covering his cheeks that Bree recalled his words enough to understand the cause of the others' mirth. Her skin colored with an even deeper shade of scarlet. Taking another step back, she tripped on her skirts.

Ruan lurched forward, grasping her arm with a steadying grip.

She stared dumbly at his fingers.

"Nae what ye were expecting, eh, Ruan lad?" Domnall's booming voice caused them both to jump. "Ye'd best be asking Robert for the ways of handling a MacBethad lass!"

"Ach!" Robert's bass joined in. "Bree did as she pleased, ye ken well enough...as with every MacBethad I've ever seen!"

Bewildered, Bree turned toward the grey haired man.

"He is speaking of my Bree, lass," Robert MacLeod explained with a lopsided and sorrowful smile on his craggy face. "Domnall's sister, in years long...since past."

"I've matters to attend. Ye should get back to the tower, Bree," Ruan interrupted gruffly. Affecting a black scowl, he let her go. As if already forgetting her presence, he grinned at Merry to swoop her into his arms.

The small girl squealed.

Bree grimaced.

How had she confused that happy sound with a scream? She frowned, angry at her own foolishness.

"The lad sees now, no?" Domnall snorted softly.

"Aye," Robert agreed congenially. "But he'll be denying it for a spell."

"I'm still here," Ruan sent them a dark look. "I'll thank ye to speak your meddlesome observations out of my hearing."

"Ruan!" Effric stood at the foot of the stairs. "'Tis happy I am to see ye!"

"My lady," Ruan bowed politely.

Effric brightened at his gesture. Her lashes fluttered before she spied Bree and then her mouth twisted in a thin line, "Bree, attend me immediately! Come, at once!"

Bree hesitated. She fleetingly wished Ruan would order her to stay, but he only watched with interest. As she passed by him, Merry pulled down his head and began to whisper in his ear.

Bree frowned. Of course, there would be no rescue for her. This was, after all, her proper place. She stomped a little on her way back up the stairs. No one noticed, and it did little to appease her growing frustration.

"Follow me, at once!" Effric hissed.

Pushing her forward across the passage, she unlocked the door of a small chamber directly opposite the stairs, motioning for Bree to enter.

Hesitantly, Bree stepped forward, there was no light in the chamber, and she could not see. Then, something struck her on the back of the head, and she collapsed forward, losing consciousness.

SPIDERS AND HANDSOME MEN

It was dark. She was cold. Her head ached and she found her mouth and hands bound with strips of cloth. She was lying on sour straw, and she dared not guess what else. Frowning, she struggled to recall how she came to be here and then remembered Effric.

She wriggled, chaffing at the bindings. Effric hadn't tied them well. Muffled sounds filtered through the darkness. She stilled her beating heart to listen. Laughter, the clinking of cups and several raucous songs revealed the sounds of the evening meal, indicating she was near the hall. Hope leapt in her breast.

It didn't take long to free her hands and her mouth shortly thereafter. Crawling through the pitch black, she located the door and wriggled the latch. It was jammed. Should she scream for help? If she did, who would come? Ruan had warned her of the men in this place. Where was he? Did he even know she was gone? Did he even care?

Something ran across her foot, and she screamed. It squeaked. She shuddered. She hated rats almost as much as she hated the darkness and riding horses. She shivered. The shock of the situation was wearing off, replaced by a rising panic.

A soft tickle brushed her skin, and she screamed again. She danced about, frantically trying to shake whatever it was off before returning to the door. She was tempted to scream for help but Ruan's warning sounded loud in her mind. It would be best to wait until the nearby sounds of merrymaking had diminished. Another rat squeaked, and she burst into tears. It had been a trying day and now her head ached. She sank to the floor, cradling her head in her hands and allowed herself to sob into her knees.

She didn't know how long she remained there, sniveling. It felt like days of torture before the door rattled. Desperate and no longer caring who stood on the other side, she bawled hysterically. It swung open and the light of the torch nearly blinded her. She launched herself forward, desperately, straight into the arms of her rescuer.

He was tall, imposing and solid. She threw her arms around his neck in pure relief.

Ruan.

He took a startled step back, unprepared, but slipped a consoling arm about her waist anyway.

What ailed her?

Why was his presence suddenly so comforting?

"I told ye!" Merry glowered at her brother. "What happened, Bree? Ye stink like a pigsty! Ach, there's a spider in your hair!"

Bree screeched, wildly flailing about.

There was a cracking sound and Ruan swore, clutching his nose. "Be still, ye wee hellion!" he shouted with an accompanying scowl and jammed the torch into Merry's hand. Capturing Bree's wrists, he deftly twisted her over his shoulder.

Bree tried to protest but he was too strong. She might as well have tried to move the walls of Dunvegan itself as he carried her through the hall, past Domnall and Robert's stunned faces, and up to the tower.

Merry trotted importantly behind, bringing the torch.

In a few short minutes, Ruan was in the bedchamber, dipping his shoulder to slide her down the length of him. Pinning her arms behind her back, he pressed her against his chest so that she felt each hard muscle, taut in his stomach. He held her there for a minute. He was uncomfortably close.

The gleam in his eye reminded her of a falcon eying a mouse.

Inexplicably, her heartbeat quickened.

Abruptly, he let her go.

"What happened, Bree?" Merry hopped to perch on top of the chest.

Bree drew a long, wavering breath and licked her dry lips. All of a sudden, it was simply too much. Tears began to flow. From somewhere deep inside, a torrent of words poured forth.

She was saying too much. In fact, she was babbling, but she could not stop. There was so much: Wat, his uncle and her mother's cold-hearted willingness to trade her for sheep, Afraig's betrayal and her father's as well. She'd never wanted to wed. No, all she'd ever wished for in life was to live in Afraig's cottage by the sea. She most definitely didn't want a forced marriage to a scowling stranger, though, at this precise moment, she was vaguely aware it was the same scowling stranger gently patting her shoulder. It didn't matter. There was Effric to fret over and now, the other odd inhabitants of Dunvegan. She'd been in the darkness with the rats. She hated rats. She hated spiders. There had been both rats and spiders in the cold. The room had smelled horrid. She could smell the vile rankness even now!

She was crying, wiping her nose on her sleeve, and then something pressed against her lips. A burning liquid seared her throat. Whiskey.

She gasped, choking.

"There," Ruan said. "That should warm ye, lass."

Bree drew a long wavering breath, startled into silence.

The corner of Ruan's lip twisted as he pressed the whiskey to her lips once more.

Shaking her head, she pushed the flask away.

"Aye…'tis vile stuff," he agreed, shrugging his shoulders. He hefted the flask several times before draining it. "I've only taken back to it this past month. I'd sworn off of drink and women years ago … I should really … be done with it all … I'm really nae certain …"

His voice trailed and it was only then Bree noticed she was standing far too close to him.

Merry had disappeared.

Somehow, she'd moved to where he sat on the chest. His powerful thighs pressed on either side of hers; his arm draped casually about her waist. She could feel his chest heaving beneath her breast as she clutched his shirt. Horrified, she willed her fingers to let go, but they clenched tighter of their own accord, digging deeper into the cloth.

His dark eyes bore into hers, and she suddenly felt as if she were drowning. From far away, she heard her voice crack, "Thank you for … coming for me."

"Thank Merry. The lass is quite smitten with ye," Ruan gave her a half-smile. He grew serious and added, "'Tis I who should be thanking ye, lass. For all ye've done for my wee sister."

Bree swallowed, remaining where she was. She should move away, but there was an odd comfort in the arm of steel encircling her waist. What ailed her? She should be running. Was she no longer capable of clear thinking?

Ruan leaned close, his lips brushing the top of her ear.

A chill crept down her spine.

"I've … had a wee bit too much … drink," he murmured as if in apology. "Ye'd best be … getting out of that gown."

Alarm rippled through her, but she could not move.

"I meant, into something else," Ruan hastily amended, clearing his throat. "Nae rid of it entirely! Aye, I know … ye have to take it off, to switch … but … ye canna stay undressed…"

The faint color creeping up his neck was strangely comforting.

All at once, he exploded, "By the Saints, woman, enough blethering! Ye just wailed your dress reeked of a pigsty! Sweet Mary! I only meant to help! Change and have done!"

Her dress did reek. She smelled as if she'd been wallowing in muck and there had been spiders. The thought of spiders creeping in her skirts made her panic once again. She leapt from his arms and began to stomp her feet, shaking her skirts in a mad dance.

He stared at her, open-mouthed.

Something tickled her neck and she gasped, trying to brush it off, "Is it gone? Is it gone?"

Ruan scowled, "Have ye gone daft?"

"The spiders!" Bree shivered uncontrollably, hysteria rising once again. She clawed the laces of her dress and had it half off before she belatedly recalled Ruan's presence.

He was staring at her with an expression she decided not to interpret.

She flushed scarlet. Clutching her dress close, she took a step back. The whiskey must be affecting her adversely.

Ruan blinked and shook his head a little then reeled unsteadily to lean against the bed. Shrugging out of his shirt and plaid he began to curse profusely as he kicked his clothing halfway across the chamber. Pitching headlong onto the bed, he rolled onto his back and covered his face with a muscled arm.

When he showed no sign of moving, Bree wasted no more time in shedding her gown and shaking her shift. The slow, rhythmic sound of his breathing signaled he'd fallen asleep. She took a long, wavering breath. It had been a trying day. She wanted to sleep herself, but a man now occupied the bed.

Cautiously, she cast a furtive glance his way.

Ruan lay on his back, naked, and carelessly exposed. Even in the darkness of the chamber, she could see every inch of him. He was lean, a mass of muscle, his stomach sculpted and his thighs powerfully built. In spite of herself, she allowed a timid yet curious inspection. Her pulse quickened as warmth flooded her.

Confused, and with a growing sense of shame, she turned her head. The whiskey must be affecting her judgment.

It was chilly.

Guiltily, she wrapped herself in Ruan's discarded plaid, the smell of heather and smoke oddly comforting. She yawned, tired. She'd have to find some place to sleep. The loud, boisterous laughter wafting up from the hall below banished any thought she might have had of venturing outside the chamber. No. Ruan hadn't been jesting when he warned that Dunvegan was dangerous, especially at night.

The tiny chamber yielded few options. The floor was unsuitable; the thin layer of rushes did nothing to dampen the cold. The bed, covered by an unclothed man, was entirely out of the question. The only item remaining was the chest.

It proved hard, cold, and bumpy. For a time, she perched on it, resting her forehead upon her knees and struggled to keep warm as the night chill deepened.

Ruan began to snore.

She shifted uncomfortably. There was no fire and the chamber grew colder by the minute. The man on the bed sighed contentedly in his sleep. She sent him a resentful stare. For a time, she rubbed her fingers together briskly. Her nose was icy to the touch. She shivered, recalling the coldness of the moors.

Ruan twisted on his side, dragging the covers with him. He appeared extraordinarily comfortable. Bree eyed him enviously. It was simply unfair that the man would lie, stripped bare, impervious to the chill while she huddled, freezing, on a hard chest.

As her nose began to drip, her convictions wavered.

Ruan's sleep was deep.

She could huddle at the foot of the bed and leave before he woke. He'd never be the wiser. He truly lacked interest in her, anyway. Domnall had said every lass lusted after him. He must have a lover.

The thought caught hold and gave her a sense of security. Of course, a man so handsome would have his pick of anyone. Relief filled her. He wouldn't be interested in her. She didn't want to acknowledge that thought was disappointing.

Time marched on. Finally, cursing herself for her weakness, and Ruan's heart was firmly taken by another, she crept to the foot of the bed.

Eager for a warm place to rest, she slid under the coverlet and huddled in a tiny ball. She reveled in the warm softness, promising she'd wake first and be gone before dawn.

***

"Such a fine, naked arse, lad!" A woman chuckled.

Groggily, Bree frowned and wished the voice would go away. She was incredibly warm. She hadn't been this comfortably warm in ages.

"Isobel?" A voice grunted in her ear.

Bree grimaced at the loud rumbling. She didn't want to wake up. She was warm. She briefly wondered what the leaden weights across her chest and legs were, but it didn't matter. It was the source of the wonderful warmness. With a smile of pleasure, she burrowed deeper, preparing to drift once again to sleep.

The weight stirred. Something tickled her cheek. Startled, she lifted her lashes to spy several strands of long, dark hair falling about her.

Ruan was examining her, with great interest, from mere inches away.

Her heart stopped.

"This thing reeks, lad. I'll have it washed."

From the corner of her eyes, Bree saw Isobel suspend Ruan's shirt at arm's length.

"Ach, and Bree, what have ye done to yer dress? It smells like a dung heap!" Isobel clucked, adding Bree's gown to the pile. "I've another for ye in Merry's room. I'll fetch it. Ne'er have I seen a lass go through gowns as fast as ye, love!"

Bree swallowed as Ruan continued to stare.

"Just lie abed with the wee wife, lad. After these latest doings, few will blame ye," the woman said, her aged face bright with amusement.

Frantically, Bree searched her memory. She'd slipped under the covers at the foot of the bed. How had she maneuvered to end up under the man?

Ruan hadn't moved. He lay half upon her, still observing in a manner she dare not interpret. Her lips remained paralyzed, but she could not find the words to say anyway. She didn't know how long they stayed there. Time seemed suspended and then from outside the window the sound of bagpipes split the air.

Startled, she jumped, her elbow striking something hard.

Ruan growled, sitting up and rubbing his jaw. "'Tis only the piper with the morning lament."

"Aye," Isobel said, bustling back into the chamber and dropping another gown on the chest. "'Tis how proper folk wake, lass."

"I'll be… needing this," Ruan growled, pulling the plaid from her and averting his eyes. Swathing himself, he pushed past Isobel just as a loud bang sounded on the door. He flung it open to reveal a grim Ewan.

"They found Sean," the blond youth said bleakly.

"Blessed Mary!" Isobel's voice caught, her shoulders sagged in grief.

Ruan sucked his breath and then banged his forehead against the wall several times before sighing, "I'll tell her."

"Your nephew... Andrew's son... Duncan..." Ewan's voice trailed.

Ruan bowed his head.

"Well, we'll never know now," Ewan cleared his throat. "His throat was slit from ear to ear."

"Blessed Mary!" Isobel repeated, but this time, her tone seemed only dutiful.

"Aye, well," Ruan said, heaving a deep sigh. "I'll be going to Jenna then."

He hesitated on the threshold, half turning her direction, but then he shrugged and pushing past Ewan, disappeared down the passageway.

Bree expelled a sigh of relief, glad the man was gone. He was unsettling, in all respects. Rubbing her burning cheeks, she met Isobel's all-knowing gaze.

"Ach, now, lass," the woman said softly, cocking her head to the side. "Out of bed with ye now, we've work to do. I'm sending ye down to the dairy. Jenna needs a wee bit of help."

JENNA'S SORROW

Ruan paused outside the dairy, reeling a little from the tidings of Sean and Duncan's deaths.

The last few weeks had been grueling—and disturbing.

They had become involved far deeper in MacDonald affairs than they should have. Now, the Mackenzie clan was tangled in the mess, keen on defending their newly acquired land from the Crown. The Mackenzies were readying themselves for a much bigger war, having suffered several attacks from Fearghus already, and some of them saw the split of the MacDonald clan as an opportunity to rid themselves of future threats once and for all.

Ruan, Robert, and a handful of MacLeods had ridden hard to meet with the Mackenzies, to ease the rising tensions, and were rewarded with some measure of success. Even though the King had greatly damaged the power structure of the Isles, including Skye, by seizing the Earldom of Ross, he could not entirely erase the relationships that had been cultivated over centuries.

It was on the way back that mysterious arrows began to fly in Ruan's direction.

The last evening, before they had rejoined Cuilen's raid against Fearghus, Ruan had narrowly missed a shaft whistling his way and had wheeled his horse toward the thickets to ferret out the culprits.

He had stumbled upon an unexpected scene. Robert stood over the body of Andrew, his half-brother, wiping his dirk on his plaid. He looked up and saw Ruan approach, but said nothing. He merely kicked a quiver of arrows across the clearing.

The arrows didn't stop with Andrew's death, but the numbers lessened.

Robert warned Ruan to avoid Andrew's son, Duncan, and then had disappeared on his horse. He was gone several days before he returned to assure Ruan that it was over.

The arrows had stopped completely then and neither Ruan nor Robert had spoken of it since. Ruan didn't want to hear if his nephew Duncan was involved. He did not want to believe the lad he'd laughingly dandled on his knee as a bairn was attempting to kill him.

Sadness weighed on his heart.

He'd never understand why his brothers had convinced their offspring that he was intent on their deaths, desiring to kill any who stood in his way of taking Dunvegan. It was entirely untrue.

He shrugged the thoughts away to focus on Jenna. Now, he must tell her that her lover, Sean, was dead.

Jenna had always been his favorite half-sister. Though some within Dunvegan named her the harlot, shunning her for bearing a child to a wedded man, he hadn't been one to find fault. How could he? She was his sister and the child was innocent. He sighed. Aye, Sean and Jenna had been doomed from the start, but there was naught to do about it now.

She must have seen him approaching. With a wail, she threw herself in his arms.

"He is dead, then!" she gasped, burying her nose in his shoulder.

"Aye, lass," Ruan sighed, folding her close.

She simply cried for a time before beginning to jabber about the bairn.

"I'll see to ye both, Jenna," Ruan said, wiping her tears with his sleeve and patting her belly. "There's no cause for fear."

A slight sound caused him to turn. Bree stood a short distance away on the path, hair hanging in damp curls down her back. The poor lass appeared wan and tired with the day just starting. Behind her, he could see Merry joining with a slow limp.

He clenched his jaw.

The women under his care were suffering. They watched him, nervously, as he guided Jenna from the dairy and down to the loch.

Morning fled into afternoon as he offered comfort and simply listened to his sister. They spent the time walking through the village and surrounding fields. She found it difficult to stay still.

He'd vowed to see to Jenna and the child's welfare from the moment she'd tearfully confessed her condition. He'd make good that promise, though he was sore pressed on how it might be done. He had nothing left. Robert would help, but he had never accepted anything from the man other than his love.

It was late when he finally saddled his horse and rode with Jenna to her tiny croft some distance away. He saw her fed and settled into a deep sleep before slowly making his way back to Dunvegan. He pondered the future. With Sean not there to help, Jenna could not manage the small croft alone. He'd barely stepped foot in the courtyard when Effric pounced upon him.

"Ruan," she smiled, plucking his arm. "I've missed ye." Her lashes lowered.

Ruan studied her with a mixture of suspicion and curiosity. He'd pitied Effric when she first arrived. That hadn't lasted long. The new Lady of Dunvegan had soon proven manipulative and despicable in her own right. She'd pursued him from their first meeting, steadfastly refusing to believe his lack of interest was genuine. Then, she became mad and he, along with the entire clan, had largely forgotten her. Yet, there was still something to pity, he reminded himself. Being wed to Tormod was too harsh a punishment for any crime.

"Ye could be laird soon!" Effric whispered, blocking his way. "Did ye hear? There is only Michael and Gerland in the way now. Andrew and his son are gone now—"

"Aye," Ruan interrupted with a frown. "Their deaths have naught to do with me!"

"But there are only three others in yer way now, and—" she said, placing her hands on his chest.

"How can ye speak so?" Ruan thundered, pushing her away.

Effric's lips thinned into a white line, "Eager to see yer new whore, are ye?"

Bree. In the past few hours, he hadn't spared the lass a single thought. Jenna's anguish had been his main concern. While fighting the MacDonalds, he'd only remembered his deathly ill, newly made wife, on occasion. By far, staying alive had been his most pressing concern.

No, the only thought that had crossed his mind about her had been a certainty that his return would find her dead.

He hadn't been in the least prepared to meet the startling green eyes, sooty lashes, and thick brown hair. Aye, she was a lass who could stir his blood should he permit it. He winced. Where was his control, his promise to himself that he'd walk away from all females before he turned into another version of his father?

He looked at his hands, fearing the violence that lay in them.

"Ruan?"

Effric's shrill voice brought him to the present. She was frowning, tugging at his sleeve, struggling between what seemed like anger and the desire to seduce him. "Come with me." She whispered.

Her prying fingers slithered down to slide under his plaid. He extricated her hand and released an exasperated breath. In the past, she'd pursued him with vigor like no other. He'd thought the matter done. Grasping her shoulders, he swung her about and threatened, "I've no interest in ye. I never will. I swear, lass, I never have!"

"But, ye can, if ye try!" she whispered, rubbing provocatively against his chest.

The lass truly was daft, there was no other explanation. "But I dinna want ye," he growled, shoving her back roughly.

"Is it Bree?" Effric snarled, her nostrils flaring.

Recalling Bree's hysteria the night before, he drew himself to his full height and said sternly, "Be ye mad or no, Effric, ye'll nae be harming Bree. If ye do, I'll lock ye in a tower myself. That, or send ye back to your father. Aye, and after last night, I'll be having ye watched day and night to prevent further mischief!"

Effric choked, turning chalk white. She glared at him briefly before scurrying away.

He wondered if she could be dangerous, or if he'd been too harsh. He'd have Ewan keep an eye on her in order to keep Bree safe. He smiled, recalling the fierce expression on Bree's face as she'd wielded the trencher to protect Merry. It had been a foolhardy act, but a brave one. Aye, he'd known from the beginning the lass had heart. Her demeanor was quiet, but she was far from weak.

Catching his smile, Ruan frowned. What was he doing? Lollygagging over a lass? No. He was done with women. They had caused him naught but trouble, and he'd do best to remember it.

"Ruan, love," Isobel's cheery voice called out from behind. "Robert bids ye come."

He fell into step at her side, gallantly hefting her basket onto his shoulder.

"Robert's told me a bit of the doings," she said in a low voice. "That yer brothers are trying to slay ye."

Ruan caught his breath. The words were stark, cold, and he didn't want to hear them. "I don't know that for certain." His protest sounded weak even to his own ears. He heaved a sigh. "Aye, well, Tormod has reason now. He's of a mind I rescued Merry to split the clan."

"Then, he's a fool," Isobel snorted. "Ye split the clan long afore that and he's a fool nae to know it."

Ruan stared in surprise.

"Can ye nae see it, lad?" she said with a smile. She raised her withered hand to caress his cheek. "Aye, there's nae a heart that does nae want ye as The MacLeod."

"Be done!" Ruan took a deep breath. "I'll have no more talk of this, 'tis far too dangerous!"

Isobel shrugged, unperturbed.

He found her reaction disconcerting. Deliberately switching the subject, he said, "Merry seems happier. At times, I can almost see her as she was, before…"

"Aye," Isobel smiled. "She's pinned to Bree like a needle in a cloth. Now, she's a lass and no mistake."

"Merry can do no wrong in your eyes," Ruan said fondly. "I should be jealous she has taken my place in your heart."

"Oh, I love our wee one, too," Isobel chuckled. "But lad, I was speaking of Bree. The wonders she has done with our Merry, in her own, quiet way."

Ruan blinked in surprise. Apparently, Isobel had fallen under Bree's spell as well. Suddenly, he recalled her curves and soft skin under his. To his horror, his cheeks tinged a slight pink. He shifted uneasily. He was much too old to blush over a woman.

Isobel reached over and tweaked his ear, "Robert's waiting for ye, love."

With that, she snagged her basket and lumbered off, leaving him standing there. He was perturbed on many accounts.

Slowly, he entered the room.

The exchange with Robert was alarming. Several respected elders of the clan stood by his uncle's side, all of them urging Ruan to rise against his remaining brothers, to slay them first before they succeeded in killing him. He didn't want to hear them. He still didn't want to believe his kin wanted his blood and he didn't want to see Robert agreeing in his own quiet way with a simple nod. That Robert wished him to wage bloodshed on his own kin was simply too much to think of now.

With a pounding head, he quitted the chamber, making his way to the great hall.

Tormod was already there, sprawling at the high table. His attention was riveted to the back of the room. Following his gaze, Ruan spied the object of his fascination, and his blood began to boil.

Bree sat quietly at a table at the far end, keeping her own company, and speaking to no one.

Hackles rising, Ruan strode to the high table, planting himself to block the man's vision.

Tormod had the grace to appear guilty, though he tried his best to cover it.

Neither spoke.

Tormod simply slouched, fumbling for his cup.

Ruan turned away. He'd have to have Ewan keep an eye on Tormod as well, though surely, even his brother wouldn't be so rash as to act on his lust for Bree.

Bree didn't notice his approach; she sat by herself, toying with her food.

He'd experienced a wide range of emotions upon waking to find her asleep in his bed. She'd been curled in the tightest and most uncomfortable ball he'd ever seen. Again, his lips quivered upwards as he recalled her horror. She'd been utterly dismayed to be in his bed where so many other women had smiled in triumph. He blinked, catching his line of thought.

Aye, the lass had every right to be dismayed. Though he no longer viewed women as playthings, how could any respectable woman believe that he didn't? He winced, recalling he'd been drunk as well, another weakness of the past. He was done with the stuff. Fervently, he vowed never to let another drop of whiskey pass between his lips again. Surely, he hadn't taken advantage of her.

Less confident, he slowed his advance, wondering if he should just leave.

"Ruan!" Merry skipped by, clasping his sleeve and pulling him forward.

Reluctantly, he allowed Merry to guide him to the table and cautiously took his place next to Bree. She tensed, but not enough to indicate he'd misbehaved. He found himself relaxing straightway.

Merry chattered, for the most part to Bree. His attention wandered to the men filing in. The majority of them spoke of the raids. Robert appeared to say a few words for the fallen and sent Ruan a look.

Ruan tightened his jaw, ignoring his uncle's unspoken question. He was not ready to wage war on his own kinfolk, regardless of their actions.

His half-brother Michael had arrived with his son, Gerland. It was odd to see them there, as they rarely visited Dunvegan. However, with Tormod childless, and the recent deaths, Dunvegan could soon be theirs.

Ruan leaned back, clasping his hands behind his neck. Tormod hated Michael almost as much as Michael hated him. It was with a healthy dose of amusement that he watched the brothers sit together at the high table, neither enjoying the company of the other.

They murmured amongst themselves for a time and then, as one, they lifted their eyes to settle on Bree.

Ruan tensed.

They were up to nothing good. Judging by their demeanor, Bree was in the center of it. He scowled, settling deeper in his seat. He could not leave the lass alone, not now.

Someone filled his cup and he absently picked at the food placed before him. At first, few shared their table, but as time passed, the crowd around them grew. The first two men asked his opinion on a dispute concerning sheep. He gave it. Several others arrived, probing what he'd do about a well run dry, caused by another diverting a stream. Another man accused his neighbor of stealing an axe, and it took quite some time before the matter was peacefully resolved. Others dropped by, to ask his opinion on some concern.

After he'd given his thoughts on the fifth matter, he paused, becoming aware of what he had been doing. These clansmen were having him settle their disputes, treating him as if he were the laird. It seemed an unwise and dangerous thing for them to do, given that Tormod and Michael were mere feet away.

Robert sat nearby, studying him quietly, a smile playing about his lips.

Abruptly, Ruan stood, tired of the entire situation. Snagging Bree, he pulled her from the hall. She kept up with him quietly and once in his chamber, stood warily by the door, as if ready to flee at a moment's notice.

"I'll nae harm ye," he said, breaking the awkward silence between them. She didn't believe him, of that, he was certain.

Mercifully, Merry had followed.

TRUST NO ONE

Bree was relieved when Merry slipped into the room.

While she was grateful for Ruan's protection in the hall, in the small space of the bedchamber, she was ill at ease to be alone with him. She was still unsure what he thought of her. Her ears tinged red every time she recalled the way she had awoken under him that morning. Now, in his presence, she could feel the color creeping on her neck.

Why was he filling so much of her thoughts of late? It must be the shock of the entire situation. There could be no other explanation.

Merry's arrival distracted her from further thoughts and Ruan gave his full attention to his little sister. He proceeded to stoke the fire and regale her with stories. He could tell a good tale and had obviously spent much time doing so.

The young girl brightened and giggled, skipping to the bed to slide under a warm plaid next to Bree. It was peaceful and they both grew comfortably drowsy, listening to the lilt of Ruan's voice long into the night.

Bree awoke early the next morning, slowly propping herself on one elbow. Merry was stretched out next to her, in the middle of the bed, dark curls framing her healing face. On the other side of Merry, Ruan lay on his back with his forearm tucked under his head. His slow, rhythmic breathing announced he was asleep, and she indulged in her curiosity to inspect him closely once more.

He was quite handsome and in spite of her best efforts to the contrary, she was beginning to think him gallant.

His lashes were unusually long and dark.

For a brief moment, she was tempted to reach out and touch them with her finger.

"Ach, what is it, lass?" he asked, his mouth quirked to one side. His eyes remained closed.

She jerked back, ashamed to be caught staring, and banged her head in the process. The noise startled Merry into a whirlwind of motion. In short order, all three tumbled from the bed, rubbing various sore points and sending each other sullen looks. With a muffled oath, Ruan strode from the chamber, slamming the door.

A short time later, Isobel poked her head through the door. "Effric's calling for ye, lass. She's wanting forgiveness."

Bree grimaced, thinning her lips. She simply didn't trust the Lady of Dunvegan.

"The lass is of unsound mind, love," Isobel said with a sympathetic smile. "But I dinna believe she'd cause ye harm. She's jealous and that is all. She seems to be making her peace that Ruan belongs to ye now. 'Tis so pleasant to see her smiling and behaving nicely. Mayhap, I can yet help the wee one."

Ruan belongs to you now? Why did those words make her

heartbeat quicken?

"I'll be with ye. I'll nae leave ye alone," Isobel promised, misunderstanding the nature of her hesitation.

Reluctantly, Bree allowed Isobel to guide her forward, still distracted by the words: *Ruan belongs to you now.*

Effric was alone, standing by the small, gilded birdcage that was placed on a table nearby. She said nothing as Bree curtsied in greeting.

"Remember?" Isobel prodded. "What ye said, nae an hour hence, lass."

Slowly, clutching her hands behind her back, Effric moved forward, stopping before Bree.

Isobel gave her a nod of encouragement.

"Aye," Effric said in a low voice. "This is what I have to say to ye!"

With a swift movement, she swung her hand up from where she'd hidden it. The blade of a small dagger glittered in the shaft of sunlight filtering through the window.

Bree simply stared in shock, but then Isobel screamed and grabbed Effric's hand as the dagger plunged forward. Bree jolted into action. With a backward twist, she leapt out of the way, flinging an arm over her face.

The blade scraped the back of her hand.

The door burst open and Ewan barged in. Taking the situation in at a glance, he disarmed Effric and subdued her within in a matter of seconds.

Bree simply stood where she was, white and shaken.

Effric began to weep hysterically. "My Ruan, she's taken my

Ruan!"

It was a chaotic scene. The chamber filled with others, among them Tormod, Robert, and Ruan. And then, Ruan stood before Bree, gently touching her cheek, but in an absent-minded way. At the same time, he was shouting at Tormod, when quite suddenly, he announced, "I'll be taking Bree away. She's done with this place!"

"Ye'll be living here!" Tormod announced, arms folded. "I'm The MacLeod, and I order ye to stay!"

Ruan gave a snort of disgust. Slowly, he moved to tower over his brother and then leaned in close to hiss, "Fie! Just ye try and force me!"

Taking Bree by the arm, he bundled her out of the castle, to the dock, and into a boat.

"Ye can stay with Jenna and help her manage the croft," Ruan explained tersely, rowing the short distance to the shore. "She needs help, and I'm sure ye've little love for the castle. I'll see to it that Effric is taken care of."

Bree swallowed and managed a nod, still in shock, she clenched her hand tightly. It was a small cut, but an unnerving one.

The boat scraped the beach and Ruan hopped out and lifted her ashore with an easy arm. He was silent, distant, as he led her to the stables. Saddling a shaggy pony, he quickly mounted, leaned down, and extended his hand to pull her up.

Bree balked.

"What is it?" Ruan asked, scowling a little.

She pressed her lips together. How could she tell the man that she hated to ride horses? She decided she couldn't, so with strength of will, she grasped his arm. His skin was warm, making her strangely nervous, but she'd no time for further distractions as he swung her roughly behind him.

"Hold on," he ordered curtly.

As the pony jolted forward, she desperately grabbed his waist causing him to cough a little. "Sorry..." she mumbled into his back, grimacing.

He didn't reply, but pried her fingers loose and repositioned them higher.

Bree frowned and cringed. She could feel his hard muscles under her hands. With her cheek pressed against his back, she could smell the smoke and heather scent of his plaid. Her ears began to burn, and she was grateful he could not see her blush.

Ruan rode in silence, directing the pony onto a sheep path that ran between two small, reed-filled lochs. A short distance away, she could see a tumbled down ruin of lichen-covered stones, an old fort of some kind.

The scenery was wild, forbidding. She wondered how far they had to go when the pony snorted and tossed its head, catching her unawares. All at once, she lost her grasp and the ground rose sharply. And suddenly she was rolling in the heather, sliding to a stop in a pile of damp, musty leaves.

For several long moments, she could not breathe, and then Ruan's concerned face entered her field of vision.

"Are ye hurt, lass?" he asked, extending a hand.

Bree gulped, a little stunned. He waited for a response before gently lifting her to her feet. Grimacing, she wiped her muddy hands on her skirt, wincing a little when she accidentally brushed the cut.

"Aye, I'm sorry for that," Ruan said quietly, catching her hand. "I'll nae be letting her harm ye again. I'm done with them all."

Bree held still. It was strange, standing on the wind swept moors with Ruan gently cradling her hand in his. She should have been cold, but instead, she was strangely warm. Then, all at once, his eyes were too much to bear. Twisting her hand free, she took a step back.

Ruan said nothing, but this time he placed her alone in the saddle and led the pony through the paths threading through the gorse and heather. It took longer. Apparently, he was in no hurry. It was oddly pleasant. From her perch, she could see in all directions, but she mostly watched the man in front of her.

Jenna's small croft was perched on top of a hill, a blue-plume of peat smoke rising far into the sky above it. Dried vines crawled over the black-stoned exterior and bits of grass grew on the heather-thatched roof. A few sheep grazed in front of the door. Ruan strode through them and they scattered, bleating at him crossly, bits of grass protruding from their cheeks.

Jenna brightened as Ruan stooped, entering the croft.

Bree paused on the threshold, watching them exchange words in low voices.

The woman caught her breath in surprise and waddled to Bree's side, "Poor lass! I never thought Effric could do such a thing! Come in now, I'm right pleased to have ye." She swept her hand in a welcoming gesture even as she leaned heavily against the door.

"Jenna, ye should be resting!" Ruan tossed a concerned arm around the woman's shoulders, drawing her to the hearth. "Think only of taking care of yourself and our wee one. I'll handle Effric."

Jenna smiled ruefully and settled into a chair with a loud sigh. "Can ye stay a wee bit tonight, Ruan? Tis hard to be alone… so soon."

"Aye, I'll return," he replied, without hesitation. He patted her stomach with a smile.

It was a possessive gesture, distinctly suggesting ownership, and then Bree understood.

Jenna was his lover. She carried his child.

Shocked, and strangely disconcerted, she glanced away. Her heart suddenly felt heavy. She was such a fool. Of late, Ruan had distracted her, sending her thoughts in confusing directions, but she'd do well to remind herself that the man hadn't wished to marry her. Clearly, he loved Jenna. She should have known. Still, inexplicably, she felt tears threaten. She clenched her fists. What ailed her? She didn't care for the man!

Ruan kissed the top of Jenna's head, "Just rest, love. Bree will do what needs to be done. I must return to Dunvegan."

Then, with a slight nod in Bree's direction, Ruan left.

Bree took a deep breath and stepped timidly into the room. "You love him," she blurted, oddly rattled. She regretted the words instantly. Why, oh why, had she said them? She sounded jealous.

"Ruan? Oh, aye, I love him with my soul!" Jenna opened her eyes briefly, long enough to raise a curious brow. "There isn't a lass for leagues who doesn't," she laughed. Then, she checked herself, eyes widening in alarm. "Oh, he's a different man, lass, grown and seen the folly of his ways. He's no longer the wild one. I'd say most of the tales are nae even true. Ye ken well enough how tales grow a life of their own."

Bree held still and then curiosity made her prompt, "Tales?"

"How many women and all… 'tis no matter," Jenna said. She shook her head, buttoning her lips, but then added, "'Tis a far fewer number than claimed, I should know. It was the carelessness of youth and nothing more. He's the sort who forgives all others but himself. He is so sure that he is beyond redemption that he canna see he is only just now worthy of love, the foolish lad. Sometimes, I think he enjoys torturing himself a wee bit too much."

Bree nodded awkwardly, embarrassed to have made Jenna speak on the matter and hurriedly searched for a way to change the subject, but then Jenna took care of the problem by leaning back and closing her eyes.

Bree grimaced, angry with herself. There was no denying it. Her heart weighed heavily. It could only mean one thing. Mysteriously, she'd developed some sort of feelings for Ruan. How could she be so foolish? She could hardly look at Jenna without feeling a strong sense of guilt.

Shaking off her darkening mood, she began tidying the tiny croft as Jenna drifted to sleep.

As the afternoon sun rose, Bree ventured into the neglected garden and set about readying it for the winter. It was peaceful to be away from the castle. Afraig crossed her mind from time to time, but she was still angry with the woman had for sending her to Scotland and to Ruan.

Ruan.

He was disconcerting, but he was kind. She could no longer deny that, whatever his past might be. Now that she understood his relationship to Jenna, there was no doubt that he'd annul their marriage. But, what would her future be? What would she do? It was a bit worrisome to contemplate. Would her father attempt to wed her off again? The uncertainty of her future weighed heavily upon her.

She frowned, pulling the dried vines and weeds vigorously, much harder than necessary.

Periodically, she checked on Jenna, but the woman slept deeply. She didn't wake until late in the evening when the aroma of the rich nettle soup and fresh bannocks Bree had made, floated through the croft. She still seemed tired, but ate heartily, telling Bree many tales of Ruan.

Obviously, Jenna loved him dearly. Her eyes crinkled about the corners as she leaned close, patting Bree on the knee and offering detail after detail of the man.

"Aye, he's the loyal sort, just a wee bit too charming for his own good. He was lonely as a lad, 'tis the only reason he was free with the lassies," Jenna repeated firmly.

Bree nodded, wincing a little, she wondered if Jenna repeated it to convince herself of the fact. The situation was entirely uncomfortable, and she was quite relieved when Jenna finally slipped into bed to nap once again.

She tidied the place and surveyed her handiwork with a pleased nod. It had been a long day, but a fulfilling one. Perhaps she could find a place to be a scullery maid. She sighed, trying not to worry for the future, but found it hard not to.

If only she could find a tiny croft, much like this one, she could just spend her days tending the garden, sheep, and geese. She could be self-sufficient. She felt a twinge of jealousy. Jenna had everything, even a man who loved her. Ruan's eyes had lit up when he saw her.

Catching the nature of her thoughts, Bree snorted, and rolled her eyes at herself. What had she been doing of late? Secretly wishing a man such as Ruan would desire her and why was she thinking that? She'd never thought such silly things before.

"You are so foolish!" she hissed under her breath as she spread several sheepskins near the fire and tossed a woolen blanket on top.

Drawing herself up resolutely, she forced her muddled thoughts to clear and focused on the work for the next day. She must be up at dawn. There was still much to do in righting the croft. She had noticed a hole in the thatching. She'd often repaired Wat's roof. She could do the same here. Tomorrow, she'd mend it.

She wondered what Merry was up to and where she'd sleep that night. Surely, someone would tell the little girl where she was, she didn't want the child to fret. As she began to worry herself, she heard the sound of boots crunching outside.

Alarmed, she sprang to her feet, angry with herself because she had forgotten to bar the door. With a pounding heart, she managed a single step that direction before it swung slowly open.

It was Ruan.

She exhaled a loud breath of relief.

Ruan flashed an apologetic smile. Indicating Jenna with his chin, he queried, "Sleeping?"

Bree nodded. A little weak-legged, she sat down on the sheepskins.

"Poor lass," he murmured, shaking his head at Jenna absently. He barred the door and added, "Effric's locked in her chamber. The elders will meet to decide what must be done with her."

Bree nodded, not really wanting to think of Effric. She smoothed the sheepskins with the palm of her hand. As usual, she felt awkward in Ruan's presence. A shadow fell and she glanced up to find him towering above her.

Ruan eyed her for a moment and then tossed a plaid next to the sheepskins. He collapsed onto it.

He was much too close and Bree pulled back, nervously.

Ruan caught the motion, but only smiled as he stretched his boots to the flames.

"Shouldn't you sleep next to Jenna?" Bree finally asked in a strained voice, silently cursing her burning ears.

"Why? Aren't ye the one in danger?" he replied. He raised a brow before adding with a good-natured chuckle, "Ye'll be in danger of running, if nothing else."

"I've nowhere to run," she admitted tightly, clutching her blanket and inching away.

Ruan extended a sympathetic hand, but she jerked sharply away. What was the man doing? Jenna surely would misunderstand. Sending him a flustered look, she yanked the sheepskins several feet away. She settled once again, turning her back with a deliberate flare. She'd no time for further bilious thoughts. He reached over and placed a light hand on her shoulder.

Bree sat bolt upright, her heart racing, but managed to summon a fierce frown. She nodded in Jenna's direction.

Ruan smiled hesitantly, obviously mystified.

"Jenna!" she gulped her explanation, hoping he didn't notice her reddening cheeks. "Jenna is right there!"

"Aye?" Ruan's dark brows knit together. He studied her before opening his fingers to reveal a small knife. "Ach, ye wee beastie, I only wanted to give ye this *sgian dubh*. I don't plan to ravish ye."

A deeper crimson rushed to Bree's cheeks, she hoped the firelight was too dim to reveal it. What ailed her thinking? Of course, the man was not interested in her! Feeling utterly foolish, she reached for the knife, but he grasped her wrist and pulled her forward. She fell heavily against his chest, startled.

"Aye," Ruan whispered, eyes glittering. "I dinna ken what evil ye've done, lass, but it must have been uncommon wicked. An innocent lass would never be so cursed as to be caught betwixt the sons of the devil himself."

Bree swallowed, keenly aware of the hard muscles upon which she lay. Her heart pounded faster. "What do you mean?" she squeaked.

"Trust no one in this place," Ruan murmured into her hair. "Least of all, sons of a MacLeod. Stay far from Tormod, I dinna ken his intent, but there's something in his voice when he speaks of ye."

Her fingers went ice-cold as he molded them around the hilt of the small knife.

Then, his jaw hardened and he sat up, pushing her away, "Move to yon side of the fire. I'm weary. Ye can plunge that *sgian dubh* in my heart if I turn your way."

Filled with a sudden fear at the mention of Tormod, Bree crept back onto the sheepskins, clutching the knife. Gone were the fanciful thoughts; ones of stark reality replaced them. Dunvegan was a harsh place, and the inhabitants were dangerous. And; no doubt, Ruan was as well.

It was a long time before she could finally sleep.

Bree awoke early the next morning to find Ruan gone and Jenna still peacefully asleep, her hand gently cradling her swollen belly.

The jealousy was not as strong and Bree felt a sense of relief. Whatever minute feelings she'd developed for Ruan were already fading. With a lighter and satisfied heart, she grabbed the water bucket and slipped outside in the cool dawn to trudge down the hill to the small stream.

The water was brown, infused with heather and peat. She grimaced. Everything about this place was brown. Kneeling by the stream, she dipped the bucket in. The water was icy cold, chilling her to the bone. She shivered, recalling her narrow escape of a frozen fate on the moors. Ruan had rescued her. She smiled, recalling how gentle he'd been, and then thoughts of him standing before her naked fled through her mind. He was handsome. She'd never thought a naked man could be appealing. Blushing at her thoughts and ashamed to be thinking of him once again, she struck the bucket.

"You are such a fool!" she snapped crossly, smacking the bucket a little viciously. "A fool! A fool!"

"Ach, lass, 'tis only a poor, wee bucket," Ruan's deep voice rumbled in her ear.

Bree jerked, startled as a hand slid over hers to pull the bucket out of the water.

He was standing behind her, and far too close. She could feel his breath on the back of her neck as he murmured, "Pray tell, what the wee bucket could have done to incur such wrath and be called a fool?"

Bree swallowed. The man was overpowering. It was hard to think. Flustered, she replied, "I was speaking of myself! I'm the fool!"

She tried to free her hand from under his, but his grip tightened.

"Ach, a fool?" Ruan snorted a little. "Over what?"

She could hardly tell him the truth. She frowned. It was hard to think, her heart was beating so loudly. She whispered, "Let me go."

"Ye find my touch so disturbing?" he asked in a low voice.

His skin was uncomfortably warm on hers. Again, unbidden thoughts of him standing so boldly naked in the chamber flashed through her mind, and she flushed scarlet.

"Ach, ye wee beastie, I'll bring the water," he said, moving to stand beside her. He took the bucket from her hands. "Ye should rest a wee bit yourself."

Nervously, Bree swallowed, watching him from the corner of her eye. His muscles rippled as he hefted the bucket from the stream.

He turned to her with a bow and said, "Please, lead the way, my lady."

There was no denying the man was charming. It was no wonder so many women had fallen for him. Bree took a deep breath, willing her heart to slow down.

She could not tread the path of where these thoughts led.

Turning on her heel, she wrestled her way back up the hill, through the slippery mud, acutely aware of Ruan following closely behind, whistling softly.

She was grateful that once in the croft Ruan's attention shifted fully to Jenna. He sat on the edge of the bed, announcing he had duties to attend to, but would return when he could.

"Take care, love," Jenna replied. She smiled tiredly as he kissed her forehead. With a deep yawn, she promptly turned over and fell back asleep.

Ruan stared at her for a little while, his brows drawn in a worried scowl. As Bree passed, he reached over and laid his fingers over her wrist.

"Watch her well," he said, rising to his feet. "I'll see if Isobel can come soon and have a wee look."

Bree nodded, pulling at her hand, but his fingers tightened.

"And rest yourself, lass," Ruan continued, his dark eyes boring into hers. "There is no cause to work so hard. Ye look a wee bit pale."

Bree swallowed uneasily, but managed a nod. She tugged her hand again.

"Ach, do ye find me so unbearable?" Ruan asked, but his eyes had narrowed and his voice sounded huskier.

"No!" Bree denied, clearing her throat hoarsely. "I'll... I'll always remember your kindness... and—"

"Remember?" Ruan tilted his head to one side, still capturing her wrist with his fingers. "Is there something about me that ye know? Am I dying?" The corner of his lip twitched.

"I meant... when our... marriage is annulled," Bree said and blushed furiously, averting her gaze. It was hard to talk to the man.

He blinked and relaxed his hold all at once. "Aye," he said, nodding curtly. "I've affairs to tend. I'll see if Isobel can be spared."

Without a backward glance, he strode to the door and was gone.

Bree looked at her wrist and then guiltily at Jenna. No, she could not rest, regardless of what Ruan said. She had to keep herself busy and her mind focused on anything other than that dark eyed and disturbing man.

The day was a hectic one. Clouds had gathered along the horizon by mid-morning, threatening rain. Bree set about working quickly. She'd discovered the hole in the roof was larger than she'd originally thought. It took longer than she'd planned to gather the heather and tie it into bundles.

Once or twice, Jenna tottered to the door and insisted that Ruan could take care of it when he returned. Bree shook her head politely, reassuring her that she found it relaxing. It was true enough. The work kept her mind occupied. By midafternoon, her heart had once again lightened. She decided she'd misinterpreted her odd feelings of the past few days. She was beginning to think of Ruan as a brother.

Bree had just clambered onto the roof with the last bundle of thatching when she felt the first rain drops fall. She smiled in satisfaction. She'd timed it well. Hiking her skirt about her waist to avoid tripping on it, she climbed up a little farther, stuffing the last bundle into the hole.

"Well done, lass, well done," she said, smiling wryly at herself.

"Aye, well done," a deep baritone agreed, chuckling.

Bree whirled to see Ruan resting against the lower ledge of the roof. Suddenly, she lost her grip and began to slide. Frantically, she grasped the thatching and succeeded in stopping her descent.

"Be careful there, lass," Ruan advised with a half-smile on his lips. His eyes trailed downwards.

Bree followed his gaze and then blushed. Her skirt had caught on heather, riding up to reveal a healthy portion of her leg. Biting her lip, she yanked it free, barely managing to maintain her grip on the slippery roof.

Then, inexplicably, Ruan's strong hand latched onto her ankle, giving it a sharp tug, deliberately pulling her, and she was sliding uncontrollably down. She collided with him full force, knocking him back off his feet. His head struck the ground, and he went limp.

Bree caught her breath, remaining where she was, but when Ruan didn't move she scrambled to the side. His dark lashes remained closed. Hesitantly, she prodded his shoulder. "R ... Ruan?"

He didn't respond.

All at once, she began to panic. Shaking his shoulder more forcefully, she raised her voice, frantically calling, "Jenna! Jenna!"

The door to the croft slammed back as Jenna charged her way. "What happened!" she gasped, dropping heavily to her knees.

"He fell back from the roof!" Bree heard her own voice shake. "I think he is hurt! He isn't moving and—"

Jenna stared at her, a little puzzled and interrupted, "The roof? 'Tis only a few feet, love."

It was true; the roof ended only a short distance from the ground.

"He pulled me down and..." Bree's voice trailed off. She didn't want Jenna to misunderstand. "I mean... I... I slid... I think I knocked him back, and he hit his head..."

Jenna bent over Ruan's face and then straightened with a growl. "Help me up, lass."

Bree jumped to her feet, supporting her elbow. "Shall I get Isobel?

Is he…?" Surely, he was not dead? Or was he? Horrified, she searched Jenna's face.

"I'll think of a suitable punishment for ye," Jenna snorted, kicking Ruan in the side. "I nearly dropped the bairn! I told ye to help the lass, nae play with her!"

Dumbfounded, Bree stared as Ruan opened his eyes and chuckled.

"Ach, 'twas far more pleasurable to watch," he said. He reached over and grabbed Bree's ankle, giving it another twist.

Losing her balance, Bree fell, landing mostly on top of him. He didn't seem to mind. Instead, he seemed to find the entire thing quite amusing.

Shaken and embarrassed, Bree scrambled back to her feet. How could the man act so in front of his lover? Not wanting to cause Jenna any distress, she said in a rush, "He is not himself! He means nothing by it! He must have struck his head!"

Clutching her skirts, she ran into the croft without daring to look at either of them. What was the man playing at? Her fingers were shaking a little as she threw a few handfuls of oats into a wooden bowl.

The door swung open and Ruan stepped inside.

"I only meant to jest, lass," he explained from the door. "I meant no harm."

Bree tensed. Summoning her best frown, she muttered, "Then, at least think of Jenna!" Could he not see how she might misunderstand?

"Aye," Ruan cleared his throat, apparently hearing.

He stood back to let Jenna pass in.

"I'm well, love, don't mind me!" Jenna assured with a bright smile.

Bree turned and stared at her, a little confused. They were both watching her, appearing somewhat confused themselves. Exchanging glances, they moved to the other side of the croft and began to discuss the state of several sheep. Returning to the bannocks, Bree focused on her work, trying to think of nothing but her list of chores.

The evening was an awkward one. Ruan mentioned that Merry and Isobel would try to come the following day, but other than that, he avoided her. He concentrated, for the most part, on Jenna.

It was late when Bree finally spread her sheepskin next to the dying hearth, Ruan and Jenna's voices still murmuring softly.

She must have been tired. She fell asleep almost instantly. She was not aware she'd even done so until she awoke suddenly, disoriented. It took a moment to recall where she was.

The sound of an axe splintering wood resounded through the croft, and any remaining lethargy was shattered. She leapt to her feet.

"Bree!" Tormod yelled drunkenly through the door. "Ye've made me angry!"

Bree gulped.

"'Tis no cause to fret, love," Jenna's voice echoed softly. "Ruan will handle him."

Ruan was already there, flinging the door open. He stood in the moonlight with arms crossed and feet planted wide.

"Ruan!" Tormod gulped in alarm, lurching back.

The brothers locked gazes and then Ruan raised a cold brow at the axe embedded in the door.

There was a deadly pause.

"Ye're here..." Tormod mumbled, licking his lips nervously.

"And why did ye come?" Ruan cocked his head to the side.

"Bree," Tormod slurred. "I've to speak with the lass."

"What matter do ye wish to speak on in the dead of night?" Ruan drummed his fingers on his arms, flexing them in preparation.

Tormod mopped his sweating brow.

"If I see ye anywhere near Bree, I'll have your head, be ye The MacLeod or no!" Ruan said through clenched teeth. "And, as violence is the only thing ye can understand, I'll leave ye with this to remember it by!"

Tormod stared blankly.

It was an unfair fight. Tormod was too drunk to defend himself. In short order, he stumbled away clutching his profusely bleeding mouth and nose. Bree's consternation warred with a deep ripple of pleasure. It was impossible to resist stealing an admiring glance at Ruan. She hoped Jenna wouldn't notice.

Ruan wrenched the axe free and tossed it on the chest with a grunt, "That should keep him at bay. I'll mend the door in the morning and I'll speak with Robert on—"

"Ruan," Jenna interrupted in a voice taut with pain. "Ye'd best nae wait to fetch Isobel. The bairn is coming."

I'M NAE IN LOVE!

Jenna suffered long into the next day and night, panting and wheezing in excruciating pain. At dawn, Isobel arrived with Merry toting her collection of herbs. She promptly put Bree to work brewing a variety of teas, some for Jenna to ease her suffering and others to keep everyone else awake.

At times, Jenna could not sit still and insisted on walking about the croft. At other times, she huddled on the chair as they rubbed her back. Periodically, Bree stepped outside to inform Ruan and those waiting with him of the progress.

With each passing hour, their anxiety grew, but she did her best to pass on Isobel's assurances that all was well. After seeing her endless suffering, Bree was convinced she'd much rather die than ever give birth to a child.

"'Tis taking too long!" Jenna screeched in agony.

"Ach, the MacLeods are ones to take their time, lass. It must be a boy...they tend to dally a wee bit," Isobel crooned and beckoned to Bree. "Here, lass. Take Jenna's hands for a spell, my fingers have gone numb."

It hurt dreadfully. With each labor pain, Jenna crushed Bree's fingers and they both shed tears.

After a time, Isobel took pity and replaced her, sending her out to keep the others abreast of the slow progress. The cycle repeated through the day and long into the night. She lost track of how many times she delivered the same message.

Evening arrived. Mercifully, there was no sign of rain. The moon hung large in the sky, the stars were bright and twinkling as she stumbled from the croft once again, yawning tiredly.

Ruan and Ewan had built a fire. Merry had joined them, leaving the croft after deeming the birthing process no longer interesting. Others from the village came and went. Someone was roasting a coney on a spit. Everyone stopped speaking when she appeared.

"Is it done?" Ruan asked, rising to meet her.

"No," Bree said, shaking her head.

Ruan was obviously worried. He had hovered around the croft from the beginning of Jenna's labor, taking little food and drink. It was rather heartwarming that he cared for his child so deeply. For whatever tales Jenna had spoken of, painting his past as a raucous and heartless man, he was now quite kind.

Collecting her scattered thoughts, she yawned again, "Isobel says these things take time, especially the first one. I'm sure your son will come soon."

Ruan broke his stride and raised his brows as Ewan glanced up from the fire.

"I'm sure all is well," Bree repeated tiredly.

"Ruan?" Ewan queried softly.

"My… son?" Ruan's brows lifted, shushing Ewan with his hand as he peered down at Bree. "Aye, I can see how that takes time."

Ewan promptly swallowed a chuckle.

Ruan shot him a black look.

"Yes," Bree agreed, feeling suddenly timid. "Isobel says the MacLeods tend to dally." She attempted a smile, but found Ruan's scrutiny unnerving.

"Dally?" Ruan repeated softly. His expression altered and he added, "In the birthing or the getting?"

It was Bree's turn to frown.

"What are ye trying to say, lass?" Ruan asked. His dark eyes gleamed strangely almost as if he were laughing. "Are ye complaining?"

"Complaining?" Bree repeated, frowning deeply. "Your son's arrival has nothing to do with me!"

"Oh? My son has everything to do with ye," he said. His lip curved in the oddest fashion. "I thought ye wanted naught of husbands."

"I… do not even have a husband!" Bree replied, a little stiffly. The man made no sense. If she didn't know better, she would think he was jesting at her expense.

"Oh?" He bent close to whisper in her ear. "Mayhap ye should spend more time in my company. Ach, with those eyes and curls ye might find things different soon enough."

Surely, she misconstrued his tone. He must be overly exhausted. Annoyed, she spun on her heel and slammed the door in his face, but not before she heard his distinct chuckle. She devoutly hoped Jenna hadn't heard the baffling exchange.

She need not have worried. Jenna hadn't heard anything. She was in the final birthing pains, crouching low over the stool and screaming loudly.

At last, the baby arrived with a high-pitched cry. Bree nearly fainted and Jenna actually did. Isobel chuckled at them both. In short order, a tiny, wrinkled creature swaddled in a plaid was thrust into Bree's arms.

"A wee lassie," Isobel said, pleased. "And she has her mother's hair."

It was a girl.

Briefly, Bree wondered if Ruan would be disappointed.

"Introduce the wee one to her kin whilst I tend to Jenna," Isobel ordered kindly. "Go, before ye faint on yer feet, lass. Ye did well."

Timorously, Bree clutched the crying bundle. She'd never held a baby before. She was not exactly sure she cared for it. It was unnerving. Isobel should not have trusted her with so precious a thing. Carefully, she tiptoed across the room and opened the door to the happy roar of the gathered onlookers. They crowded close, Ruan grinning widely, Merry at his side.

"Your... daughter," Bree said nervously, relieved to give the infant away before she accidentally dropped it. She searched his face, wondering if he'd be disappointed that it was not a boy.

Ruan's dark eyes narrowed.

Unaccountably, she felt a twinge of disappointment. "A daughter is... as fortunate as a son," she said, compelled to defend the helpless baby.

"Aye, I thought as much, after that last conversation with ye, lass," Ruan snorted. He threw back his head and laughed. "Just who do ye think Jenna is?"

All at once, Bree tensed uncertainly.

Ruan caught her chin and forced her eyes to meet his. "By the Saints! I thought ye knew she was my sister!"

A smattering of laughter rang about her.

"Faith, lass, I share the same father with every lass within a league of this place, and that includes Jenna!" Ruan leaned forward, playfully tweaking her nose.

She'd thought she blushed before, but she was gravely mistaken. Her skin felt aflame as a tide of crimson swept from her head to her toes.

With a rich laugh, he pushed past her into the croft, carrying his newly born niece with him.

***

It was very late before the croft was silent once again.

Isobel had returned to Dunvegan, and Jenna slept peacefully with her newborn daughter. Bree curled in front of the fire in the tiny, uncomfortable ball she seemed to favor; Merry, as always, by her side.

Ruan tipped his chair back, balancing on two legs. He enjoyed tormenting Bree. His pulse leapt at every flash of her green eyes. Those eyes were dangerous. He should be ignoring them, but in spite of his best efforts, he was finding it impossible.

She'd been mortified to discover Jenna was his sister. While it was amusing, the misunderstanding was confounding in another sense. What a scoundrel she must have thought him! Already, she must have heard many of the tales. He wondered which ones. Most were not even true, but he knew there was little hope of convincing her of that.

He was annoyed to find his thoughts perpetually revolving around Bree.

How could he forget that most women were greedy and troublesome? Aye, and the reputable women saw him only as a rogue, incapable of love and loyalty. Even Bree thought he'd brought his own wife to serve as a handmaiden to his lover. What manner of beast did she think him? He could not fathom women.

He slammed the chair back on all four legs.

The noise startled the bairn. As the thin wail cut the darkness, he ruefully slipped outside the croft into the cold night wind, hoping to clear his mind, but he failed miserably. His thoughts remained on Bree. Not wanting to think what that might mean, he finally returned to throw a plaid next to Merry and force his eyes shut.

Sleep was long in coming.

By morning, they were all exhausted.

The infant dozed only in fitful spurts, doing a grand job of keeping them awake the rest of the time. Jenna, though tired, didn't appear to mind in the slightest, she'd obviously met the love of her life. While fascinating to observe, he suddenly felt smothered by females, all of them exceedingly complex. Even the tiny one Jenna had brought into the world the night before was already tormenting him. How was he going to feed her, along with the rest? He had nothing left to his name.

As the sun rose, Bree stumbled about, making porridge while burying yawns in her sleeve. She did her best to avoid him, and, for the most part, succeeded quite well. Why did he find that a challenge? Repeatedly, he caught himself seeking ways to spark those green eyes into life.

He was daft.

He shook his head to clear it. He had to leave the croft before he turned mad. With great relief, he discovered several loose stones under the window, and Ewan's arrival gave him the perfect excuse to escape. Pointing to the stones he announced, "I'll be off to mend these."

There were plenty of shells in the bucket to grind as mortar, but he needed to breathe the fresh salty air. He simply had to remove himself from the intoxicating influence of so much femininity in one place. The door of the croft closed behind him with a satisfying thud. He leapt easily over the low stone wall and made his way to the pale, yellow beaches. Kneeling, he scooped up handfuls of small snail shells and dried seaweed, absently letting them run through his fingers. This had always been one of his favorite places.

He was on the beach for only a short time before he spied Bree and Merry coming his way, fighting the wind. Alarmed, he dropped the bucket, but Merry's wide smile indicated nothing amiss.

"Isobel sent us to help," she informed him, skipping happily. "She says we need a wee nip of fresh air."

Bree was not thrilled to be there. That was readily apparent. She watched him warily and he caught himself smiling like a fool, unable to stop. She was such a suspicious lass. He had never quite met one like her before. Who could resist the challenge? After showing her the shells to gather, he offered the bucket merely as an excuse to capture her hand. Unable to comprehend at first, she waited politely for him to let go. As his fingers trailed over her wrist, his amusement grew and her indifference shifted into confusion.

She pulled her hand away.

"Ach, lass, I dinna bite," he said. Then, from under half-closed lids, he added suggestively, "Well, perhaps I do, but those that I do dinna seem to mind much."

"It is no affair of mine," Bree replied stiffly, bending to pick up a shell.

If he were honest to himself, he was a wee bit insulted. Aye, more than a wee bit, his pride was grandly hurt. Rare had been the lass to resist his charms. Not that he was charming her, he hastily reminded himself. He folded his arms irritably. What would she do if he swept her in his arms and soundly kissed her? Catching the thought, he swore abruptly and halted mid-step. What was he thinking?

He nearly tripped over Merry. Aye. Bree's suspicion was catching. Merry observed him with a dark scowl, her brows drawn together in a manner that promised trouble. He opened his lips, feeling the need to defend himself, when he spied Robert riding hard toward him.

"Tidings!" Robert shouted, pulling up beside him. "Come to the hall at once. Bring Bree."

***

With a sense of growing dread, Ruan marched into Dunvegan with Bree in tow.

The noon meal forgotten, the clansmen gathered around an exhausted and battered young boy seated in Tormod's chair. Upon spying Ruan, his small face lit, and he leapt into his arms. Ruan staggered a step, unprepared, but hugged the lad in return.

"Ruan!" the lad gulped. "Fearghus... Fearghus..."

"Take a breath, Colin," Ruan placed a comforting hand upon his head.

It took some time, but Colin finally managed to impart the details. Fearghus had raided the clan borders, burning several fields and a handful of crofts. After seeing his kin locked in their croft and the roof set afire, the lad had escaped.

Ruan blanched.

He wanted to retch. It was his fault. He'd caused this. Fearghus was striking back with vengeance. Sick at heart, he collapsed on the nearest bench.

"This blood is on yer hands, Ruan," Tormod announced loudly. He inspected the faces of the men around him eagerly, obviously expecting a chorus of agreement.

Grim silence greeted his display.

"Aye," Ruan murmured finally. "'Tis true enough."

A ripple of disagreement circled the hall.

Tormod licked his lips, nervously.

"Nay," Ruan said. He stood, holding up his hand and addressed the clansmen. "I'm the cause, but I'll set it right."

They erupted into a cheer.

"'Tis no fault of yours, Ruan!" a man said.

Others took up the words.

"Silence!" Tormod thundered. He looped his hands over his paunch, and his chin jiggled in indignation. "If Ruan had nae attacked Fearghus, this would never—"

"If ye'd never wed Merry off then Ruan wouldn't have needed to fetch her," Robert interrupted calmly. "We should ride at once. Fearghus may nae be yet finished, and we should head him off."

Agreement circled the hall.

"Ye'll be riding, too?" Robert asked Tormod coolly. "Michael and Gerland as well?"

Tormod took an involuntary step back. "Aye, Michael and Gerland, of a certainty, but I should be staying here to… to deal with… matters."

Ruan's head snapped up. Recalling Tormod's unexpected appearance in Jenna's cottage, he turned upon his older brother. "I'll nae hesitate slaughtering ye if you touch her, Tormod. Make no mistake."

Tormod's flaccid cheeks rippled as he lifted his jaw. "Dare ye threaten The MacLeod?" He hissed.

"Aye," Ruan replied, unrepentantly.

Several nearby clansmen nodded in open support.

"Ruan's wife inspires such loyalty?" Tormod spat in their direction, but he paled, obviously unnerved.

"We all love Bree," Robert's voice rang clear, nodding at the men to return to their seats. "Ewan will see to Bree's safety whilst we are away." Robert continued evenly. "The young pup canna come with us; 'tis best to keep the Earl of Mull from this matter."

"Ye should be riding, Tormod," Ruan said and folded his arms in a direct challenge.

"Matters of import require my attention!" Tormod raised his voice, but it sounded thin, almost wavering.

"Then, Ruan shall lead," Robert announced. He lifted his arm, holding it high. "He is a MacLeod!"

The clansmen in the hall roared in response, "A MacLeod! A MacLeod! Ruan MacLeod!"

Tormod's face drained of color.

Ruan laid a hand on his uncle's arm. "A word, Uncle?"

Under his brother's intense scrutiny, he drew Robert away.

Once outside Tormod's hearing, he scowled. "What are ye doing? I've nae agreed to your daft scheme, and I'll nae have these men..." The shouts reverberating in the hall drowned the rest of his words.

Taking Bree and Ruan by the arm, Robert shepherded them from the place, a pleased smile upon his lips.

"What have ye done?" Ruan accused Robert, angry. "Are ye daft? I'll nae have these men thinking I aim to split the clan!"

"'Tis nae in yer hands now, lad. And what happens next is a matter for the clan," Robert replied. He smiled indulgently at his nephew. "But we must avenge Colin first, and when we return, we'll have a gathering of the clan to discuss what needs to be said. Now, be off to the stables, I'll meet ye there in a wee bit."

Ruan's scowl deepened as he made his way in silence, dimly aware Bree was still following him. If Tormod hadn't wanted him dead before, he certainly would now. The show of support in the hall had all but sealed it. He wished the clansmen had remained silent. He sighed. Why would Fearghus do this? The level of violence was unusual. The man had mostly settled for stealing cattle and sheep in the past.

As he walked into the stables, he ran headlong into Ewan.

The lad jumped back, dropping the saddle slung over his shoulder.

"Nay," Ruan said, and shook his head. "Nae you, lad, we ride without ye today. Your father has no place in this."

Ewan opened his mouth to protest.

"Besides, I need ye for other things," Ruan continued. "Ye'll have to guard Bree, though I don't think Tormod will go near her. 'Tis best to be safe." Ruan grasped him by the arm and pulled him forward. "If I don't return, take Merry and Bree to Cameron."

"Aye!" Robert nodded, joining them to hear the last part. "'Tis a braw plan. Mayhap, we should send them both sooner until matters are settled."

"Settled?" Ruan turned on his uncle. "I told ye, Robert, I'll nae be the cause of brother fighting brother—"

"And ye will nae be, I swear it, lad," Robert interrupted, clasping him firmly on the shoulder.

Ruan stared at him skeptically, before addressing Ewan, "Do ye understand, lad?"

"Aye," Ewan agreed with a nod, albeit a reluctant one.

The stables bustled with activity. Men led the horses from the stalls while, out on the road, Ruan could hear the rasping of metal as others inspected their weapons. Ruan stalked to his mount, observing Bree from the corner of his eye. She was grim-faced, twisting her hands together tightly. He felt an odd surge of protectiveness mixed with something he knew he should deny and something he didn't want to acknowledge.

"I never wanted a wife," he muttered to Ewan, slamming the saddle onto the back of his horse.

The beast stamped in response, tossing its head.

Ewan raised a brow, but said nothing as he helped adjust the cinch.

"Ach, and even if I were stuck with a wife, I never wanted a respectable one!" Ruan scowled.

Ewan cleared his throat.

Ruan didn't appreciate the light dancing in the lad's eyes. Swinging himself into the saddle, he leaned down and growled, "Aye, she means nothing to me. There's no need for that. She sees the truth of what I am. The poor lass wants to run far away and can ye blame her?"

The horse stomped skittishly and Ewan grabbed the animal's head with a steadying hand.

"Aye and I've no yearning for her, anyway," Ruan swore under his breath. Surely, that was true. Surely, he could convince himself that was true. He pounded the pommel, frustrated, knowing it was not. "She's even more bothersome than most!"

The horse stepped sideways under the attack.

"Have ye nothing to say?" Ruan thundered, glaring down at Ewan.

"Nay," Ewan answered. His eyes twinkled in a manner dangerously close to amusement. "I'm nae the one fooling myself."

Ruan frowned, but raised a querying brow.

"I'm nae the one falling in love," Ewan explained with a cocky grin.

At the word, love, Ruan kicked the horse. It leapt forward in response. He pulled the reins sharply and the animal reared in displeasure. It was preposterous. Though he'd never truly loved a woman, he was certain it took much longer than Ewan implied.

The men were almost ready. He had to be going.

Pressing forward, he watched Gerland and Michael mounting their horses. Nearby, he saw Merry clinging to Bree, threading her arms around her neck. Her brown eyes were large with unshed tears. He longed to comfort his small sister and wondered if there would be a time that she wouldn't have to worry for his return.

Then, his eyes shifted to Bree. Her face was white. Aye, he longed to see the poor lass at ease, and those lips smile. Overwhelmed by a strong wave of protectiveness, he raised his voice to address the clansmen that were not going, "Ye can tell Tormod if he even looks at my wife that I'll flay him alive. Aye, be he The Macleod or no!"

Cheers erupted at this.

He grimaced at the light in Robert's eye as he said, "And I'll be holding each of ye to that, I swear!"

He had no authority to order them to do anything, but they didn't seem to mind. Instead, they only roared louder, pounding each other on the backs, as if he'd just announced he was splitting the clan. He frowned.

Ewan's lips cracked into a broad grin.

Masked by the deafening clansmen, he barked in the lad's ear, "If I dinna return, Ewan, take them both to Cameron. Both. Give me your word!"

Ewan touched his finger to his lips. "I swear to the last drop of my blood!"

Ruan nodded once in satisfaction and then pulled the horse sharply once again, to stop before Bree and Merry. "I'll return, my

Merry wee lass," he promised, placing his hand over his heart. "This will be the last time, I swear, that ye'll have to fret so. I'll take ye wherever 'tis ye wish."

"Paris?" Merry asked, her chin trembling.

"Aye, I swear that I'll take ye to Paris, my Merry lass," Ruan said, before turning to Bree. Against his will, her expression made his heart thrill in response. It was admiration. She was looking at him with admiration. Aye, Ewan was dangerously perceptive. He was falling for the lass. He was a fool to deny it. For the first time, he wondered if it would be possible to win her love even as he was astounded that he desired to try. Aye, he was a fool to try. He did not even have a shilling in his name.

"Aye, when I return, we'll be talking, *mo ceisd*," he finally said and then he thundered away.

***

It was a week from hell.

They rode hard, sleeping little, as they hunted the men responsible for the unholy attack.

Several times, in the heat of battle, Ruan found arrows assailing him from behind, as in the previous raids. One succeeded in grazing his shoulder. He shared his suspicions with no one, but it heightened his state of alert. Perhaps he was foolish, but he still did not want to believe his own brothers were trying to kill him.

They had found some of the raiders camped in the mountains near several crofts. The encounter was over before Ruan could even order that they be kept alive for questioning. He exchanged heated words with Michael and the others over the loss of the opportunity to gather more information.

It began to rain.

They sloshed through the mud, their bare knees and plaids soaked, as they scoured the moors for signs of the raiders.

A few days later, they stumbled upon another encampment.

Again, Ruan found his attempts to take the men alive thwarted and this time by Gerland.

It was maddening.

The entire incident was unusual, from the manner of Fearghus' initial attacks to the fact that though these men were dressed in MacDonald plaids, they did not wear them properly. He could have sworn they were shouting in French as the battle ensued. One swarthy man was definitely Spanish. He'd heard him praying aloud as he lay dying on the moors. Gerland's sword cut it short. It made little sense and Ruan was perplexed how they came to serve Fearghus. That is, if they were in the man's service at all.

The day was particularly gloomy. The clouds steadfastly refused to let the sun's rays penetrate their forbidding layers. Ruan spent the night scouting the perimeter of the nearby forest. It was late when he finally returned to the others and discovered Robert had ridden with Michael to investigate a new set of tracks.

Ruan sat tiredly before the fire. Someone thrust a leg of fowl and a few bannocks into his hands. He adjusted his plaid, stretched his long, bare legs with a brooding scowl, and ate quickly. He didn't trust Michael or Gerland. He was concerned for Robert's safety.

He was asking what direction they had taken when a wail sounded from the men around him. Springing to his feet, he saw Robert's horse following the others.

It was without a rider.

He didn't recall mounting his horse; suddenly, he was just reining alongside Michael. His attention focused solely upon the grey-faced man his brother bore in his arms.

"He's dead," Michael said, his voice sounding as if it were from far away. "There was nothing we could do."

"Aye," Gerland murmured in agreement.

Finally finding his voice, Ruan asked hoarsely, "Did ye slay the man who did this?"

"He escaped," Michael answered. "We stopped, trying to save Robert."

Ruan bowed his head, willing the tears to come, but they were strangely absent. His heart sank. He was responsible for this, first the crofters, and now his uncle. Their deaths were upon his head. He could not think.

"We must return to Dunvegan," Michael said. "This pursuit is over."

Ruan followed, saying nothing. He watched them break camp and mount their horses to return.

He didn't join them. Instead, he remained on his horse, vowing he wouldn't leave until he'd avenged Robert's death. He wheeled the animal toward Dunscaithe, paying no heed to the handful of men choosing to follow him. A mad quest, Michael had yelled after him, but Ruan brushed off his brother's warning.

Time passed in a haze.

It was late the next day and they had been following a set of tracks for hours. As the sun sank low, Ruan caught sight of the elusive horseman and pressed forward with a surge of renewed energy. Charging down the hill, he burst through a copse of trees in hot pursuit.

This time, the arrow whistled without warning.

This time, it didn't miss its mark.

Ruan crumpled from his horse without a word.

MO CEISD

Over the week, Merry fretted for Ruan's safety, and Bree found she did the same. It was odd how she wanted to be his wife, now that the possibility of him not returning loomed. They spent their days in Jenna's croft with Ewan constantly at their side. They watched the lad absently fiddle with his dirk. It was a comforting gesture. They knew he wouldn't hesitate to use it.

In the evenings, Ewan entertained them all, including the still nameless infant, with tales so wild they could not be true, in spite of his insistence otherwise. It was then, in the darkness of the night, long after Merry had drifted off to sleep with her head in Bree's lap, that Ewan told Bree how Ruan had ridden to save the young girl. He was an unusual man, and against her better judgment, she found her heart quickening. *Mo ceisd*. Ruan had called her *mo ceisd*. She puzzled over the meaning of the words: my problem. It was not surprising he considered her a problem, but he spoke in such a disturbingly gentle tone. She shivered. He was a troubling man, an enigma.

The day came when the men returned bearing Robert's body, a death that sent a ripple of shock through the entire clan. Ruan's choice to remain behind and to hunt the killer would have won him even more hearts hadn't they already been his. A day passed and then several more. They all worried, even Ewan, though he tried his best to conceal it.

"He's a strong man. He'll be fine," he told them for the fifth time.

Late the following afternoon, Silas pounded on the croft door, insisting Bree and Ewan return at once to Dunvegan. Ill tidings, was all he'd say, but there was a glint of satisfaction in his eye. Bree followed the priest with a sinking heart. They heard Effric shrieking long before entering the hall and Bree knew something was dreadfully wrong.

Tormod paced before the fire with his hands clasped behind his back. He pointedly ignored Effric, who had collapsed in a crumpled heap on the floor. She was wailing, pulling her hair and scratching her cheeks in the most alarming manner.

"Dead," she sobbed her voice cracking. "Dead!"

Michael leaned on the edge of the table, casually swinging his leg as Isobel sat nearby, simply staring into the distance, nose red-rimmed and her face grey.

Bree's heart skipped a beat, and it was suddenly difficult to breathe.

"Dead," Effric whispered.

"Aye," Tormod sneered, obviously pleased. "Ruan's dead, Bree. Ye are a widow."

They all stared at him, dumbfounded.

"'Tis no cause for concern, lass," Tormod continued pompously. "I'll see ye well taken care of, well taken care of indeed."

Isobel's voice shook with emotion. "The lass should be sent to her father."

"I'll be taking Bree away now," Ewan rasped, placing his hand on his dirk.

"I should have tossed ye out months ago!" Tormod roared, he raised his hand and motioned to several men lounging about. "Lock this hag in her chamber and send the Earl's whelp home. I've no place for either!"

It was over quickly. Ewan struggled valiantly, but he was no match for four well-armed men. A sharp blow from behind rendered him unconscious. Bree gasped in horror as they lugged him away.

"Ye'll pay for this," Isobel shouted, as they hauled her from sight.

Effric ran after her, screeching.

Silence blanketed the hall. In a matter of minutes, Tormod had destroyed Ruan's plans for their protection. Bree watched, numbly, as the man smiled and rubbed his fingers together in glee.

"Ye are a right winsome lass," he leered. "Aye, one that can give an heir."

She stared, still in shock and unable to believe the implications, but as he moved closer, she managed to blurt, "You are wed!"

Tormod's mouth gaped wider, his beady eyes slowly roved over her body as he said, "Effric is mad. None would deny an annulment!"

There was some truth in that. Surely, surely, her father would rescue her, but her heart sank, knowing he could not be swift enough with Tormod's intentions degrading by the minute. She took a step back, but he followed. Frantically, she fished for the small hidden knife Ruan had given her, not allowing herself to think of the man himself yet, and then Tormod's hands were suddenly upon her.

"Aye, it matters naught of Effric." He licked Bree's neck and thrust his tongue in her ear. "I'll get my heir on ye now."

"No!" Bree shouted hoarsely, unsheathing the knife and lashing out.

Tormod grabbed his ear, cursing, as blood spurted between his fingers. He raised his hand and struck her across the face. She lost her balance, but he pulled her close with his free arm. He was a large and strong man, and she struggled in vain. He held out his hand, staring numbly at the blood on his fingers. A deep gash ran over his cheek.

She'd nearly sliced off the top of his ear.

"Ye'll pay for this," Tormod grated, grabbing a handful of her hair and forcing her lips on his.

She gagged. His mouth tasted of whisky and onions. There was the sound of ripping cloth, and his hands were on her flesh. She struck back with renewed vigor, twisting away to scream. He struck her, harder this time. Her vision blurred as a pain shot through her head. For a minute, she was unable to move. He was pinching her, pushing her toward the table when a slight movement by the fire caught her attention, and her heart leapt with joy.

Ruan leaned heavily against the wall, grasping it for support. His skin was white, but his dark eyes were filled with a rage that warmed her soul.

"Ruan!" she gasped in relief.

"Ach, ye canna be mourning him," Tormod grunted, pressing against her as his lips descended over hers once again.

As Bree watched, Ewan appeared as well, but Ruan was already moving toward her.

"Aye, she canna mourn me," Ruan's cold voice hissed as he pressed his dirk against his brother's throat. "Nae when I'm still alive."

Tormod froze in disbelief.

Bree could feel his heart pound against her breast, and then she pushed him back with all her strength. This time, he let her go.

"Ye should be dead!" Tormod mouthed, his lips pale and convulsing as he gasped for air.

"Nay, ye failed again," Ruan's voice was low. He stood stiffly, hunching to one side and swaying on his feet before asking her, "Are ye well, lass?"

He pulled her briefly into a protective embrace she hadn't known that she wanted until she stood in the circle of his arm. She leaned her cheek against his broad chest, nodding and swallowing a gulp. At that moment, she understood why Merry worshiped him.

Clansmen filed into the hall.

"Ye've some explaining to do, Tormod," someone shouted from the crowd.

"Aye," Ruan's voice dripped with a passionate anger. "But I'm scarce in the mood for it. I've sworn already if ye touched my wife, I'd slit your throat, brother or no, and The Macleod or no."

Letting Bree go, Ruan pressed his dirk deeper into the flesh of Tormod's neck, its blade glittering in the shaft of sunlight streaming into the hall.

Tormod squealed, sounding remarkably like a stuck pig, but then Ruan gave a sudden gasp. Bree watched in horror as his eyes rolled in his head, and he fell back even as Ewan stepped forward to catch him.

A bright red stained his shirt.

"He's wounded!" Tormod wheezed, clutching his ear and feeling his neck, as if to assure himself he was still whole.

"Ye'd best pray he will nae die," Ewan said grimly.

Suddenly, a scream reverberated in the hall accompanied by a flurry of voices. Whispers circled the gathering and then Isobel ran into their midst, tears cascading down her cheeks at the sight of Ruan. She hugged him fiercely to her breast in obvious relief, even as she pointed frantically toward Tormod's chamber.

Confused, Bree glanced through the parting clansmen.

Effric's lifeless form hung suspended by a rope thrown over a beam, still swinging slightly. Her head angled sideways. As they watched, a slipper slid off her dangling foot to land amidst the rushes with a soft thump.

***

Effric's suicide cast a grim pall, but happiness abounded over Ruan's unexpected return.

"The lass just could nae bear to think him dead," Isobel repeated, shaking her head as they laid Ruan on his bed with great care.

"Robert?" Ruan moaned upon waking. He grasped Isobel's arm. "I must speak to him, can ye send him in?"

Isobel paused and quickly blinked tears away.

"What is it?" Ruan frowned.

"Ye must rest, love," Isobel said. She laid a hand on his forehead. "Aye, ye've a bit of a fever. 'Twill likely worsen soon."

"I must speak with Robert!" Ruan insisted, knitting his brows to deepen his frown. "I...was hunting Fearghus' man... I think... why was I doing that?" he stopped, confused. "I'm sure some of them were

French."

"Robert is resting," Isobel replied, patting him on the cheek. "I'll leave ye with Bree now, and go fetch the webs. We must halt the bleeding, love. Drink this whilst ye wait."

Ruan accepted the whiskey with a tired smile, but there was a furrow between his brows and then his lids fluttered closed.

Thrusting a basin of water and a cloth into Bree's hands, Isobel reassured, "He's a strong lad, love. Clean him. I'll return shortly."

Giving Bree's shoulder a comforting squeeze, she left and for the first time that day, Bree allowed herself a shaken breath of relief, but it was a relief that didn't last long.

The blood coloring Ruan's shirt was alarming.

With a somewhat timid touch, she picked at the dried blood caked with sweat and grime. She tried to be gentle, but it proved impossible. Fearing he was bleeding to death under her hand, she tugged the shirt over his head, and he erupted into a struggling mass of muscle, wrestling with the confining cloth. Panicking, she yanked the shirt hard, ripping it off.

"Sweet Mary!" Ruan bellowed. His hair stood on end as tears of pain wet his lashes. "Are ye trying to slay me, lass?"

Bree opened her mouth, wanting to shout back, but fell silent as she caught sight of the wound cutting his naked chest. She'd never seen such a thing. The flesh was purple and black. The swollen gash was encrusted with blood and matted hair. She covered her mouth with her hand.

"The men had to …dig the arrow… it was fair dark… he…" Ruan explained weakly and then, blanching, fell silent.

Bree nodded once, and reached for the wet cloth with a shaking hand.

"Just turn your head when you retch, lass."

It was too much. She could no longer ignore the rising nausea. She'd a brief impression of dark, amused eyes as she rushed to the chamber pot and was violently ill. After several minutes, faint chuckles emerged from the bed, and she returned, cheeks flushing.

"Forgive me," she whispered in a strangled voice. "I've... never seen..."

She winced and picked up the cloth, dabbing his chest and wondering if she should dash to the chamber pot again.

"I've had worse," he said, attempting a weak smile.

Bree swallowed, wringing the cloth, and asked, "You... don't do this, often, do you?"

"Aye, do ye mean if ye'll have to?" Ruan gritted his teeth in pain, but managed a half-smile. "I hope not."

Bree smiled feebly, then dabbed the gash again.

He gasped.

"I'm sorry," she gulped, and drew back in alarm.

"It has to be done," Ruan gave a resigned sigh. Spying the whiskey flagon Isobel had tossed him, his lips widened into a grin.

He didn't flinch much after that, she thought wryly as she continued her gentle assault. The wound was hardly half-clean, and already the water in the basin was as red as blood. Her nostrils flared at the smell. She moved the basin to the other side of the bed in the effort to control her riotous stomach.

"Ye've nae done this before, have ye?" he murmured, voice

sounding thick.

"No," Bree shook her head. "I've never seen such a grievous injury."

"Nay, *mo ceisd*, nae that," Ruan's voice sounded guttural, sensual. "I meant touched a man's naked chest."

Bree pulled back sharply, upsetting the basin. As the bloody water tipped into the bed, she lunged for it. Ruan grunted in pain as her elbow dug into his stomach.

"I'm sorry!" she gasped.

Red stained the covers and she wanted to retch again, but she was distracted as Ruan's strong fingers closed about her wrist to pull her close.

"Ach, there's nae harm done," he said, with a wicked glint in his eye. "I can think of nothing better than to lie in bed, drinking whiskey, with a lass bare to the waist draped over me."

Bree froze. His words were shocking, but she was even more astonished at her own reaction. Her heart fluttered and her pulse began to beat erratically.

"Aye, well, and here I've been told ye were dead, then sore wounded. Now, I find ye half-drunk trifling with a bonny lass," Isobel chuckled in obvious relief as she swept into the room, followed by Ewan. "I told ye he was a strong one, Bree!"

Blushing, Bree attempted to jerk free, but Ruan gripped her arm with a firm, yet gentle pressure. His touch felt like fire. She bit her lip.

"Cover up, Bree," he murmured, eyes deliberately dropping as his lips twitched. "Ewan shouldn't see ye like that."

She drew her brows in confusion and then glanced down. She

gasped. She was indeed bare to the waist. Tormod had ripped the entire bodice and a healthy part of the shift as well. Flushing an even deeper crimson, she scrambled to pull the tattered cloth together. How dare the man laugh at her! She'd been concerned for his life, cleaning that odious wound, and he'd been drinking and ogling her the entire time. Lifting her chin, she allowed her anger to show, but his expression made her suddenly uncomfortable. There was something there besides humor, something that made her wish to run and stay at the same time.

"Robert," Ruan said. He gripped Ewan's arm tightly. "I must speak with him, lad."

Ewan tensed, but then nodded, and said, "Aye, but 'twill have to wait."

Ruan frowned. He struggled, as if to rise, but collapsed back in pain and then promptly fainted.

"Aye," Isobel said. She pursed her lips grimly. "He's half out of his head, but 'tis well enough for now."

Then, Merry was there, launching herself hysterically at Ruan, causing him to wake again as Isobel bustled about, issuing crisp commands. In short order, she had them all scurrying until Ruan's wound was dressed and the bed covers replaced.

"There," Isobel said, nodding with satisfaction after Ruan dutifully drank the last of some broth. "Ye are feverish, but as strong as an ox. This is a scratch compared to that last set ye came home with."

Ruan smiled tiredly and turned his head.

Ewan and Merry were hustled out the door and Bree found herself faced with a hot tub of steaming water sprinkled liberally with herbs and a new shift draped over the foot of the bed.

"He'll be fine, lassie," Isobel said. She reached over to pinch Bree's cheek as she passed. "Clean up, the water is growing cold, and I've need of the tub."

With that, she left Bree alone.

Suspiciously, Bree eyed Ruan.

He appeared asleep, but he'd fooled her before.

She watched his slow, rhythmic breathing for some time before the events of the day began to resurface. Remembering Tormod's hands, she peeled the torn gown away with growing urgency. Yes, she needed to wash away his stench and the smell of Ruan's blood. She managed to bite back sobs that emerged from nowhere. Stepping into the tub, she set about scrubbing her hands fiercely. She was washing her hair for the fifth time when Isobel entered.

"By the saints, lass, why are ye shivering in that icy water?" Isabel gasped. Snagging the linen toweling, she plucked Bree out of the tub and rubbed her briskly, clucking, "There, lass, no more tears now."

Bree gulped, unaware she'd been crying.

"Into bed now!" Isobel herded her toward the soft, warm blankets. It would have been quite inviting, if only Ruan was not lying in them.

She balked.

"He will nae be moving for at least a week," Isobel said, and pushed her forward. "And ye've naught to fear, even if he did." There was a twinkle in her eye as she bundled her in.

There was no point in resisting. Bree had seen Afraig in that same mood often enough. It mattered little. Isobel would be gone in a few, short minutes, and she could do as she pleased. She drew the covers under her chin and waited as the bath was emptied and removed, all the while fighting the temptation to look at the man less than an arm's length away. When Isobel sat at his side and placed a hand on his forehead, she finally did. His lashes were unusually long and black. She glanced down at his lips, overwhelmed with the odd desire to touch them with her finger before noticing Isobel's knowing smile.

"He'll be right well soon enough, lass," Isobel promised again, and then hurried out the door.

She'd scarcely gone when Ruan murmured. "Forgive me for nae getting here sooner, lass. I'll nae let Tormod touch ye again."

The sooty lashes lifted and his dark eyes burned hers.

"You're awake," she breathed, rattled. He was uncomfortably close.

Amusement crossed his face. "Aye. I've never been asleep."

Horrified, she drew back, falling out of the bed in her haste to get away. With heated cheeks, she scrambled up from the rushes.

"The... entire time? You were watching the entire time?" It was more of an accusation than a question.

"Aye," his lips curved. "Ye've nothing to be ashamed of."

She stood with fingers clenched and tears streaming down her cheeks.

"Don't weep."

The gentleness in his tone only served to unleash the tears.

"Be done!" his voice altered to a familiar harshness. "Get in bed!"

Bree collapsed in hysteria, not even sure why she was crying, only that she was unable to stop. It had been a day filled with many emotions, so many that she could no longer ignore them. She began to babble how Silas had told them he was dead and then there was Tormod. The mere mention of his name made her ill. What kind of man was he? He'd thrust his tongue down her throat. She could still taste the rank mixture of onions and rotting teeth. Gagging, she wiped her mouth on the back of her arm. She sniveled on the floor until firm fingers closed over her arm, drawing her up from the rushes. Something pressed against her lips. A familiar liquid seared her throat. Whiskey. She gasped, choking.

"There. That should rid ye of the onions."

It took several moments to realize Ruan had moved across the bed to pull her up.

"You should be....resting," she gulped, wiping her tears with the back of her hand.

"I will, as soon as ye get in bed," Ruan replied with clenched teeth, he tried to rest on his elbow, but collapsed in pain.

"You shouldn't move. You will cause yourself harm!" Bree hiccupped, with open concern.

He raised a brow, then wincing in pain, gingerly eased himself back. "Trying to keep me now?"

She stared at him, confused, and then a moan escaped his lips.

His body began to shiver.

In less than an hour, he came down with a violent fever.

**

Bree spent the next three days at his side, filled with remorse. If he died now, she'd forever feel she'd cursed him. He'd saved her several times, and she'd done nothing, but cause trouble in return.

Isobel assured her the fever was to be expected, and that it would heal him. She insisted that Ruan was young and strong, and that he'd seen worse, but Bree found it hard to believe. She stayed at his side through the long days and nights, wiping his sweating brow and forcing liquid between his parched lips.

Except for the occasional moan, Ruan suffered in silence.

THE ESCAPE

Late in the evening on the fourth day, Ruan opened his eyes.

"I kent ye were the strong one!" Isobel's kind smile swam into view. "Ye've too much to live for."

He squinted, reliving the arrow, its brutal removal, and the ride back to Dunvegan in a haze of pain. Then, Tormod's leering face hovering over a terrified Bree flashed into his mind.

"Bree," his lips were cracked and dry.

"Aye, she's asleep on the pillow there, love," Isobel said, nodding with her chin.

Unusually weak, Ruan turned his head with a great effort to find Merry at his side. She lay with her head nestled on Bree's shoulder. Both were asleep.

Suddenly, he was overwhelmed with emotion.

"Aye, those two never left yer side," Isobel explained with an indulgent smile.

Merry sat up, her lips split into a wide grin before she launched herself to smother him with kisses.

Ruan smiled tiredly and tousled her hair. He caught a glimpse of

Bree over Merry's shoulder. Her presence made his heart pound, and he closed his eyes, oddly shy. He lacked the strength to open them again.

It was some time later that he woke again, feeling much stronger.

At his side, Bree stirred in her sleep. With a sigh, she rolled, lifting an unconscious arm as if to encircle Merry. To his surprise, she shifted his direction, dropping her arm across his chest, and threading her leg through his.

He took a deep breath, his mind flooding with a host of distracting thoughts as his throat constricted at her soft touch. She nestled closer. Her hair was everywhere, exuding the faint scent of lavender. He took a deep breath of the heady fragrance.

Aye, he was a fool.

There was no denying it: he was smitten.

His behavior degenerated from that moment on.

Careful not to wake her, he shifted back and studied her in fascination, keenly aware of her hand resting lightly on his thigh. As time lengthened, the location caused a pleasurable panic, and with a slight reluctance, he repositioned her fingers to rest instead on his stomach. It hardly helped. A heat began to burn. His attention riveted on the softness pressed against him, his palm involuntarily skimming lightly over her hip as her leg entwined deeper with his.

She was so achingly soft.

Flushed with desire, he fought to control the primal urge to crush her close and cover her lips with his.

"Hold still," Bree mumbled, her lashes still closed. "You'll wake your brother."

"He's awake," Ruan whispered in her ear.

After a moment, her eyes flew open.

They both moved at once and Ruan winced at the sudden pain.

"I... forgive me!" Bree said and bolted up in the bed, pressing her hands against her cheeks.

Ruan didn't reply, dismayed with himself. Sweet Mary, why was he so weak? Why could he not remember he was done with women? Aye, he knew he was smitten with the lass, but all the more reason to avoid her. He didn't want to harm her, to turn into his father and see her cower in fear. Nor, did he have even a hovel to offer her as shelter. No, it was better to avoid the entire thing.

She left, hurriedly, and Isobel returned to cajole more broth and gruel down him, refusing to let him speak to Robert. He managed to finish the entire bowl before succumbing to sleep once more.

He woke with a start, in the dead of night, jolted by the memory of Robert's death.

With a gasp, he sat up.

Vaguely, he was aware of Bree and Merry asking him what was wrong, but he was too overwhelmed to reply. A weight descended, threatening to crush him. Robert had died. Aye, and it was his own fault. He was responsible for his uncle's death. Aye, he had to rescue his sister, but he must have gone about it the wrong way. Now, innocent crofters and Robert were dead because of his choice to ride without thinking of the consequences. Why had he acted so rashly? Surely, there must have been another way.

"What is it?" Merry's tremulous voice echoed in the shadows.

How could he tell her?

Bree lit a candle. Her hands were shaking.

He was frightening them.

"Robert," he finally said, his voice sounding strangled. "I…remember."

No one said anything. What was there to say?

He staggered out of bed, brushing Bree's offer of assistance aside, and welcoming the pain shooting through his shoulder. It allowed him to focus on what he had to do. He had to leave this place. Soon, before he caused more harm. Staying in Dunvegan was no longer a choice.

"Ye shouldn't be about," Merry warned. "Isobel will nae be pleased."

He didn't reply. He stepped to the window, throwing open the shutter to stare into the night sky. He could hear the sea beating against the castle, a sound that he always found comforting. At periodic intervals, Merry insisted he return to bed, but he ignored her, finding the cold air cleansing to his thoughts. At length, he settled on a plan. The first action would be to take Bree and Merry to Cameron.

They were both asleep when he finally returned to the bed, knowing he must rest. He'd need his strength in the days ahead. Unusually tired and weak, he settled next to Merry and willed sleep to come, but sleep proved fitful.

As the sun rose, Merry rose with it. She frowned, pointing to a small red stain on his shoulder. "I told ye to rest," she glared. "I'll fetch Isobel."

He smiled, a little, as his sister disappeared into the corridor. She'd changed in the past few weeks, even stronger now than before her fateful wedding night. Bree was still asleep, obviously exhausted, her curls cascading over the pillow. He studied her from under half-closed lids, ignoring his quickening pulse, and wondered if he'd ever see those green eyes light with mirth, or those lips smile. Suppressing a sigh, he staggered to his feet, experiencing pangs of sadness over Robert's loss. He'd almost made it to the window once more when the door opened and Isobel entered, followed by Ewan.

"Ho!" the blond lad laughed and caught him as he lost his balance. "'Tis too early to be about!"

"I must be leaving," Ruan grated between clenched teeth, but allowed Ewan to escort him back to the bed.

"Nay, ye must rest," Isobel disagreed, vehemently. "At least a week."

"Nay," he said, in a tone of finality. "The longer I stay, the more harm I'll cause for everyone, myself included."

They could not dissuade him, Isobel and Ewan both tried.

In the end, he won.

They knew he'd leave anyway, and none could argue against the fact that Tormod wanted him dead. And now with Robert out of the way, he was more likely to succeed. His concern was not so much for himself, but for those who might come to harm in the attempt to thwart Tormod's plans. No, he insisted, he must leave that night. His wound was painful, but manageable. He could sit on a horse ... barely.

Isobel insisted on accompanying them for Merry's sake, but Ruan knew she was worried about him. It was decided that Isobel and Merry would leave to assist Ewan in securing suitable horses and hide with them a fair distance away. Once it was dark, Ewan would return to find a boat and ferry Bree and Ruan to the hiding place. After which, Ruan made Ewan promise he would return to his father. The lad was ill set against it, and it took Ruan the better part of an hour to convince him to return to Mull for the present time. Traveling over Skye and onto Inchmurrin would be dangerous. Ruan was certain Tormod would follow them, but he could not let Ewan know that.

He sighed.

If all went well, they would be in Inchmurrin before the week's end. Aye, in leaving Dunvegan for good, he'd be leaving his soul behind, but he'd do it. He'd send for Jenna and her bairn later, after Cameron took him as his sworn man. He knew Cameron would resist accepting him as a sworn vassal, but Ruan had no choice other than to try. He had nothing to offer but his arm and his loyalty. Of course, Robert, the proud clansman that he was, would not have wished it, but it was the only way to avoid any more bloodshed.

At the thought of his uncle, Ruan sighed again, feeling a deep, burning pit in his stomach. He willed tears to come, but they still wouldn't form. His guilt was strong, but it was too late now for Robert and the crofters and he must move on. He squared his shoulders. In time, he could mourn. But now, he must act.

Ewan left, with obvious reluctance, to escort Merry and Isobel out of the castle and there was nothing for Ruan to do but wait and rest. Bree seemed nervous. He could not blame her. She paced in front of the small window in their chamber, trying her best to ignore him. Torn between amusement and guilt, he turned away. He had to conserve his strength if he was going to ride all night.

He woke to Bree's light touch, and a curl fell forward and tickled his nose. He hadn't meant to sleep. For a brief moment, he felt no pain, no remorse, only a wave of desire. His hand covered hers of its own accord. Her eyes widened in the candlelight, but then a wave of pain seared his chest and the moment was lost. He growled, recalling all at once that he soon must ride a horse through the cold, wet night.

Bree pulled her hand free as he gritted his teeth and forced his legs over the edge of the bed and attempted to stand. An unexpected wave of dizziness assailed him. He would have fallen, if she hadn't been there. They almost fell anyway; he was much heavier than she was.

"Sweet Mary," he hissed between his teeth. He grasped her shoulder tightly as nausea rioted with the pain.

"This isn't wise," Bree swallowed, the worry evident in her voice.

"I'll be fine, lass," he lied with a grimace. He forced his feet to move forward out of sheer discipline.

Swathed warmly in his plaid and with his sword and dirk belted into place, he felt somewhat stronger. Bree had helped him more than he liked. Under any other circumstances, he would have enjoyed the experience of her shy, timid touch, but thoughts of his uncle were foremost in his mind.

Navigating the narrow, spiraled stairs proved difficult, but he got it done and his confidence that he was strong enough grew with each step. At the bottom stair, Bree snuffed the candle and listened carefully before opening the door.

The way was mercifully clear, and they slipped out of the castle and down to the sea-gate undetected.

The cockman guarding the gate was snoring, propped up against the castle walls, and there were gaming pieces scattered on the walkway.

Ruan scowled at the man's negligence, and then Ewan stepped forward, grinning in the moonlight.

"He's drunk…finally," he said, indicating the man with a nod. "It took all evening."

"'Tis fair ridiculous that ye succeeded at all," Ruan muttered in disapproval as he made his way to the waiting boat. He managed to jump into it without assistance though he experienced a dull jolt of pain.

Bree followed quietly.

"Are ye certain this is wise, Ruan?" Ewan queried softly, as he dipped the oars into the water.

"Aye," Ruan said, nodding. He didn't add that he had no choice.

Ewan rowed in silence.

The loch around the castle was a still, black pool of shadows that reflected the bright moon illuminating Dunvegan and the hills behind it in a scene that would be burned into his memory forever. Part of him would always belong to these hills and the heather slopes melting into the jagged, sea cliffs. The castle glimmered bright, nestled on the edge of the loch with the dense forests and the village behind it. He watched it slowly disappear and savored each glimpse until it was finally lost from sight.

Ewan rowed for some time before the shore drew closer and they could see a dark line of trees.

"You're late!" Merry cried out as they came ashore. She bounded into the water and helped pull the boat aground. "We were worried."

"Ach, lass! Leave that to the lads," Isobel called. "Ye'll be getting wet!"

Ruan waded ashore and tousled Merry's hair and said, "I'm afraid ye canna be rid of me that easily, my Merry wee lass."

"I don't need ye anymore," Merry replied. Dimples appeared on her cheeks. "'Tis Bree I was fretful about."

A surprised smile jerked Ruan's lips. He cast a side-length glance as Bree joined him, wringing the hem of her dress. Her face was pale in the moonlight and looked taut and worried. Without thinking, he gave her shoulder a comforting squeeze.

They both stiffened at once.

Hastily, he snatched his hand back. He turned to Ewan and spoke rapidly to mask his discomfort, "Did ye find it much trouble to take the horses, lad?"

"Nay," Ewan shook his head and smiled. "Tormod will nae be missing these two for a few days." He pointed to the animals tethered a short distance away.

Ruan inspected them with a frown. They were ancient, creaking beasts. Ruan doubted if Tormod would ever miss them at all. "Two?" he muttered, less than pleased.

"We'd best start," Isobel said. She looked up from tying a small bundle onto one of the saddles. "Merry and I will ride the dapple. Bree, ye'll ride in front of Ruan so ye can guide the horse if he faints. Which, by the look of ye, lad, is fair likely."

Ruan tensed at the thought of Bree in such extended, close contact, but the nagging pain of his wound reminded him Isobel spoke wisely enough. With Ewan's assistance, he succeeded in mounting the beast and sat stiffly as Ewan caught Bree about the waist and tossed her into his lap.

He clenched his jaw. Her curls were everywhere. His brows furrowed into a deep line. He had to keep his wits entirely about him. He could not afford to be distracted. Impatiently, he brushed her hair away and warned in a low voice, "Keep your hair out of my face."

She stiffened and twisted her hair into a braid as Isobel and Merry said their farewells to Ewan.

Ruan cast his eyes about, seeking to keep his thoughts away from the slender, wriggling form planted firmly between his thighs. He was annoyed that the pain of his wound failed to prevent his body rousing in response. "Hold still," he growled.

With Isobel and Merry ready at last, they exchanged their final farewells and rode away, leaving Ewan standing alone in the moonlight.

Ruan lost track of the countless times he had ground his teeth together on that unrelentingly, torturous journey. It was a small miracle any teeth remained. Every step the horse took jarred his wound unmercifully. Bree proved a constant distraction, but one he'd rather not have. Her softness pressed against him could cause his body to respond with lust, should he allow it.

He wiped his forehead with the back of his sleeve, and inadvertently caught a strand of her curling hair. An image of her asleep, hair fanning across the pillow, flashed in his mind, and a surge of desire stirred his blood.

"By the Saints!" Ruan swore aloud and swatted at the low branches overhanging the path.

They followed a stream winding along the edge of a steep and stony ravine for some time until the terrain turned marshy. Cliffs rose in the distance and when they arrived at the base of them, they entered a thick wood that blotted out any light the moon might have given. The going was slow. After what seemed like hours, a break in the trees afforded him a glimpse of the sky. Dawn was approaching. The dull light grew brighter as they wound uphill through the woods and out onto the open moors.

In the distance, he could see the Old Man of Storr turning pink in the rising sun. He drove them at a faster pace. It seemed to take forever until they finally arrived in the shadow of the black precipices.

"We'll rest here a wee bit," he murmured, dismounting in relief. He was exhausted and in severe pain, but they had made it. Tormod would not think to look for them here so soon.

"Ach, I'm right glad to see these rocks," Isobel grumbled, sending Ruan a sharp glance. "Ye rode as if auld cootie himself was behind ye, lad."

Ruan snorted. No, *auld cootie* hadn't been behind him. He wanted to shout that the devil had been sitting in his lap, with a wealth of curls blowing in his face.

Isobel took one look at him and pushed him down onto the nearest stone. Pursing her lips, she said, "We should have waited. Ye were too hasty, lad."

A haze of fatigue settled over Ruan. "Aye, and that is exactly why no one will ever believe we were foolish enough to leave," he sighed heavily, attempting to rise. "The horses—"

"The lassies can care for them." Isobel frowned. "I'll nae have ye falling ill again. I've nae the time for it."

Ruan didn't resist. Sliding to the ground, he leaned tiredly against the boulder and bowed his head. A warm plaid dropped about his shoulders. "Thank ye, Isobel." He yawned.

"You are welcome," Bree replied, hesitantly.

Surprised, he opened an eye. She attempted a smile, but her lips were too tight. He watched as she joined Merry to struggle with the saddles. Part of him wished he had the strength to help—he'd make short work of it—but the rest of him enjoyed the fascinating way in which she moved. Tilting his head, he allowed his gaze to rove over her slender figure, enjoying the pulse of his blood before becoming aware of the nature of his thoughts.

Expelling a sharp breath, he clamped his eyes firmly shut.

REENAN

Ruan seemed gravely ill. His skin was grey and he was in obvious pain. A fresh, red patch of blood stained his shoulder.

"He should be abed, foolish lad," Isobel mumbled, searching the saddlebags for her bundle of herbs. Her expression was grim.

"He is strong," Merry said loudly, too loudly.

Bree squeezed her hand in comfort.

They watched Isobel clean his wound and sprinkle it liberally with herbs. Once satisfied that it was no longer bleeding, she leaned back on her heels. "Bree, love, I'll need a wee bit of help."

Prepared to be squeamish, Bree stepped forward, but this time the expected nausea didn't arrive. His wound was healing remarkably well, and she found his muscular chest occupying her thoughts instead.

He was lean and strong and his skin was warm to her touch. Several times, she fought the urge to run her fingers through his hair.

Finally, they were done and she became aware of Isobel observing her with twinkling eyes. Bree ducked her head to hide the color rising in her cheeks.

"Ach, now, we should rest a wee bit," the old woman said. "A lassie on each side should be enough to keep him warm."

In short order, Bree found herself promptly tucked in next to him with Merry on the other side.

Isobel dusted her hands, surveying her handiwork with satisfaction. "I'll watch for a spell. Rest while ye can. I'm sure the lad will wake soon and have us moving once again."

Bree expelled a breath and burrowed deeper in the plaid. She could feel Ruan's steady breathing. He generated an enormous amount of heat even though he was ill. His eyes remained closed and this time he did not awake under her curious inspection. His lashes were incredibly long and black. Once again, she experienced an urge to touch him, especially the curve of his lower lip.

Catching the nature of her thoughts, she frowned and instead forced herself to ponder what lay ahead.

She awoke some time later.

A thick blanket of fog had fallen, draping the mountains above them in mist and cloud. It was growing late and the sun struggled to shine weakly from its position low on the horizon. Thunder muttered far away, signaling the arrival of a storm as fine droplets of rain caressed her cheeks.

Cautiously, Bree slipped from under the plaid and discovered Isobel had fallen asleep on her watch. Ruan hadn't moved and he appeared much the same. Merry snored, nestled on his shoulder.

Bree glanced around. The horses were grazing a short distance away, their forms large, moving shadows in the mist. All was silent. If Tormod had followed, he'd have to be extremely fortunate to find them in this fog

She breathed deeply in relief and then shivered. It was growing colder. Ruan needed shelter and warmth. A fire would help, if she could even start one in these conditions.

Searching for something dry to burn, she scouted around the edge of their camp and came across a small gully with several old trees at the bottom. Hoping to find some fallen branches, she moved toward them. Loose stones slipped and slithered under her feet as she descended and arrived at the bottom. As her first step sank rapidly into the mire, she scrambled back in alarm. She'd heard many tales of unfortunates happening upon a bog. Their deaths were gruesome, sinking slowly before they disappeared entirely, never to be seen again. Reluctantly, she decided the trees were impossible to reach.

From the corner of her eye, she saw a flash of movement. She turned quickly to see a form flitter through the mist and up to the opposite side of the gully. Suddenly uneasy, she lifted her muddy skirts, climbed the wet heather to the top, and ran back to the camp.

Ruan was awake, leaning on Merry's shoulder as Isobel paced frantically in circles. Upon spying her, they all exhaled in overt relief.

"'Tis dangerous here, lass!" Isobel exclaimed, rushing to her side and clasped Bree in a bosomy hug. "There are steep stones and bog pits all about! I feared the worst!"

"Aye," Merry chimed.

Ruan opened his mouth, but whatever he was going to say was lost, as his brows rose in surprise, and his attention focused over her shoulder.

Whirling, Bree found herself staring into the curious gaze of a young woman with intensely blue eyes and white skin sprinkled liberally with freckles. She was short and slender and her blonde hair was twisted in a loose braid that fell down the length of her back. One of her arms was thrown around the shoulders of a boy about ten years of age, and a smaller child peeked cautiously from behind her skirts. Both children shared her complexion and build.

"Ach, lad," the woman squeezed the boy's arm. "'Tis nae cause for alarm here, methinks. 'Tis just a few weary travelers, by the looks of them, love."

"Reenan!" Ruan's deep voice called out.

The woman jerked in surprise, craning past Bree, and her mouth fell open. "Ruan! Why, 'tis a wee surprise to see ye! What brings ye here, man?"

Ruan's lips cracked into a smile, but it caused him to break into a bout of coughing. He winced in pain and leaned hard against Merry.

Reenan rushed to his side.

He managed a weak grin as she guided him to the nearest boulder. "Aye, but your bonny face is a wondrous sight!" he said.

"What are ye doing here, lad. Ach, yer hurt!" Reenan touched his shoulder, but withdrew her hand as he exhaled sharply.

Shaking her head, she ordered the boy, "Laddie, bring the cart. We'll get this daft one out of the rain! I never would have seen ye if it hadn't been for the lass poking by the bog, and even then, with all the mist, 'tis a miracle!"

"Bree, love, 'twas dangerous there," Isobel clucked, shaking her head.

Bree felt her ears redden.

"Aye, but I'm pleased she did," Ruan grunted, struggling to his feet.

Looping an arm of support around his waist, Reenan frowned. "What happened, lad?"

The gesture was an intimate one and Bree wondered just who, exactly, this Reenan was. She was quite fetching and Ruan was obviously happy to see her. She found herself frowning.

"I thought of coming to ye," Ruan was saying through clenched teeth. "But, with Sean gone, I'll nae be wanting to cause ye trouble, and trouble is sure to follow me."

"There is nothing unusual in that," Reenan said with a husky laugh. "Though 'tis well Sean is up north, he still wants yer blood for that last kiss."

Ruan snorted with a crooked grin, "I was drunk; I dinna ken who 'twas."

"Ye shouldn't hurt a woman's pride so," Reenan teased in reply. "Well, ye'll be staying whilst ye get yer strength back and there's an end to it. I've missed ye so, though, ye'd best know that Lorna is with me now."

Ruan's brows tightened and he fell into another bout of coughing.

Reenan chuckled, "Aye, well, there's a bed ye regret lying in, no? I told ye, time and again, lad, that–"

"Ye'll be meeting Bree," Ruan interrupted, nodding in Bree's direction. "My wife."

The shock was apparent in the woman's expression. She belatedly masked it with a smile. "Wed! Ruan wed! Heaven knows how many tried to accomplish that! To think I would live to witness the mighty Ruan in love!"

"I've said naught of love," Ruan gave a deep-throated growl.

Bree didn't know what irritated her more, the fact that she was hearing of a Lorna and the many women trying to wed him, or that he'd just announced that he didn't love her. Of course, he didn't love her. She knew that, but it was hurtful to hear just the same. She whirled and stalked after the horses, no longer wanting to observe their reunion.

The horses hadn't strayed far. She grabbed their bridles, but they ignored her feeble attempts to move them. Placidly chewing the dry stalks of grass, they eyed her for a few moments before shaking their heads free and stepping away. She shot them a poisonous glare.

"I'll help," a small voice chimed.

Bree turned to find a girl, slightly younger than Merry, grinning at her. She possessed the same shock of blonde hair and the brilliant blue eyes as her mother, and Bree wondered just how many children Reenan had.

It took the girl no time at all to have the horses obediently following and Bree found herself trailing behind with a grimace.

A rickety cart rolled into view, already loaded with their belongings and Ruan settled amongst them. Reenan leaned over to murmur something in his ear as she tucked a plaid under his chin.

His temper suddenly exploded. "Will ye have done, woman!" he roared. "Above all others, ye know I'm incapable of love and I've naught to my name! The past is dead and buried."

"Ach, things like women rarely stay buried," Reenan sniffed.

Ruan choked again.

"Her husband died three months past, and she's my cousin. I can scarcely turn her out."

Ruan growled.

"Ye've nae told me what brings ye this far out," Reenan switched subjects. "By the look of ye, 'tis nae good news."

"Nay," Ruan replied, blanching a little. "'Tis ill tidings of the worst sort. Robert is dead."

She stared at him for some time and then wordlessly patted his shoulder. Motioning to her son, the cart lurched forward. Isobel joined Reenan to sit in the front and Bree followed with the children.

The cart creaked so much that further conversation was impossible, not that Ruan appeared as though he wished to speak. He lay in the back with his eyes firmly closed, and mouth shut tight.

Bree's thoughts wandered to Lorna. She was obviously his lover, or had been. She frowned deeper. Lorna would almost assuredly be beautiful. Her jaw tightened, wondering why it bothered her. She had no real claim on the man. They were riding as fast as they could to Cameron, where Ruan's first action would be to seek an annulment of their marriage. She glanced away.

The fog was so thick it was difficult to see. At times, the mist lifted to reveal they were traveling away from the mountains, passing by rugged rocks and grassy slopes. She could see the trunks of slender birch and the occasional pine.

It was not long before a large croft arose unexpectedly out of the mist. The acrid smoke of a peat fire billowed from the roof. The door flew open and out popped several more children, all of them chattering in excitement.

Encompassing them into a sweeping hug, Reenan bundled the

entire lot into the croft.

They had scarcely entered the croft when a tall, willowy woman stepped forward from the shadows.

Bree sighed.

Lorna was far more beautiful than she had imagined. She was the kind of woman who reduced others to the status of dowdy with a mere look. Her fiery, red hair framed a flawless, creamy face. She shared the same radiant, blue eyes as the rest of her kin. As those luminous eyes fell upon Ruan, her face suffused with pure joy, and she launched herself into his arms.

It was simply too much.

Not entirely sure why, Bree spun on her heel and slammed the door of the croft with guilty pleasure. The pleasure was short-lived. Her heart felt oddly heavy.

The mist had parted to reveal a short line of trees next to a low, stone building not far away. Moving toward it, she berated herself. She was jealous. Somehow, she had let the man under her skin. How could she?

She headed toward the small stone building, and rounded a corner to nearly trip over a flock of geese. The birds scattered, squawking and flapping their wings. Bree mumbled an incoherent apology their direction and plodded ahead.

A shadow fell across her path, and she glanced up to see Ruan's inscrutable face. He blocked her path.

"Wait," he said hoarsely. "'Tis nae what ye think. Well... some might be... I should explain, I think." He licked his lips and added, "Perchance."

If she hadn't known better, she'd have thought him nervous. He seemed inordinately self-conscious. And then, the image of the beautiful woman in the croft crossed her mind. No doubt, he wished his wife gone so he could be with Lorna. That thought hurt.

Angry, she attempted to charge past him. The scuffle was brief. As her knee headed for his groin, he swung her about with consummate skill, pinning her arms behind her back and against his chest.

Panting with exertion, she stopped struggling, brown curls covering her face in wild disarray. Let him think he'd won; he'd have to loosen his grip soon. He was still weak. Growing angrier, she blew at the hair from her face. Images of him kissing Lorna paraded unbidden in her mind. Wanting to banish the thoughts, she stamped her foot in frustration, inadvertently grazing his shin.

Ruan swore under his breath. "I'll thank ye to hold still," he hissed through clenched teeth.

Not quite knowing what possessed her, she tossed her head back against his chest and deliberately attempted to push him away.

He twirled her again to face him, there was something in his expression that made her pause, but then she shook her head, regaining her anger. "Let me go! It is best not to keep your lovely Lorna waiting!"

Ruan's expressive eyes shuttered instantly as his grip tightened about her wrists.

She winced.

"Ach, now, lass," Reenan's voice startled them both. "Ruan never loved that beastie. She was a blunder he'll nae repeat and that was over three ago!"

Ruan swore under his breath.

"He's mended his lustful ways, lass." Reenan continued blithely. "Ye've nothing to fret over."

"Be done, Reenan!" Ruan frowned in her direction.

"She should know Lorna and the others mean nothing to ye," Reenan replied stoutly. "They were a scheming lot, foolish lad. Ye still canna see how much of a victim ye truly were, ye blind fool!"

"Others?" Bree murmured, rankled.

"Reenan!" he barked. "Ye've said plenty!"

"Ach, nae nearly, and 'tis only right she knows. She's yer wife," Reenan snorted. Then, her voice lowered, teasing, "I'll have ye know, I almost believed ye, 'I've no time for love-'"

"Keep your tongue behind your teeth, woman!" Ruan thundered.

Reenan clucked her tongue, raising a wicked brow. "Only if ye speak with Bree, 'tis only right."

He gritted his teeth. "I've had precious little chance! Ye gab worse than a fishwife!"

"No need to fash yerself," Reenan hummed, unperturbed, and with a pert grin.

"Fires of Hell!" Ruan lost control and shouted. "'Tis no small wonder Sean leaves at every chance!"

"I'll be running along," Reenan continued as if Ruan hadn't spoken. "Now, don't be shy telling him what he deserves to hear. I've long warned him he'd pay the price of his folly."

"By the Saints, woman!" Ruan pleaded. "Away with ye!"

Reenan puckered her lips, and with a decided sparkle in her eye, she gathered her plaid close and set off back toward her croft.

To Bree's relief, he abruptly let her go. She took a step back and rubbed her wrists.

"Forgive me." The softness in his voice startled her, and she looked up, surprised.

"I...did nae mean to hurt ye," he grimaced, indicating the red marks on her skin with a slight nod. He reached out.

She turned her head away.

"Aye," Ruan's brow darkened. "I'm a man of all manner of sin, beyond redemption. I've no desire to remember the past and there's naught I can do about it now. 'Tis done."

Bree held her breath. It didn't sound as if he were eager to rush into Lorna's arms. The thought was pleasing, even as she was struck by jealousy that he had rushed into her arms in the past. She frowned, lifting her chin a little.

He lifted an inquisitive brow.

They locked gazes for a moment, and then Ruan swayed a little on his feet.

"Come," he said gruffly. "I'd best be getting back whilst I can."

He set off toward the croft, and she followed. The crunch of his boots on the rocks was the only sound to break the silence between them.

When Ruan lifted the latch of the door, he was deluged with excited, squealing children.

From the corner of her eyes, Bree searched for Lorna, but to her relief, the woman was not there. And then, she was being pulled inside by Isobel and set to work slicing onions and cabbage for the fish stew already bubbling in the cauldron over the fire.

Ruan slouched on a stool near the fire, playing with the brood of children at his feet. Jiggling the smallest on his knee, he tickled the others as they clambered around. After a time, they settled down at his feet as he recounted stories of faraway places.

Shutting out the sound of his lilting voice, Bree helped Reenan ladle the stew into wooden bowls, and then Isobel called them all to eat.

The meal was boisterous and the croft filled with the laughter, but Bree found it difficult to participate. She sat quietly, eating her stew, observing the scene with what she finally acknowledged was outright envy.

She was jealous of everything, jealous of the happiness around her, and jealous of Ruan's relationship with Reenan. She was definitely jealous of Lorna and the fact Ruan had kissed the woman and had never kissed her. She blushed hotly at the thought and focused on her food.

For the first time in her life, she admitted what she'd never allowed herself to think before. She wanted what Reenan had, a cottage of her own with healthy, happy children. Her attention shifted to Ruan. If she were honest, she wanted a real husband. But she wanted a husband who would love her alone. One who was never tempted by exquisite women with willowy figures and soft, red hair, and with the name of Lorna.

She must have been staring, for Ruan lifted a quizzical brow her direction and for several, long moments their gazes locked again, and then, she glanced away. She spent the remainder of the meal, fidgeting and playing with her food until Ruan excused himself and left the croft without explanation.

Bree drew a deep breath, trying not to be upset, but failing miserably. She sat, frowning into her cold stew until Reenan shoved a bucket into her hands.

"Ach, I've forgotten the sheep," the woman announced. "Milk the ewes, lass. They're in the back, four of them. Best get at them afore 'tis too late." She moved away to boot her children playfully. "To bed with ye, young ruffians. 'Tis an early morning for the lot of ye, time to gather hay!"

"Aye, we might be in for a spell of bitter weather," Isobel chimed in as she began to stack the wooden bowls on the table.

Grasping the bucket, Bree slipped outside, grateful for the excuse to escape. She took several steps toward the pen before she realized she didn't have a clue how sheep were milked.

"It can't be much different than a cow," she muttered crossly as she tried to avoid all thoughts of Ruan. Apparently, he was not done with Lorna. He'd obviously left to seek her out. In all likelihood, he was kissing her in a heated passion that very minute. He was supposed to be ill.

Gripping the bucket tightly, she clambered over the low rock wall and into the sheep pen. It was dark, but the clouds were rapidly moving away to uncover the moon. The silvery light cast an eerie atmosphere about the place.

From nowhere, tears threatened, and Bree frowned at herself. Biting her lip, she resolved to protect her foolish heart and focus on her task. She sought out the nearest ewe.

Suddenly, she heard voices. She hesitated, searching in the darkness and then Ruan's deep laugh filtered from behind the gnarled oak at the far end of the pen. The sound of the soft, dulcet tones in reply filled her with anger and humiliation.

It was one thing to imagine him with Lorna. It was quite another to hear the proof.

Then, Ruan swore. His voice was loud, angry.

Against her better judgment, she cautiously crept forward.

"Yer cruel. Why have ye changed so?" Lorna's voice was thick with tears.

When silence greeted this question, Bree crept closer, peering through the thicket.

In the moonlight, she could see Ruan standing with his feet planted widely apart and his arms folded.

Lorna moved closer and tried to slide her arms about his neck, but he pushed her away with a gesture of annoyance.

"Do ye want to see me beg?" Lorna snapped, before assuming a sultry pout. She trailed a finger over his chest. "Ye've seen me do many things, have ye not?"

Bree creased her brows in a frown.

"I'd rather nae see ye at all," Ruan retorted, batting her hand away. "I'm done with ye. I was three years ago."

A feeling of elation fought with jealousy within Bree's heart, as she huddled behind the tree.

Lorna's mouth hardened. "A heartless wretch that is what ye are! What can ye see in that horrid lass?"

"Bree is my wife," Ruan replied, in a voice edged with steel.

"Wife!" Lorna repeated haughtily, nose wrinkled in distaste. "Aye, so, ye got a bairn on her, is that how 'tis? Forced to wed her?"

"I'm done with ye and that includes speaking," Ruan said, with a derisive snort. "I'll grant ye the courtesy no more, though I will say one last thing—I'm grateful."

"Grateful?" Lorna repeated softly, a sly smile playing about her lips.

"Aye." Ruan nodded once.

Bree winced.

"Aye," Ruan repeated, sidestepping as Lorna advanced again. "For showing me how dangerous a net can be woven when a man is nae mindful what bed he lies in. I've nae made that mistake again."

Lorna jerked as if slapped.

Ruan slowly folded his arms, glaring down at the red-haired woman before him in the silence that followed.

Finally, Lorna gathered her shawl close. "The bairn wasna yours," she hissed. "I doubt ye can even father one!"

When he remained silent, she spun on her heel and disappeared into the thickening mists.

Bree held her breath, ashamed to be eavesdropping, but pleased Lorna was gone, and then Ruan moved. Guiltily, she bolted, and ran through the soft, warm bodies of the curious sheep. They bleated, stamping their feet.

"Who is there?" Ruan called out.

Bree leapt over the low wall and burst wildly into the croft.

Isobel and Reenan glanced up from the table, startled.

"What is it, Bree?" Isobel asked, concerned.

Bree paused for a moment, catching her breath with a pounding heart, and then she blushed furiously. She could hardly admit she'd been spying. Not knowing what to do, she covered her warm cheeks with her hands.

"The milk, lass?" Reenan prodded gently and with a mystified smile of encouragement. "Ach, then, go on and fetch it."

Fumbling with the latch, Bree stepped out once again into the falling darkness. The air felt cool to her flaming cheeks.

When a careful perusal showed no obvious signs of Ruan, she expelled a deep breath of relief as she climbed back into the pen and moved toward the tree to retrieve the bucket. She hefted it up and turned, running headlong into a dark figure.

Screaming instinctively, she swung the bucket above her head.

ATTACKED BY A BUCKET

While not prepared for the attack, Ruan managed to lift his good arm to ward off most of the blow. The bucket only grazed his cheek. Aye, he should have known the lass would attack. Her nerves were as taut as a bowstring. With a muffled curse, he wrenched it from Bree's hand and lunged forward to subdue her as a matter of self-preservation.

He caught her about the waist and pinned her against the tree.

"Fires of Hell, but ye are hard on a man!" he shouted, as the beguiling green eyes filled with the shock of recognition. Aye, he examined her appreciatively; she made a man hard as well. Succumbing to his baser instincts, he pushed against her harder.

Her eyes widened in surprise.

Aye, he quite liked her there. "You're a wee vicious thing, aren't ye?" he breathed, his pulse quickening at the softness under him.

"What do you expect?" Bree responded, a little breathlessly. "Attacking me in the dark?"

"Me? Attacking?" Ruan touched his cheek gingerly. "I wasna the one wielding that bucket as a weapon!"

"Be thankful it wasn't your ...!" She faltered, moving to pat her skirts, searching for the *sgian dubh* he'd given her.

"Aye, this?" Ruan grinned, shifting his weight to unsheathe the small knife in question. "'Tis twice now ye've lost it. 'Twill do ye no good with me. But then, perhaps I'd best keep it." He twirled it, eyeing her with deep amusement. "I might live longer in comfort that way."

She glowered in an obvious attempt to intimidate him, but succeeded only in appearing fetching, like a kitten drawing its tiny pink mouth in an endearing hiss. He focused on her mouth and her full lips. They were lips that he wanted nothing more than to claim.

Sweet Mary, what ailed him? Why couldn't he remember he had naught to his name. He shook his head as if to clear, it but found himself staring into her eyes. They were interesting eyes, brewing deep with emotion.

All at once, he forgot what he'd wanted to say.

She was holding still beneath him and he could feel her heart beating rapidly, but then, it might have been his own. He moved closer. Her skin was so warm. His lips almost touched her ear.

"Ruan?"

Reenan's voice cut through the darkness. A shaft of light fell on them through the croft's open door.

"Aye," Ruan pulled back, clearing his throat.

Bree moved away to jump over the low wall of the pen, and he followed.

"Ach, there ye are," Reenan said with a nod, stepping back as he loomed up behind Bree. "I was a wee bit worried about Bree, though needlessly, it seems."

He followed Bree into the croft.

With blue eyes dancing in open merriment, Reenan eyed him and subjected Bree to the same intense scrutiny.

He scowled.

"I'll find the bucket and milk the sheep, lass," Reenan said, with a knowing grin. "I did nae mean to intrude."

Ruan saw Bree flush hotly.

He turned away, inexplicably finding he was doing the same.

Aye, he knew the truth. He wanted her to be his wife, not just in name. Somehow, she'd grown on him, though, in all likelihood, she didn't feel the same. Aye, the wee lass had never wanted to be wed at all. He'd heard himself from her that all she wanted was to live with Afraig in a cottage by the sea.

A cottage was not even something he could afford to give her. He clenched his fists, ashamed that he had nothing to give.

"Ye should rest, lad," Isobel said, rising from the low stool and beckoning him to the fire. "And I'll be looking to that wound now. We canna have ye ill with another fever."

Ruan watched impassively as Isobel changed the dressing once again and Reenan returned with the milk, and then tucked her brood securely under their covers.

Pulling a heather-filled pallet close to the dying fire in the center of the croft, Reenan said, "Ye'll sleep there with Bree. Merry and Isobel can join me." She blew out the candle.

The room fell into darkness, the only light a dull, warm glow from the open hearth. The giggling snorts of the children gradually lessened until they were finally asleep.

Ruan remained as he was, seated on the stool, thoughts fixed on

Bree.

She glanced nervously his direction several times, but when he made no move to join her, finally settled on the pallet and burrowed under the covers.

It would be a mistake to sleep next to her.

He waited.

When she fell into a pattern of soft, rhythmic breathing, he rose to peer down at the slight form of his wife.

He was exhausted. His shoulder ached, and the prospect of sleeping on the cold floor was less than appealing. At least, he tried to convince himself that was the reason as he slipped in next to her. Bree tensed immediately, and he pulled her close, telling himself he sought only to prevent an attack.

Her hair tickled his cheek.

Her spine was rigid and he was sure she was holding her breath.

Moving onto his back, he wondered what she was thinking, but was oddly too shy to ask. He scowled. Aye, in all likelihood, she was already planning what she'd do once their marriage was annulled. He winced at his stupidity. What was he dreaming of? The lass didn't care for him.

With his brows drawn in a dark line, he prepared for a miserable night, but, surprisingly, sleep found him quickly.

Only a short time later, the sun streamed through the open door to warm his face.

Reenan was busy at the table.

Bree was nowhere to be seen.

"Ach, yer awake, ye muckle fool," Reenan smiled in greeting.

"Aye and a braw morning to ye as well," Ruan scowled, leaning up on an elbow.

"'Tis afternoon," Reenan dusted her hands clean and came around to stand at the foot of the pallet. "Ye should just kiss her and have done, ye great, foolish beast."

Ruan's eyes widened in surprise as he rose to his feet.

"Aye and I know ye heard," Reenan persisted, laying her hand on his arm. "She canna see how smitten ye are, and–"

"She has no reason to love me," Ruan said. He shook her off, aggravated. "And can ye blame her? I've nothing to offer!"

"Ach, ye'll sort that out soon enough, lad," Reenan replied, and placed her hands on her hips. "No lass could have a more loyal or gentle husband."

"Aye, I've sense enough to see that loyalty and gentleness are poor companions in the cold of winter if ye've naught to eat and nae peat to burn! I've nae roof, nae land, and certainly nae love left in me. The likes of Lorna have seen to that as well!" Ruan found himself shouting. He glared, and then added, "Besides, I've no doubt Bree loathes me." With a shrug, he signaled the matter done.

Reenan burst into a hearty laugh. "How can ye be so blind? A lass that watches ye like she does feels many things, and none of them is near loathing. Open yer eyes, man. 'Twill take only a wee bit of wooing, and–"

To his utter relief, Reenan's brood burst inside to smother him with hugs and to push him outdoors. Thankful to escape their prying mother, he followed them to find Bree and Merry unloading bundles of hay from the cart under Isobel's guidance.

He moved to help, but all three sent him a stern look.

"Ye'll be leaving soon enough," Reenan said, appearing to push him onto the nearby rock wall. "Sit and rest now. Ye'll be needing yer strength sooner than ye like, I'll warrant."

He sighed, hearing the wisdom of her words, and closed his eyes, soaking in the warmth of the sun.

After a time, Isobel bundled the children into the cart to gather more hay, leaving Bree to stack the bundles against the croft.

It suited him well. He folded his arms, observing her from half-closed lids.

Fleetingly, he allowed himself to forget his concerns and to wonder if Reenan could be right. Maybe the lass didn't loathe him at all. She'd held still in his arms, not once, but twice last night. What would she do if he did kiss her? Would she strike out, or would her lashes close and her lips part?

His pulse raced and he found himself standing next to her, bending down to lift one of the bundles with his good arm.

"You should be resting," Bree said. She frowned, reaching to snag it from his grasp. "Reenan said you should sit!"

He playfully pulled it away, just a little, and laid his free hand over hers. "Aye, but these wee bundles weigh less than a feather," he replied. "I canna harm myself with dry grass."

His put his left hand over hers, waiting to see if she would pull away, but she held still. Her cheeks tinged a slight pink. That was hardly the response of a lass who despised him. His pulse quickened. Perhaps Reenan was right; he might win her heart if he were careful.

She tugged the bundle again, and he relinquished it, choosing instead to sit back on the wall.

"Aye," he said, feigning weakness simply because he desired to stay in her company. "Mayhap, I should rest a wee spell longer."

Concern suffused her features, and he almost felt guilty for misleading her.

"I can manage," Bree agreed. "It is easy enough."

He smiled, watching her work in silence for a time. She was nervous, uneasy. He searched for something to say, wondering what she would enjoy talking about, when he spied Lorna rounding the corner of the croft. His heart sank. The woman seemed intent on slithering in his direction. As Bree curiously followed his gaze, he succumbed to a rash impulse.

Rising to his feet, he seized Bree's arm, pulling her off balance. She fell against him. As her astonished face lifted his way, his lips descended to cover hers.

Her mouth was warm, soft, and startling.

He'd kissed many women before, but had never experienced a sensation such as this. For the briefest of moments, her lips opened in response, and he was overwhelmed with a fierce heat that threatened to bring him to his knees. He wanted to cherish, protect, and take her all at once. His hand cradled the back of her head. His fingers twined through her hair of their own accord. She seemed to melt into them, but then, Merry called out, and the moment was lost.

Disconcerted, Bree pulled back.

A small part of him was pleased to notice her hesitation. She didn't seem angry, but he was mostly shocked at his own actions. Where was his control? He'd just vowed to move slowly, to win her heart. Now, he'd undoubtedly ruined his chances.

"What happened?" Merry joined them, her brows furrowed. "What are ye doing?"

Clearing her throat, Bree ducked, and began vigorously tossing the hay into the pen.

THE KISS

Rattled, Bree heaved a sigh of relief as Merry led Ruan away. Her cheeks were still flaming; no doubt, they would remain crimson for days. He must have kissed her to infuriate Lorna. While secretly thrilling, it was vastly disappointing.

Once Lorna had gone, his intent had apparently been accomplished for he had simply walked away.

She didn't know whether to cry or to be angry.

She settled on berating herself. She must have kissed very badly. He'd suddenly become distant, and he hadn't even said a word.

He'd simply left, using her to rid himself of Lorna. So, why could she not stop thinking about his lips on hers? His kiss was forceful, gentle, and commanding all at once, much like the man himself, far more intense than she could have possibly imagined.

It took some time to clear her thoughts.

When she returned to the croft, she found Ruan asleep on a pallet. His face was still pale.

"Ach, the lad will be fine, lass," Reenan promised, as she shooed her children away from the pile of fresh bannocks. "He just needs a wee bit of rest before taking ye on to Cameron."

Bree bit her lip and nodded.

They moved quietly about the croft that night, and when Reenan blew out the candle, she quietly took her place by Ruan's side.

It was difficult to sleep, at first.

Even asleep, the man's presence was overwhelming. His lips were incredibly distracting. She wished he'd never kissed her, because she suddenly wanted to experience more. She frowned, turning away.

Somehow, she had to gain control of these strange emotions. After all, he was trying as hard as he could to take her to Cameron where their marriage would be annulled.

Eventually, she fell into a fitful asleep.

The sound of a creaking door signaled it was time to wake. She looked up to see Isobel framed against the gentle pink dusting the sky. "'Tis time to be leaving, Ruan," the woman said.

"Aye," Ruan's deep voice breathed close to her ear.

Swallowing, Bree turned to find him propped on an elbow, staring down at her.

They didn't speak.

And then, Ruan reached over to brush the hair from her face, his finger trailing her cheek.

Bree gulped.

"The ship sails with the tide, lad," Reenan yawned in the darkness behind them. "I've asked several of the lads to drop by this morn to show ye the way."

Ruan moved away and sat up. "I'm in your debt, Reenan."

"Aye, as always," she chuckled.

Bree watched him rise, too confused to interpret his actions, but she was soon too busy helping Reenan with the morning meal and packing their things to give it further thought.

In short time, they were ready to leave and she stepped outside, peering at the brown heather rolling in gentle waves with the wind. It was odd. Only a month ago, she'd have leapt at the chance to leave Skye, but now she felt a twinge, wondering if she'd ever return.

She felt a little sad, but only a little, as she joined the others to bid their farewells.

"Have a wee bit of patience with the man," Reenan whispered in Bree's ear, giving her cheeks an affectionate tweak. "He's–"

"Aye and I'll see ye soon, Reenan," Ruan interrupted, clasping a hand on her shoulder and prying her away before she could speak more.

"Ach, love," Reenan protested. She tossed her head and shrugged. "Then, suffer with yer way. If ye but listen–"

"Aye and I've listened," Ruan cut her short. He nodded briefly at Bree. "'Tis time we left."

With final farewells said, they joined several men dressed in brown, MacDonald plaids and saffron yellow shirts. Ruan apparently knew them well. They clasped arms in fond greetings as they moved down the path at a brisk pace.

"Where are the horses?" Merry asked, skipping along.

"They belong to Reenan now," Isobel replied, tossing a small cloth bundle over her shoulder. "We'll be walking to the boat, lass. 'Tis only a short step away."

"She's right welcome to them," Merry said, with a disdainful sniff. "They were useless beasts anyway."

The small girl continued to chatter, bouncing ahead to join Ruan, and Bree gratefully fell back behind them all. Though she was unsure of what Reenan had wished to say, it was obviously something Ruan knew and disagreed with. She frowned, wondering why the man had to occupy her thoughts so fully. With a conscious effort, she forced her attention to the scenery unfolding about her.

The fog had been so heavy on their arrival that she hadn't realized they were close to the sea. The path to the shore was rough and steep, a narrow passage between two cliffs that led to a fine sandy beach. Above her head, gulls glided on the wind, crying mournfully.

A large vessel was in the water. Several more men jumped on shore and greeted Ruan warmly. The wind blew in gusts, preventing her from hearing their words, but judging from the startled looks sent her way, she was grateful. She'd no desire to hear Ruan explain her presence. She knew the man thought he was stuck with her. She frowned.

The boat was old, but seaworthy, filled with kegs and boxes, it was already riding low in the water. Assuring her it was safe, the men lifted her aboard, and she settled in the back with Merry.

They launched almost immediately. There was no piper playing to keep time, and, for that, Bree was grateful; instead, the men broke into bouts of song, mingled with roars of laughter. Ruan was the loudest among them.

The waves slapped against the boat, and Bree grimaced, willing her stomach to stay at ease.

The vessel glided forward, but as they progressed, the wind and waves strengthened. Soon they were bobbing back and forth in a sickening, swaying motion. She tried to concentrate on the dramatic coastal scenery slipping rapidly past her, but it was not long before she lost the battle and leaned over the edge, violently ill.

She spent the remainder of the day, resting her cheek on the side of the boat, afraid to retch again.

The sun was well on its descent when Isobel called out, "'Tis almost over, love, Eilean Donan is a welcome sight, even though they be Mackenzies."

Cautiously, she raised her head to see a castle perched on a rocky islet a short distance away. Long-horned sheep grazed on the rugged faces of the great tree-clad slopes cradling the loch. The wind had died and the loch appeared smooth as glass, rendering the last leg of the journey much easier until, finally, the boat ground ashore.

A group of men appeared on the dock, led by a large, rotund man bearing the name of Simon Mackenzie. His broad face broke into a wide grin to see Ruan.

"Aye, 'tis twice I've seen ye in a month now, lad," Simon laughed, as they clasped one another in greeting. "Please dinna give me tidings of the MacDonalds that I'll nae want to hear!"

"'Tis my own affair this time, Simon," Ruan's deep voice replied. "I'm on my way to Cameron."

"Ach, now there's a lad I've sore missed!" Simon chuckled as they moved away, exchanging bits of news.

Bree closed her eyes, lacking the will to move as the men unloaded the kegs and crates. After the rough passage, it was pleasant to sit in the late afternoon sun, even though she was still on the infernal boat. The sudden dips as the men walked about threatened to upset her stomach, but she failed dismally in summoning the strength to disembark.

Hands slipped around her shoulder and under her knees, jerking her up in one, swift motion. She yelped, startled, and her eyes flew open.

"Ach, *mo ceisd*," Ruan breathed softly in her ear. "Ye canna sleep here."

Mo ceisd. His tone made her heart race, even as she frowned at the words that still labeled her a 'problem'. However, there was no time to think as he swung her over and into Simon's waiting arms. The man promptly placed her on the shore and Ruan leapt down to join her.

"Your... shoulder!" She floundered, uneasy over his nearness.

"Ach, I used my good arm, lass, and ye weigh nae more than a feather," he said with a half-smile. His hand lifted toward her, but Merry promptly appeared from nowhere to snatch it.

"Come!" the small girl said a bit petulantly, tugging at his fingers. "I'm weary of waiting!"

With a laugh, Ruan led them from the sea loch to the narrow steps leading to the castle, moss and golden seaweed clinging to the black rocks on their path.

Passing under the open gatehouse, they had scarcely stepped foot in the courtyard before they were accosted by an angry man, with grizzled gray hair and a lacework of scars over his left brow. "Ruan!" he shouted. He placed his hand menacingly on his dirk as he added, "How dare ye come here, after what ye've done!"

Ruan's brows climbed in surprise, "And what do ye mean by that,

Dougald?"

"As if ye dinna ken!" The man shouted, his chin trembling.

A small crowd began to gather, eyeing them with interest.

"Ach, well…" Ruan knit his brows. "I'm at a loss—"

"Ye'll wed my daughter, my Sheila, this very night!" Dougald raised his dirk, brandishing the blade. "I've no desire to harm ye, lad, but I will if ye don't make this right! I've always thought ye a man of honor, until now!"

Ruan frowned. "Sheila? I'm nae sure…" His voice trailed off in confusion upon spying Dougald's fierce expression. After a minute, he continued. "Aye, well, I'm certain Sheila is lovely, Dougald, but I'm already wed!"

Dougald stared and then cursed. He took a step forward, but paused as a young woman pushed her way through the thickening crowd. She stepped from the circle of observers, belly heavy with child.

Ruan's eyes narrowed as understanding dawned. "Aye," he said coldly. "This must be Sheila."

"I've naught but ill to see," the angry father spat. "Ye canna wed my daughter as ye should now!"

"The bairn isn't mine," Ruan's voice grew colder. "And I've no recollection of seeing Sheila afore."

"Aye, be truthful, lass." Simon said, stepping up in support of Ruan. "Even Ruan canna get ye with a bairn when he's nae here."

"He was here!" the girl whispered, her lips white. "He came with the Earl of Lennox. He… was drunk, and… and…"

"That was nigh on twelve months ago," Simon snorted. "And I

know he touched no one. Ach, even if I dinna ken, ye've some time yet afore that bairn is dropped."

"No!" The girl shook her head, desperately. "'Twas nae even nine months, and the bairn is late." She covered her head in her arms, sobbing, as several women sympathetically drew her away.

Doubt crossed her father's face for the first time.

Voices rose and then everyone was speaking.

Taking a deep breath, Bree slipped away from the crowd in search of an escape. She wanted to hide, if only for a few moments, until she lost the sudden urge to cry. She stumbled through the courtyard, and found a spot next to a wall of kegs and crates.

A hand touched her shoulder.

She looked up as Ruan caught her chin in his hand and forced her eyes to meet his. "The bairn isn't mine," he said.

She swallowed and finally forced herself to reply, "It... really is none of my affair."

"Oh?" he glared at her angrily. "Ask yourself why I'm here, explaining this to ye, then!"

She looked away, but then a new thought struck her. The words came out before she could stop them. "I'm sure there are plenty of children about that *do* belong to you!"

His dark brows drew into a scowl, and she felt oddly ashamed.

"I have no bairns! If I did, ye would have known," Ruan replied with a clenched jaw. "Ye think I'm uncommonly vile!"

Bree bit her lip and glanced away. As much as it hurt to admit, she was only an obligation to the man. She was certainly never desired. He'd obviously forgotten the kiss. He hadn't mentioned it. But then, it hadn't been a real kiss to him. She found herself repeating dully, "It...really is no concern of mine. You will soon be free to do as you please when our marriage is... annulled."

There was an awkward silence.

"Aye," he said finally, his voice cold and distant. "'Twill nae be long now, then. I've no desire to be chained in wedlock."

A jumble of emotions greeted his words. Inexplicably, the anger of rejection outweighed all others. She raised her head and allowed the hurt in her eyes to show. "That is well, for I've no desire for you as a husband!"

Ruan's dark eyes burned in response.

"Aye!" he retorted. "I've nae bedded a woman these past three years, and I'd rather pull out my own eyes and tongue with hot pincers before I ever touch another one and that includes ye, lass! 'Tis right thankful I'll be to be rid of ye!"

They stood there, breathing hard, then, as tears threatened, Bree struck out, pummeling his chests with her fists, wanting to make him go away. He stared, stunned, eyeing her fleetingly before stepping back.

What possessed her? She'd never behaved so irrationally in her entire life.

"Come, lass," Isobel's calm voice unexpectedly asserted itself. "Merry, take her up to the hall."

***

"I used to think ye understood lassies uncommon well, lad, but ye've proved of late ye know less than most," Isobel said, with a kindly chuckle.

"Aye and I've no desire to learn," Ruan snapped, attempting to brush past her, but she caught his arm.

The old woman smiled. "Well, ye might wish to try a wee harder with this one, love."

Ruan gave a snort of disdain. "She wants nothing to do with me." Aye, and he'd only himself to blame. "I'm sure ye must have heard. She wants her annulment and a cottage by the sea."

"Well, ye've hardly been talking to the wee lass, if she thinks ye still want this marriage annulled, love," Isobel laughed a little. "She likely thinks that kiss of yours meant nothing to ye."

"Kiss?" Ruan frowned, flinching in embarrassment. Of course, Isobel must have seen.

"Aye," She laughed, reading the nature of his thoughts. "What exactly have ye said to her about it? I'd say nothing, judging by what just took place."

He didn't have to reply. She knew him too well.

"Love, how could ye be so foolish? She probably thinks–" Isobel began.

"Be done!" Ruan interrupted. Taking a deep breath, he continued in a softer tone, "Thank ye for your concern, but I've had my fill of this for now."

Thankfully, she nodded, but her aged eyes were twinkling.

Eilean Donan's hall was alive with merriment. The candles burned brightly in the large iron chandelier suspended from the heavy oak timbers spanning the ceiling. Torches flickered on the walls.

Only a month ago, he had ridden here with Robert, to ease the Mackenzie concerns over Cuilen's clan. He clenched his fists a little.

Aye, Robert had been alive then. It wasn't so long ago.

Simon had informed him that The Mackenzie had left with a band of men. He hadn't told Ruan where they had gone. He didn't have to. Ruan knew they were headed north, to Fearghus. To know that Fearghus was now dealing with Mackenzie trouble suited him just fine. His only regret was that he hadn't killed the man when he had the chance.

Lady Elspeth Mackenzie was already presiding at table when he entered; she beckoned to him immediately, giving him no time to search for Bree. Not that she wanted to see him, he reminded himself as he bowed over the lady of the castle's wrinkled hand.

He'd always enjoyed Lady Elspeth's company. She had a rare wit and, in spite of her advanced age, a sharp mind. He was saddened to find her health had deteriorated since their last meeting, only a month ago, but her spirits were high. She seemed frail and tired easily. After only a brief conversation, she kissed him a warm farewell and retired to her chamber.

He found Bree almost immediately.

She sat with Merry at the farthest table close to a window, appearing miserable. He suppressed a sigh. The lass detested him, that much was plain. There was little point in wooing her. He flushed, wondering how he could have even considered such a daft scheme.

It must have been the wound.

In any case, 'twas for the better. He had other, weightier matters to consider, such as the damage he'd inflicted on the clan. He could not think of Robert's death, not yet. Disheartened, he swung his leg over the bench and took his seat opposite her.

"Forgive me," Bree said, as he sat. Her voice shook nervously.

He blinked, surprised, but said truthfully, "There is nae need for that." He shrugged.

"No, that is not true. You have been very kind to me," Bree continued earnestly, the color high in her cheeks. She didn't meet his eyes, instead she trailed her finger back and forth on the surface of the wooden table. "I had no cause to speak to you so, especially since I haven't thanked you as I should... for... what you have done. You have rescued me more than once and..." She faltered uncertainly.

In spite of his best efforts, his pulse quickened. His dark thoughts disappeared. Almost of its own accord, his voice deepened, and he leaned forward with a suggestive whisper. "Aye and what is the proper way to... thank me?"

Merry began to tap on the table loudly, giving a long, loud sigh of boredom.

Bree appeared a little confused, but said firmly, "I... thank you."

He took a deep breath, relieved at her innocence.

Her company obviously addled his wits. One moment he was ready to return her to Domnall, and the next, he was flirting with seduction. He clearly needed space and time to think. Sitting there was a mistake. Standing abruptly, he gave a gallant bow and said, "Aye, then I've been thanked, and there's nae harm done. We leave at dawn; be sure ye rest well."

Merry was frowning at him. He reached over and tousled her hair; he'd have to deal with her later. Right now, he wanted to be gone. He ducked to join Simon and several others a few tables away and distracted himself with their company long into the night, long after he saw Bree and Merry settling to sleep in the corner. Finally, scant few hours before dawn, he sprawled across the table and slept, exhausted.

All too soon, Simon was shaking him awake as the soft morning light filtered in the hall.

He staggered to his feet, bleary eyed and still tired.

"Aye, lad," Simon said with a knowing grin. "Ye'll sort it out soon enough."

Ruan squinted and replied, "'Tis too early to speak in riddles, Simon."

"I'll wager neither of ye slept well." Simon punched him lightly on the shoulder and nodded with his chin.

Following the man's direction, Ruan spied Bree peering out the window.

She yawned, stretching her neck, seeming somewhat sad. The desire rippled through him, to sweep her in his arms and assure her all would be well. Only, he could not promise that, and he was highly uncertain she fancied hearing him say anything. Belatedly, he realized he was staring and hadn't answered Simon.

He turned, but the man was gone.

Isobel arrived, and Ruan sat on the edge of the table, absently swinging his leg as the others gathered their things. They had oatcakes and fish along the way, and after he'd given his thanks for the hospitality, he led them out into the crisp morning air.

Clouds hung low in the west and the wind was rising.

It promised to be a wretched day.

Bree and Merry huddled in the back of the boat, plaids drawn against the biting wind and Simon refused to let him take an oar. The shore was scarce over a stone's throw away, so he didn't insist. It was just as well, his shoulder was still sore.

Simon quickly led them to the stables.

Ruan dipped his head under the low door, entering, as Simon pointed to three beautiful mares.

"Lady Elspeth insisted ye have these," he said with a smile.

They were stunning animals.

"These be far too valuable," Ruan said. He shook his head. "I canna accept them."

"Aye," Simon replied with a laugh. He handed the lead of the first to Merry. "She told me ye'd say that and that I was to tell ye she'd forever be in yer debt for saving the laird."

"Ye saved the laird?" Merry danced sideways, her black eyes snapping with interest. "From which clan?"

"I saved the laird from a chicken bone… hardly worth the horses," Ruan frowned.

Merry was rightfully disenchanted. She led the mare out of the stable, chattering to Simon. "Three? Does that mean I ride my own?"

"Nay," Simon answered. He tossed Ruan a couple of bridles before following her. "Ye'll ride with Isobel, ye canna manage one of these beasts on yer own yet, I'd wager."

"How much would ye wager?" Ruan heard Merry's impertinent reply.

He smiled.

"Merry!" Isobel warned.

Ruan chuckled. Simon would lose. Merry was one of the best horsemen he'd ever seen. Still smiling, he stepped around the front of the mare, almost tripping over Bree.

"Ach, lass, what are ye doing here?" he asked, catching his balance and pulling up short.

"Simon said you needed help," Bree said. She stepped back quickly. "He said your shoulder…"

Ruan peered through the open door to see Simon walk past, grinning widely. He suppressed a sigh. Apparently, only he could see that the lass detested him. "Aye, well, ye can ready your horse, then."

He tossed the remaining bridle, but instead of catching it, she instinctively raised her arm to cover her face. It fell to the barn floor with a jingle. They both reached for it at the same time, his fingers brushing hers. She straightened, stiffly, tugging the bridle free from his grasp.

"Ach, forgive me," he said, feeling a little remorseful. "I did nae mean to frighten ye, then."

She was standing close.

The heady fragrance of lavender rose between them. He wondered how she always smelled of it and began to feel much more than simple remorse. It was difficult to step away, but he did. He returned to his task, but watched her hesitantly approach the mare with overt reluctance.

She apparently didn't like horses.

He patted his mare's withers absently. He smiled, a little, as Bree pushed the bridle at the mare's nose, as if the animal would bridle itself.

"Ye have to open her mouth, lass," he said, finding himself by her side, grinning. "Like this."

He reached around, nicking the bridle from Bree's grasp and expertly slipped it over the animal's ears. It was only then that he realized he was too close, arms virtually encircling her. The back of her head tickled his chest. She twisted, clearly expecting him to step away, but he was strangely rooted to the spot. Her brows creased in confusion, and as the silence between them lengthened, he wondered if she could ever put her distaste of him aside.

"You'll not be kissing me again," Bree said at last, lifting her chin a little.

It was Ruan's turn to be surprised. Tilting his head to one side, he murmured, "Odd… that ye'd be thinking of a kiss."

"I wasn't," she answered, flustered. Her cheeks were turning pink. "I… I…"

"Yes?" he pressed, as a small flame of hope kindled in his heart; what if she were only shy? Could it be that she hated him less than he feared?

"Nothing," she said, turning her head to the side. She moved to leave, as if expecting he'd let her go.

He knew he should, but instead, he leaned close and whispered, "I think ye want another."

"No!" she squeaked. Placing her hands on his chest, she half-heartedly attempted to push him away.

Ruan didn't move. Her actions were far too fascinating.

"I don't want to be kissed and forgotten!" she said with difficulty. This time, she shoved him, in earnest.

He stepped back, caught slightly off-guard, but quickly seized her wrist and yanked her back into his arms. Sweet Mary, Isobel had been right. He was an ignorant fool. "Who could kiss ye and forget?" He asked softly. "Aye, I kissed ye, and I've thought of nothing else since."

Bree's lips parted in surprise.

"Aye, I've kissed many, lass, but yours was the first that ever terrified me." He slid his hand up her back, pushing her closer. "That is why I haven't spoken of it."

She blinked and her brows crinkled, "Terrified?"

"Of what 'twould be like to lose ye," he whispered, revealing his innermost fear but no longer caring. "I don't want to let ye go, lass. Do ye still want this marriage annulled?" If she pushed him away, he'd suffer a pain beyond imagining, but she didn't. Instead, she melted. He lifted his thumb, lightly tracing her cheekbone.

Then, he felt a swift kick on the back of his knee.

He leapt back, startled.

"What are ye doing?" Merry pulled him away from Bree, her small face a mixture of anger and fear. "Did she fall off her horse?"

"Ach, but ye are slow in getting these horses ready, lad," Simon bellowed loudly, obviously in a kind warning that he was entering the stables. "I'll lend ye a hand."

Bree took advantage of the commotion to escape, but he already knew Isobel had been right. He should try harder with this one. He just might win her heart, and he might yet prove worthy of it. Mood soaring, he made quick work of the horses and led them out of the barn.

"Ruan lad, give a hand here," Isobel called, pointing to her horse.

He obliged, lifting her into the saddle.

"Thank ye, love," she said, pursing her lips. "I'm thinking we should head for the blacksmith afore leaving."

"Blacksmith?" Ruan raised a curious brow.

"Ach, we need to get ye a pair of hot pincers to pull out those eyes and tongue of yers, lad," Isobel replied with a chuckle.

Color tinged his cheeks, but his heart was too light to do more than send her a mildly exasperated look.

UNEXPECTED CONFESSIONS

Bree didn't know what to think. Ruan's unexpected confession, the soft gentleness of the man, his touch of tenderness had thrown her emotions into a state of turmoil. Surely, he was not toying with her. If he were, she'd gladly find her knife, wherever the infernal thing was, and cut his heart out. The thought startled her. She no longer recognized herself, but it felt right.

Simon offered a friendly hand to toss her onto her horse, and she wondered if she should tell them she'd never ridden on her own before. As she landed in the saddle, the beast snorted, and she clung desperately to its mane. It bolted a few paces before Simon deftly caught the reins and handed them to her with a wide grin.

From the corner of her eye, she watched Ruan swing unaided into the saddle, saying his farewells. He was obviously healing well. The man was distracting. His carved lips, expressive eyes, and the way he'd held her close filled her mind, but then the horse beneath her moved and all other thoughts fled.

She'd always hated riding horses.

Desperately, she tried to control the horse, but it didn't appear to notice her attempts.

Isobel and Merry trotted past, followed by Ruan, and she was relieved when the beast fell into line, but they had hardly left the village when it appeared to change its mind. It ambled after the others for only a short distance before stopping to nibble a withered tuft of grass, blithely ignoring her feeble tugging of the reins.

A burst of wind ripped through the glen, followed by scattered drops of rain.

"Move!" she growled for the fourth time, kicking the beast with her foot.

It finally twitched an ear and snorted, but continued to chew. Even that minute of a response was progress, and she smiled, pleased, but was disappointed to discover it had merely detected Ruan's return.

"Ye have to be firm with a horse, *mo ceisd*," he said, reining to stop beside her and reaching over to cup his hand over hers.

Bree blushed furiously, feeling out of depth. His touch felt like fire. "She is ignoring me," she managed to mumble, refusing to meet his eyes.

"The more fool she," he squeezed her hand softly before leaning back to swat the beast on the rump.

The horse lurched forward, flattening her ears, but dutifully trotted as long as Ruan rode behind to prod her forward. They joined the others, and Ruan again took the lead forging ahead to scout the road, but never straying far.

As soon as Ruan left their company, the mare sauntered to a stop. Bree prodded the animal in vain, but there was no doubt it was a creature of the most perverse nature. It had known from the start exactly who was in charge. As long as Ruan remained out of sight, it frolicked down the road enjoying its freedom to the fullest, prancing where it willed and helping itself to every tasty tidbit to be found, whether it grew on the next hill or in the opposite direction. As time wore on, it began to scratch its back against the trees, though Bree was certain its true intention was to rid itself of the nuisance of a rider.

It began to rain, in earnest.

Isobel and Merry offered advice, but when Ruan returned late in the afternoon, she was on the verge of tears. The mare had wandered into a thicket on the steep side of the hill, nearly scrapping Bree off into the middle of a gnarly tree. She held up her arms, protecting her face from the branches whipping past but more to cover her eyes from the precipice plunging beneath her only a short distance away. She was certain the beast was now plotting the best way to kill her.

"She thinks she is a mountain goat!" Merry's chirping laugh rang in the drizzling rain.

Bree shut her eyes tightly as the horse continued its perilous climb.

"Just hold on, lass," Ruan called out gently, a decided note of amusement in his voice. In moments, he'd joined her to extricate the beast from its precarious location, taking the reins from her cold fingers, and tying them to his saddle.

Once on level ground, Bree allowed her eyes to open. She glared at the horse, wondering how she could possibly devise a suitable punishment for the beast.

It serenely ignored her.

Isobel eyed the grey clouds grimly, talking of snow.

"Inchmurrin is a fair distance," Ruan said. "We still have far to ride this day."

Isobel groaned, refusing to budge. "'Tis too wet, lad, and even though ye care nae to remember it, yer wound is nae fully healed."

Bree huddled in her wet plaid, ignoring their conversation as their voices rose and fell.

Finally, Ruan sighed. "Ach, we'll go just to the hill, though we should press on to the village."

"Nae if we catch our deaths getting there!" Isobel grumbled.

They forged on, and as darkness fell, stopped before the shadowy shape of an abandoned croft. Only a small portion of the roof remained.

Bree slid wearily from the saddle, stiff, sore and barely able to move.

She was entirely unprepared for the sharp hoof lashing out, planting itself squarely on her shin. She pitched forward, sprawling in the mud, gasping in pain to lie where she was, thoroughly wet and ears aching.

Ruan's strong arms lifted her to her feet, and then her temper flared.

Shaking free of his grasp, she tripped over her wet skirts to stand in front of the obstinate mare and began to shout. The beast's ears flattened as she informed it of its black heart and the fact it was only fit to be fed upon or worse. She racked her brain, thinking of all the uses for horseflesh, ranging from simple hides to boots, at times hopping on one leg as pain radiated through the other, shouting until her voice grew hoarse.

Gradually, she became aware of Merry laughing, and then Ruan slipped his arm around her waist, and half carried her into the derelict building.

"Ye forgot armor," Merry said with a giggle. "I don't think I've ever eaten horse, what does it taste like, Ruan?"

"I've never eaten one, my Merry wee lass."

Bree could hear the smile in his voice. "That horse is evil!" she said, voice trembling.

"Aye, she is uncommon creative," Ruan said with a chuckle, holding her close in the darkness longer than necessary before letting her go. "I'll find something to burn."

It took some doing, but a fire finally sputtered, casting an eerie light upon the black stones. Isobel doled out more oatcakes and herring, but Bree stared at hers with little appetite. She sat by the fire, watching the steam rise from her plaid as it dried.

When Ruan returned with the fourth armload of wood, Isobel insisted it was enough.

"We'll nae need more than that, love. Sit before ye catch ill!" She fussed with worry.

It had been an exhausting day, in all respects, but Bree was entirely sure she wouldn't rest if Ruan chose to sleep next to her. Everything seemed to be changing between them. She wanted to drive him away and throw herself in his arms at the same time. It was confusing.

Accepting his bannocks and herring, he joined her by the fire, stretching out at her side. As his thigh brushed hers, she stiffened, but he didn't move away and oddly, she didn't, either. To slow her rapid pulse, she focused her attention on Merry; the child had fallen asleep with her head resting in Bree's lap. Gently, she smoothed her raven locks as Merry smiled in her sleep.

No one spoke; they simply listened to the fire crackle and hiss at the occasional raindrop seeping through the damaged roof.

Time passed, and as the temperature plunged, Bree's ears began to ring. As her chin drooped in exhaustion, she felt Ruan's gentle hands pulling her down to rest her head on his warm shoulder. His voice rumbled comfortingly beneath her ear.

She fell asleep, feeling warm and safe.

The dawn was cold, but dry, as Merry jumped to her feet, waking them all with, "Ruan, can I ride the horse, please?"

Bree opened her eyes as the warmth beneath her cheek heaved.

"Ach, Merry," Ruan groaned, sitting up slowly. "Can ye at least wait until the sun rises?"

"The horse?" Merry repeated. "Please?"

Her brother turned to her with a grin, reaching over to tousle her hair. He whispered something and the small girl collapsed into giggles. Bree sat up slowly, certain she was the victim of some jest, but if it ended with her not having to deal with the animal, she was satisfied.

As Merry gleefully skipped out of the abandoned croft, Ruan turned to peer down at her through half-closed lids. "Ye'll ride with me, lass."

Bree meant to nod, but the movement caused her to wince in pain. Her throat ached and her ears burned in pain.

Ruan lifted her lightly to her feet. "Are ye well?" he asked, dark eyes filling with concern.

She succumbed to a bout of coughing that ended with a sneeze.

"Bree, are ye ill?" Merry asked as she rushed into the dilapidated structure. "Isobel, Bree is ill!"

Isobel responded with a groan and a sneeze of her own.

The day deteriorated rapidly, in all respects.

It grew colder by the minute. Snow began to fall, and both Isobel and Bree worsened. Ruan's mood took a dark turn. Bree knew he was worried; his mouth eternally twisted in a grim line, whenever he looked upon them.

Merry rode the mare with consummate skill, eager to scout the road ahead, but Ruan cautioned her against straying too far from his sight. Their constant bickering over the matter made Bree's head pound. She spent the day huddled under Ruan's cloak, grateful for his warmth and the strong arm circling her waist. If she hadn't been so ill, she'd have found it a disturbing ride, but as it was, she spent little time fully conscious.

At noon, they dismounted, allowing the horses to take water from an amber colored stream as a biting wind swirled around them.

Isobel's condition had worsened.

Ruan studied her, gravely concerned, and then made a decision. He'd head north, to a village almost a day's ride in the wrong direction. "If Tormod is following, he'd never dream of searching there," he explained. "Aye, at this snail's pace, he'll find us for certain."

His voice sounded unusually far away, as if he were speaking under water.

Frowning, Bree attempted to turn her head, but found her neck too swollen to allow it.

She gasped in pain.

"Fires of Hell, lass," Ruan pulled back her plaid for a closer inspection. "Ye look worse than Isobel!"

"I'm ... fine ..." she attempted to croak, but stopped abruptly. It was too painful to continue.

His cool fingers brushed her forehead, "By the Saints, ye are burning, lass! Merry, ready the horses, we are leaving. If we push hard, we can be at the Inn by nightfall."

"We've little coin," Isobel protested weakly, though perking up at the mention of the Inn.

"Aye, but we've no need of Bree's horse; she canna master the beast anyway," he grunted, gently lifting her into his saddle and mounting behind.

"'Tis most unfair!" Merry complained loudly. This set off another bout of quarreling. Merry objected with every possible argument to keep the horse to which Ruan simply replied, "No".

Gratefully, Bree leaned against his warmth, finding comfort in the deep rumbling of his voice and promptly closed her eyes.

She didn't open them again until it was very late.

Snow was falling when they arrived in a small village composed of little more than the Inn and two other buildings. The Innkeeper examined Bree dubiously, refusing them at first, but in the end, he was unable to resist the trade of such a fine horse for lodging and far less coin than its worth.

The room was in the attic, tiny but clean. There was a large bed tucked under an eave, with a small one next to the fireplace.

"It's more than I could have hoped for, love," Isobel said, as she sank gratefully in the covers with a sigh.

***

The first thing Bree noticed was that she could swallow.

The second was she could hear.

Everything seemed unusually loud, the murmur of voices below, the soft crackling of the fire, someone breathing close by and the intermittent rustle of paper. She was warm, dry and comfortable. She stretched, wiggling her toes gratefully against the coarse linen sheets before striking something warm and solid. She simply enjoyed the heat for a time before, with great reluctance, she lifted her lashes to wince in the late morning light.

"Are ye feeling better, *mo ceisd*?"

Ruan's deep voice rumbled from under her ear, and she glanced up, startled. He was holding a book, stretched lazily on his back by her side, shirt undone, as he peered down at her with a mixture of amusement and concern.

Bree rubbed her cheek, embarrassed to be sleeping yet again on his shoulder. She was making a habit of it.

"Ye've been half out of your head these past few days," he offered when she made no move to speak. "Five, to be exact."

Five? She frowned in disbelief. Surely, she hadn't been ill for five days, but then, jumbled memories returned. Someone had poured liquid down her raw throat. Strong hands had rubbed her aching back and a soft voice had whispered *mo ceisd* more than once. She sighed. The man continually called her a problem, and she supposed she was. "I'm sorry to be such a bother."

"Bother?" Ruan shook his head. "'Tis no fault of yours ye took ill."

"I … cause you a lot of… problems." She looked away, feeling unaccountably shy.

"Aye." He chuckled. "But ye seem to be speaking of different ones than what I have in mind at the moment, lass."

Bewildered at his suggestive tone, she turned back to meet his inquisitive eyes. "I only meant… you call me a … problem, quite often of late…" Her voice faded.

"I call ye a problem?" he asked, brows knit. He appeared genuinely perplexed.

"It is nothing," Bree said, shaking her head, embarrassed.

"Nay, please explain," Ruan insisted. He pulled her chin up, forcing her to meet his gaze. "I'm fair confused, *mo ceisd*...." He hesitated only a moment before his lips began to widen in a smile. "Ach, I've never called ye a problem, *mo ceisd*, nae once."

Bree frowned. "You… just did, twice."

"Nay, lass." His voice deepened as his hand slid to the back of her neck.

The man's touch was like fire, making it distractingly difficult to concentrate on his confounding words. His hand glided down her shoulder and arm to thread her fingers through his. Then, he drew her hand to his chest, slipping it under his shirt, pressing her palm against his naked skin. She jerked and blushed scarlet.

He leaned close, whispering, "*Mo ceisd*... has a different meaning…"

She gulped, her hand still touching his bare chest. She knew she should move it, but her fingers refused to budge.

He slid half on top of her, pressing her back into the pillows. "Aye, I should have just used the English, my heart." He pushed closer, his lips touching her ear, his breath hot on her neck. "Aye, that is what I've been calling ye… my heart."

Bree caught her breath, heart pounding. He stayed where he was, lips lightly brushing her neck. It was simply impossible to think.

"Aye, *mo ceisd*." He took a deep breath and slowly withdrew her hand from under his shirt, adopting a rueful expression. "I've had every intention of moving slow with ye, but ye make it right difficult on a man."

She really didn't want him to leave, but she was a little unsure if she was ready for what might happen if he stayed. She found herself blushing again.

"I'll fetch ye something to eat," Ruan murmured, rising from her side and buttoning his shirt. "Ye must rest and gain your strength."

She watched him go, secretly admiring his muscular figure and then mystified at her thoughts and still exhausted, allowed her heavy lids to fall once again.

The next time she woke, the sun had fallen. The smells of the evening meal wafted up from below, accompanied by the occasional hearty laugh. She was alone. Her dress lay neatly folded at the foot of the bed, and she hurriedly slipped it on. After several minutes, she ventured down the narrow, creaky steps to the common room of the tiny inn.

Hesitating in the shadows, she peeked at the bustling scene. All the locals seemed to gather here, men, women and a few children. All chattering loudly, all dining on what looked like more porridge, herring and bannocks. The thought of eating fish and bannocks again was hardly appealing.

In the corner, Merry and Isobel sat alongside an elderly man, and then she saw him. Ruan was almost in the center of the room, leaning comfortably against a table, laughing down at a buxom young woman standing very close.

Bree's heart pounded loudly in her ears. As she watched, the woman tittered, sending Ruan a seductive pout. Feeling utterly betrayed Bree whirled, almost running up the steps as hot tears collected under her lids.

She was a fool.

Of course, with all the beautiful women incessantly throwing themselves in his path, he could hardly maintain an interest in someone such as herself. Throwing the door open with a gulp, she stepped into the room only to be promptly caught from behind.

"Ach! Why are ye running from me, lass?" Ruan captured her about the waist, reeling her to face him.

"I'm not!" she lied, trying to pull away, but he was too strong.

"I'm nae a fool!" he said, his dark eyes smoldered. "I ken well enough ye've little reason to trust me, but this is beyond absurd! I hardly spoke to the lass! Even if I did, 'twould have no meaning!"

"She seemed quite...pleased!" Bree gulped, a crease forming between her brows.

"Ye think I ken naught of loyalty?" He bristled with a scowl. "Do ye think I'm that desperate to bed anything?"

Perhaps she was being unfair, but it was difficult when she was an obligation to him, nothing more. He'd never have picked her on his own; and, she was quite plain. At that, she did burst into tears and tried to pull away. "She was beautiful!"

Ruan let her go and she escaped to the opposite side of the room, sniveling and wiping her tears with her hands, feeling raw and foolish. There was a short silence, one in which she didn't dare look at him. She heard his footsteps behind her soon enough. Strong fingers gently grasped her shoulders, turning her once more his direction. He leaned down to look into her face.

His expression softened. With eyes crinkling in some form of amusement, he said, "Aye, I suppose there are many bonny lasses, and I may see many of them, but whatever they may be... they will never be Bree."

Thinking of the future bonny lasses they had yet to meet, Bree frowned, turning away. "I'm certain I'm nothing compared to... to..."

"All the women of my past?" He finished for her, giving his lip a bitter twist.

She was not thinking that. However, now that he mentioned it, she wanted to hear his answer. She nodded.

"Aye, well, honestly... I canna recall much about them, and I've no desire to do so. Back then, I thought only of myself and I never thought of the pain I caused. Aye, 'twas considered manly to have your way with women and leave when ye tired of them." Ruan's eyes held an expression of embarrassment mixed with shame. "But, after seeing the pain my mother suffered and Jenna's...My eyes opened to my folly. If ye could only know...'tis because of my past that I truly cherish ye more and will be all the more fiercely loyal. I ken well enough what ye are, and I'll do anything nae to lose ye."

It was a good answer, and her heart warmed a little.

"I'll spend the rest of my days proving it to ye," he said, his thumb gently traced her cheek.

Yes, she was falling for the man. She had been, since the moment she had met him.

"'Tis Bree that I want, ye wee fool, the most suspicious and untrusting lass in the Highlands," he said with a smile. "Why would I wish for aught else?"

At that, she looked away and whispered grimly, "But you didn't choose me!"

Ruan's expression lightened. "Aye, I did."

"You thought I was Aislin—" Bree shook her head.

He laid a finger on her lips and slid his hands down her arms to encase her fingers with his. "It matters naught how we met, but I do know one thing, lass, and I know I chose ye. I remember quite well the day I did."

At that, her interest was piqued.

"Aye," he said, as he pulled her close. His voice dropped into a husky whisper. "When I rode away with Robert…" His voice faded at the mention of Robert, breaking a little with sadness.

Bree's hand lifted of its own accord to touch his shoulder briefly in a gesture of sympathy.

He held still and then continued. "Aye, that day…I knew I wanted ye. 'Twas that day I decided I would try to win your heart, even though… I'm nae worthy of it and I've little to offer ye, lass."

She caught her breath, surprised.

"I thought to court ye slowly, *mo ceisd*," he said ruefully. "But, then I was wounded and we had to leave… and I kept thinking ye did nae want me nor trust me to provide for ye… and… I *still* canna promise ye a roof…"

They stared at each other, and then his eyes took on an expression that made her heart pound.

Leaning close, he whispered with some difficulty, "Words are useful, but then… there are times that one should simply… feel."

His hot breath blew against her neck, sending shivers down her spine.

Mesmerized, she saw his mouth come closer.

This was no light, tender brushing of the lips; the kiss was overpowering and sensual. His tongue immediately sought entry, parting her lips with a demanding mastery in a deep exploration that made her senses reel. She experienced the strangest sensation that she was a mere observer standing several feet away, for she'd never melt against him in such abandon, or open her mouth wider to invite such an achingly sweet possession. She desired nothing more than the touch of his tongue on hers and the uncertainties, the jealousy, simply vanished.

Somehow, they had collapsed sideways onto the bed; he pushed her back, hands skimming the curve of her hips before sliding to unlace her bodice. He was kissing the side of her neck and a throaty moan escaped her lips. His fingers slid under her gown, slipping it over her shoulder and his mouth followed it. The most exquisite of sensations burned through her, and she arched closer in his arms.

There was a loud whack as Ruan fell sideways off the bed.

Bree scrambled back to see Merry wielding a broom, pummeling her brother as he sprawled on the floor, protecting his head with his arms.

"Merry! Stop!" he shouted, voice muffled by the floor.

"What kind of a beast are ye?!" Merry shrieked hysterically, jabbing him repeatedly with the broom.

"Ach, Merry!" Isobel chuckled from the door.

"He was licking Bree!" the little girl screeched, lunging for Ruan as he attempted to move.

With a swiftness that belied her age and bulk, Isobel deftly disarmed the little girl and tossed the broom aside.

However, Merry was not one to abandon a cause so lightly; she threw herself in a flurry of kicking and biting, once more knocking Ruan down. He fell against the wooden bed frame, striking his head against the post with a loud thud.

"Fires of Hell!" he shouted. "Get her off me!"

Smothering her laughter, Isobel caught Merry's ear and pulled her off. "Merry, he was nae doing aught that he shouldn't have done, weeks ago."

"But 'tis disgusting!" Merry protested, twisting to Bree. "He was hurting ye!"

Bree hurriedly shook her head in denial. Despite the humiliation of the situation, she could not have the little girl thinking her brother had caused harm.

Merry's mouth dropped open and a look of pure betrayal suffused her pointed face. "Ye liked it?"

"Ach, lass," Isobel smiled, pushing Merry roughly to the door.

"Someday, ye'll find love yerself, and ye'll see then that it can be a good thing. Now, 'tis time to eat."

"'Tis revolting!" Merry shouted. "I'll never let a man lick me!"

The door closed behind them with a bang.

Bree took a deep breath and wriggled back into her bodice, not daring to look at Ruan.

He rose to his feet with an exaggerated groan. "I'd best see to the wee spitfire," he said. He paused, looking down at her before leaning down to kiss the top of her head and to ask in a whisper, "So, did ye like it?"

She blushed scarlet.

JEALOUSY

Taking a deep breath, Ruan closed the door softly behind him. He was grateful for Merry's interruption. He did not want to rush with Bree. With a mere flash of those green eyes, she'd ignited an inferno of passion and he winced at the readiness of his body. One moment, he'd been angry and in a keen distress over her lack of trust. The next, he had found himself lying on her, trailing his tongue on the soft swell of her shoulder intent on undressing her as quickly as possible. Aye, where was his honor? How could he think to bed Domnall's daughter when he could not even provide for her? But, all such honorable thoughts fled with memories of her soft skin. He wanted to rip her clothing with his bare hands, devour every inch of her and shout, not in anger, but from the sheer intensity of what burned inside him. Aye, she was quiet and shy, but her lips were alive with a passion he'd never tasted before.

However, it must wait until he secured a place as Cameron's man. It was the right thing to do.

Straightening his plaid, he headed down the stairs to focus on Merry. She sat with Isobel in the far corner and when she spied him, slammed her tankard down with a loud clash.

Several pairs of eyes turned their way.

Ruan scowled. With Merry's current mood, they would likely provide full entertainment for those gathered there that night.

Isobel smiled as he took his seat, but catching Merry's black expression, she murmured a warning. "Be nice, lass."

"What were ye doing?" Merry asked bluntly, glowering.

Ruan squirmed, twitching several fingers in the silent plea for her to lower her voice. She inspected him up and down, waiting, and when the silence became unbearable, he licked his dry lips. "Doing?" He feigned ignorance, only temporarily delaying the inevitable.

Merry raised a wicked brow and then stood to hover over him, raising her voice. "Why were ye licking Bree?"

Ruan winced. Grasping her arm, he yanked her down on the bench as a round of chuckles circled the room.

"Be done!" he snapped roughly, but his heart melted at Merry's genuine distress. She was scared. In his recent confusion of late, he'd all but ignored her.

He sighed.

Aye, she was his wee sister, the one he'd been fighting for, but she was also the reason he was in his current predicament, he added wryly to himself. He pulled her into a warm hug. "Forgive me, Merry. I've been selfish, a bit distracted of late."

She was rigid at first, but then clung to him tightly. "Aye," she nodded, but added with a devilish grin, "but I haven't missed your constant pestering."

Ruan raised a brow, thrilled to see her smiling. "Pestering?"

"You're a bit smothering, treating me like a bairn. 'Tis nice to have Bree distract ye." Merry's humor disappeared in an instant, and she pulled out of his embrace, rising from the bench to stare at him in disgust. "But I did nae think ye were going to lick her! Why would ye?"

Ruan shook his head, taking a deep breath. It wouldn't be the last time he regretted Fearghus still walked, if only he'd done more than wound the man in their last meeting.

"Were ye... trying to make her cry?" Merry frowned.

"No!" He replied vehemently.

Merry's eyes were large, dark, glowering. "I did nae think ye'd ever hurt a woman, even if ye were drunk."

Ruan leaned forward, gently cupping her chin in his palm. "I've made many mistakes, and I've hurt many people, but nae like ye think, Merry. I swear it. When a woman loves a man, she... finds... pleasure in those things. It doesn't make her cry."

"Oh?" Merry's lips lifted in a sneer of challenge. "Does Bree love ye?"

The voices in the room hushed, more than one person strained forward to hear his reply.

He exhaled an exasperated breath.

Isobel spared him, waving a hand and pointing to Bree hovering near the bottom of the stairs.

"Bree, love, take a seat," the old woman called, grabbing Merry's wrist and pulling her down onto the bench next to her. She sent her a fierce warning to behave with her brows.

Ruan settled back, watching Bree's approach. Everything about her heightened his senses, affecting his very breathing, from the tumble of brown curls cascading over her shoulders, to the curve of her lips, to the slight unconscious swaying of her hips as she walked. Several men gawked at her longer than he liked, and he sent them a dark look. They obligingly returned to their cups.

Bree timidly took her seat next to him, nodding shyly in greeting, and he let his gaze rove over her figure. Desire surged in him. He wanted to pull her close and thrust his tongue between those sweet, glistening ruby lips.

A burst of pain exploded in his knee, tearing him from his thoughts. He swore as Merry kicked him again, apparently for good measure.

"Are ye being foolish?" the little girl hissed.

Ruan frowned suspiciously, drawing his knees out of her reach. She hardly appeared frightened or upset. No, this time, her brown eyes were seething with jealousy.

The Innkeeper's wife appeared. "About that dress," she said to Isobel, tapping a finger on her chin. "I've a lass the same size, and she's a gown or two that would serve ye quite well."

"Bree's smaller than most," Isobel pursed her lips as both women eyed Bree speculatively. "It has to be right warm, though. The snow is already falling in the mountains."

Bree frowned, confused.

With a slight smile, Ruan studied her through half-closed lids, settling back again to continue his bold appraisal when a sharp jab in his hand once more jolted his attention to Merry. The vixen had stabbed him with the end of her blunt knife.

"Be done, Merry!" he barked, in unexpected pain. "Ye've no cause to be jealous!"

"Jealous? Of Bree?" Merry's nostrils flared. "I *like* Bree!"

"Then, what is the problem?" Ruan glared, rubbing his hand. She'd almost drawn blood.

"You!" she spat, on the verge of tears. "I don't like ye, nae anymore!"

In the past, he'd simply have swept her into his arms, and a hug would have healed the pain. However, this suddenly new Merry was complex. He didn't have the foggiest notion of what she meant nor what thoughts were running rampant behind those snapping eyes. Temper flaring a little, he glared. "By the Saints, Merry! Now is nae the time to turn into a bloody woman! I'm tortured enough with Bree. I canna be guessing about ye as well!"

At that, Bree frowned a little. "Tortured?"

He blinked. "I only meant … ye are a wee bit … bedeviling … at times—"

She glanced away.

"Aye, I've heard ye call her meddling and troublesome," Merry announced.

Bree's green eyes flashed alive.

Taken aback, Ruan turned on his sister. "Are ye daft?"

"I heard ye, telling Ewan, afore ye left on the raid," Merry replied with a hostile flare of nostrils. "Can ye deny it?"

"I can scarce recall what I might have said then," Ruan said. He glowered at his little sister before turning to Bree. "And I'm sure I only meant ye were troublesome … on occasion … but nae like either of ye are thinking!"

Bree said nothing, her lips tensed a little, but she took a deep breath, and helped herself to a bannock.

"Aye, well, I've never heard ye complain of all the other women ye said enjoyed ye, Ruan." Merry piped, dark eyes tightening maliciously.

Bree's hands clenched a little at the mention of other women, and Ruan drew his brows into a firm scowl. "Ach, Merry! This time, ye are speaking far out of turn! There is no cause for such impertinence!"

"Ye've said yourself, time and again, that ye had many, many, many women –"

"Many, many, many?" Ruan repeated, slamming his fist on the table. "What devil are ye possessed with, lass?"

To his surprise, Merry's mouth shut instantly with a gulp as she burst into tears. Isobel laid a comforting hand on the little girl's shoulder, pursing her mouth in disapproval, and even Bree sent him a dark look.

He stared at all three of them, at a loss, and then stood abruptly.

A quick glance about revealed what he had feared. He was the sole amusement of the entire common room. He met their gaze boldly and executed a bow with an extra flourish. He kicked the door open and strode across the courtyard to the stables, swearing loudly.

At least the horses were understandable.

***

Across the table, Bree could feel the heat of Merry's anger. The little girl furrowed her brows in a deep line and stuck her tongue out at Ruan's disappearing back.

"Yer right cantankerous of late," Isobel said. She pinched Merry on the cheek. "'Tis time for bed."

"I'm nae tired," Merry growled.

"Aye, but ye've tortured Ruan enough for one day," Isobel answered, with a chuckle. Rising, she forced Merry to stand. "'Tis time to sleep, ye can torment him again in the morning."

Not wanting to be alone, Bree followed them back to their attic room.

It had been a confusing day.

Merry was bundled, still protesting, into bed and Isobel settled next to her with an extended sigh. Sounds from below drifted their way as Bree slipped under the covers. Someone began to sing. Others clapped their hands, and she found herself wondering what Ruan was doing and with whom. Her imagination had taken a dark turn when the door inched open, and she felt a wash of guilt. She really was a nastily suspicious 'lass'. She hurriedly turned away, feigning sleep.

He stumbled a little in the darkness, cursing under his breath, and dropped a small bundle on the bed.

"These are a warmer dress and shoes," he explained shortly. "I'm nae a wealthy man, but at least they are new."

Bree sat up slowly.

She'd never had anything new. She traced the weave of the cloth with a finger, at a loss for words.

"Ye can try them on in the morning," Ruan yawned, stretching beside her and folding his arms under his head. "We leave at dawn."

She ran her fingers over the shoes, striving to understand the man next to her, and her thoughts swerved in directions she seemed to be traversing more of late. His dark eyes, the strong line of his jaw, his nearness made her blood tingle. How could she actually sleep?

To her utter annoyance, he promptly drifted off.

Sourly, she scooted as far from him as she could, clutching the bundle to her chest.

She awoke to the sound of Isobel's voice ordering Merry to rise.

"Why did we have to sell that horse?" Merry grumbled, struggling with her dress. Her head emerged and she added pointedly, "I can actually ride it!"

Bree sat up slowly. Ruan was nowhere to be found.

Isobel stood by the door with her things already tied in a bundle. "Bree, love, bring our wee beastie down when she is ready. 'Tis time we left."

"I'm ready," Merry growled, stomping after Isobel and slamming the door.

A draft of cold wind rattled the shutters as Bree swung her legs over the bed. She blew on her fingers and shook out the new dress. It was blue and made of thick wool. A pair of green stockings rolled onto the floor next to the leather shoes. She dressed hurriedly, staring at the new shoes peeking from under the hem of the dress. She smiled, thinking of Ruan and the way his eyes crinkled when he laughed.

The door flung back and Merry trudged in, kicking it shut and yelling, "Ye fobbing, mewling, beef-witted maggot!"

In spite of the shock, Bree's lips twitched.

Merry glowered in response.

"You are so much like him," Bree finally said.

The little girl folded her arms and scowled.

Bree's smile widened.

For a moment, the little girl seemed as if she'd leave, but then she sidled to the edge of the bed, hands twisted nervously behind her back.

"He loves you more than anything, Merry," Bree said softly. As the little girl's eyes lit, she knew she'd guessed the source of the problem. She sighed. "He just doesn't know what to do with me. He has a kind heart, and he's … stuck with me."

"See that he doesn't love ye," Merry whispered. Her words were harsh, but her tone pleading as she lunged, wrapping her thin arms about Bree's neck.

There was a shrill whistle from the bottom of the stairs.

"Isobel wants us," Merry murmured. Taking Bree's hand, she pulled her down the steps.

The common room was empty except for Isobel. She pointed to two bowls of porridge, watching Merry cling to Bree with a pleased twinkle in her eyes. Her lips wisely remained sealed. They had almost finished eating when the door opened and Ruan entered. He didn't notice her at first, striding over to give the Innkeeper and his wife a warm farewell, but then he turned and spied her. An expression crossed his face that curled her very toes as he took in the blue dress and the leather shoes. Then, Merry jumped up, moving to block his view and Bree bowed her head.

When she looked up, he was gone.

Sighing, she followed Merry out of the door, wrapping her plaid close.

The two horses were saddled and ready. Isobel mounted with a groan. "I'll be grateful when this day is done."

"Why canna I ride my own?" Merry grumbled, stomping her feet. She squawked as her brother caught and easily tossed her behind Isobel.

"Ye'll be riding with Isobel, lass." Ruan cut her complaints short. "That's an end to it."

At his dark scowl, Merry snapped her mouth shut, but her brows drew into a scowl of her own as he swung easily into the saddle behind Bree.

Bree swallowed a sigh. It promised to be a miserable journey, not for the weather, which was perversely bright and beautiful, but for Merry's venom and Ruan's disturbing nearness. Even though the beast had been the spawn of evil, she suddenly regretted the loss of her horse. Almost anything would have been better than suffering the intense hatred radiating from Merry while perched in Ruan's lap.

They set out in the crisp, morning air. A heron flapped lazily overhead, long legs trailing, as it followed them curiously for a time. They left the trees and headed into the barren wilds, and she saw nothing for leagues save the lonely tracks of rabbit and deer.

"Aye, 'tis a bleak place," Ruan said, seeming to sense her thoughts. "But bonny in its own right."

Bree furrowed her brow, inspecting the wide expanse of brown heather and mud for shreds of beauty as the cold wind bit her face.

Ruan laughed, "Your silence seems to disagree."

"What is so amusing?" Merry called from behind, craning around Isobel's girth for a better look.

Ruan didn't reply. Instead, he kicked his horse forward and upon reaching even ground, broke into a canter to cover a great distance. By evening, they had left the barren moors, traveling alongside a river for a time that eventually drained into another loch. The terrain here was green with pine trees and little snow.

The sun was sinking low on the horizon when they reached a small village; several cottagers raised their hands in greetings as they arrived. An elderly man called Ruan's name as they reined in before a large croft.

"'Tis right glad I am to see ye, lad," the man said with a grin, revealing several missing teeth. "'Tis been far too long."

"Aye." Ruan laughed as he dismounted and slapped his arm around the man's shoulders. They walked to the side of the windowless croft as several young girls emerged from within. Bree slid stiffly out of the saddle, staggering a little as her feet hit the ground, but Isobel's ready hand caught her elbow, providing support.

"Step inside, love." The woman nodded encouragingly. "'Tis my kinfolk."

The evening passed in a haze.

The humble croft filled with family members spanning three generations; there were so many that Bree lost count. One of the girls passed bowls of porridge made with oats and a little meat and Bree dutifully swallowed a mouthful between yawns. She allowed her heavy lids to close, just for a moment, and awoke sometime later to a pleasant burr beneath her ear.

"Aye," Ruan laughed heartily. "'Twas nae my grandest moment, to be sure."

Isobel and several others attempted to stifle their laughter.

"Ach, ye've woken the lass, love," Isobel said. She leaned

forward to brush a lock of hair from Bree's cheek.

Bree blinked and slowly sat up. She was on the floor next to Ruan and had been sleeping with her head upon his chest. She frowned in sleepy confusion.

"We'd best rest." Isobel struggled to her feet. "We should leave at dawn, though I'd love to stay a spell, mayhap next time."

Ruan yawned, placing a gentle hand on Bree's shoulder and pulling her back to his side.

She tensed a moment, unused to the intimacy of his gesture, but gradually felt drowsy and safe. She nestled closer, sliding her hand over his chest, unaware her fingers had slid under his shirt until she felt the heat of his bare skin. Her eyes popped open as he audibly caught his breath, but he didn't move her hand. She could feel his heart quicken beneath her fingers, and it was strangely comforting to discover he was not all that much different than herself. Neither spoke, nor moved, and finally, her lids closed once again, and she succumbed to the irresistible call of sleep.

As dawn painted the morning skies, Bree was yet again on the back of a horse, with Ruan planted solidly behind her. Merry's mood had blackened even further. For the fifth time that morning, she had kicked Isobel's horse forward, forcing the animal to quicken its pace to edge in front of Ruan, thereby allowing her to twist and send him a poisonous glare.

"Be done, Merry," Ruan's deep voice resonated.

Merry didn't reply, instead she tossed her hair and lifted her nose in disdain. A few minutes later, she glanced over her shoulder again, sending Bree a black look.

"Merry!" Ruan warned.

"Ye don't have to hold her like that," the little girl observed waspishly.

"I'm not ... holding her any special way," Ruan growled in reply, even as his fingers slid slowly back and forth over Bree's hip. "And, even if I were, 'tis no concern of yours."

Merry's nostrils flared.

They plodded in silence for a time, Isobel's horse gradually slowing until they were abreast. Without warning, Merry's foot lashed out in a spiteful kick, this time striking Ruan squarely on the shin.

"Ye bloody wee beast!" he shouted.

Merry smiled, practically purring.

Snorting in exasperation, Ruan urged his horse faster, out of his sister's reach. They pressed forward, traveling south over moors and down steep ravines. Bree forced her attention to the landscape in the attempt to avoid the disturbing heat of the man behind her. After several hours, what she'd found dull and gray before became more interesting in a rustic, wild sort of way. The smell of the damp leaves, the rustle of the evergreens, was almost comforting. She smiled at herself. She must be falling ill from boredom.

Then, Ruan began to speak, asking her about her childhood, and the things she liked. She was shy at first, but as time wore on, their conversation became easy and warming to her heart. They stopped several times to rest the horses and eat bannocks and apples, laughing, and each sharing parts of themselves the other found surprising.

Merry glared, chewing her apples in silence.

As the afternoon wore on, the wind began to howl, and icy

droplets of snow occasionally stung her cheeks. Pausing on the shores of a small loch, Ruan briefly considered making camp, but he gave into Merry's insistence that they move on, so great was her fear of the kelpies in the water.

The sun hung low on the horizon before they finally halted before a tiny stone cottage nestled amidst the dim shapes of rustling pines. The elderly couple greeted Ruan like a son, attempting to press their meager supper into their hands, but Ruan would have none of it. After seeing the women safely bundled into the small barn nearby for the night, he spent several long hours gathering peat and mending a fence until the night made it impossible to see.

As darkness fell, Isobel spread her plaid in the hay near a large cow softly chewing her cud, and sank down upon it with a loud, exaggerated sigh.

Exhausted, Bree dropped next to her, curling in her plaid, and Merry burrowed close. She could not help but smile at the little girl; she displayed no signs of jealousy the instant Ruan was out of sight. The thought of Ruan triggered a host of other thoughts, few of them unrelated to his powerful kiss and fiery touch. Ashamed to be dwelling on such things, she forced her eyes shut, but she found sleep elusive.

It was late when Ruan finally stumbled in, disturbing several of the hens from their slumber. They squawked, ruffling their feathers as he stretched and settled next to Bree, throwing his plaid over them both.

He was asleep in moments.

Bree waited until his breathing fell into a slow rhythm before surrendering to the temptation to turn his way. The sky had cleared and dim moonlight filtered through the open door, illuminating the man who occupied her thoughts with increasing frequency. She stared, a little guiltily. He was unusually handsome. She propped her chin on her hand, indulging in her curiosity, wondering what it would feel like to be the object of his desire. His carved lips beckoned her touch. Finally giving into the temptation, she timidly touched one with her finger.

Gradually, she grew aware his eyes were open.

Suddenly ashamed, she moved away quickly, but he caught her hair and twisted her face back towards his. Sliding his hand around the base of her neck, he pulled her slowly down. Her resistance melted with the first touch of his lips.

The kiss was slow, different from the passionate invasion of before, and having an even more powerful effect. Her heart beat wildly as his lips embraced hers with extraordinary tenderness and her mouth opened of its own accord, inviting him deeper. He took his time, exploring her lips, and she lost herself completely to the wealth of sensations rippling through her. As his hand slid down her spine, she shivered involuntarily, and she could feel his lips smile into hers.

It was enough to break the spell.

With flaming cheeks, she pulled back.

Ruan sat up, resting his forearm across his knees. He stared at her for a time before whispering, "'Tis just as well, lass. 'Tis the wrong time and place for this."

She watched him step outside, feeling a mixture of relief and disappointment. Her mind was still racing sometime later when he returned to her side. After encircling her in a possessive arm, he fell asleep. To her astonishment, her lids grew heavy, and she quickly followed, feeling secure.

Bree awoke with a gasp.

The shock of the water was so cold it made her skin burn.

Ruan sprang to his feet, flinging his wet hair. He drew his dirk in one swift motion, only to shove it back when he spied Merry standing with an empty bucket dangling from her hands.

"Fires of Hell!" Ruan shouted. "Why? Why, Merry? Why?"

"Ye overslept," she piped cheerfully, but with brows drawn in a disapproving line. "Dawn has come and gone."

It was not quite true, the sky outside had barely begun to lighten.

Bree began to wring her skirts, having mercifully avoided most of the water, she observed brother and sister from the corner of her eye. Ruan glowered, shaking his wet hair. He was soaked, having endured the brunt of the onslaught. Then, he lunged toward his sister.

Merry valiantly stood her ground much longer than any other would have done in similar circumstances, but as Ruan reached her, she hurled the bucket his way and bolted. Easily deflecting it, Ruan dashed after her and scooped her up with one strong arm.

"Be done!" he barked. "I'll nae have ye behaving this way!"

"I would ye'd never met her!" Merry hissed, clenching her fists. "From the beginning ye only noticed her and now 'tis worse. The rest of us are thrown away!"

Her chin was shaking, her eyes large with unshed tears and Ruan's frustration visibly evaporated. With a heavy sigh, he enveloped her in his arms.

"'Tis nae true, Merry," he finally said. "I'll always love ye, I'm just a bit… ye'll have to be patient. There are times when ye need to let me be, lass."

Merry's back straightened and she kicked his shin once again. "Then, ye don't really care! Ye don't think ye are wrong!"

"I'm not!" He howled in pain.

"Aye, ye are!" she shouted at the top of her lungs. "I'm still your sister! Ye wouldn't even notice if the MacDonald came and snatched me away, ye only see Bree!"

Ruan paled, he said nothing as Isobel entered the barn.

"What is all this shouting, lad?" She asked, knitting her brows in concern.

Merry pushed past her and after a moment Ruan followed, leaving Isobel to eye Bree, still dripping wet, with curiosity.

"Aye," Isobel finally said. "They'll sort it out, lass. Let's be off now, it might snow."

They bade their farewells to the elderly couple and mounted their horses. Brother and sister were uncommonly subdued the remainder of the morning and they all traveled in silence. It was early afternoon and they had just cantered to the bottom of a hill and into a small thicket of trees when Ruan motioned to a gurgling stream.

"We'll water the horses," he announced curtly.

It was a pleasant enough glen. The gnarled trees moved softly in the cold wind as several deer nearby lifted their heads in languid curiosity, observing them for a time from a safe distance before returning to their grazing.

Bree shivered, rubbing her stiff neck when a strange whistle chased by a thud startled them all.

Stunned, she stared dumbly at a feathered shaft of a quivering arrow, embedded deeply in the trunk of a slender tree before Ruan knocked her down to the ground, shouting.

Several more whistles thudded about them and then Ruan was on his horse. Crouching low over the animal's neck, he brandished his dirk as three men, their faces swathed in cloth to hide their identities, appeared from seemingly nowhere. He wheeled the beast into them before leaping off to take one down. The other two fell back, endeavoring to avoid the frightened beast before recovering to resume their advance.

Bree didn't have time to be afraid. Instead, she found herself coldly calculating, picking up several sharp stones to throw. One of the rocks hit its target, bouncing off the man's head with a sickening thud that caused him to lurch her way. Then, all at once, she found herself focused solely on her own survival, trying to escape his brutal advance.

He lunged toward her, raising his sword with a curse, but then Ruan was there, plunging his blade through the attacker's back until it protruded from the man's belly. The man clawed at it fruitlessly before sinking to the ground without a word.

It was over, almost as soon as it had begun, Isobel still hovering nearby, clutching Merry in a protective embrace. Both were pale and silent. For a time, Ruan simply stood, blood dripping from his sword, and then one of the men groaned. Slowly, he knelt, and pulled the cloth from his face with visible reluctance.

He stood with a curse, turning white.

Bree stepped closer and then her heart leapt into her throat.

Gerland, Ruan's nephew, lay in the wet grass, blood trickling from his mouth.

"I'm cursed!" Ruan hissed between his teeth. He ripped the cloth coverings from the remaining two men and choked, "These are my own kinsmen!"

"Ruan," Gerland gasped, lifting a weak hand.

Slowly, Ruan returned to kneel stiffly by his side.

"Aye," Gerland said with a wheezing, bitter laugh. "Ye always wanted Dunvegan. Only my father and Tormod stand in yer way now."

Ruan's dark eyes widened, startled. "I've never lusted for it to warrant killing my own kin." He whispered hoarsely.

Gerland's jaw clenched in pain, and he gritted his teeth. Blood flowed through his hands clutched over his chest. The wound was fatal and they all knew it. Finally, he managed a grim smile. "I ken that well enough now, uncle. Nay, I always knew it. I was… too weak to stand against father… I seek yer forgiveness, ere I leave this world."

"'Tis I who should seek yours," Ruan wept, placing his hand over his nephew's trembling fingers. "I've brought nothing but death upon us all. Robert, Albin…"

"Nay, listen!" Gerland said. He struggled to lift his head, adding, "Their deaths are on father's head, nae yours! Tormod hired the men from the north, to burn the crofters, to make it look like Fearghus…The plan was to slaughter both ye and Robert, but they only succeeded with Robert. I was there when father ran him through, it wasna Fearghus…'twas father!" He reached up, fiercely grabbing the front of Ruan's shirt. "This blood is nae on yer head, I swear it!"

Ruan held still.

"I canna do it," His nephew's voice cracked. "Father told me to kill him… I could nae. I…I was seeking father's forgiveness by trying to …kill ye, but I … canna slay ye, either."

Ruan bowed his head.

"Forgive me, uncle." Gerland whispered.

"Aye, die in peace, lad," Ruan replied in a low voice.

It didn't take long.

At last, Gerland groaned, then blood gushed from the corner of his mouth all at once, and he went limp.

Ruan didn't move for some time. Finally, he rose and whispered, "The fault is mine, lad. I should have stopped this, long ago."

"Let us be gone!" Isobel tried to pull Ruan away. "Ye dinna ken 'twas him, lad, ye canna have known."

"No!" Ruan shook his head. He collapsed to his knees. Horrible, great sobs ripped from his chest. "Robert! Robert!" he gasped, choking on his tears.

Bree rushed to his side, and he clung to her, weeping, repeating Robert's name.

"Aye," Isobel murmured. Her face was grey. "'Tis time ye wept for him, lad."

It was some time before his tears finally dried and a deep sadness covered his face.

"We must go, love," Isobel crooned softly. "Michael could be here soon."

Ruan shook his head, rising to his feet grimly. "Aye. I hope he is."

"'Tis too dangerous to stay here," Isobel said, shaking her head.

"I canna leave my nephew here to be eaten by carrion," Ruan grated.

There was no dissuading him.

He lifted Gerland's body onto his horse, taking him a good way to the top of the mountain. There were many stones and it didn't take long to place them over the body. When they finished, Ruan stood for some time before shouting, "Tormod! Ye are no longer a brother of mine!" Tears were heavy in his voice.

Timidly, Bree touched his forearm in a comforting gesture. To her surprise, he whirled upon her, crushing her wordlessly to him, and then lifting her onto the horse said, "We must ride quickly."

They mounted in silence, urging their horses on with great haste, riding the day and long into the night. As an eerie mist descended, they happened upon an abandoned croft and slept. In the morning, Ruan made an announcement.

"Inchmurrin is too dangerous," he said. "Michael will be searching that path. I shall take us to Stalcaire, one of Cameron's smaller holdings. 'Tis nae far."

These words were greeted with smiles. These soon turned into frowns as he pushed them hard on paths that seemed nothing more than goat tracks through the brush. The way was difficult. They rode for hours, rising with the dawn, stopping only in exhaustion and never daring to light a fire.

Bree's stomach continually growled, gnawing in hunger. Aside from a few bites of bannocks swallowed hurriedly as they rode, none of them had eaten much the past few days. After the bannocks were gone, they subsisted on a mixture of oats and water.

Ruan was tense. He slept little, but as the days passed, there were no further signs of pursuit.

They galloped across stretches of the moors, down ravines and around treacherous bogs, until finally, one late morning, they crested at a rise to see before them a loch, large and deep, that gave birth to a river. Stands of birch trees graced the surrounding hills, a stream running through them like a thread of silver. At the edge of the loch, on an islet, perched a small castle.

"Stalcaire," Ruan announced. "One of Cameron's small holdings. We should be safe here whilst I send word to him."

"'Tis nae Inchmurrin, but 'tis wonderful to behold," Isobel said. She smiled in anticipation of a dry bed and a hot meal.

Ruan didn't reply as he pushed forward over the scant earth-covered rocks down to the shore. As they neared, he slowed his pace, frowning at the banners streaming from the castle walls. Sounds of music drifted their way, accompanied by loud guffaws of laughter. Drawing his brows into a brooding scowl, Ruan urged his horse straight to the boats. Several clansmen leapt up in alarm, but upon recognizing him, relaxed and lifted their arms in greeting.

"Come for the feast, Ruan?" one of them asked with a grin.

"Feast?" Ruan repeated.

"His lairdship will be grateful for yer presence," the other man stated.

"The Earl is here?" Ruan's brows lifted in surprise.

"Aye," the man said, nodding solemnly.

"At last, a wee bit of good fortune!" Ruan heaved a sigh of relief, dismounting. "Take me to him, at once!"

He swung Bree down from the horse, lightly brushing her forehead with his lips. She tensed a little, but he didn't seem to notice as he focused his attention on Merry.

"Ye'll be safe now, ye wee beastie," he said, pinching his sister's cheek. "'Tis time ye met Cameron."

"Aye and I'm sure I'll be delighted," Merry grumbled blackly as she followed them all into the boat.

They had scarcely stepped foot in the courtyard when a deep baritone rose to greet them. "It has been far too long, brother!"

The man approaching them with the sleek grace of a cat could be none other than Cameron, the Earl of Lennox. His presence, his every move spoke of elegance, wealth and power. He was long-legged and handsome. Chiseled lips curving in an almost outright sensual manner accented his face. He was of the same age and height as Ruan. Though his hair was several shades darker, they could easily have passed for blood brothers.

Ruan moved close, wearily clasped forearms, and leaned forward to murmur in Cameron's ear.

The man listened, saying nothing, as his dark, compelling eyes swept over them. Then, patting Ruan on the back with a long-fingered hand, he captured Isobel's fingers between his and raised them to his lips. "Ah, 'tis a wondrous sight to behold ye once again, fair Isobel."

Isobel blushed.

Turning to Merry, he executed a courtly bow. "Last I saw, ye were but a wee terror and now I stand before the fairest maiden in Skye. Soon, the mere touch of your hand will be worth a king's ransom."

Merry's mouth dropped open and then her dark eyes began to sparkle.

"I see your charm is fatal to the young as well," Ruan remarked dryly.

"'Tis a gift from the powers that be," Cameron said. His eyes crinkled in what seemed a minute display of humor.

"Aye, but is it a gift from above or below?" Isobel murmured congenially.

Cameron's expression flickered with interest as his attention shifted to Bree.

"Bree," Ruan cleared his throat. "My… wife."

Brows lifting ever so slightly, he cast Ruan a curious glance. "Ruan? Wed?"

"Aye." Ruan's expression grew unreadable.

Bree felt her cheeks redden.

For a fleeting moment, Cameron regarded Ruan in open disbelief for a moment before gallantly kissing Bree's hand. "My Lady Bree, I stand in awe of the rarest of women, but I see your dazzling beauty played no small part in bringing Ruan to his knees."

It was impossible not to smile back at the man.

A NIGHT OF PASSION

Ruan indulged in a prolonged stretch accompanied by an exaggerated yawn.

The sun was setting, casting long shadows across the chamber. From the window, the waning light had turned the loch into a sheet of silver, with not even a ripple on its glassy surface. He must have fallen asleep. He'd bathed, changed into fresh clothing and had sprawled across the bed for a brief moment, but apparently the day had almost passed.

He smiled, a little, recalling Bree's abrupt shyness as he stripped in preparation for his bath. She'd suddenly remembered a promise to Merry and had hurriedly left.

Aye, he'd have to think about what to do now they were safe. His original intention to annul the marriage was unthinkable, and though he suspected she felt the same, he'd never actually discussed the matter. Grimacing in thought, he strode from the chamber and down the steep newel stair in search of Cameron.

He was easy to find.

The Earl of Lennox sprawled before a crackling fire in the small vaulted chamber behind the hall, impeccably dressed in a fine silk shirt and richly woven black breeches. A plump wench balanced on his knee. He was attempting to kiss her as she giggled and tipped a bottle between his lips.

Ruan eyed him thoughtfully.

Cameron only drank when he was upset, and it was exceedingly difficult to upset the Earl of Lennox. Women were the only thing that reliably distressed the man, but he had made it a practice to avoid them. The wench meant nothing. Time and again, he'd seen Cameron's playful act. It never went beyond a kiss. He'd never shared Ruan's brash predilection of casual dalliances.

Not that he did himself, anymore, Ruan thought firmly as he strode into the room.

"Ah, Ruan!" Cameron's face broke into a wide smile.

Ruan paused. Rarely did the man display anything but exceptional self-control. He lived under a guarded mask of restraint, even when relaxed and in the company of friends. His overt display of emotion meant only one thing.

"Ye seem drunk," Ruan stated, folding his arms. "Exceedingly drunk."

Cameron smothered a laugh.

"In fact, I've only seen ye this drunk on your wedding day…days." It was difficult to speak to Cameron concerning marriage. Though he was a year younger than Ruan, he was already a widower six times.

"Aye, ye always were an unusually astute man," the Earl said. He raised his brow to the wench and sent her a sultry look, "I'd warn ye to avoid him, lass, only he's a changed man, now that he's found himself a wee wife."

Ruan frowned, eyeing the woman darkly, and said, "The Earl has had enough of your company."

She looked as if she'd protest, but thinking the better of it, she disappeared with a quick nod.

Cameron didn't seem to mind, but he did heave a growl of exasperation when Ruan appropriated the wine.

"Are ye wed again?" Ruan prompted suspiciously.

The Earl gave a derisive laugh and shrugged. "I'm drunk."

Ruan sighed. He was beginning to lose track of Cameron's marriages. "Who is this one?"

Ignoring the question, Cameron lurched to his feet and stumbled into the hall. Grasping the edge of the high table to steady himself, he searched for another bottle of wine. Upon finding none, he swore, grasping the closest candlestick and dashed it to the wall.

"When?" Ruan asked, grasping his friend firmly by the shoulders to guide him to the nearest bench.

"Ach, this one is nine months gone with a bairn," Cameron laughed, but it was a mirthless laugh.

That was a surprise, but the Earl gave him no time to wonder.

"Nay, 'tis nae mine," the man supplied. He ran his hand through his raven hair. "Another bairn of the King's...'twill be his third that I have in my keeping."

"Then why did ye wed her, lad?" Ruan blinked in surprise.

Cameron looked away but said, "'Twas at the request of the barons. If I had nae wed her, one of Cochrane's kin would have and we canna allow that man to gain more power than he already has. She has kinfolk in both England and France that he'd use against us."

Ruan knew that Cameron detested court affairs, but he could never escape from being deeply mired in them. And, he was far too rich and powerful to remain unwed. It was a shame, the lad was an honorable sort that deserved to find love. Thoughts of love reminded him of Bree and he was suddenly aware he was beginning to grin like a fool.

Cameron hadn't noticed. He was still speaking.

"Heed me well! Cochrane's up to some devilry against the Earl of Mar, but the King is blind. He follows the man like a fool!" Cameron allowed a faint expression of disgust. "Ach, the fool is nothing more than Cochrane's puppet! 'Tis time we dealt with the man!"

The words hung in the air and Ruan wasn't entirely certain if he was speaking of the King or of the King's unscrupulous favorite, Thomas Cochrane. In either case, those words were too dangerous for a man of his position. It only proved that the Earl was exceedingly drunk. "Enough, Cameron. 'Twould nae be wise to be overheard," he said.

"Aye," Cameron agreed and closed his eyes.

"Aye," Ruan nodded.

Silence fell between them.

"Ach, I'm a cursed man," Cameron said finally. "The lass was terrified to wed me, convinced she will nae live the year. Aye, 'tis the only reason I agreed to this madness. I've no faith myself that she'll live past the month of May."

"Nonsense!" Ruan growled in reply.

Cameron lurched back to the table, but this time to splash water on his face from a silver bowl, "Heaven forgive me, but I've never have I met a more disagreeable lass. Aye, she is bonny, in a hard, rotten sort of way ..."

He stumbled a little to the nearest bench and collapsed onto it, covering his face with a hand.

Several servants hovered under the archway uncertainly. Ruan waved them away. The Earl was in no shape to eat or face the numerous guests who always flocked to his table. The silence between them lengthened once more and Ruan found his thoughts wandering to Bree.

It had felt so right, that night in the stables, to hold her close, and to touch her soft skin. He'd wanted to kiss the curve of her neck and more. He still did. He stretched on a nearby bench, lost in thoughts of Bree, and it must have been at least an hour later before he grew aware of Cameron quietly observing him.

"I never thought to see the mighty Ruan wed, trapped by a lass," the Earl commented impassively. "I thought ye, at least, would keep your wits about ye to remain free."

Ruan gave a heavy sigh, suddenly feeling the weight of recent events. "Nay, 'tis I who trapped her," he admitted reluctantly. "I ruined her life to save Merry, poor lass."

Cameron listened as he recounted the events of the past few months, ending with Robert's death and the subsequent journey.

"Tormod and Michael fear ye," the Earl stated, twirling an empty goblet in his hand. "And they are right to do so. I've long said Dunvegan should be yours. We all know it. Tormod has no heir, and I doubt he'll ever get one, Silas is still a priest, and Michael... he deserves death for Robert. None of them warrant aught else after what they've done."

"Aye," Ruan agreed in bitter reluctance.

Cameron sent him an appraising look, "'Tis the first time I've heard ye agree... in words, though I've long known your heart. I told ye some time ago, lad, that it should be done, but ye swore to never spill your brothers' blood."

"Tormod and Michael... I no longer consider brothers. But, I must think on what must be done later," Ruan replied, brushing him aside. "I have more pressing matters for which I must ask your aid."

The Earl's lip twitched in faint amusement. "I've asked ye for help oft enough. I've never found it so terribly difficult."

"This is different," Ruan scowled.

"Aye, asking for help is a sight more humiliating than giving it," Cameron's brow creased in laughter, but his lips remained set in a grim line.

"Merry's annulment–" Ruan began.

"Consider it done," Cameron said, waving his long fingers.

Ruan released a pent breath, relieved. He could only trust Cameron to that extent. When the Earl of Lennox said it would be done, it simply was.

"And, yours? Shall I have your marriage annulled as well?" There was a smile in his voice, though his expression remained serious.

Ruan's scowl deepened.

"My lord!" a piercing voice echoed in the hall. "My lord Earl!"

A woman swept into the hall, tall and willowy, beautiful in a chilling way. Her hair was blonde, twisted in intricate loops to frame her face and her fingers dripped with sparkling gems. A large sapphire draped her long, white neck. She waddled as she walked, belly swollen, heavy with child.

"My lord," she repeated.

Cameron didn't respond to the sound of her shrill voice, but his mouth tightened in a way that made Ruan pause.

It was as close to expressing revulsion as the Earl usually came.

The woman came to a stop before them. Her brows creased with annoyance as her tone sharpened. "My lord!"

Slowly, the Earl rose to his feet, extending a graceful hand to his newly made wife. "Ruan, allow me to introduce ye to the ..." he paused briefly and a small ripple of alarm crossed his face. Shaking his head slightly in the obvious attempt to clear his still wine-muddled thoughts, he continued, "The... Eighth Countess of Lennox, Helo... Heloi—"

"Heloise," the woman finished for him. She blinked, obviously annoyed, and murmured, "And I'm the Seventh Countess of Lennox."

Cameron bowed, faintly discomfited, but it was unclear if it were for the fact he'd forgotten her name or what number she occupied in the long parade of wives.

"I'm honored to make your acquaintance," Ruan replied dutifully.

She smiled and fluttered her lashes flirtatiously.

Her blue eyes were sharp and tiny, and for some odd reason, reminded Ruan much of a vulture. Already, he understood Cameron's distaste for the woman, but found his thoughts interrupted by the arrival of the other guests.

Cameron's table always swarmed with those seeking to gain the Earl's favor, a fact that Ruan knew he hated. The man detested frippery and idle gossip. To watch him, no one would have ever known. Even still drunk, he moved in the hall with sinuous grace, slipping artfully through a host of conversations.

After introducing Ruan to several visiting personages from France, he returned to the high table, attentively assisting the Countess with a strong hand and doting on her as if theirs were truly a love match. Ruan shook his head, amazed at the man's ability to mask his true emotions, but all thoughts of Cameron and his new situation fled as Isobel arrived with Merry and Bree in tow.

Ruan's heartbeat quickened at the sight of Bree. She shyly approached a little stiff in a new gown of a soft, green silk that clung to her slender form in the most pleasing of manners. A blue ribbon captured her hair, but a curl had already escaped its binding to frame her cheek. The simplicity only served to enhance her beauty, and he could only stare.

"My Lady Bree, please join me," Cameron raised his voice, beckoning to the empty chair on his right.

Something in Cameron's tone caught Ruan's attention as the Earl held out his hand, eyeing Bree in an overt appraisal. His blood began to burn, and he found himself striding forward, suddenly not wanting her anywhere near the man. Cameron, who could seduce any woman, wed or unwed by merely walking into the room.

"I see!" Cameron mused with a faint glimmer of humor. "This is nae mere dalliance, lad."

Ruan met his gaze boldly.

The corner of Cameron's lips curved upwards. Clasping Ruan briefly on the shoulder, he gallantly addressed Bree. "I shall call ye, my dearest sister Bree."

"And, what of me?" Merry brazenly interrupted, her dark eyes taking in the entire scene.

Cameron's eyes lit with a smile amidst the circle of laughter. Kissing Merry's hand, he seated her next to Bree with a flourish and signaled the meal to commence. Merry promptly forgot further complaints as platters of mutton, coney and roasted pheasant arrived with pickled eggs, almond cakes and bowls of stewed pears. As the servants poured the fine French wine, the traveling jongleur arrived.

Ruan settled next to Merry, enjoying her cheerful mood before letting his thoughts center once again on Bree. What had come over him? He trusted Cameron. Why had he inexplicably behaved like the fool? He leaned back for a better view. She was obviously uncomfortable, sitting stiffly next to the Earl, her right hand gripping the arm of her chair with white knuckles. Cameron was attempting to set her at ease, speaking to her warmly as he cut and served generous portions of each platter, seeing Bree's trencher well supplied before tending to his disapproving wife.

Suddenly, Merry blocked his vision. "What are ye looking at?" she asked sourly.

Ruan affectionately tousled her hair and managed to win a reluctant smile from her sullen lips. "Ye've nothing to fear, lass," he murmured, setting about carving her a healthy portion of meat.

They had scarcely finished the second course when the Countess stood abruptly, her porcelain skin blanching even whiter. "The bairn," she said, clutching her belly. "'Tis the time!"

With a courteous nod, Cameron murmured, "I wish ye the best of fortunes." Waving to a nearby maid, he commanded, "Send for the midwife."

The Countess sucked in her cheeks. "I've only … been wed two days, 'tis… too soon for yer curse to take hold on me ... isn't it?" Her voice fell and fear crossed her face.

Cameron didn't respond. His expression remained impassive as she left. Then, with a graceful, regretful bow, he excused himself from his guests and retired to the small vaulted chamber attached to the great hall.

After a moment, Ruan followed, joined by Merry and Bree.

The Earl stood before the fire, ignoring their presence, as he poured and drained several goblets of wine. Upon emptying the bottle, he reached for another, but Ruan intervened.

"I think ye've had plenty, lad," he murmured, skillfully extracting the bottle from Cameron's grip.

Cameron took a deep breath and lifted a scornful brow. "Odd, isn't it? I've been wed six… eight times and I've yet to bed any named 'wife'".

Ruan furrowed his brows.

It was going to be a long night.

Cameron fixed him with a baleful eye, and then turned to Bree, "Aye. My first marriage was in England, at the tender age of eleven, an arrangement by my mother against the King's wishes. Her name was …"

"Her name was Camille," Ruan supplied, shoving a chair closer to

Cameron with his foot. "Sit, lad, before ye fall."

"Nay, Camille was my third wife." Cameron disagreed, bitterness heavy in his voice.

"Camille was the first, the weakly lass," Ruan said patiently. He'd recited this list with Cameron many times, and over the years, it had only grown. "Your wedding night was spent reading poems before your mother insisted ye stay away for your health. She died a week later."

"Ah, yes," Cameron conceded, turning back to Bree. "She left me wealthy, or I should say wealthier. I've still yet to see the lands I gained from her."

Bree glanced at Ruan while nodding politely, obviously confused. He gave her an encouraging smile only to find Merry's elbow in his ribs.

"Merry!" Ruan scowled in warning.

Merry scowled in reply.

"Anna, my second wife was a wee bairn, another English lass," Cameron continued, his voice distant, oblivious to his audience. "I gave her a doll, tucked her into bed and left. She survived three years, the only one that lived past the first year," he said. He turned to consult with Ruan once again. "The foul death of the English, was it not?"

Merry's frown deepened and Ruan returned it with one of his own.

"Nay, the Keiths... disposed of her... in retribution for... ach, 'tis no good to be bringing up the past, lad," Ruan replied.

"The foul death of the English, was it not?" The Earl repeated, his voice growing harder.

"Nay," Ruan sighed. "Ye must be thinking of Elizabet, the third wife."

"Bree will be staying with me this night," Merry informed him in a whisper.

"Aye, Anna had only been dead two weeks before I was wed again to Elizabet." Cameron's tone was flat. "If I hadn't left during the wedding feast to fight the Keiths, I'd have fallen victim to the plague as well."

"She is sleeping with me!" Merry hissed.

"The fourth, I canna even recall the lass!" Cameron turned upon Ruan, his brows furrowed in a tight line.

"She was the widow," Ruan sighed in reply, attempting to hurry the conversation. "She was already long ill. Ye didn't even meet her for the wedding. 'Twas when we were fighting the English. The fifth ran off with her lover afore the wedding night and was killed when their horse plunged over the cliff."

"Aye and the sixth drowned herself afraid my touch alone would cause her an unholy death." His lips curved upwards in a half-smile, but there was no mirth in it. "Aye, I suppose it did..."

"That... should not be your burden." Bree cleared her throat, nervously twisting her fingers behind her back. Again, she looked to Ruan in uncertainty.

He sent her a warm smile in reply.

"Ye'll have her marriage annulled!" Merry's demands were only getting louder.

"Be done," Ruan said, clasping Merry's shoulder. "Bree is nae danger to ye, lass. Think of her as a sister."

"Ye mean to keep her?" Merry was outraged.

"Ach, Merry!" Cameron said, sending her a bemused look. "Ruan's in love with the lass. He clearly wants to devour her. I've never seen him look at a woman so."

Ruan's brows lifted in surprise. The man was evidently becoming intoxicated once again. Sober he never betrayed confidences of any sort, including those he only suspected. Although, Ruan supposed, it should be obvious to all that he truly had fallen in love. He glanced at Bree curiously, seeking her reactions.

Her eyes were downcast, but her cheeks were pink.

He smiled.

"Say that isn't so!" Merry insisted, tugging his arm. "Ye said ye would annul it and be done!"

"Merry, the cause is lost," Cameron said. He snagged the wine from Ruan and threw back his head to drain it in several long, impressive gulps. His hand was unsteady as he pointed to Ruan. "Now that ye've happily wed, ye've only given me another thing to envy."

Ruan regarded him in open astonishment. "I've naught for ye to envy, surely!"

"Freedom," Cameron answered. "And now love. Aye, 'tis naught to envy, my friend." His tone was mocking.

"Freedom?" Ruan repeated, astounded. "Ye've more freedom than I!"

"I doubt many would see it that way," Cameron countered, his words slurring a little as he rubbed his temples with his long fingers. "Your wife is exquisite, but 'tis plain to see her heart is pure and kind. That is a thing of dazzling, rare beauty."

Ruan was again surprised at the surge of jealousy running through him.

"Ach, ye love her," the Earl of Lennox said. He shifted unevenly. "I've seen ye desire women, but I've never seen ye jealous over one."

Concerned with Cameron's ever-loosening tongue, Ruan made up his mind. With several long strides, he caught the Earl deftly as he collapsed. "Come, lad. 'Tis time ye were in bed."

He was grateful that Cameron gamely complied in silence. He guided the man out of the chamber and up to the narrow stairs leading to his private rooms. After depositing him on his bed, Ruan returned to find the vaulted chamber empty.

For a time, he gazed into the fire, brooding, wondering if Bree was distressed, if Cameron's words had caused her to find disappointment in him.

Finally, he permitted himself to search for her.

***

Bree lay next to Merry, brushing the little girl's hair back in slow, soothing strokes. The instant Ruan left, Merry's animosity disappeared. Now, she was tearful, clingy, and immediately seeking the comfort of Bree's arms.

Cameron's talk of love had been particularly disturbing, for Merry, because she was certain it meant Ruan would stop loving her, and for Bree, because Ruan hadn't fervently agreed with what the man had said.

She sighed, slightly ashamed to be pining for Ruan's love.

While he'd kissed her and implied that he loved her, he'd never actually said the words.

She felt foolish.

She sighed, wondering just exactly when she'd falling in love with the man herself. It had happened so gradually, she couldn't point at the exact time. After a time, satisfied Merry was asleep, she extricated herself from the child's embrace as the door of the chamber opened and Isobel marched in.

"I canna believe the arrogance of that high-handed harridan! Ach, what an ungrateful crone!" Isobel's chin jiggled in outrage. "Sending me from her side, nae wanting common folk to touch her noble skin or that of her wee bairn!"

Bree stared, uncertain of what to say, but she need not have worried. Isobel was not listening. She stomped about the chamber, shaking out the plaids, refolding them, stoking the fire, and rearranging everything in her path as she complained bitterly about the arrogant Countess and how the poor young Earl deserved more than a shackling to the Personification of Conceit herself.

Somewhere in the middle of the tirade, the door creaked open once again, and Bree felt a warm hand slide over her shoulder. She jumped, but Ruan was prepared, skillfully twisting her out the door and pulling her up to his chamber before she could scarcely react. The room was dark; the fire had long since died. Moonlight streamed through the open window. There was a chill in the air, and she shivered, though, not entirely from the cold.

"I've rarely seen Isobel so riled," Ruan chuckled a little.

"The Countess seems…" Bree began in Isobel's defense, but the thought fled as Ruan crushed her close. His lips descended to devour hers for several long, glorious moments before he wrenched away. He pressed her back, hard against the door, and she felt his breath on her cheek.

"I... canna bear to lose ye, lass," he whispered in her ear. "If I were an honorable man, I'd have this marriage annulled."

Her heart filled with an ache of disappointment so deep that she almost missed his next words.

"I must be off to Dunvegan and soon. I... canna make ye mine, I might... not return. Domnall or Cameron could find ye another husband if I—"

"No!" Bree said, and pushed him back violently. "I don't want another husband!"

The thought was preposterous.

He fell back a few paces, but then he reached to pull her fiercely against his chest.

She stood there, encircled in his arms, feeling the rhythmic breathing of his chest. "I feel... safe with... you," she confessed softly.

Ruan expelled a deep breath and then whispered, "I dinna say ye are safe, lass, and I ne'er said I was an honorable man. If ye only kent what I've been thinking this past hour... a maiden would perish from blushing."

Oddly, she smiled.

"My heart wants to make ye mine before I go." He nuzzled her ear and nipped it. "Aye, with no thoughts of how ye'll be fed or if, heaven forbid, I leave ye with a bairn, where either of ye will live—"

"Then, do not go!" she interjected, disturbed at the thought that she might never see him again.

He straightened. "'Tis a matter of justice... for Robert, at least, if no one else. I owe him that."

A slight pall settled over them, and Bree sighed. Would she never truly have what she wanted? A cottage filled with laughing children and a husband, and, not just any man.

She wanted Ruan.

She could agree to have the marriage annulled or wait patiently for his return, but from deep inside, her emotions began to burn. She wanted to reach out and take her dream before it slipped away. She was weary of waiting for someone else to deliver it. Lifting her hands to run them over his hair, she whispered what she truly felt. "Then, I'd rather be a widow of one day."

He moaned, and then pressed her hard against him. "I love ye, *mo ceisd*, like I've never loved another."

The words warmed her very toes.

"I should nae be reckless—" he groaned, smothering her with kisses.

Bree made up her mind. She'd have this night, regardless of what the future would bring. Surrendering to her desire, she arched close. "Be reckless, then."

Ruan caught his breath and then smiled even as his brows knit into a scowl. "If ye don't leave now, woman, I'll never let ye."

Sliding her hands up his chest to touch his cheek, she whispered, "I'm not leaving."

***

Bree awoke with the dawn and Ruan's thigh possessively pinning her to the bed. Recalling the events of the night before, her ears reddened. The chamber was in disarray with pillows and covers strewn across the floor, a chair tipped sideways.

He'd been quite vocal, speaking of his desires before making good on a decent number of them. Her cheeks burned, and she now understood precisely why a maiden would perish from the blushing.

The man possessed the passion of an animal and the loudness of one as well. He'd awakened a side of her that she hadn't known existed. She'd become almost savage herself, knocking him back and biting his neck, causing him to shout in ecstasy. In the light of the morning, she was shocked by her conduct, but was distracted from further thoughts as Ruan's warm hands slid around her, pulling her close.

He hungrily kissed her throat and chills ran down her spine. She shivered and he chuckled.

"Aye, I forgot to ask ye last night, lass," his voice rumbled in her ear. "Did ye want this marriage annulled?"

Frowning, a little, she shifted to look him in alarm. "Do you?"

His dark lashes lowered.

She stared at him uncertainly.

"I'm mocking ye, lass," he said with a chuckle. "'Tis far too late for an annulment, my wee... wild beastie."

Recalling his continuous shouting, Bree blushed, murmuring, "You were hardly... discreet ..."

"I found myself attacked by a wee hellion!" he smiled unabashedly. "I never dreamt ye would be so vicious, though, considering how challenging ye've been from the start, I should have known."

At that, she blushed harder, covering her cheeks with her hands.

Ruan laughed, rolling her over to rest on top of him. "I'm exceedingly pleased to find ye brutal, and now I'm thinking I should be right relieved ye've been forgetting to wear the knife I gave ye."

She followed his gaze to her *sgian dubh* lying on the floor. She moved to pick it up, but he deftly twisted her again to lie under him. His kiss was gentle, but deepening into a burning passion when a knock rattled the door.

"Cameron needs ye, lad," Isobel's muffled voice sounded from the other side.

Ruan frowned. "Aye?"

Isobel paused before replying, "They have sent for a priest ... The Countess is dying."

With a sigh, they rose and dressed hurriedly.

They found Cameron in the small vaulted chamber staring silently out of the open window, oblivious to the cold wind. Bree huddled close by the fire, watching as Ruan joined the Earl, clasping him warmly on the shoulder.

Cameron didn't move, but he did speak. "I truly am cursed."

"Nonsense," Ruan scowled. "'Tis nothing to do with ye."

Cameron surveyed him impassively. "Can ye truly say that? This is the seventh woman to die with my name. Regardless of what I said as a drunkard last night, I wish the lass no harm."

"Aye, but 'tis an extraordinary set of circumstances, that is all," Ruan replied firmly. "Childbirth is a dangerous thing. The others were mishaps, one already ill ... one murdered..."

"Aye, but they are all dead," Cameron replied. His tone was aloof. "It matters nae how it happens."

"My lord," a wizened, old woman cleared her throat as she hovered in the doorway. "The priest has arrived. The Countess calls for ye."

Cameron straightened slowly. After a time, he bowed politely in their direction and then allowed the old woman to lead him away.

Ruan sighed, joining Bree before the fire. He lightly traced a finger over her cheek, but neither felt like speaking.

It was not long before Cameron returned. His handsome face was drawn and pale as he informed them, "She is dead."

Bree shivered.

He stood in the center of the chamber, forbidding and detached. "I…have rarely seen so much blood."

"My lord!" The ancient woman had returned. This time, she clutched a small bundle to her breast. "The wet nurse has come. Do ye wish to see yer daughter before she is taken away?"

Cameron remained where he was, giving no indication he'd heard.

"Allow me," Ruan said, and stepped forward. He lifted the small infant carefully from her arms, murmuring, "Give him a wee bit of time."

The woman nodded once and disappeared.

There was something mesmerizing about the way Ruan gently cradled the baby, never had Bree seen a man appear more virile and handsome. All at once, she wanted to kiss him, take him to his chamber, and repeat the entire night of before. Their eyes caught. She blushed hotly and glanced away.

"I suppose this is my third daughter," Cameron observed dispassionately. He made no move to touch the infant. "Or shall I say the King's."

"One day, ye'll have a bairn of your own," Ruan said.

"I've no need of a bairn," Cameron answered in icy, clipped tones. "I now have three heiresses to my estates. I could even use a few more as I've land to spare. I'm sure the King will provide."

"Have ye ever even held a bairn?" Ruan raised a suspicious brow.

"I'm sure I must have wedded one, once or twice," Cameron replied in a mocking tone.

Thrusting the infant into the Earl's arms, Ruan ordered, "Hold the wee lassie."

Cameron obligingly held the bundle, cold and distant. The infant began to whimper. The Earl peered at the child briefly before shoving the bundle back at Ruan. "She needs a wet nurse, nae me."

With that, he quit the room.

As Ruan sought out the wet nurse, Bree went in search of Merry.

She hadn't seen the little girl the entire morning, and it was unusual. She knocked on the door to Merry's chamber, only to find it swing open, creaking on its hinges. Hesitantly, she stepped inside. "Merry?"

The chamber was tidy, apparently empty, with nothing amiss. She turned to leave when she heard the door close with a thud. Whirling, she beheld a paunchy, cloaked figure holding Merry tightly, with one hand clamped over her mouth and the other pushing a blade against the little girl's neck.

"Do nae speak a word!" a familiar voice hissed.

It was Silas, the priest.

She could not allow herself to feel fear, to wonder why he was there. Instead, she forced herself to act.

"Leave her be," Bree swallowed, her voice shaking a little. The fear radiating from Merry was overwhelming. "Take me, not her!"

"Aye," Silas laughed as the hood fell back. "I'm taking ye both."

As he moved forward, Bree shouted, "Run, Merry!"

Desperately, she reached for the *sgian dubh* Ruan had playfully hidden in her boot that morning, but a sudden burst of pain exploded from the back of her head and then darkness descended all at once.

FEARGHUS

As the servants lit the candles lining the main hall, Ruan leapt up the steps to Cameron's private chambers, two at a time, with a growing sense of dread. At first, he had thought Merry and Bree were with Isobel. When he finally sought the woman out, they discovered that neither Merry nor Bree had been seen for quite some time. A quick search revealed no sign of them anywhere in the castle grounds.

He pounded on Cameron's door.

"What is it?" Cameron asked, his brows arching in concern.

As they headed back down the stairs, Ruan heard Isobel's scream. His heart leapt into his throat as he strode into the hall.

Isobel was cradling Merry close to her breast, but any sense of relief Ruan felt was instantly gone as his little sister turned to him. Pushing away from Isobel, she launched herself at Ruan. An angry bruise was already spreading over her jaw and a jagged cut marred her neck, but it was the horror etched on her face that made his heart stand still.

"They took her!" Merry sobbed, clutching Ruan desperately. "Silas and another man took her back to Dunvegan! Ruan, ye have to get her, I love her! I'm sorry! I'm sorry! I don't care if ye love her too, just bring her back! Promise me, ye'll bring her back!"

It was too much to feel. He stared in shock only for a moment before spurring into action. Now was not the time to experience even a shred of emotion.

He must act.

As Cameron lifted a hand, dispensing crisp commands to his men, Ruan wordlessly bounded to his chamber. It took only a moment to collect his weapons, and then he was back in the hall.

"I'm coming with ye," Cameron stated, throwing his cloak over his shoulders.

With a curt nod, Ruan headed for the boats.

A group of men awaited them on the shore, battle ready and on horses, and then they were galloping into the falling darkness, with twenty more of the Earl's men preceding them down the road.

They didn't need to speak further.

They knew where they were going.

Dunvegan.

***

Bree's ears rang incessantly and her stomach heaved. Someone had stuffed a rank smelling gag in her mouth and drawn a hood over her face. Vividly, she recalled Silas' leering presence in Merry's chamber, but how she'd ended up securely tied to the back of a horse was a mystery. Judging by the soreness of her ribs, a significant amount of time had passed. She wriggled enough to maneuver the hood to the side, allowing a partial view of the horse's hooves squelching in the foul smelling mud. It was growing dark and she could smell the rain in the air.

From the corner of her eye, she spied another horse. There were at least two captors. Fervently, she prayed that Merry had escaped.

They began a sharp ascent, a steep and stony climb. Several times, the horse stumbled, jarring her unmercifully.

"Hold!" a man's voice called from the darkness ahead.

The horses reined in sharply.

"What took ye so long?" a gritty voice from close by startled her.

"'Twas nae an easy task," Silas grated from inches away, apparently the rider of her horse. "Cameron guards his castles well. We were fortunate they were in great need of a priest."

She shivered as hands untied and lifted her down. She forced herself to be limp, feigning sleep, but it was not necessary. Her abductor dumped her unceremoniously on the ground and tossed a plaid over her head.

"Where is the wee one?" another voice queried.

"I had to leave her behind," Silas growled. "They were growing suspicious of the boat."

Bree's heart leapt. Merry had escaped. Then, a new wave of anxiety rose. Surely, Silas would have drawn the line at harming his own sister. And then she remembered that she was the man's relation now as well, and he was showing little concern for her. She began to fret.

"I've little tolerance for yer constant bungling!" the gritty voice inserted itself again. "Ruan will be on yer trail. We must press on."

"Nay!" Silas responded angrily. "I've had enough of ye! I'm leading this raid, and–"

"Fool!" the man hissed in response. "I'll be patient with ye no longer!"

There was the sound of rasping metal, and at that, Bree's eyes flew open. She managed to shake the plaid to the side just in time to witness the last moment of Silas' life. He stood with his sword raised as he faced a bald, burly man she'd never seen before. Several others leaned against their horses, watching in mild interest but making no move to intervene.

It was over quickly.

Silas was no swordsman.

The man disarmed him with a single stroke before his blade slashed the priest's throat.

With a slight gurgle, Silas sank wordlessly to the ground.

Bree gasped.

"We leave at once," the bald man announced. "I'll nae have this fool lead Ruan right to us. The boat is waiting; we must lose nae time!"

She held still, frozen with shock, as he approached. His steel fingers crushed her wrist as he dragged her to his horse and tossed her in front. Mounting quickly behind her, he locked his arm about her waist in a vice grip that would afford no opportunity for escape and ordered his men to move.

It was a grueling ride. They traveled long into the night, stopping for only short periods of rest. The weather deteriorated, the gusts of cold rain driving through her plaid, stinging her face and hands.

Before dawn, they rested under a ledge of rock in a narrow ravine and huddle close to a small fire. Bree found herself bound securely, tossed to the side, and then ignored completely. The men spoke loudly.

Their spirits were elated with their success, and she soon discovered the bald man's name was Angus, he and his companions were Fearghus' men, on their way back to Duntulm.

Fearghus!

This discovery brought her to a near state of panic. Ruan would never think of searching for her in Duntulm. Her mind raced, why did they want her? Was she a trap for Ruan? She listened carefully, but she found answers to none of these questions.

At dawn, they rode as if the very devil chased them. For the most part, they kept her hooded, ordering her from the start to remain silent. Twice she summoned courage to speak, but each time Angus rewarded her with a sound smack across the face so fierce that she feared it had cracked her jaw.

"Ye'll nae speak, woman!" he shouted, planting his beefy face within an inch of hers. "I've no patience for it and if ye even attempt to escape, I'll bring yer head alone back to Fearghus! He will nae mind much!"

Bree gulped. She didn't try again after that.

Time passed in a blur.

They resumed their mad dash, and she managed only a few glimpses of her surroundings. The lone hawk soaring in the sky, tree branch rustling in the wind, but it meant little. She didn't recognize any of the terrain. She only knew she'd never been on these roads before.

They stopped rarely, subsisting on the occasional bannock and draught of water. She spent the majority of her day propped before Angus, gritting her teeth and nursing her sore jaw, as the horse jostled her unmercifully. At night, they rolled her in several plaids and slept on either side of her to ensure no chance of escape.

Tears flowed in those long, dark nights until she fell into an exhausted sleep amidst the damp heather, the smell reminding her of Ruan. She knew in her heart that he was following, and it gave her some measure of peace, but only a small measure. He wouldn't think to look in Duntulm. No, her destiny was in her own hands. She had to escape. Panic, fear, and despair roiled within her, at times threatening to render her helpless, but she could not give up, not now when she had too much to live for.

It was thoughts of Ruan that began to steel her resolve in those nights and the days that followed. She had to survive. She had to escape. She fought desperately to bring her fear in control and doubled her efforts to find a way to elude her captors.

The cries of many gulls heralded their impending arrival to the sea. The sounds of pounding waves roared in her ears as they cantered down the beach to a waiting boat.

Bree's heart sank. Her doom was fast approaching, and she hadn't yet found one opportunity to escape.

"Aye, 'twill nae be long now!" Angus rubbed his hands, apparently pleased with their progress. "Fearghus will reward us greatly for yer bonny face!"

Bree clenched her jaw and glared at him.

"Ach, what ye think makes no difference to me," the man laughed as he shoved her into the boat. "We'll be dining well enough soon and raising our tankards high with a wench or two on our knees!"

The men broke into cackles of anticipation as the oars dipped into the water.

Bree closed her eyes tightly, willing her panic to subside. Soon, they would entomb her in Duntulm, and whatever Fearghus desired of her; it was surely nothing good. She had to escape. Jumping overboard was not an option. She could not swim.

"Aye, ye canna escape," Angus informed her with a laugh. "There is nothing ye can do, lass."

Cursing her transparency, she didn't lift her head to look at the man.

The winds turned violent, large waves tossed the boat mercilessly, sending her sprawling to the bottom. Her captors paid little attention. They no longer seemed to mind the fact her hood had slipped to her shoulders, allowing her to see. She cautiously peered over the vessel's side at the coastline rapidly disappearing.

Soon enough, she saw the brown expanse of Skye on the horizon, gradually forming into in the rolling hills topped with stone columns. As they drew closer, she could see the scrubby trees and the tiny dots of sheep and goats.

Tears slid down her cheeks. Vainly, she wished Ruan would somehow magically appear. Her heart was heavy. She could still feel the *sgian dubh* tucked safely in her boot, but she'd little chance to use it with her hands and feet perpetually secured. Not that she'd have a chance against these battle-hardened men, anyway. No, she could not escape yet, but she had to remain vigilant.

The storm prevented further progress, and the men put to shore to wait it out. They built a fire and shared tales and ale long into the night. Someone tossed her a piece of bread as an afterthought. From listening, she learned they would reach their destination early the next morning, providing the clouds would lift. She remained alert, watchful, but Angus was ever at her side. Finally, she fell asleep, overwrought with dread of what the next day might bring.

The next morning, the dark clouds had lifted enough to allow them to continue their journey, and they sailed north. It was not long before the gloomy walls of Duntulm rose before them on a lofty pinnacle of rock, hovering over the surrounding lands like a sinister giant crow.

Bree shuddered, trying her best to quell a rising sense of panic. Merry had almost died here. She knew once interred in those walls the chance for escape virtually disappeared. Try as she might, she could not see any course of action to prevent it.

Angus flanked her side at every moment.

The boat finally ground to the shore and the man lost no time hefting her easily over his shoulder. Followed by several men, they hurried up the steep slope. With her hands and feet securely bound, she could hardly even wiggle in the man's iron grip.

She clenched her jaw and raised her chin, willing the threatening tears to disappear.

The castle was dark and forbidding, the inner courtyard rank, and falling into decay. Loud raucous laughter greeted their arrival. Angus gave a cheer, hefting her upwards as if she were a prize, as he made his way through the gathered men and up to the private chambers of the castle laird.

"I have returned, my lord!" he bellowed, rapping the door with a single knock.

"Enter," a thin, reedy voice replied.

Angus pushed the door open, swinging Bree down from his shoulder to her feet as he entered the chamber.

It was dark, illuminated only by the light of a single candle.

Bree was unable to see, but it made little difference. Assailed by a putrid stench, her eyes began to water.

"My lord," Angus murmured, as he bowed in the general direction of the bed. "I've brought Ruan's wife, Bree. The MacLeods failed in catching Merry. I've already paid them for their carelessness."

In spite of the situation, Bree's heart leapt at the first indication that Merry was unharmed.

A gaunt face with sunken eyes peered through the shadows. "Then, ye ken well enough what's to be done." The voice said in a hoarse whisper.

"Aye, my lord, it shall be done."

"Bring her closer," Fearghus whispered. He beckoned with a frail finger.

Placing his finger in the small of Bree's back, Angus prodded her toward the bed.

Her feet were still bound, and she nearly fell on her face.

"Ach!" Angus grunted in annoyance as he slashed her bonds with his dirk before shoving her roughly forward.

Bree caught her balance, barely stopping herself from falling on top of Fearghus. Up close, the smell was even more overwhelming, and it was all she could do not to cover her face and gag.

Fearghus' cheeks were hallowed, the bones of his face sharply prominent. His skin was transparent, hanging from his body like dry paper.

It was obvious the man was dying.

"Aye," he acknowledged. "See what Ruan has done to me? Do ye see why he'll pay?" His eyes burned with pure hatred.

Bree could not help it. She turned her head to the side and gagged.

"Aye!" Fearghus rasped, his voice shaking from the strain. "I'll see ye ruined by Tormod first and then the both of ye will die. I'll nae leave this world until 'tis done and nae until I see Ruan's head on a pike!" He pushed the covers down weakly, enough to reveal a rancid, oozing wound on his leg.

The stress, journey, and lack of food now ending with the sharp waft of rotting flesh suddenly became too much for Bree.

She crumpled in a dead faint.

TAMING THE BEAST

Ruan rode hard, the hardest he had ridden in his life, but fortune conspired to make his path difficult.

Rain fell in sheets, swelling the rivers to impassable heights that forced them to change course several times. He slept little, pressing on as fast as humanly possible. No one complained. They were loyal, fighting men, and they knew what was at stake.

They stopped only long enough to prevent the horses from floundering. But, even then, Ruan could not sit still. As the others took the opportunity to stretch or lie on the ground, he would walk some distance away to scream in pure frustration.

Cameron always followed, standing with Ruan until he sank to his knees amidst the heather, too overwrought to scream anymore.

"Ye must rest," the Earl admonished gently, "Ye'll be of little use to the lass should ye collapse along the way and our path will only become more treacherous in Skye."

"I'll kill Tormod!" Ruan promised in broken whisper. "And Michael as well!"

"If I dinna slay them first." Cameron drew his mouth in a thin line and clasped him on the shoulder.

Bree never left Ruan's thoughts.

Repeatedly, he had replayed the last day in his mind.

Why had he left her alone? Why had he assumed she was safe? Why was it taking so long to reach her? He was ill at the thought of what fate she might be suffering. When he did find her, would she hate him for taking so long?

Sleep eluded him. He arose before dawn, waking the others.

"We should sail for Dunscaithe with haste before we head to Dunvegan." Cameron broached the subject as they readied their horses.

"Nay," Ruan said. He shook his head grimly. "I canna afford the delay."

"Aye, but ye must nae lose. Now is the time to claim Dunvegan, and ye canna do it with my men alone," Cameron insisted. "'Twill only delay matters by a day and in the end, may save Bree sooner."

"Every moment is precious," Ruan disagreed, even though he knew the Earl spoke words of wisdom.

At length and after much debate, he begrudgingly acknowledged the value of Cameron's plan. It wouldn't serve Bree well if he were to die before reaching her. Having Cuilen at his side would accelerate the ending of the matter, but his heart ached at the delay.

They reached the ships late in the morning.

He thought he'd die from impatience, but at last, they were shoving off, setting sail for Dunscaithe.

The winds favored them and they arrived in Dunscaithe as the evening rays glistened on the sea. Their feet had scarcely touched the shore before they were met by horsemen, Cuilen and Domnall among them.

"What brings the Earl of Lennox to Dunscaithe, unannounced and in great haste?" Cuilen asked, dismounting to bow respectfully.

"Ye look awful, Ruan lad," Domnall interrupted, his shrewd gaze turning into outright alarm. "Is Bree safe?"

Ruan covered his face with his hands and turned away. How could he tell the man his daughter was anything but safe? He was at a loss for words.

Dimly, he heard Cameron's calm voice provide a quick explanation.

"I'm coming with ye, lad! I'll slaughter Tormod myself!" Domnall shouted hoarsely.

Suddenly overwhelmed, Ruan sank to his knees, covering his head with a groan as hot tears wet his lashes. He clenched his fists. Why was everything taking so horrendously long? Why could he not protect Bree from what she was experiencing this very moment? He wondered if this nightmare was ever going to end.

"She's a strong lass, Ruan," Domnall said, laying a heavy hand on his shoulder. "She's a MacBethad. She'll surprise ye, lad."

"Aye, now ye must only keep hope in yer heart," Cuilen advised. He reached down, offering him a hand. "We've time for nothing else. We must act."

The words were comforting but only a minute amount.

It didn't take them long to ready the boats. Cuilen had trained his men well. They set sail at once, but again the rough seas impeded their progress. They managed only a few leagues before the winds forced them to put ashore for the remainder of the night.

Ruan spoke to no one. He stood on the shore, screaming into the wind, caring little of what others might think.

At dawn, the winds died and the mists descended. They sailed up the coast for quite some time before the sun finally penetrated the mist, parting the clouds to reveal the stark and haunting peaks of the mountains drifting by.

Ordinarily, these sights would have thrilled Ruan's heart, but now he felt nothing. He could only think of Bree, and the fact that he was descending upon Dunvegan to accomplish the very thing that his brothers had feared the most, the thing that had never been in his heart. He sailed to claim Dunvegan as his, to wrest power from their corrupted hands.

In the distance, the familiar cliffs and beaches appeared, and his heart began to quicken. Soon, Bree would be safe. Soon, he'd be done with these men he no longer considered brothers. No more would they harm Bree or his clan. Soon, it would be over. He clenched his fists, willing her to hold on just a wee bit longer.

They stormed through the sea-gate and into the castle. They had been prepared for resistance, but there was none. Even the three men who briefly touched their swords didn't qualify as such.

Ruan advanced unchecked, and in minutes burst into Dunvegan's main hall to find it empty, with only Michael hovering uncertainly behind the high table.

"Ruan, what is this?" the man asked, licking his lips.

"Ye ken well enough what 'tis!" Ruan thundered. He leapt over the table, catching his brother about the throat and bodily pinning him against the wall. "Where is Bree?"

Michael's lip lifted in a snarl. "She's nae here."

Ruan unsheathed his dirk, pressing the blade firmly against Michael's throat. "Where is she?" he repeated in a deadly voice.

Michael took a deep breath and then smiled, angrily baring his teeth. "Aye. She is Tormod's by now. He left for Duntulm this morning. A gift, Fearghus called her. I'm sure he's had her many times—"

"Silence!" Ruan roared. He pushed the blade deeper as Michael fell silent. He closed his eyes, his heart breaking. Duntulm. They had taken her taken to Duntulm, how could he have known?

"Aye," Michael hissed viciously in his ear. "Ye came to the wrong place!"

Ruan clenched his jaw and shouted, "Why did ye do this? Why? What have I ever done to ye?"

"'Tis simple, Ruan," Michael answered with a long, slow laugh. "Ye live and that is enough."

Ruan shoved him harder against the wall, half in frustration, shouting. "It makes nae sense, man! I never would have taken Dunvegan like this!"

"Oh?" Michael pointed to the men standing behind him. "Why do ye think we wanted ye dead? 'Twas only Ruan the clan saw as their laird, from the time ye finished yer fostering. Aye, 'twas only yer name on their lips! We kent 'twas only a matter of time afore ye murdered us whilst we slept! Ye've done exactly what we've expected, all along. Ye came back to this place to wrest it from the rightful heirs!"

"Nay!" Ruan clenched his jaw. "I would ne'er have come like this if ye hadn't taken Bree!"

"Much blood has spilled on yer account!" Michael accused. "'Tis on yer head!"

"Nay, 'tis upon yours and I'm done with it, ye black-heated dog!" Ruan replied, lifting his chin. "Ye've spilled enough blood, including Robert's."

"Fie! Robert deserved to die," his brother said, relishing the words. "I took pleasure in it, with my own hand. He never dreamt I would do it, the fool!"

Ruan's jaw hardened.

"This is nae news to ye," Michael stated with a surprised brow.

"Gerland told me, ere he died." Ruan clenched his fingers tightly around the hilt. "Ye can die knowing ye slayed your own son."

"Gerland?" Michael's face turned grey. "Ye murdered him? My own Gerland?" At that, he stooped and drew a knife from his boot.

Ruan was grateful.

It made it much easier to kill him.

As Michael crumpled at his feet, Ruan felt Cameron's long fingers clasp his shoulder in a gesture of support.

Ruan straightened, feeling nauseated, and whispered, "She's nae here!"

Cameron turned to his men and, raising his arm, ordered, "We sail to Duntulm, at once!"

"Aye," the men in the hall agreed as one.

Ruan closed his eyes, praying they were not too late.

***

Dazed, Bree slowly sat up, her muscles stiff and sore. Confused, she looked around. She had been lying on the floor on a pile of ragged plaids in a cheerless chamber. The small window afforded little light and there was no fire on the hearth. A bed stood in the center, dusty and devoid of any coverings, the chamber pot had fallen to the side, revealing a black, dry scum.

The door rattled and opened. It was a formidable door, studded with iron nails and with its own iron padlock.

She swallowed, remembering she was a prisoner.

"My, my," a dour-faced woman clucked as she entered the chamber. She was holding a wooden tray and peered down at Bree with a thoughtful eye. "That's a mighty fine gown ye have there, lass, and the boots…I'm of a mind that I know of a lass who deserves them more."

Bree squinted, a little confused.

"Aye, take them off, ye will nae be needing them," the woman ordered, placing the tray on the floor and kicking it close to Bree with her foot. The bread rolled off and the wooden bowl lost most of its water. "Ye can eat after; I'll have my gown first."

Bree stared, dumbly at first. As the woman's expression darkened, she hurriedly complied. Perhaps she could overpower the woman, tie her up, and escape. She still had Ruan's *sgian dubh* in her boot. She began to untie the fine gown Cameron had given her, inching closer to the knife when the door opened and two more women entered.

"Ye'd best hurry, Elizabeth," one of them stuttered. "The MacLeod will be here right quick!"

"Aye, hurry, lass!" the woman said, stepping close to Bree and ripping the laces.

"What are ye doing, Elizabeth?" the other woman asked, but then as understanding dawned. "I want the boots!"

"No!" Elizabeth snapped, yanking the gown over Bree's head. "I'm taking them both, and that's an end to it. Hurry, before Tormod comes!"

As the women squabbled, Bree slid the knife free and quickly hid it in the plaids she'd been sleeping on. She could not fight all three, but she still hoped an opportunity for freedom would present itself. The fact that Tormod was coming was both good and bad. While she knew his intentions, she also might be able to twist the situation to her advantage.

First, she knew she must calm her frantic mind.

The women stripped her down to her shift, mourning the fact they could not steal that as well, so fine a shift it was, but as Tormod's voice bellowed from below, they scurried out of the chamber like rats, taking her belongings with them. It was no matter; she forced herself to take a calm breath, reminding herself that she had the knife.

Quickly, she formed a plan; she'd hide the knife under the heather mattress and convince Tormod she wanted him and when he was not looking, plunge the knife somewhere to gain her freedom. She quailed a little, and didn't define the 'somewhere'. If she thought about it too much, she wouldn't be able to do it.

Searching through the plaids, she had just grasped the handle of the knife when the door flung open. Fear gripped her heart. Her plan was already failing.

"Bree!" Tormod stumbled in, a little bleary eyed. He searched the chamber before spying her on the floor. His lips split into a lecherous grin. Slowly, he eyed her boldly and shut the door. "Aye, I told ye that

I would make ye mine!"

Her hands began to shake. Frozen with fear, she watched him approach as if in a dream, but as his fingers closed in over her wrist, her lethargy shattered. Panic flooded her. It took every ounce of her will not to scream and fight the man.

"Bree," Tormod whispered in her hair, beginning to grope her. "Aye, Ruan will nae save ye this time!"

The mention of Ruan threatened to bring tears, but she had no time for them. Forcing the words, she managed a tremulous croak, "My lord... I...I've always wanted to be yours, not Ruan's."

His hands stopped. Cocking his head to the side, he knitted his brows in a confused frown. "What is this?"

Bree's throat closed. She tried to speak, but the words failed to form. It was impossible to think.

"Bree," he murmured again, apparently already forgetting the matter. His lips puckered, targeting hers.

Unable to control herself, she wriggled free. She had to get the knife. As she bent, he seized her arm and hefted her over his shoulder.

"I'll have ye now, ye spitfire," Tormod grunted, striding to the bed and throwing her down upon it.

As he lunged, she managed to roll off the other side, landing with a thump on the floor.

"Bree!" Tormod roared.

Frantically willing her beating heart to still, Bree licked her lips and said, "Aye, my lord. I want you, like I want no other!"

"'Tis enough talking from ye, now!" Tormod bellowed, reaching for her.

Desperately, she slid her gown off her shoulder and fluttered her lashes.

He paused. His lecherous grin returned.

"My lord," Bree whispered, in what she hoped was a sensuous voice. "Not on the bed, come to the floor, 'tis...much more...thrilling that way."

Tormod blinked, confused, but as she ran to the pile of plaids, he began to smile stupidly. "Aren't ye a wild beastie!"

Her knees were shaking so badly, she half collapsed in the plaids. He moved toward her, his gait uneven and his words slightly slurred. Perhaps the man was drunk. The thought gave Bree a little more confidence. Allowing herself only to focus on success, she slid back onto the plaids in what she hoped appeared an invitation. It was not nearly as graceful as she'd planned it to be.

She need not have worried.

The man grinned like a fool. "Bree, aren't ye a little minx!" Then, he paused, suddenly suspicious. "What of Ruan?"

"Ruan has nothing." Bree tossed her head, forcing her lashes to lower and flutter again. "You are The MacLeod, a man of power... and..." Her words faltered. There was nothing positive about the face leering closer. "And... power, very... powerful... with much... power..."

Frantically, she searched for something to say, but it didn't matter. He was not listening, but leering at her breasts, his tongue slightly hanging out of his mouth.

He lunged, sliding his arms around her and plunging his tongue down her throat much quicker than she'd anticipated. Even drunk, the man was strong. Her body fought of its own accord, ignoring her frantic attempts at control. However, he apparently didn't notice, or else enjoyed the struggle.

His lips found hers, but she managed to twist enough to continue her desperate search for the knife. His mouth tasted of whiskey, onions, and rotting teeth. She wanted to retch. She could not find the knife. The plaids were sliding in all directions, and she wanted to scream out of frustration and fear.

Almost weeping, she wildly patted the floor.

She was on the verge of screaming when she felt the cool handle slip into her fingers. Without hesitation, she plunged the blade into the nearest target.

Tormod gasped.

Hysterically, she withdrew the blade and plunged again.

This time, it struck something hard and stuck.

Tormod fell back, eyes popping in shock as he clawed at the knife embedded in the side of his neck. His grip loosened and Bree scrambled away, but he miraculously revived and staggered to his feet, regaining control.

"Bree!" he bellowed, but this time, his voice filled with rage and vengeance.

She swallowed a scream; he was going to kill her. She leaped for the bed, searching for something to defend herself, but she found nothing. She stumbled, tripping on the wooden bowl. Grasping it with cold fingers, she swung it at him with full force.

There was a crack as the bowl hit him on the side of the head. He tottered back, losing his balance to fall. His head struck the wooden bed frame with a loud thud.

He slid to the floor without a sound.

For several, long, interminable minutes, she hovered where she was, waiting for him to rise to his feet, but he remained with his face down on the floor, not moving. Finally, she tiptoed closer, unable at first to believe she'd accomplished her goal, but as the minutes passed, it became apparent that she had.

Her heart lurched.

Now was her chance!

No one was looking for her; they all assumed she was in Tormod's clutches. She must hurry before the man woke and called for help. Quickly, she ran to the door and cracked it open, peeking outside carefully. She exhaled a loud sigh of relief to discover no one there.

Slipping down the passageway, she crept past several open doors along the way. Both chambers proved empty. The third room revealed a chest. She could hardly escape the castle wearing only a shift. She ruffled through its contents, finding a pair of breeches, a yellow shirt and a plaid. Perhaps she could masquerade as a lad.

Dressing quickly, she took a deep breath, preparing herself for whatever lay ahead and marched out into the passageway, seeking for a way to escape the castle. First, she had to steal a horse. They would find her too quickly if she left on foot. She wouldn't let herself consider the fact she was unable to ride one. Instead, she focused on escaping the main keep and locating the stables without drawing attention.

It was easier than she'd expected.

The inhabitants of the castle were scurrying, in a state of distress.

Apparently, the boats on the horizon had been identified as more MacLeods arriving.

"MacLeods!" a woman hissed, pressing a basket of linens into her hands. "Ye can take these to Maud, I'm off! I'm nae fool enough to be caught here again! We just fended off the MacKenzies, ach, and now the MacLeods?"

Bree watched the woman go, wondering briefly what they had to fear from more of Tormod's men, but she shrugged her curiosity aside. She had to leave before Tormod woke and discovered her gone. He'd be furious. She'd never survive a second encounter. It was luck that he'd fallen victim to her attack, and the thought of him lying so still, silent on the floor, gave her a momentary pause. For a brief moment, she wondered if she'd killed him. Surely, she hadn't. It could not be so easy. Brushing the thought aside, she focused on the stables.

Setting the basket aside, she fled down a side passage, bursting through a door as several men ran past with clanking swords. She ducked back inside until they had gone and then slipped into the courtyard.

There were a group of buildings to the side, and she ran to them as fast as she could. Destiny conspired to help her, for the first door she slipped through was the one she sought, and she found herself confronted by the sight of several horses tied to a post. They flicked their ears nervously at the commotion outside.

Bree closed her eyes, enjoying the momentary sense of relief, before mustering the resolve to approach the first animal.

It was a fearsome beast, and the largest horse she'd ever encountered. It was a massive mound of hooves and muscle that stood proud as if it knew well it was utterly magnificent. It snorted and tossed its shaggy mane.

Steeling her nerves, Bree inched forward. "You will have to do," she said, gritting her teeth.

The horse flicked its ears and stamped its foot in warning.

"Ach, what are ye doing?" a sleepy voice from her elbow made her jump. "Step away from the laird's horse!"

A wave of fear washed over Bree. They had discovered her. Her shoulders drooped and her heart beat frantically, but then a determination rose from deep in her soul. Faking a commanding attitude, she whirled to find herself facing a young lad. "You must saddle this beast at once for me! Be quick!"

The boy frowned, though already a little more uncertain than before. "'Tis the laird—"

"Do not think to question me!" Bree interrupted. "Make haste! I've a message that cannot be delayed! Do you really want me to return to Fearghus and tell him that a lowly stable boy has delayed this message of great import?"

The boy blinked, but began to scurry, collecting a saddle and bridle along the way.

"Be quick!" Bree snapped. "Or I shall cut off your..." Words suddenly failed, her heart was pounding so loudly it was difficult to think, so she said the first thing that came to her mind, "...nose!"

The threat worked.

The lad doubled his efforts and in minutes, she found the pawing beast saddled, bridled and ready to ride.

She could not afford to hesitate.

She didn't let herself think.

Struggling onto the animal's back, she kicked it viciously. She was nearly unseated as it sprang out of the stables and thundered through the gate, causing the lone man guarding it to watch her disappear, dumbfounded, and absently scratching his chin.

Bree desperately clung to the saddle.

The animal was powerful, apparently thrilled to be free, and she simply let him run until she could collect her thoughts. Once satisfied Tormod's men were not following, she addressed her next concern, and that was how to control the wild beast running freely beneath her.

As they plunged down a rolling hill, she tugged the reins, trying to bring him to a halt.

The beast blithely ignored her first attempt.

She tried again.

When met with no response, she allowed her fear to give her strength. With a scream and a loud curse, she yanked the reins, commanding the animal to halt, letting loose with every curse she'd ever heard before in her short life.

Much to her surprise, the horse slowed its pace, flicking an ear her direction.

Bree repeated her performance and found herself rewarded with two ears flicking both her way.

To her utter astonishment, the animal slowed to a stop.

"I've had enough of you!" Bree continued, voice shaking so badly the words were scarcely recognizable. "From this moment on, I am the master! I am, not you! You will listen to me and follow my every request! Do you promise to listen?"

The horse snorted and stamped a hoof, but didn't move.

Bree swallowed, clasping her trembling hands. She was shaking everywhere and on the verge of hysteria. She forced the thought away, there was no time to sob right now, and she must make her escape complete.

Darkness was falling quickly. She had to find shelter and hide; surely, they had discovered her missing by now and would soon be on her trail. She kicked the horse and he eagerly leapt forward, gathering speed with each step until she tugged on the reins to slow him. To her surprise, he followed her bidding.

A forest loomed ahead.

It would have to do; she would hide in the thickets. At least the skies had cleared, and it promised not to rain.

WHICH CLAN SHE FAVORS

Ruan boldly strode into Duntulm, Cameron and Cuilen flanking either side. Fearghus was no fool, not with the host of boats on his shores. He didn't even attempt to a fight. A group of MacDonald clansmen bowed in low respect, informing them that Fearghus wished to speak.

Ruan was impatient, taking the steps two at a time, until at last, the door to the laird's chamber swung open, and he was inside.

The stench made him gag.

"Aye, come to finish off what ye started?" Fearghus rasped from the darkness.

As his vision adjusted to the light, Ruan saw the man's pallid form on the bed, his breath ragged, eyes bright with fever.

The smell of death was in the air.

"Where is Bree?" Ruan demanded, striding forward. "Tell me where she is, *at once!*"

"Aye, I wanted to see the look on yer face, ere I depart this world." Fearghus grinned, gloating. "Tormod's had at her, this past hour! Ye'll find yer woman ruined –"

Ruan bounded to the bed, grasped the man's throat, and bodily lifted him from the bed. "Tell me where she is! Now!"

"Tormod is in the east tower," Fearghus whispered with a smirk. "'Tis too late—"

Shoving him back on the bed, Ruan ran from the chamber, Cameron close at his heels. The castle inhabitants fled before them as they bounded up the steps, kicking in the doors of the chambers as they ascended. The fifth door revealed a man lying on the floor.

It was Tormod.

There was no sign of Bree.

Filled with rage and drawing his sword, Ruan descended upon his brother. He was tempted to behead Tormod upon the spot, but he needed to find out what had happened to Bree first. Restraining himself with difficulty, he only pressed the blade upon his brother's neck as he half-lifted him from the floor.

Tormod was oddly still.

Noting the coldness of the man's flesh, Ruan peered closer and spied the vast pool of blood that had formed on the floor.

Protruding from Tormod's neck was the handle of the *sgian dubh* that he'd given Bree.

Cameron dropped to his knee and placed his long fingers on Tormod's white lips. "He breathes still," he said. "But, nae for long."

No man could survive losing that much blood.

Tormod's lashes fluttered weakly. "Ruan," he mouthed feebly. "Cold...very cold."

"Where is Bree?" Ruan shouted. "What have ye done with Bree?"

"Bree?" Tormod repeated, and then his eyes rolled back.

He was dead.

"Aye, she must have escaped," Cameron stated, eyeing the chamber in disgust. "I shall have the men search."

For the first time, Ruan allowed hope to blossom in his heart. "Aye," he murmured, smiling. "She's a MacBethad."

***

It had been a cold night. She'd walked in circles to stay warm, hugging the shaggy horse for warmth at times. So great was her relief to be free, she'd scarcely noticed any inconvenience. As dawn colored the sky, she once again headed south, following the coastline as closely as she could and ignoring her hunger pangs.

She was afraid to stop. Yet, she was afraid to press on. She didn't know where she was, but there was no sign of pursuit. She prayed fervently that she was leaving Fearghus' land and avoiding Tormod's. She reached the hilltop and saw the Old Man of Storr rising in the distance. Tears of relief sprang into her eyes.

Reenan.

Reenan would know what to do. Her cottage had been close to the shore, in the shadow of the mountain. She could find it. With renewed hope, she kicked the horse into a gallop, surging with hope and reveling in the warmth of the sun's rays beating upon her skin.

The Old Man of Storr grew steadily closer as the power of the animal beneath her filled her with a sense of wonder. She marveled at the change in herself, that she could actually enjoy riding a horse. The beast seemed to sense the change, responding to her commands with respect instead of resentment.

Some time later, she pounded down the lane that became familiar and suddenly widened into Reenan's croft. She pulled up short, astounded she'd actually found the place just as Reenan and her children burst out the door, mouths agape.

It was only then that she allowed herself to cry, but the tears that flowed were mostly ones of relief.

The children tied the horse to a tree as Reenan led her into the croft, plied her with porridge, and guided her to the bed. She pitched headlong onto the heather pallet and closed her eyes, and fell into an exhausted sleep.

***

Ruan had spent the better part of the night distraught.

They all had searched the castle, but there was no sign of Bree.

He had returned to Fearghus' chamber to question the man again. Upon hearing of Bree's escape, Fearghus had let out a scream of pure frustration. The further knowledge that Tormod, Michael, and Gerland were now all dead and Ruan was the undisputed Laird of Dunvegan had caused the bedridden man to suffer some kind of seizure.

Ruan shoved Fearghus back upon the bed and held his dirk to the man's throat, "Aye, I'd slit your throat now and have done, if it weren't for the fact that I might need ye still."

Fearghus gasped and his lips took on a purple hue.

"Ye'd best pray I find her soon," Ruan said in a low voice as he dug the blade into the man's flesh, "'Tis the only way ye'll find a quick death."

"I'll stay and watch this black-hearted dog suffer whilst ye look again," Domnall offered. Picking up a bottle of wine from a nearby table, he pulled the cork out with his teeth. "A sudden death is too grand a one for the likes of ye, Fearghus."

"Aye." Ruan and Cameron agreed in unison.

"See that he lives until we return," Ruan ordered, moving toward the door.

As he left, he saw Domnall raising the bottle of wine in a toast.

"To yer health, Fearghus!" Domnall's voice was heavy with sarcasm. "And a slow journey to the Gates of Hell!"

Ruan strode out the door with Cameron at his side.

They searched every part of the castle, and Ruan was nearly giving up hope when he noticed the stable lad nervously following him.

"Ach, lad." Ruan frowned, addressing the lad for the fourth time. "What is it?"

"I…think I saw her, yer lairdship," the lad croaked, licking his lips nervously. "She was dressed as a lad, told me to saddle the laird's own beast, or she'd cut off my nose."

Ruan blinked, exchanging a dubious glance with Cameron.

"I swear it," the lad insisted. "I'm telling ye true! She was a wee thing with brown curls and all. I knew she was nae a lad, but she… she was very commanding, right fearsome, insisted on the best horse and set off through the gate at sundown."

"I see." Ruan nodded in distraction, finding the story preposterous.

"Aye, she could barely stay seated," the lad added, shaking his head. "'Tis a wonder she did nae fall."

Ruan paused, scowling a bit, and gave the lad his renewed attention. "She could nae ride?"

"Nay, my lord, nae a whit!" Came the reply.

Elation surged through him.

Cuilen didn't ride with them. Instead, he stayed to see Fearghus' passing. As uncle to the infant Fearghus had begot with his niece, he was now the overlord, and there were many matters to be set straight.

Domnall, Cameron, and a handful of others followed Ruan with haste, riding to the moors in search of fresh tracks. They headed south, while several other parties fanned out in different directions.

Ruan scowled, wishing desperately for a good tracking hound, but he'd scarcely finished the thought when he spied fresh hoof prints in the mud, pointing due south, and all at once he knew in his heart the tracks belonged to her and where she was going.

"She's headed to Reenan!" Ruan broke into a wide grin, his heart growing lighter with each passing minute.

Domnall and Cameron followed, but they didn't share his optimism.

Several times, Domnall pulled rein, suggesting they return for hounds, but Ruan insisted and pressed on, and soon after, they spied Fearghus' magnificent beast tied to a tree outside Reenan's croft.

"Aye!" Domnall barked in outright relief. "She's a MacBethad."

"Nay, she's a MacLeod!" Ruan turned on the man, a wide smile on his lips.

"Get in there to your wife, lad." Cameron permitted his lips to twitch upwards in the semblance of a smile. "Ye can both fight anon as to which clan she favors."

**

Bree was having the most wonderful dream.

She was cradled in Ruan's arms; he was holding her close, whispering how much he loved her, repeating the words over and over. It was a dream she never wanted to end. She wanted to revel in his embrace and listen until the end of time.

She burrowed closer, but then something soft and wet touched her cheek and her eyes flew open.

Disoriented, she stared in confusion. She was still in Reenan's croft, but Ruan was there, holding her close, his tears falling onto her face. She was too afraid to move, afraid the illusion would disappear, and then she heard her father's grating voice.

"Aye, she is a MacBethad. I told ye from the start that she was a strong, Highland lass."

With a gulp, Bree lurched forward to throw her arms around Ruan's neck.

He fell back on the floor with a surprised laugh, half dragging her out of the bed, but she didn't mind. Tumbling after him, she began to babble, asking first of Merry, and then telling him of Silas, and ending last with Tormod.

"I stabbed him." She frowned, lifting her head from his chest for the first time. "I…do not know what happened to him. He was so still. Surely, I …I didn't…" She could not bear to think she'd killed a man, even one as evil as Tormod. She confessed her fear in a whisper. "I think I might have killed him."

"Nay, I did," Both Ruan and Cameron answered in unison.

"Aye," Cameron amended curtly. "We *both* finished him."

Flooding with relief, Bree lifted her head to see Cameron, Domnall, Reenan, and her entire brood gathered close where she huddled in Ruan's lap on the floor. Suddenly shy, she pushed away, but he'd have none of it.

"Nay, lass," Ruan said, hooking a finger under her chin. "I'm never letting ye go again. I'll have ye as my captive until the day I die."

He bent to kiss her warmly on the lips. It made her tingle down to her very toes.

"Aye, lass, I told ye from the start that ye would love him." Domnall chuckled. "'Twas plain to see that ye were meant for each other.

***

They left the next morning, sailing a boat up the coast to Duntulm. Bree had spent the night in Ruan's arms, taking comfort in the soft rhythm of his chest rising and falling beneath her cheek. Neither of them had slept much, they had simply enjoyed each other's presence.

"Aye, 'tis good to see ye found love, Ruan," Reenan had said, giving him a sisterly peck on the cheek.

Ruan had thrown back his head with a roar of pure laughter. After lifting Reenan up and twirling her in a circle, he set her down and enveloped her in a warm hug. "I'll be expecting ye at Dunvegan, every year, to celebrate the birth of our newest bairn."

Bree had blushed scarlet amidst all the laughter.

However, now on the boat, she found his words worrisome. As if sensing her mood, Ruan reached over and kissed the top of her head. "What is it, *mo ceisd*?"

"Dunvegan." She frowned. "Surely... we aren't going back, are

357

we?"

His dark eyes widened a little in surprise. "We must! Dunvegan… is ours now, love. 'Tis our…home."

Home? The thought of Dunvegan as her home was absurd. The dark, gloomy castle filled with even darker memories was not the cottage of her dreams.

"'Twill nae be the same, lass," Ruan assured. "As the Lady of Dunvegan now, ye can do with it as ye please."

"I've always dreamt of a cottage by the sea," Bree said and grimaced. "Not a castle."

Ruan threw back his head and laughed.

With a sigh, she laid her head on his shoulder.

THE GIFT

A month or so had passed. The morning held the hint of spring.

Bree stretched luxuriously.

She'd been having a decadently passionate dream of Ruan covering her skin in a multitude of kisses. She held still, not wanting the dream to end, but when it only grew stronger, she lifted her lashes to discover his dark, handsome face smiling down at her. She opened her lips to speak, but he promptly cut her off with a demanding kiss and swept her into a tide of emotions amidst his perpetual shouts of ecstasy.

The morning hour grew late before Ruan laughingly pushed her from the bed with his foot.

"I've had a wee surprise waiting for ye since last night, lass," he said. "But ye kept on…distracting me."

"The fault is all mine?" Bree questioned, sliding back under the covers.

After several moments, he groaned, nuzzling the hollow of her throat. "Aye, ye wee wild beastie."

Adopting his accent, she whispered. "Perhaps it can wait a wee bit longer, aye?"

He kissed her passionately before jumping out and upending the covers to roll her out of the bed once again. "No more of these wily ways! I've something to show ye."

From the floor, she watched him dress hurriedly. She could not help but admire the man; he was the finest of specimens, in both body and heart.

He dropped her gown over her head.

"Ye have to be clothed for this surprise, lass," he announced. "Stay here whilst I find it."

Mildly curious, she slipped into her gown and waited.

Much had happened since returning to Dunvegan. Merry and Isobel had arrived shortly after. Merry was cheerful, and her mood had only improved upon hearing Fearghus had died a miserable death. The little girl had stood in the hall on the first evening to offer Bree and Ruan an official toast to their "forever, long-lasting, and truest of loves".

Gone was her jealousy, never to return.

Dunvegan had brightened considerably by the day, in part due to the presence Jenna and her no longer nameless daughter, Morag, but there was still much to do. While she thought being The MacLeod suited Ruan, particularly well, she was uncomfortable with thinking herself the lady of the castle.

A knock at the door broke into her thoughts, and she smiled. "Yes, my love. I'm ready for your surprise." She hopped on the bed and rolled on her back, playfully covering her face with her hands.

The door creaked open, soft footsteps approached.

"My wee lassie," familiar soft tones whispered in the room.

Bree sat up. "Afraig!" She cried, launching herself at the tall, angular woman standing in front of Ruan.

EPILOGUE

"What a brawny, wee son ye have," Cameron said. He lightly touched the tip of the infant's nose as he lifted a mocking brow at Ruan. "And ye still say ye have naught?"

"Are ye jealous?" Ruan eyed the man.

Cameron tensed a little even as he smiled elegantly. "I've no desire for a bairn."

Ruan laughed. "Aye, well, if ye insist, ye can be a wee bit jealous."

Cameron handed the baby back, but something in the man's face made Ruan pause.

"What is it, lad?" he scowled in concern.

"The King bids me to court," the Earl replied in a distant voice.

It was not good news.

Ruan gave his friend a sympathetic look. "Mayhap ye should find a lass and wed her before ye go. Surely, there are a few ye fancy?"

"I would never curse someone I fancied with an untimely death! I've no desire to touch another lass for the remainder of my days." The line of Cameron's mouth tightened a fraction. "I've enough blood on my hands. I'll nae wed again."

Ruan said nothing. They both knew the chances of that were slim. Cameron was simply far too politically valuable to remain unwed.

"Forgive me," The Earl said, and bowed. "This is a joyous occasion."

"Nonsense," Ruan protested, but they were interrupted by the arrival of Afraig and Isobel.

"'Tis time for the laddie to be fed," Afraig said.

"'Tis too soon for that!" Isobel frowned. "He must be bathed."

"Ach, after he is fed," Afraig disagreed, reaching for the child in Ruan's arms.

"I'll have a say in what Ruan's son needs," Isobel almost growled, laying a possessive hand on the baby's head.

"Bree's son is quite famished," Afraig said, glowering in return. She placed her fingers firmly on the child's leg.

"Aye, but—" Isobel began, glaring outright.

"Be done, dearest of ladies," Ruan interrupted, laughing at them both. "Shall we allow Bree to decide?"

They both snapped their mouths shut, having the grace to be embarrassed as Ruan bowed, leaving them in Cameron's company. As he entered his private chambers, he saw Bree peering out the window.

Her expression made him hesitate.

"What is it, *mo ceisd*?" he finally asked, uncertain.

"The pipes ..." she said, craning her head forward.

He could hear the pipes below, mingling with the waves and the plaintive calling of the gulls.

"...And the heather on the hills ..." she continued, "...the amber bubbling burns, the ferns, and the silver birches ..."

Turning to face him, she stooped to kiss their son's forehead before sliding her arms about his neck. "...the shining blue sea...the magic of this place," she whispered. "I see now why you love it. This place *is* beautiful."

"Aye," Ruan agreed with a smile, but he was glancing down only at her and their son cradled between them. "Aye. 'Tis this that truly is."

The End

Coming Soon

The Bedeviled Heart

The Highland Heather and Hearts Scottish Romance Series
Book Two

Kate placed a protective hand over her expanding belly. She was noticeably rounder now. The bairn was a strong one, constantly kicking her through the night.

She stood in the courtyard, soaking up the sun while listening to the plaintive wailing of the gulls. It was an unusually warm day for winter. Dunvegan was peaceful; she'd spent over a month in its walls. The laird and his lady treated her with such kindness that she was beginning to hope she'd found a suitable home.

She tried not to think of the Earl, but he was always in her thoughts. She heaved an exasperated sigh. He'd probably already forgotten her existence. It hurt to admit it, but Lady Elsa was right. Such a powerful man would scarcely think twice of a simple maid.

Adopting a bright smile to mask the wretchedness she was feeling, she returned to the kitchens and snagged a platter of meat. "Add more," she ordered the cook, pursing her lips in disapproval. "This is for the laird's table!"

The man shook his head, but followed her bidding in a jovial manner. "Feeling a bit pert, are ye, lass? Ye must be feeling a mite better."

"I'm feeling much better," she said, with a sunny smile. She almost felt she belonged in the place. Another month and it would feel like home.

On her way to the hall, she met her aged aunt.

"Ach, be careful there, love," Isobel warned, a smile crinkling her old face. "No need to exhaust yerself."

"I'm well, auntie," Kate sang cheerfully, ignoring the riotous rumblings of her stomach. Aye, this babe was proving difficult. It was still impossible to eat, and she was markedly thinner. At times, it was almost unbearable to bring the dishes from the kitchens, but she'd managed to control her nausea thus far. "Ach, ye wee one, you must help your mother, now." She whispered fondly to her belly.

Dunvegan's main hall bustled with preparations for the holidays. Several children played boisterously amongst the tables. She stumbled a little, lifting the platter over their heads as they sped past.

The laird of Dunvegan caught her arm, steadying her with a brotherly hand. "Ach, Kate, why don't ye rest a spell?" he suggested. He smiled in kind concern before adopting a stern expression to shout after the lads, "Be watchful, ye wee hellions!"

"I'm well, my lord." Kate dimpled a smile at the man.

He and his lady were exceedingly kind. Several times, the laird had pressed her to reveal the father of her bairn. She knew he only sought to defend her, and while she was grateful for his protectiveness, how could she betray the man she still loved? It mattered nothing that he'd forgotten her. She should have known it would end like this. He was an Earl, far beyond her reach. Her own foolish heart had landed her in this predicament.

Raising her chin resolutely, she wrinkled her nose a little at the smells drifting past. "There is no cause for your concern, my lord."

One of the lads returned to whisper excitedly in Ruan's ear.

"Here?" Ruan's dark brows lifted in surprise. "Now?"

Kate turned away, fighting a wave of nausea. Placing the meat on the high table, she descended the steps carefully to the kitchens once again to wait for the goose. She chatted idly with the cook until it was finally ready and was pleased her stomach lurched only a little as she made her way back to the hall.

This time, Ruan was standing before the high table with his dark eyes focused upon a cloaked figure blocking her path. He clasped the man's shoulder in a familiar manner as his face flooded with concern. "Ye look right awful, lad. What happened? Surely, ye've nae been wed again?"

The wave of nausea returned with vengeance.

Covering her mouth with a hand, Kate attempted to step around the newcomer to rid herself of the platter as soon as possible. A sudden waft of onions caused the bile to surge to her throat. Unable to stop herself, she dropped the goose and fell to her knees, retching violently.

She became aware of the man's fine leather boots only after she had soiled them.

Horrified, she clutched her hands over her mouth, not knowing what to do.

"Kate?"

Oddly, the voice reminded her of Cameron.

"Kate?!"

Her mind went blank and then Cameron's astonished face entered her field of vision.

"Kate! It *is* you!" he whispered, his face registering complete shock.

"What is this?" Ruan's deep voice inserted itself. "Do ye know the lass, then?"

Ignoring him, Cameron slipped a hand under her arm and lifted her to her feet. "How can ye be here? I've been searching everywhere! Everywhere! I've been distraught!"

He did look awful, thinner, and grimmer. Dark stubble graced his chin. She'd never seen him so unkempt. However, even disheveled, he still exuded an air of grace. She shook her head with a wry smile. The man simply could not be anything but handsome, no matter what he did. Lady Elsa was his true match; they made an impressive couple.

"Kate!?" the Earl searched her face. "What happened? I'm at a loss how ye came to be here...of all places?"

Obviously, he hadn't yet noticed her prominent belly. Instinctively, she shrank back, trying to make it smaller. It was silly. Her situation was far beyond hiding now. Her thoughts were a complete muddle and she was entirely unprepared for the sudden turn of events.

"Explain yourself, lad!" Ruan's deep voice cut in. "Surely, ye canna be the one the lass is running from?"

"Running?" Cameron briefly glanced at him, mystified, before turning to Kate. "Running? Why—" he stopped abruptly as he spied the smooth curve of her belly. His eyes widened, "What is this?!"

Kate's lassitude vanished. Drawing herself to her full height, almost reaching his shoulder, she replied fiercely, "'Tis no reason for ye to be distressed, my lord Earl!"

Clutching her belly possessively, she tried to bolt, but he blocked her with an easy arm.

"So... *this* is why... ye ran?" he asked, searching for words. He swallowed several times and then whispered, "Why didn't ye tell me? This is nae cause for shame!"

"Surely...'tis nae...*your* bairn?" Ruan asked, astounded. His brows were in his hairline.

Kate gulped as tears filled her eyes.

What was she doing?

She simply never wept!

Tears were such a useless waste of time.

"Come, Kate." Bree's quiet voice filtered through the confusion. "Let's find some of Isobel's tea to settle the nausea."

Gratefully, Kate latched onto the Lady of Dunvegan's arm even as Cameron held out his hand to prevent her departure.

"Nay, lad," Ruan said. Catching Cameron's arm, he wheeled him about. "Kate is safe here. Let's speak on this matter first. I never dreamt I'd be taking ye, of all men to walk the earth, to task over this!"

Following Bree, Kate scurried out of the hall.

To be continued ...

ABOUT THE AUTHOR

Like many of us on this planet, Carmen Caine wants to live in another time or world. She spends every moment she can scribbling stories on sticky notes that her kids find posted all over the car, house, and barn.

When she is not working as a software engineer, she is busy ferrying her kids to various appointments, writing lyrics for her husband's songs, taking care of the dog Tigger and his heart condition, attempting to tame her three insane cats, scratching her three Nigerian Dwarf Goats behind the horns or coddling her flock of thirty bizarre chickens from around the world.

Carmen Caine also writes Young Adult Paranormal Romance under the name of Madison Adler.

Follow Carmen Caine on Twitter:

http://twitter.com/CarmenRomances

Follow Carmen Caine on Facebook!

http://www.facebook.com/carmen.caine